CHASING ELIZABETH

MYSTERIES & MATRIMONY, BOOK 3

JENNIFER JOY

FREE EXTRA SCENES

Want access to free bonus scenes?
Join Jennifer Joy's Newsletter here!

CHAPTER 1

*E*lizabeth Bennet flung off her covers, morning chill and anticipation prickling her skin and awakening her senses. She had to leave quickly if she were to leave at all.

Every floorboard groaned. Every breath thundered. Every brush of fabric as she donned her costume scratched. Sounds nobody heard during the daytime deafened at dawn, and no matter how many times Elizabeth had performed this same routine, the nerve-tingling urgency and panic never ceased to accompany her.

She could not risk waking the household.

Plaiting her hair and pinning it in place, she reached in the dim light for the brooch she always left beside her book on the bedside table. It was her favorite — the one Uncle Gardiner had bought for her in Italy ages ago, before the war. Elizabeth ran her finger tenderly over the uneven stones — emerald malachite; bright turquoise; vibrant lapis lazuli; and aventurine in Spring grass green, Summer sun yellow, and Autumn orange — carefully arranged in an intricate, miniature puzzle creating a colorful mosaic of the Italian countryside. She would travel there. Someday.

Until that blessed day, Elizabeth wore her uncle's thoughtful gift on the lapel of her riding habit with pride. Were it not for her dear aunt and uncle's efforts on her behalf, she doubted her father would allow her and her sisters to venture so far as even London.

That Aunt and Uncle Gardiner had persuaded him to allow Elizabeth to accompany them North through Derbyshire the approaching summer — where her aunt had spent most of her youth — was a modern-day miracle. They might even travel farther to the Lake District. Elizabeth hoped so.

Less than two months remained until her grand adventure. Forty-seven days to be precise. Forty-seven days which could not pass by quickly enough to suit Elizabeth.

Her morning escapades were her only relief from the tedium of watching the clock tick through the never-ending days.

Elizabeth tiptoed down the hall to the stairs, skipping the creaky fourth step from the bottom.

She paused, holding her breath and listening. Nothing.

Heart in throat, she checked the time on the mantel clock in the drawing room, suspecting the hour before the device confirmed it. The soft glow of dawn's first light meant she would not have to tarry about Longbourn until it was safer to walk alone through the fields. It was bad enough for a young lady, a gentleman's daughter, to deprive herself of an escort when stories of spies and highwaymen filled the newspapers.

But, of what use was stolen freedom if she was unwilling to seize it? Of what use was life if it was not lived fully? She was not careless. Her father knew the path she walked, and he knew she would be back at home by breakfast. She walked quickly, with purpose, and she always carried in hand whatever stone or twig she could find should she require it for her defense (although it felt silly and unnecessary, for nothing of significance ever happened around Longbourn.)

With a sigh of relief, Elizabeth backed away from the front door, watching the upstairs windows should a candle appear. Then, turning, she ran across the drive, every step lighter than the one before. This was the moment she lived for — the glorious anticipation of what was to come, the energizing prospect of seeing Tempest.

The air was damp from yesterday's rain, but the path Elizabeth had worn through the fields connecting her father's estate of Longbourn to Lucas Lodge had dried enough to lose its slickness. She would have to exercise greater caution today lest Tempest lose her footing on the saturated earth.

Her dear friend Charlotte Lucas stood in front of the stables, beside her father's groom.

Elizabeth hoped she had not kept them waiting long. Tossing her stick to the side and scampering forward, she shouted, "Good morning!"

Charlotte held her hands out, greeting Elizabeth with a warm smile. "I was hoping you would arrive earlier than normal," she said, looking over her shoulder at the groom as if to say *I told you so.*

Mercer's face creased in a smile as wide as Charlotte's. He had been the groom at Lucas Lodge stables since Sir William had purchased the estate before Charlotte was born. Mercer and Charlotte had taught Elizabeth everything she knew of horses and equestrian skill.

She teased, "After two days of poor weather, Papa would have had to lock me in my room to keep me away."

"Nonsense," Charlotte retorted, allowing the groom to help her onto her mount. "Mr. Bennet would never do something so contrary to his character, and if he did, I imagine you would climb out of the window. He is not ignorant of your morning activities, and yet he has not prohibited you from coming."

"Not directly," Elizabeth mumbled. Her father did not prohibit much at all where his family was concerned, lacking the initiative required to exert himself in setting such limitations or the persistence to enforce them. But he held strong feelings against the two things Elizabeth longed for the most: travel and a horse of her own she was free to ride whenever she wished. One complemented the other, and both promised everything Elizabeth lacked in her life: adventure. The thrill of having new experiences and meeting new people with customs she had only read about — would *only* read about, if her father had anything to do with it — would have to wait another forty-seven days. An eternity in Elizabeth's mind.

Not wanting to waste time dwelling on things she would rather not, she turned to Joe, the stable boy. He held a grumbling bay mare tightly by the reins.

"I see you have selected my favorite this morning,

Mercer," she said. Flipping the forelock out of the horse's big, brown eyes, Elizabeth rubbed the star underneath. "Good day to you, Tempest. I have missed you dearly."

The groom's eyes smiled, adding to the creases lining his face. "Ay, Miss Elizabeth. Tempest needs a good run. She is restless today." Taking the reins from Joe, who looked relieved to hand them over, Mercer led Tempest to the mounting block. Elizabeth settled onto the sidesaddle while he checked the girth one more time, a cautious habit of his that both she and Charlotte appreciated. Those who extolled the propriety of riding aside had never had their feet trapped under them when their sidesaddle slipped. Elizabeth would have disregarded such pious arguments and ridden astride, but she was not so foolish as to believe her reputation — and consequently, that of her family — would not suffer if she chose to rebel against society's restrictive rules. It did not, however, prevent her from dreaming of dressing as a boy one day merely to experience what it was like to ride astride as the men did. Shocking!

Tempest pulled at the reins.

"You are restless, too, are you?" Elizabeth said in a soothing tone.

"Much like the lady who rides her, I should say,"

Charlotte said, leading them past the length of the stables to the open fields beyond.

Elizabeth chuckled. "We are a match. I am grateful you have held on to her as long as you have."

Charlotte sighed, her smile fading as she looked at the bay mare. "Nobody wants her, poor girl. George has tried to sell her several times, but her temperament is too strong. My brother is not one to give up, though. He heard of a gentleman who is planning to let Netherfield Park soon, and he intends to offer Tempest to him for a price few would refuse."

Elizabeth's heart sank. Tempest was not obstinate or headstrong. She merely knew what she wanted and accepted nothing less. Was that so wrong? Should a lady — er, horse — not have a mind of her own? Must she always succumb to the will of others obediently, without question?

Forcing a lightness she did not feel, Elizabeth said, "Someone is to let Netherfield Park at last? Now, that is good news!" She prayed he would be a kind master to Tempest. Too many treated spirited horses harshly in an effort to break them, and Elizabeth could not bear to think Tempest might subjected to such a life.

"It is rumored he is unmarried," Charlotte added with a sly smile.

Elizabeth tensed. "And so the race begins," she muttered.

"Indeed. My mother is already scheming."

"As will mine as soon as she finds out. The poor gentleman will sooner wish he had not settled in Hertfordshire when the matrons chase after him like a fox in the hunt to be caught like a prize for their daughters' matrimonial felicity."

Despite her comment, Elizabeth understood her mother's tenacity. Still, understanding did not make it any less painful to witness her mother's ruthless persecution of prospective husbands for her five unmarried daughters. Especially when Elizabeth was in no hurry to marry. She knew what she wished for in a husband, and she would accept nothing less.

Charlotte smiled softly. "I only hope he is slightly past his prime. Old enough to have developed an appreciation for maturity and sensibility. In looks, I would rather he be plain. That would suit me nicely, for no woman wishes to marry an ugly man. However, I do not flatter myself that I shall marry a handsome one."

"You do not give yourself enough credit, Charlotte," Elizabeth exclaimed. "What of love? Do you not wish for a man to stir your heart? You would have me believe you could be content with a stodgy clergyman when I have always seen you more suited to a dashing army captain."

"I am not like you, Lizzy. I am not romantic. Give me a cottage and a constant heart, and I will declare myself happy enough."

Elizabeth rebelled at the thought. She wanted more — for herself, as well as for Charlotte and her own sisters. Surely, the world contained enough love matches to suit them all … if ever she could see more of it.

Knowing better than to voice her concerns aloud to her overly practical, exceedingly rational friend, Elizabeth changed the subject. "Did you read the latest news in the papers? About the British spy who thwarted a ring of smugglers selling secrets to the French?"

"I am only shocked they have not yet bestowed a clever *nom de guerre* on the gentleman. Some combination of color and flower," Charlotte said dryly.

Elizabeth laughed. "Like The Scarlet Pimpernel? Or The Pink Carnation? Or The Purple Gentian? Perhaps they will call him The Yellow Archangel, The White Orchid, or The Jolly Daisy."

"Jolly is not a color. You know what I mean, Lizzy. The papers feed the romanticism of their readers to sell more copies. He will have a name soon enough, and young ladies and old alike will swoon over his daring adventures."

"You must admit that being a spy *is* a rather romantic profession."

Charlotte shook her head. "I fear for you. You only have one more year until you reach your majority, and I can attest to how swiftly the time goes by … and how cruelly … when you have no prospects and must face the disappointment of becoming a burden to your family."

Elizabeth could not stomach the commonly held view that a lady's sole purpose in life was to marry, and to marry well. "It is not so bad as that, Charlotte. You have time. There is more to life than matrimony."

"You would do well to clear your thoughts of romantic notions before you must settle down and marry. It is our duty."

Those were provoking words. Charlotte knew that. Her controlled expression revealed nothing, but something must be wrong. Charlotte never incited an argument when her calm sense proved more effective in making her point.

"You are particularly practical this morning, Charlotte. What has brought this on?"

Charlotte looked over her shoulder. As usual, Mercer rode behind them — at a sufficient distance to allow them private conversation while offering protection.

Whatever Charlotte said was not meant to be overheard.

For the second time that morning, Elizabeth's heart lodged in her throat.

"I can confide in you, Lizzy, I know," Charlotte whispered. "I overheard my father talking with my brothers."

Charlotte admitting to eavesdropping? This bore ill.

"The estate is in debt, and unless John marries into a fortune — a vain hope, I know as well as you do—" the words tumbled out of Charlotte's mouth only for her to cut them short.

Elizabeth huffed. She held little compassion for irresponsible older brothers. John Lucas would not marry just anyone. Oh no. He had been brought up for greater things and now, past the age of forty, he required not only a fortune but also a title. Anything to wash the tint of trade from his name and to be addressed by something grander than his father, Sir William … who had at least done something other than marry to secure a knighthood and the title that came with it.

"I see you understand my predicament," Charlotte said, her voice quivering. Emotion never overcame Charlotte, and the hopelessness in her tone tore at Elizabeth's heart. This was grave.

There had to be a way out. "What of George's horses? Can they not save the estate?" Elizabeth asked.

George Lucas was the second son. Unlike his elder brother, he was responsible. Once Sir William had sold his interests in trade, along with all means of increasing his fortune, George had taken up the only method of gain society permitted gentlemen. He bred and trained horses.

Charlotte sighed. "It is not enough. One of our stallions would have to sire a racehorse or some other impossible scheme for the *ton* to take notice of us. George does well enough, and I am grateful he does what he can, but we cannot forget to take into account my eldest brother's habits. It is a pity he is to inherit instead of George. My future would not feel so precarious…"

Elizabeth understood precarious futures. The Bennet daughters' interests were not provided for any better than Charlotte's were, and Elizabeth's mother lived in constant dread of her husband perishing before all five of her offspring married and settled.

As much as Elizabeth wished for a love match, she

knew that if she did not find it in a timely fashion, she would soon enough find herself in the same situation as Charlotte — desperate and on the edge of spinsterhood without a penny to her name. A burden to her family.

She shook the dreadful prospect from her mind. This morning was not providing the release she craved at all. If anything, she felt encumbered. Trapped. Defeated.

No, never defeated! She would not succumb, nor would she allow Charlotte to wallow in gloom and doom. Not when they still had their freedom and sense enough to plan a better solution. Why waste the beauty of a new morning full of promise on distressing possibilities which might never come to pass? No. Elizabeth possessed too much hope to fall prey to the depths of despair.

"… And so, you see how the responsibility to marry into a fortune falls onto me," Charlotte said. "Forgive me if I seem downcast, but it is a desperate situation. I am neither very young nor sufficiently pretty."

Elizabeth snapped, "I will not hear you speak ill of yourself, Charlotte. Not when you are the most sensible, wise lady I have the privilege of knowing. Any gentleman would be fortunate to have you for his wife."

"If he got past my lack of fortune, connections, and youth."

"Superficial matters of no consequence." Elizabeth dismissed the lot with a wave of her hand. "Or need I remind you of my lack of fortune and connections?"

"Ah, but that is as far as our similarities go, Lizzy, for you are both young and quite pretty. There is a vivacity about you which will draw gentlemen like flies to honey."

"Flies! I would sooner swat the troublesome creatures away! I have no patience for bothersome vermin, nor would I wish you to suffer their company. I most certainly would never agree to marry one. Would that we could away to London … or anywhere other than here! What I would give for one season away. For you to meet a gentleman worthy of your sensible heart. For some excitement before we must succumb to marriage."

Charlotte laughed. "Marriage is not a disease! No wonder you dread it."

Pleased her humor had restored lightness to their conversation, Elizabeth said, "I do not dread marriage. Not really. I only fear I will have to marry before I have a chance to do anything consequential. Is it too much to wish for one adventure to cherish forever? I could endure almost anything so long as I was allowed that. You are not the only one who can be practical, Charlotte. I know the likelihood of my meeting a man I could love with my whole heart and soul is slight in Hertfordshire. I am convinced the gentleman I would gladly marry resides outside the county, and, yet, my father is determined to keep me from traveling."

"He agreed for you to travel with your aunt and uncle."

"And I am grateful. I am. However, I know very well that he will deny every future request, just as he has done in the past. He believes I ought to be content with Mr. Pinkerton's books and one short trip when I fear they shall only whet my appetite."

"Oh, Lizzy, I am sorry." Charlotte did not argue against what she knew to be true.

"We are a pitiful pair this morning. Let us not behave like damsels in distress. We are masters of our own fate, Charlotte. Captains of our own destiny."

"In a just world, perhaps."

Elizabeth frowned. The world was not always just, and until that changed, Charlotte would accept the first hand offered to her, and Elizabeth would have to continue sneaking out of Longbourn for the Lucas Lodge stables at the crack of dawn. Which reminded her...

"We should get going if I am to return to Long-bourn before breakfast. Are we going to ride or not?" Clucking her tongue, Elizabeth tapped Tempest's flanks and leaned into her right hip in expectation of the thrill of a good gallop.

CHAPTER 2

*F*itzwilliam Darcy rubbed his thumb over the monogrammed casing of his compass as he oversaw the packing of his last trunk, eager to take his leave before his return to Pemberley was postponed yet again. He had not set foot on his estate for nearly three years. A reprieve was well past due. Lord knew he had earned it.

He was tired. Weary. In sore need of a brief retreat to the familiar. To the verdant fields he knew as intimately as the back of his own hand; away from mucky roads and crowded towns. To families and tenants he had known his entire life; away from malicious strangers and two-faced traitors. To the warmth of his own fire and the comfort of his own bed; away from smoky tavern chimneys and bug-infested mattresses.

Darcy needed to go home. He needed to see his sister.

Since his cousin Colonel Richard Fitzwilliam had recruited Darcy, Georgiana had taken residence with their aunt Matlock. It was safer, and Georgiana enjoyed the company of her cousins in town.

Surely, she must miss the place where she had been born and had grown into a young lady. Surely, she missed it as badly as he did. Georgiana had not implied otherwise in her last letter. Other young ladies might resent being pulled away from the entertainments of town at the height of the season, but not Georgiana.

Darcy would collect her that morning, and together, they would return to Pemberley.

Pemberley. The tension in his shoulders melted away. He thought more clearly at Pemberley. Problems became more manageable at Pemberley. He could forget about the war and his role in it at Pemberley. Darcy opened the lid of his compass, looking down at the engraving on the inside. *Home is where the heart is.* Darcy's father had often quoted Pliny the Elder's words.

Though Darcy stood in his bedchamber at Darcy House, his heart was already at Pemberley. At his home.

One fortnight. That was all he required. One

fortnight after a three-year interim. Then he would get back to work. He would see his assignment through to his satisfaction.

A knock on the door pulled Darcy's thoughts back to the present. Gone was the glorious silence he had anticipated at his Derbyshire estate, replaced with the noise of London — clambering carriage wheels, horses' hooves, and voices getting louder as they drew nearer.

Wilson, Darcy's trusted valet, closed the trunk and hobbled to the opening door. Wilson never complained of his old army injury, and Darcy never spoke of it. They each bore scars in their own manner.

"The colonel is here," Wilson said as the gentleman in question breezed past the valet, charging into the room.

Darcy's stomach twisted. Richard was highly respected among the tightly knit circle who knew of their clandestine activities, but Darcy would not disguise his displeasure at seeing his cousin in uniform in his house. "What are you doing here?" he asked.

"What? Nary an offer of brandy? How do you know I have not come to congratulate you on the success of your latest mission?" Richard teased.

Darcy did not laugh. Richard always used charm

and humor to get what he wanted, and his use of it put Darcy's senses on alert. If anything, it convinced him that this was not a social call. Leo had sent him.

Wilson did not send the last trunk downstairs where the carriage awaited to convey him and his master to Pemberley. He stood at attention at the door, awaiting orders. He, too, knew something was amiss.

"What do you want?" Darcy asked, watching as Richard helped himself to the contents of the decanter on the bedside table.

Pouring another glass and handing it to Darcy, Richard said, "To a job well done! I salute you, Cousin."

"It is too early in the day to imbibe."

Richard shrugged, tossing back the contents of his glass. Smacking his lips together, he grinned. "It is not too early when one has been up all night, and it is never too early to celebrate. The papers caught wind of the story, and they have printed a flattering account of how the French spies were thwarted once again by an anonymous son of England." He produced the offensive article from his breast pocket.

Darcy turned away from it. "They glorify unlawful rebels in the same paragraph in which they extol the cleverness of the men who prevent them from selling secrets to the enemy."

"Allow me to reassure you on that point. They said nothing of your cleverness."

Darcy glared at Richard.

The ingrate's grin widened. "You ought to embrace your fame, Darcy. When the war is over, they will proclaim you a hero. Already, there is talk of your *nom de guerre.* I am rather partial to The Oxford Orchid, although I admit there is a romantic appeal to The Crimson Carnation."

Darcy's fists clenched. "Ridiculous!"

"Do you prefer The Purple Pansy?"

Darcy should have accepted the drink Richard had offered him. Then he would have had something to throw at his cousin's smirking face. But Richard would love to provoke Darcy to anger, and so that was precisely the reaction of which Darcy would deprive him.

Taking a deep breath and feeling his cheeks cool, Darcy said levelly, "I do not wish for fame. My sole desire at this moment is to see Georgiana and return to our proper place."

Richard sighed. "I suspected as much. Left to your own devices, you would hide away at Pemberley like a hermit as you did before. You do know that is why I convinced you to occupy your time for a more worthy cause?"

"I have not set foot on my estate in three years, Richard. Three years!"

"Has it really been that long?" Richard rubbed his hand over his face, looking every bit as exhausted as Darcy felt.

Seizing the opportunity presented to him, Darcy said, "I am leaving. Do you want a lift as far as Matlock House? I intend to collect Georgiana and be on our way within the hour. She is expecting me. I already spoke with our director at Leo, and he agreed that a fortnight at Pemberley was reward enough for the latest capture."

"About that," Richard said, gesturing to the chairs by the unlit fire. "Pray hear me out before you decide on the direction of your coach."

"It is already decided," Darcy enunciated, wishing to Heaven he had told the butler to deny Richard entrance until he could depart. What had been a mere twist in his stomach seconds ago was quickly turning into a sinking sensation.

"Yes, well, The Four Horsemen rallied quicker than we had supposed. We received word only this morning." Richard's eyes bore into Darcy's.

Darcy sat, his ears buzzing while his cousin prattled on. The Four Horsemen were the plague of

England, disguised as modern-day Robin Hoods. Their supposed generosity had bought the allegiance of an immense network of smugglers and ruffians who lined their pockets with blood money.

He had been so close to catching them. He knew their names. Sir Leonard Sharp. Sir Benedict Voss. Sir Harcourt Grant. Sir Erasmus Clark. Gentlemen of fortune. Gentlemen held in high esteem. Gentlemen influential among the upper classes as well as the lowest. All knighted by King George and friendly with the Prince Regent. All suspected of treason by the elite branch of the British government with whom he worked.

Darcy had been so close to catching them, but just as they had done many times before, they vanished, leaving a middleman who guarded his silence as vigilantly as a monk to take the blame. The middleman's family had since come into some money — enough to purchase a comfortable cottage in the country. Darcy pressed his fingers against his throbbing temples. Had life become so cheap, a price could be put on it? A life for a country cottage?

The Four Horsemen denounced the extravagances of the Prince Regent while they grew their wealth at the expense of those who would offer their lives in exchange for a meager cut of the spoils. They were despicable. The lowest of the low. They had to be stopped.

"I knew that would get your attention, Darcy." Richard nodded at Wilson, who immediately began unpacking the trunk.

Darcy was too numb to stop him. Duty trumped desire. Pemberley would have to wait. Georgiana would have to wait. Drat it all! Cooling his disappointment, he asked, "What can you tell me?"

Richard leaned forward, clasping his fingers together. "Only enough to alert our agency to upcoming trouble. Leo suspects The Four Horsemen have ties to a family in Hertfordshire. As you know, the men themselves are never seen together, but each of them individually has been seen in the presence of a gentleman we wish for you to befriend. He may very well prove to be the link which will lead us to the vipers' den … and, we pray, to their capture. I have made all the arrangements." He sat back, squirming in his seat.

Darcy watched his cousin warily, his sense of foreboding growing with every crossing and recrossing of the colonel's feet. Why was he nervous?

Clearing his throat, Richard added, "Next week, it is my hope you will accompany Bingley to a comfortable estate he recently let near Meryton."

"Bingley?" Darcy shot up from his seat, unable to remain still. Pacing before the fireplace, he demanded, "What on earth convinced you to involve Bingley in this?"

Richard joined him, stopping Darcy with a firm grip on his shoulder. "Only my confidence in your extreme discretion and incomparable skill." There was no humor in his voice now.

Charles Bingley had been Darcy's friend since their Cambridge days. Bingley's innocent belief in the good of people had often put him at a disadvantage to which Darcy's skepticism often came to the rescue. Darcy had saved Bingley from harm, and Bingley kept Darcy's optimism from dying (no small feat when every day his faith in the good of humanity was put to the test.) It was a friendship of opposites restoring balance, and Darcy resented Richard for manipulating, and potentially endangering, his one truly good friend.

Darcy shoved his hands through his hair. "But Bingley? Of all people, Rich, why him?"

"I am sorry. Truly, from the depth of my soul, I am. Bingley was interested in letting an estate in Hertfordshire. You know how he is."

Darcy groaned. "Half of London knows of his plans."

"Exactly. So, when we found out the property

was located right where we need you, and he was finally convinced to let the estate—"

Darcy interrupted, "Convinced by you, I presume?"

Richard bunched his cheeks with a grunt. "It was not difficult. Persuading Miss Bingley was another matter, but her objections calmed considerably when I suggested the almost certain possibility of you joining their party."

"I hate you."

With a wide grin and another squeeze, Richard released his hold on Darcy's shoulder. "That is the spirit! I will give you details as I am informed, but for now, all I know is that you must travel with Bingley to Hertfordshire in a week's time. Miss Bingley will ensure her brother sends you an invitation to accompany them. Your mission, should you choose to accept it, is to travel with them to Netherfield Park so you may befriend the gentleman we have seen in the company of The Four Horsemen. Do you accept?" Richard extended his hand.

Darcy stared at the appendage, the enticing vision of Pemberley blurring Richard's hand. How badly he wanted to refuse. But he could not. Bingley was no match for The Four Horsemen, and Darcy would hate himself for all eternity should his friend come to danger when he could have prevented it.

Softly, Richard added, "I am sorry, Darcy. I did not intend to involve Bingley, but Leo does not have the freedom to spare one man when the lives of thousands are at risk."

Darcy could only nod. He knew how it was, as callous and unjust as every war fought before.

"This is the last one, Darcy. I feel it. One last mission, and then you may ensconce yourself at Pemberley."

Richard did not understand how cruel it was to kindle his hope after he had snatched it away. "You cannot know what you are doing to me. I miss it so badly, I ache."

"That ache has nothing to do with Pemberley, Darcy. It was there when I dragged you away after your father died. It is the people you miss. You are lonely."

Darcy shot him another glare.

Richard held up his hands. "When you meet the right young woman, you will learn the true meaning of home."

Utter nonsense. They were spies. They did not get close to anyone. It was too dangerous. What did Richard know of love and women?

"What shall I tell Georgiana? She is expecting me." Would she be as disappointed as Darcy was?

"My mother has taken care of that. With the

London season in swing, there is much to distract her here. Georgiana will not have time enough to miss her grumpy older brother. In fact, I believe she was relieved when I gave her the news." Richard shoved his hand closer to Darcy. "Do you accept?"

Darcy shook before he could convince himself not to or take offense at his cousin's presumption. "The gentleman I am to investigate, what is his name?"

"Sir William Lucas."

Darcy mulled the name over in his mind as Richard detailed the connection between him and The Four Horsemen.

Sir William was a gentleman of fortune with an estate bearing his name. His humble origins in trade made him a favorite with lower classes, but the gentle class also respected him. More significant was this: Sir William had been knighted by King George. Just as each member of The Four Horsemen had.

There were too many similarities to ignore. By all appearances, The Four Horsemen had recruited another member.

CHAPTER 3

*D*arcy excused himself from the group, earning nothing more than a frown from Mrs. Bennet, who was too pleased with her eldest daughter's success in securing a dance with Bingley to overlook his own oversight toward her remaining four daughters.

Since he avoided dancing with Miss Elizabeth, Darcy decided it best to forgo dancing altogether that evening. He had work to do — work which would increase the safety and security of every person at the assembly. If that was not justification enough, he could not conjure a better one.

Skirting around the edge of the room, Darcy took advantage of his superior height to observe the villagers, tradesmen, and scattered gentry crowded into the assembly room. There was a notable lack of higher society, thus explaining to some degree the rashness Mrs. Bennet allowed herself. With nobody to check her — for Mr. Bennet had clearly given up on the task long ago, if indeed he had ever attempted to improve his wife — she felt free to indulge her vulgar speech. Several times her voice perforated Darcy's thoughts and intruded the conversations he attempted to listen to with estimations of his and Bingley's wealth along with doting praise over Miss Bingley and Mrs. Hurst's gaudy gowns.

Miss Elizabeth, on the other hand, made her neighbors smile everywhere she went. From the tenants with frayed coat collars to the ladies turned out in their finest, and the shopkeepers decked out in their wares, she conversed easily with all and left each group she addressed happier for having received her attention.

To his perplexed first impression of a lady caked in mud were added the more complementary endowments of lively, observant eyes, an oft present bright smile, and laughter that tinkled like chiming bells.

She captured his attention, and Darcy could not fathom why. Too many times, his vision settled on her when he ought to have been following the movements of Sir William.

It perturbed Darcy to feel an instant connection

to the young lady. There must be a valid, logical reason for it. His instincts were too acutely trained to mislead him, and time and again, his gaze wandered to the impertinent miss. Miss Elizabeth.

Thus presented with a problem requiring immediate solution, Darcy studied Miss Elizabeth more fully as she flitted from one group to the next, her eyes frequently tracking the location and activities of her sisters (especially the younger ones.)

It occurred to Darcy that Miss Elizabeth fitted the profile of an excellent informant. She clearly possessed the confidence of every being in the building. No doubt, she used her humor to diffuse tense situations as well as to extract information others struggled to attain (such as himself at that moment.) She was insightful enough to watch her sisters and possessed the initiative required to prevent disaster before it could start. She reminded Darcy of Richard.

That was it! He understood now. He was only drawn to Miss Elizabeth because she represented someone familiar to him in these unfamiliar surroundings. She was also close to Sir William's eldest daughter, who had presented herself briefly after Miss Elizabeth had sped away on her horse earlier that morning.

He had not been distracted by her at all. He had

only recognized in her the traits he often sought out in a valuable asset. Miss Elizabeth would be a worthy partner ... were she not a female. It was a pity his instincts had not accounted for her gender. Darcy could not in good conscience involve her in his assignment. Never let it be said that Fitzwilliam Darcy endangered the life of a lady.

However, while Darcy wished for his mission's sake that his best means of befriending Sir Lucas was not a female, his frequent gazes in her direction could not rebut the fact that Miss Elizabeth was unquestionably a member of the fairer sex ... and that her similarities to Richard did not venture beyond certain tells of character.

She glided with a nimbleness which rivaled the athleticism of many of Darcy's acquaintances employed by Leo.

While her incident with the mare lent itself to the conclusion that she had much to learn in regards to horsemanship, she had known to kick her feet free of the stirrup and her skirts in the split-second before she fell. Either she was not so inexperienced as the scene suggested, or she had too much experience tumbling from racing equines. Darcy guessed the former, as only a fool would risk the latter. And he was convinced Miss Elizabeth was not a fool.

"This is nothing like what we are accustomed to,

is it, Mr. Darcy?" a voice which was not Mrs. Bennet's, but which was equally unwelcome, said.

Darcy frowned. How strange he should compare Miss Bingley to Mrs. Bennet … which, naturally, led to the passing observation that Miss Elizabeth seemed quite distinct from her mother.

He really must stop thinking of her. She was not the informant he sought, and his repeated attempts to regain focus when Miss Elizabeth persisted in invading his thoughts was onerous. As were Miss Bingley's incessant interruptions.

Miss Bingley smiled, clearly pleased with her observation and emboldened to deepen her cut against the assembled. "I would not be surprised if someone should release a pig any moment!" She must have believed her disdain to be clever, for she chuckled under her gloved fingers.

Darcy could not bear her company a moment longer. The crowd too closely resembled the assemblies he had attended near Pemberley. Out of respect for his own hard-working tenants, he would not share in her unseemly derision.

Excusing himself to continue about the room, he watched Sir William for the better part of the next hour. He was a marvel — a true master. Not once did the gentleman's disguise falter. No calculating looks or hardened eyes. No unexplained absences or sly glances. Had Darcy not witnessed Sir William's insightful cut to Miss Bingley and heard his naming of Sir Erasmus, he would have been the last gentleman in the country Darcy would ever have suspected of treachery.

Darcy was confident of his abilities, but Sir William exceeded his level of skill. Darcy despised disguise. He hated hidden motives and lies, and it was plain to see that Sir William was lord of all such traits. To confront him directly would be a grave mistake.

From whom, then, could he extract information without arousing suspicions (other than Miss Elizabeth, of course)? Sir William's family? One of his friends? A longtime servant? A close neighbor?

Mr. Bennet came to mind. Sir William had introduced him heartily. He was one to watch, and soon Darcy found himself standing along the back wall, where he could more discreetly observe Mr. Bennet debate with two of Sir William's sons.

Mr. John Lucas was the firstborn, and the male equivalent to Miss Bingley so far as Darcy ascertained. His cravat was folded with greater care than the occasion required, and the frequency with which he partook of his snuffbox and peered downward through his eyepiece at everyone gave the image of a determined dandy with delusions of grandeur. He had not presumed to dance with any of the ladies present, much like Darcy (but for vastly different reasons, Darcy presumed.)

The character of Mr. Lucas' brother was much more difficult to sketch. George Lucas possessed none of the airs of his older brother. To the contrary, when George Lucas was not deep in conversation, he sought out the ladies who sat on the chairs lining the fringes of the ballroom floor for want of a partner.

Where Mr. Lucas proudly scorned his social inferiors, George (Darcy would think of him by his Christian name to avoid confusion) was considerate. While Mr. Lucas was unmarried (and, from his appearance, around the age of forty), George often sought out the attention of his wife and their three children. His eldest, a girl with two missing front teeth, giggled while they turned about the room with her feet on top of his boots just as Georgiana had done with their own father once upon a time. At Pemberley.

George Lucas was a family man through and through, resembling his father in his amiable manners and attentiveness to everyone. But that knowledge, and the likelihood that Sir William had established a treasonous liaison with The Four Horsemen, lent Darcy motive enough to keep a watchful eye on George. At a time when many families suffered to keep their estates whole under the weighty demands of the taxes levied against them, how far would he go to secure his extensive manor and property for his family? Especially if his father demanded it of him?

Darcy drew nearer to the trio, careful to appear as if he were intent on the dancers and not on their conversation.

Mr. Bennet said, "Ah, but is it fair to assume that your definition of justice is the same as mine, or anyone else's in the room for that matter?"

What an interesting question. Darcy would never presume to speak for others, but he did not wane in his own estimation of right and wrong.

Mr. Lucas yawned.

George, however, rubbed his chin before replying, "Had you asked me that same question a few years ago, I would have insisted that justice is as plain to distinguish from injustice as black is from white. But the war has a way of changing perspectives and including more shades of gray I would never have acknowledged before."

"Even values and morals? That is a bold claim, indeed," countered Mr. Bennet, rubbing his hands together with a smile which implied a love for thoughtful conversation. He was the sort of man to get so lost in theory, he never got around to practical application.

George answered, "I do not speak of values and morals. A good man will always live by the norms he demands of himself or risk losing all self-respect."

Mr. Lucas rolled his eyes and dangled his eyepiece in one hand.

George added, "Perhaps an example will clarify my meaning. Let us consider taxes. Would it be just for a gentleman to refuse to pay an unreasonable tax when he has no way of knowing if his money is being used for an honorable purpose? I, for one, would gladly pay a tax if I knew the funds would be used to supply warm blankets, nourishing food, and quality horses to the men for which I assume such taxes are intended. However, it is a bitter drought to swallow when I read of Prinny's extravagant residences and immoderate parties."

Mr. Lucas scoffed, although Darcy imagined he would not have been above attending one of those parties, had he been invited.

Mr. Bennet leaned back against his heels. "Perhaps so, from a gentleman's point of view. But you can hardly expect a king's son, born into privilege, to understand our plight. Does that make him unjust ... or merely ignorant?"

"Both. Any man can learn if he has the inclination. Ignorance is dangerous, and any man's insistence on remaining so when he is in a position of great power and responsibility is a horrible injustice to the people who by law and tradition must look to him and submit to his authority," George replied.

Mr. Bennet bowed his head, his shoulders slumping. "Ay, that it is," he muttered.

George's eyes widened, and he clapped his hand on Mr. Bennet's shoulder. "Pray do not misunderstand me, Mr. Bennet. When I spoke of ignorance, I never meant to imply—"

"It is true, though, is it not?" Mr. Bennet interrupted. "It is the reason I allow my girls more intellectual liberties — and less opportunities — than is generally approved of by society. Had I not been ignorant of my son's—"

"Charlotte tells me Miss Elizabeth is counting the days to her tour with the Gardiners. Mrs. Gardiner will be happy to pass through Derbyshire, I imagine," George said, preventing the older gentleman from uttering what he had been about to reveal.

Darcy strained to listen. Any mention of Derbyshire was of interest to him, and he could more easily join their conversation now the subject had been broached.

Recovering himself, Mr. Bennet began, "About that…"

"What is the countryside compared to the luxuries and diversions of town?" Miss Bingley's imperious tone at Darcy's opposite side overpowered Mr. Bennet's revelation.

Darcy bristled. Her timing was horrendous. Not only had Darcy been about to learn about Miss Elizabeth's journey to Derbyshire, but George had expressed some contrary views regarding justice and their Prince Regent which merited further conversation.

Miss Bingley whined, "To think we are missing the theater for this! I do not know what Charles was thinking." She fanned her face, and for the second time that evening, Darcy could not help but notice the similarities between her and Mrs. Bennet.

"You could ask him," Darcy suggested, moving away from her lest she think him encouraging. If he moved to the other side of the conversing trio, he could still listen for another opportunity to join their conversation without drawing attention to himself. Maybe then, Miss Bingley would go away.

"He is busy dancing. I should very much like to dance, but there is a shocking deficiency of suitable gentlemen here." She arched her neck and looked up at him expectantly.

"I do not intend to dance," he said, more determined than ever to commit to his decision. He could not have voiced his determination with greater precision.

Just then, several dancers circled the refreshment table, and a few ladies sat waiting for their next partner. One of them was Miss Elizabeth. Several of the "unsuitable" gentlemen to whom Miss Bingley had referred looked her way. One of them had the gall to take a step toward her.

Miss Bingley huffed and stormed off in the opposite direction.

Darcy struggled to tune his attention on the conversation, of which he had missed a goodly portion by now. To his vexation, he was too keenly aware of Miss Elizabeth sitting so near where he had stood moments ago. There were dozens of empty chairs lining the walls around the room. Why had she chosen *that* one?

His jaw tightened and his fists clenched. *Focus, man, focus!*

"It is difficult to maintain loyalty to a monarch who flaunts his wealth while his subjects suffer," George said.

Delicately sniffing his nose, Mr. Lucas said, "It is a wonder nobody has taken affairs into their own hands."

"How so?" asked Mr. Bennet.

Darcy held his breath to overhear the reply.

"For example, my father—"

"Darcy!" called Bingley jovially. "What are you doing standing in a corner when you ought to be dancing?"

Darcy crossed his arms over his chest. It was either that or strangle his friend. How would he ever complete his mission if everyone seemed intent on interrupting at the most inconvenient times? He shot Bingley a glare meant to silence him, but it was too late. Mr. Lucas' revelation about his father was said, and he was now regarding Bingley through his eyepiece.

The moment was lost. Another vital clue had slipped through his fingers.

Shaking with repressed frustration, Darcy seethed, "I do not wish to dance."

"Do not be stupid, man. There is more than one lady sitting for want of a partner." Bingley babbled about how lovely Miss Bennet was, adding, "Look! There is one of her sisters sitting down just behind you, who is very pretty, and I daresay very agreeable." Of all the women in the room Bingley could have indicated, he nodded at Miss Elizabeth. Darcy did not need to look behind him to see. He was well aware of Miss Elizabeth's position in the room.

Taking a step toward Miss Elizabeth, Darcy's

heart leapt into his throat when Bingley said, "Do let me ask my partner to introduce you."

To the very lady with whom Darcy would deny himself the pleasure of a dance for the danger she posed to him? On a night full of distractions and impediments? When Bingley himself had caused Darcy to miss the most valuable piece of information he had collected about Sir William until now?

It was too much.

Darcy snapped, "She is tolerable, but not handsome enough to tempt *me*. I am in no humor at present to give consequence to young ladies who are slighted by other men. You had better return to your partner and enjoy her smiles, for you are wasting your time with me."

The harsh words effectively carried out what Darcy had meant them to. Bingley left in a confusion of shock and apology.

Darcy knew better than to look behind him, but Bingley's flustered reaction prompted him to ignore his intuition.

The flush in Miss Elizabeth's cheeks and the rapidity with which George asked her to dance told Darcy that Bingley had not been the only person to hear his insult.

George scowled disapproval, as was to be expected. Darcy knew he deserved it. Unable to attack his tender friend, he had attacked a young lady whose only fault had been her uncanny ability to distract him. He had acted unjustly.

He felt like the raincloud that ruined the parade and melted the children's sweets. How could he have been such a brute when he was a gentleman?

However, it was Miss Elizabeth's smile and the defiantly humorous twinkle in her eye that cut Darcy to the core. How could she possibly be so gracious as to spare him a smile after he had insulted her vanity?

CHAPTER 4

ONE WEEK LATER, NETHERFIELD PARK

*D*arcy could not rest. Tonight, he would meet Sir William. The gentleman had invited Bingley to the Meryton Assembly the day before, and Bingley had been happy to assure Sir William of their attendance.

Darcy wished he had been there for Sir William's call, but he had not counted on the swiftness of Bingley's neighbor in welcoming him to the area. It could not have been helped. Darcy required his fastest mount, and when his groom suggested they stop at the farrier's before continuing on to join their party, he had seen fit to acquiesce.

The delay had meant a missed opportunity, but not all was lost. There were advantages to meeting his mark in the crowded, celebratory setting of an assembly. Darcy could scrutinize Sir William in a setting comfortable to most, surrounded by the family and friends the gentleman had likely known all of his life. It was a favorable environment for even the most accomplished traitor to let down his guard. Would Sir William reveal a glimpse of his clever cunning — of his duplicitous nature? Darcy counted on it.

The fields were damp from a week of thunderstorms and rain, but the weather had taken a turn for the better. The cerulean morning sky beckoned Darcy to steel his nerves and sharpen his thoughts, as fresh air and exercise always did. A copse of trees at the top of a rise drew his eye. Darcy hoped it would give him a view of Lucas Lodge.

Leaving the slumbering residents at Netherfield Park behind, he headed to the stables where his groom, Oakley, readied his horse. Oakley and Wilson had stuck with Darcy since their first assignment. Darcy trusted them implicitly.

At his insistence, Richard had sent two more Leo agents to pose as servants at Netherfield Park — a gardener to keep watch outside and a footman to protect the residents inside. Darcy would no more endanger his friend than he would trample the bluebells and orchids scattered over the rolling fields.

Directing his chestnut gelding up a narrow path, he mulled over the little he had learned since his arrival and considered how best to proceed.

He would not appear to advantage at the assembly, he knew. How could he beside Bingley, with his open manners and easy laughter?

Darcy had always been guarded and wary by nature, but years of association with Leo had made him more so. His life, and the lives of others, depended on his discretion. However, it came with a cost. While distrust and suspicion served him well in his assignments, it often alienated Darcy from society. He had many acquaintances but few close friends. For three years, he had not widened his circle. He could not rightly do so.

And now, he was in Hertfordshire to ingratiate himself with the Lucases. He would have to try harder to behave the charming gentleman and thus gain their confidence. The success of his mission depended upon it. His prompt return to his sister and Pemberley lay in the balance.

Taking a deep breath of fresh air, Darcy pushed his horse forward to the top of the knoll, wishing the time between now and the assembly would pass with merciful speed.

He heard the pounding of hooves in an alternate rhythm to that of his own steed. They grew louder the closer he came to the top of the rise. Darcy veered off the path to allow the approaching galloper the right-of-way, avoiding the puddles slick with mud and regretting his choice when his horse had no other option but to trample a cluster of orchids shaped like white and green butterflies. *Oxford Orchid.* The name popped into his mind unwelcome. Blast Richard! Thanks to his infernal cousin, flowers were ruined for Darcy.

Whirling around to face the path, Darcy watched in horror as the racing horse startled at his sudden movement, the mare losing her footing as her mistress lost her seat.

SEVERAL THOUGHTS PASSED through Elizabeth's mind in the split-second it took for her to fall to the sloppy ground. First and foremost, sidesaddles were an evil invention of man. Good thing she had freed her feet from the stirrup without getting too tangled in her skirts (another questionable invention when it came to riding.) Second, this never would have happened on Tempest. Third, and more important, who else was riding on her and Charlotte's favorite path at the same early hour?

Two polished boots appeared not two feet in

front of her nose. A deep, velvety voice said, "Are you hurt?"

The gloved hand that hovered by her face was so clean, Elizabeth hesitated to take it. She lifted her own hand from the slippery muck to confirm what her damp skin and garments suggested. She was covered in mud.

She looked up at the mannerly stranger, the morning sun casting an angelic halo around what she prayed was merely an apparition, a figment of her overactive imagination. The chiseled jaw, firm chin, and the arch of concern in the dark brow of the handsome man standing over her certainly fit the appearance of a dreamy hero.

Elizabeth blinked, but he did not disappear. Nor did she wake to find herself at Longbourn, tucked into her warm bed. In fact, she was getting cold. She looked down. Yes, the mud was real. The man was real. Her humiliation was real.

Clenching her fingers into fists, Elizabeth stifled a groan. What a lovely predicament she was in. As if it was not bad enough to be thrown from a horse when she considered herself a skilled horsewoman, it had been observed by a stranger who would always associate this unfavorable moment with her. That he was handsome only added to her vexation.

"Pray allow me to assist you," he said, moving his hand closer to her.

Handsome and a perfect gentleman. The affront against Elizabeth's vanity multiplied. And yet, reason told her she could not ignore him and remain in the puddle all day. It was a quandary made of her own foolish self-consciousness. She could not extract herself from the muck without making a worse disaster of her riding habit, but neither did she wish to dirty his pristine kid leather gloves.

Stuff and fluff, she was being ridiculous! There was nothing to do but make light of her situation. Then, maybe, the stranger would understand her blush to be the result of laughter instead of shame. Shame at her own bruised vanity (for, what import did she place on others' opinions of her?) and for her delayed reaction. One would think she had suffered a blow to the head.

"Are you injured? Did you hit your head?" the stranger asked.

Ha ha! There it was. She could not take offense with his question when she had thought the same only a moment before. If anything, she must applaud the gentleman's sound deduction.

By the time Elizabeth's smile reached her eyes, it had developed a sincerity of its own, and she laughed heartily as she placed her hand in his. "I thank you, sir. I assure you the greatest injury I suffered was to my pride."

The stranger pulled her to her feet before she could catch her breath.

Now that the sun did not blind her, she considered the gentleman. His eyes were the same color of the lapis lazuli on her brooch. Life was especially unjust against her that morning.

It became imperative that she explain. "The mud is slippery—" She cringed. Of course, mud was slippery. "And, mercifully soft."

Elizabeth bit her lips together before she said anything else nonsensical. Maybe she *had* hit her head during the fall. She wiped the mud from her brooch, avoiding his gaze until she had collected enough of her dignity to look him in the eye.

The gentleman watched her. He must think her mad. Or worse, foolish. She was tempted to offer another explanation, but the twitch at the corner of his lips stopped her. Whoever he was, he was not immune to the humor of their situation. It was some comfort — enough to latch on to.

Her tension eased and her embarrassment subsided, Elizabeth felt amusement bubble up inside her.

"Lizzy!" cried Charlotte from behind her.

Elizabeth startled. She had forgotten all about Charlotte. Pulling her gaze away from the mystery man, who only then dropped her gloved fingers and stepped away, Elizabeth wondered how long he had been holding her hand. How long had she been staring into his eyes?

Her cheeks burned once again. How could she act like a moonstruck maiden in the full light of morning? Had Elizabeth observed herself, she would have poked fun at her own folly and nonsense.

Mercer gathered the mare's reins before she stepped on them — something that only occurred to Elizabeth to do when she saw it done. Some horse-woman she was! The gentleman must think her completely inept.

She had never felt more helpless. Elizabeth did not like it one jot, and she determined not to continue in the same manner for a second more.

Defiantly avoiding so much as a peripheral gaze at the gentleman lest her senses take leave of her once again, Elizabeth turned to Charlotte. "I am well. I ought to have known there might be other riders along the path instead of charging heedlessly ahead, and now I have received my due punishment." She pulled her mud-caked habit from her body, the further consequences of her present state chilling her like another dash of cold puddle water.

Elizabeth's heart hammered against her ribs. "My father!" she gasped, feeling physically ill. There would be no hiding what had happened from him. The line she walked to maintain the freedom she cherished was a fine one … and she had crossed it.

The poor gentleman behind her had every right to think her a complete hoyden with abominable manners, but if she did not return to Longbourn before her family gathered in the breakfast parlor, her father would use this incident to forbid her from ever riding again. That it was her own doing smarted the worst.

Collecting the reins from Mercer and rushing him to assist her atop the dreaded sidesaddle, Elizabeth mounted, and with a heartfelt "Thank you!", she threw an apologetic smile behind her as she took off past gaping Charlotte toward Lucas Lodge.

Of what use were polite introductions when her freedom was on the chopping block? Elizabeth determined not to concern herself about the mannerly gentleman. She had graver matters to worry about.

However, the hint of his smile stuck with Elizabeth all the way back to the stables, and the image kept up with her as she ran to Longbourn where her and Jane's maid, Emily, paced by the washing line.

Oh dear. Elizabeth's worst fear was unfolding before her eyes.

"Miss!" Emily gasped, inspecting Elizabeth from top to bottom and seeing the tremendous task before her.

"I am sorry. Perhaps it looks worse than it is?" Elizabeth hoped so. The habit was the only attire suitable for riding in her possession, and she had been hard-pressed to acquire it.

"It is not that, Miss. It is just that … Mr. Bennet is breaking his fast and he has already asked about you."

Elizabeth's heart sank. She was too late. "Drat," she whispered.

Thinking quickly, she peeled off her gloves and habit, handing them to Emily. "Let us hope my gown is not so messy as to arouse suspicion. We will cause too much fuss if we enter together. Allow me to go upstairs first, then I will give you a signal from the window."

Emily's subsequent frown did not inspire any encouragement. "At least, clean your face, Miss," she said, handing out a recently washed linen.

Elizabeth reached her fingers up to her cheeks, brushing off dried chunks of dirt and giving rise to the vain hope that the gentleman had not seen enough of her face to recognize her again.

Scrubbing her face, she thanked Emily. And, straightening her shoulders, Elizabeth entered the residence through the kitchen. If she could sneak through the back of the house, she might make it to the stairs without being seen. She would change into a clean morning gown and join her father in the breakfast parlor where he would not suspect anything was untoward.

Raising her finger to her lips in greeting and plea to the cook, Elizabeth tiptoed down the hall to the stairs, each step carrying her closer to the solution to her predicament.

Three more steps.

Her fingers grasped the bottom of the banister. The landing was in sight. She would take the stairs two at a time and be in her room in a trice.

This just might work!

"Lizzy? What are you doing sneaking around? Have you no pity on my poor nerves? Such tremblings all over me. Such pains in my head and beatings at heart, I can get no rest by night nor by day," her mother whined behind her.

Elizabeth froze in place, her foot poised over the first step, her hopes of escaping notice effectively dashed. Of course, her mother would start the day earlier on the morn of the assembly where their new neighbor — a gentleman of fortune and his friend of an even greater fortune — were supposed to attend. Elizabeth would not spoil her mother's excitement by mentioning how she had most likely chanced upon one of the two gentlemen. Mama would be thrilled, and she would want a detailed account of their meeting — a conversation which must be avoided at all costs.

Smoothing her skirts and plastering a smile on her face, Elizabeth turned, praying that her mother was alone in the room … or with her sisters … or with anyone else but Papa.

Ribbons, feathers, and dried flowers cluttered the couch where Mama sat. But, much to Elizabeth's disappointment, she was not alone. Papa sat beside her. His eyes were fixed on his "sneaking" daughter's muddy hem.

Elizabeth swallowed hard, rushing to allay his fears before they led him to Thomas. "As you see, I am completely unharmed, although my gown cannot claim the same," she teased, praying her father would raise his eyes to meet hers with the mischievous twinkle he so rarely displayed since her brother's death nearly ten years ago.

His gaze remained fixed on her hem. "You

suffered an accident?" he asked, finally looking up. There were tears in his eyes.

Blast. He was thinking of Thomas.

"I daresay the mud puddle fared worse than I did, although I look the worse for it," Elizabeth teased again.

Mama interfered. "You ought not go out alone as you do, Lizzy. We live in dangerous times! What if you met with a spy or a highwayman? Men such as them never marry," she exclaimed, fanning her face with the bonnet she had been trimming and unraveling the ribbons braided along the brim.

Elizabeth opened her mouth to say she had not met with anyone outside of the usual, but she quickly closed her mouth before she uttered a falsehood. She was already in enough trouble, and she did not want to drag the strange gentleman into her mother's argument.

"You will not be fit to be seen tonight, then how are you to give a favorable impression on Mr. Bingley and his friend? It falls to Jane and you, if you are so fortunate, to catch one of them. Our futures depend upon it!" The last of the bonnet's ribbon drifted to the floor, no match against Mama's vigorous fanning. "Such flutterings and spasms! You cannot know what I suffer."

Elizabeth clasped her hands together. "You are

right. I will be more cautious. If you give me leave, I will arrange for a bath immediately."

As she had hoped, her mother waved Elizabeth away to see to more important matters while she returned her attention to her bonnet.

But before Elizabeth had cleared the threshold, Papa spoke. "Pray keep your promise, my Lizzy. I have already lost one child. I could not bear to lose my favorite daughter as well."

Heartbroken tears prickled Elizabeth's eyes and anger tightened her throat. Why must she pay for the recklessness of her brother when she was nothing like him? Could her father not see the difference?

She stood frozen in the doorway, wanting nothing more but to escape and knowing she must hear her father out first. Holding her breath, she waited for him to continue.

He said, "I aim to speak to Sir William today about this matter."

Here it came. The moment she had dreaded since Mercer had taught her to ride along with Charlotte's younger sisters.

Papa's voice echoed as if he were speaking from another room, as if she were not standing a mere four paces from him. "You are not permitted to ride again. Do you understand?"

Elizabeth crossed her arms over her chest, the blow striking her harder than she had anticipated. She reached for her throat, unable to breathe.

"Oh, but, my dear," said Mama, "Sir William will not be able to attend to you with all the preparations he must see to before the assembly tonight."

Elizabeth was grateful to her mother for changing the topic, for once Mama got on the subject of a ball she was not easily veered away from it.

Papa sighed. It was his custom to enjoy an evening of quiet reading while the remainder of his household danced at the assembly. "Then I have no option but to attend the assembly so that I might have a word with him."

Her throat too tight to utter a word, Elizabeth bowed her head. She backed out of the room to the steady stream of her mother's prattle about gowns, marriageable gentlemen, and her expectations for the evening.

If only Elizabeth had not lost her seat when the mare startled. Tempest would not have shied. If only she had been riding Tempest. But Tempest belonged to Mr. Bingley now.

Closing her door, she leaned against it and slid down its length to the floor. She hoped Mr. Bingley was a kind master.

Maybe her father would reconsider. Maybe he would not speak with Sir William at all. He so rarely prohibited anything — except where she was concerned. No travel. Now, no horses. If this was her privilege for being his "favorite," she would gladly concede the honor to any one of her sisters.

Guilt pricked her conscience. Elizabeth could not wish such an evil on any of her sisters when she wished them all as happy as she wished to be. She would find a way out of this suffocation.

Through her blurred vision, she saw a wrapped parcel on the table beside her bed. She rose to see what it was. "My Lizzy" was written on the brown paper in her father's pen.

Elizabeth's stomach knotted. Of all the days Papa could give her a gift, she had shown up late from her ride covered in mud. Wretched daughter she was!

Beside his gift was a letter from her aunt Gardiner. It would contain news and plans of their upcoming journey. As badly as she craved good news, Elizabeth resisted the urge to open the letter first, reaching for her father's gift instead.

Peeling the paper off the rectangular object, Elizabeth read the title of the book. "*A General Collection of the Best and Most Interesting Voyages and Travels in All Parts of the World*" by John Pinkerton. The sight of it should have warmed her heart, but it made her heart sick. She had memorized the first volume before she realized what the tome stood for. Her father apparently thought that so long as she could read about the places she wished to see, she had no need of actually seeing them.

"I am never going to make it outside England," Elizabeth whispered to herself. How could she when she had not managed to travel any farther than her uncle Gardiner's residence in London?

Thank goodness she had her adventure to the Peak District with Aunt and Uncle to look forward to!

She flipped the book open to its contents. Several chapters were dedicated to Derbyshire. Her heart stirred. That was one of the stops Aunt and Uncle planned to take on their travels. First, Derbyshire and the Peak District to the north. Then, the Lake District. Then, the world. Or so Elizabeth dreamed.

Setting the book back on the table, she opened Aunt Gardiner's letter. She read the words. Then, blinking hard, she read them again. And again. They did not change no matter how she wished they would. Uncle Gardiner's engagements were too heavy to allow for a trip to the Lake District that summer. They would have to postpone their trip until the following spring.

The following spring! That was a whole year from now. An eternity.

Elizabeth collapsed — dirty gown and all — on her bed, the brooch she traced under her fingers little consolation as disappointment gripped her chest and dampened her cheeks.

CHAPTER 5

"I am certain Mr. Darcy agrees with me, do you not?" Miss Bingley ceased arguing with her brother to cast Darcy a furtive glance.

Darcy dared not agree with Miss Bingley on any topic lest she presume that a shared opinion raised her in his estimation.

Before Darcy composed a proper rebuttal, she continued, "Really, Charles, I am shocked you prefer the country over town when the season has started. We could be entertaining friends and going to the theater instead of to this rustic assembly."

Bingley fussed with his hat, mindlessly bending and twisting the brim. It was no small wonder he went through so many of them.

"It was our father's wish, Caroline, and it is mine,

to establish myself as a gentleman with an estate of my own. I have taken the counsel of those wiser than me to let an estate at which to learn. Would you have me wait until hunting season, when we will want to host our friends, and I will not have enough time to dedicate to learning? I prefer to begin now, to take my time and understand fully, while I am at my leisure."

Darcy recognized Richard's sound reasoning in Bingley's argument.

Miss Bingley pouted. "You are too easily persuaded. I daresay you will fall head over heels for the first country maiden to show herself agreeable, and you will be worse off than you were before we left London. I should like to see you insist on learning estate management when you are distracted by a pretty face. It is a good thing Mr. Darcy is here to keep you in check, for you seem intent on paying neither me nor Louisa any heed."

Contrary to Miss Bingley's claim, Darcy had no intention of interfering with his friend's amorous objectives. His focus must be solely on his mission: Gain Sir William's confidence and let him lead Darcy to The Four Horsemen.

Fortunately for Bingley, Mrs. Louisa Hurst had seen fit to ride more comfortably in the other carriage with her husband. Otherwise, she would certainly have added to her sister's assault against their brother.

"And what of it?" Bingley lifted his chin. "I should be so fortunate to fall for a young lady as pure and gentle of heart as she is handsome of face."

Miss Bingley huffed. "Precisely the sort of lady from which you ought to keep your distance! You do not know how ladies truly are, having been raised with Louisa and myself as your most intimate examples. You think all ladies are as accomplished, well-mannered, and full of grace as we are, but pray allow me to warn you that most are meanly deceptive."

Self-aggrandizing, pretentious, and conceited were more suitable adjectives, Darcy thought.

She added in a huff, "They think nothing of condescending to conniving arts to capture a gentleman's affection. Especially those who consider themselves beauties."

As if she had not tried every artful device apart from a manipulated compromise to capture his attention. Darcy tried to ignore her.

Bingley, however, rose in the defense of his unknown future bride. "Must all handsome young ladies be accused of malicious, artful designs? Can they not, too, be as sincere as a lady without fair features? You are too harsh on your sex, Caroline."

"If managing an estate is as involved as you

imply, what makes you think you will have time to court a young lady? You would do better to remain unmarried until your affairs are in order, as Mr. Darcy has done."

"I am not like Darcy. I would soon become lonely at an estate without a wife to keep me company."

Darcy held his peace. Bingley clearly had no idea of the soothing effect an oasis brimming with pleasant memories could have on a disquieted heart, but he refused to take sides with Miss Bingley. She flattered herself enough without any assistance from him.

The brother and sister's conversation faded along with the creaking and squishing of the carriage wheels along the miry road. As much as he wished for Bingley to attain his aims and be happy, Darcy had more urgent matters to ponder. Who was Sir William? Darcy wished to be better prepared before he met the man, but the little he had learned only added to his caution and fueled the image of a cunning adversary. The Four Horsemen did not associate with ordinary men.

Sir William would be a powerful foe — one who gave the impression of an inoffensive, obliging fellow with excellent manners, well-liked by his neighbors and, as such, immune to suspicion.

Bingley had already been misled about the

gentleman's character. When Darcy had asked his opinion of Sir William, he had nothing but compliments to utter. Never had he met a man more courteous. But Bingley saw everyone in a favorable light and, therefore, was not a reliable source of information.

Sir William's ability to mask his deviousness so thoroughly made him a powerful rival. Darcy would have to exercise extreme caution. He could not make any mistakes tonight.

If only he could find someone intimately acquainted with the Lucases — someone who understood the true nature beneath Sir William's carefully maintained façade. An ally to point Darcy in the right direction, someone already in the family's confidence.

"...do you not agree, Mr. Darcy?" Miss Bingley said yet again.

Darcy clenched his jaw. Her assumed intimacy and frequent interruptions were growing tiresome.

Rubbing his finger over the monogrammed compass attached to his fob, Darcy reminded himself of his goal. He would not allow his growing irritation at Miss Bingley to distract him from his purpose.

Narrowed focus sharpened his senses and restored his impassivity. By the time the carriage stopped in front of the assembly room, he was ready — eager — to face his enemy.

NOTHING COULD HAVE PREPARED Darcy for the rotund man with merry red cheeks who greeted them in his role as the Master of Ceremonies. At first appearance, Sir William was precisely as Bingley had described him to be: friendly, obliging, courteous, and all attention to everybody. There was a good amount of pride in his manners, but not of the offensive kind. He wore his rank with the same self-satisfaction with which an officer donned his first red coat. And while he spoke eagerly and often of St. James, his rise in status had rendered him courteous rather than supercilious.

Had Darcy not known better, he would have been inclined to like the gentleman. Sir William's garrulous speech and the sincerity he achieved in his engaging manner marked him as one of the most accomplished spies Darcy had ever met … and he had met more than his fair share over the past few years. Most men in Sir William's position were quiet, secretive. Not he. He lived large, so committed to the success of his act, he was not afraid of drawing attention to himself.

Darcy understood now why Leo had sent him. Sir William was like no other villain he had ever met.

"If you need an introduction at St. James, I would be honored to oblige," the older gentleman offered with a bow and an accommodating smile.

Miss Bingley scoffed at his offer, her face in high color. It was an expert cut straight to the quick for one who believed herself the social superior of everyone in attendance at the assembly.

How had Sir William discerned her character so accurately in the few minutes since they entered the large room to deliver such a direct cut?

Darcy was in awe. Cunning and deceit he could handle, but he had never met a foe who used open manners so skillfully as Sir William. For the first time since his first mission, Darcy felt he was in over his head. Getting the information he required from Sir William would be his greatest challenge to date, and it was the one mission in which he genuinely could not fail.

Sir William continued, "I only recently returned from London where I had the good fortune to renew an old acquaintance. Perhaps you know Sir Erasmus Clark?"

Darcy froze. Was Sir William so bold as to name one of The Four Horsemen aloud?

The sly gentleman, his eyebrows raised in bushy question marks, turned his attention to Darcy, looking him straight in the eye so that Darcy's blood went cold. Did Sir William already suspect? How could he?

With all the indifference in his possession, Darcy held his gaze. "I know of Sir Erasmus, but I cannot say we are intimately acquainted."

Haughtily, Miss Bingley said, "My acquaintances are limited to the first circles."

Had Sir Erasmus been born into nobility, she would have pretended an acquaintance, but knights were only one step above a commoner (despite their obscene wealth.) Since they could not be used to heighten her position in society, she did not waste her time with them.

Darcy, however, rose to meet Sir William's challenge. "He is highly respected in certain circles."

Sir William leaned closer to Darcy, as if he meant to share a confidence.

Darcy held his breath, his pulse drumming in his ears.

"Sir William, now is not the time for private conversations when we look to you for introductions!" a shrill voice interrupted. "How can we welcome the new residents to Netherfield Park properly if you do not perform your office? We do not want them to think we lack in social graces nor neighborly affection."

Already inclined to dislike the screeching madam, Darcy followed Sir William's trajectory of sight to a plump woman drowning in lace and wielding a fan like a sword as she cut through the crowd. She dragged five ladies behind her, all of them young, and, Darcy would wager, all of them unmarried. The meaning behind the squealing matron's words were painfully clear.

His tête-à-tête with Sir William thus brought to an immediate halt, Darcy sought to extract himself lest he expose his increasing aggravation. Until he set upon a pair of fine, brown eyes. He knew those eyes.

Darcy could not help but note that the face surrounding said features, now fully visible for him to appreciate without the splotches of mud inhibiting his view, was equally fine.

Her pert nose suggested she was no stranger to mischief, as the circumstances of their first meeting confirmed. The firmness of her chin suggested a strength of character uncommon in most young ladies in society. The twitch tugging the corners of her lips implied a sense of humor. Given her good humor after having been thrown from her horse, he concluded that the lady was one to make the best of any situation no matter how unfavorable. The blush on her cheeks was as rosy as it had been that morning, and the way she chewed her bottom lip while peeking at her mother suggested she possessed more manners than Darcy had believed from someone who had run away after receiving his assistance. Darcy had not known what to think of her, but there was no denying she had left an impression.

The young lady beside her, a fair-haired maiden whose pale complexion confirmed a less adventurous spirit than her sister, also blushed as her mother prattled to Sir William about what Darcy knew not. He could not bring himself to pay attention to a word she said. Nor, apparently, did the gentleman who came up to stand behind her. His eyes contained the same mirth and curiosity his fine-eyed daughter expressed, but he did not look in the least embarrassed about his wife's presumption. Nor did he pay her any particular tender regard when he said rather sarcastically, "Your ability to converse without taking in breath is remarkable, my love, but considering how easily your nerves are unsettled, I recommend you pause to breathe at once before you swoon."

Sir William must have been accustomed to the lady's manners. He lost no time in performing the service she had insisted upon.

Darcy committed their names to memory. Miss Elizabeth Bennet. That was the one which lingered in his mind.

He ought to ask her for a dance. Surely, he could indulge in a reel during his mission.

His mission! Sir William. The Four Horsemen. Pemberley.

Darcy clenched his jaw and his fists. How easily he had been distracted! He was as flighty as Miss Bingley had accused her brother of being.

To his chagrin, Darcy found his gaze once again straying to Miss Elizabeth.

He knew then that he must depart from her company.

For a brief moment, he had been inclined to delay his investigation and ask her to dance. It deeply troubled Darcy that such a desire should provoke him to distraction at that moment, and with a young lady he had last seen covered head-to-toe in mud.

CHAPTER 6

*E*lizabeth accepted George's proffered arm, resisting the temptation to look over her shoulder at Mr. Darcy. Turning would have ruined the effect of her regal bearing in which she strove to prove how far above his snub she was. Like a queen teaching a lesson to an unmannerly peasant. Now, there was a picture to restore her humor!

"Serves him right for refusing to dance with you and every other lady in the room," George said as they joined the dancers in the quadrille.

Her anger, having sparked to a brilliant and brief flash, dwindled in favor of curiosity. Not that Elizabeth had forgiven Mr. Darcy — far from that! Only that she was now sensible enough to reason on his actions in a way she would have rejected a moment before. "I wonder why a gentleman would bother coming to an assembly if he is disinclined to dance," she mused.

Mr. Darcy had been watching — or perhaps it might have been more accurately stated, studying — everyone at the assembly, but he had not danced at all. Not even with the ladies of his party, one of whom Elizabeth was certain had exercised all of her feminine wiles in an attempt to secure a dance.

"Could it be pride?" Elizabeth wondered aloud when she and George met on a turn.

She was inclined to believe Mr. Darcy too lofty and proud for their company, but his intense interest in observing the crowd created doubt. His was not the look of disdain, but of interest — of, dare she say it, curiosity. That was a quality about which Elizabeth understood a great deal.

Curiosity was fast becoming the theme of the evening. Mr. Darcy had certainly aroused hers. The man was intriguing, and since he was also very pleasant to look upon, she had stolen several glances of the gentleman over the past few hours. With his height, attractive features, and reported wealth, he could very well be proud … but there was something else about him she could not quite ascertain.

George considered his answer carefully, as was his custom. He never made decisions lightly nor offered his opinion without sufficient consideration.

After some time, he finally spoke. "If the gentleman possesses pride, I am inclined to believe it well-deserved. His comment was rude, but did you see his reaction once he realized you had heard him?"

Elizabeth scoffed. "How could he have doubted I heard his insult? A true gentleman would not have said what he did at all." That was not proof enough to forgive him in her mind. George would have to do much better than that to restore Mr. Darcy to her good opinion.

"You make friends easily, Miss Elizabeth. But even with the advantage of your ability, I daresay you would suffer from a degree of anxiety at being the new lady amongst a pack of unfamiliar faces. Add to that the general hum of the less discreet who speak of the newcomer's income and status, and a man not given to making friends easily would soon find himself at a tremendously uncomfortable disadvantage."

She could not rebuff his sound reasoning. Especially when her own mother was one of the "less discreet" of whom George referred.

He must have sensed her willingness to listen, for he continued, "How would you like to be looked upon by every single person in an assembly room, assessed and scrutinized and the main topic of conversation? Reduced to nothing more than your annual income and social status so that all the maidens and their mothers might make you the object of their ambitions? It is enough to test the mettle of any man. No, Miss Elizabeth, I will give Mr. Darcy the benefit of the doubt and choose to believe his comment to be a rare lapse in gentility and not a permanent stain upon his character."

Elizabeth twisted her mouth. George's arguments were sound even if they were overly generous. Then again, did not her reluctance to embrace them reveal a resentment which reflected poorly on herself and threatened to ruin a perfectly lovely evening — the one and only high point in a dreadful, traitorous day? Her spine straightened at the thought. She was not so weak-willed to allow herself to be influenced by the whims and moods of others, most of all by a stranger who had no hold over her at all.

She sighed resignedly. "You would make me sympathize with Mr. Darcy after he insulted my vanity. Very well, I will overlook his poor display of manners this time. However, I still wonder why he bothered to come if he did not intend to widen his circle of acquaintances."

George grinned. "You take an interest in the gentleman. I saw you glancing his way several times."

Elizabeth's cheeks warmed. "He is new, a novelty. I must entertain my mind with something, and Mr. Darcy offers an interesting puzzle."

Her partner's grin widened. "A puzzle you would like to solve?"

Could her face burn any more than it did at that moment?

"I apologize, Miss Elizabeth. I ought not tease and torment you as I do my own sisters. I have no doubt you are correct in your estimation, and I must say it does not surprise me that you are drawn to the complexities Mr. Darcy's character seems to offer. He reminds me very much of Tempest."

Elizabeth gasped in mock horror. "Mr. Darcy would not be amused at your comparison of him to a temperamental mare!"

George laughed, and she laughed freely with him. She could not remain resentful against Mr. Darcy for an ungentlemanly comment when he would unquestionably take offense at her current conversation and subsequent merriment. She had yet to meet a gentleman who could stand to be laughed at, and she supposed Mr. Darcy was no different.

But there was truth to George's assessment. Tempest had been a challenge, and yet she had been Elizabeth's favorite in the Lucas Lodge stables.

Another sigh escaped her lips. "I miss her, you know."

George met her gloved palm, his smile replaced with the tender look he often gave his children when they needed comfort. Elizabeth felt as though she was ten-years-old again.

"I miss them when they leave the stables, too," he said softly. Then, his smile returned. "But Mr. Bingley is a kindly fellow who will treat her well, of that I am certain. And, he has danced twice with Miss Bennet. If they marry—"

"You are as bad as my mother, George Lucas! Two dances are nothing when the ratio of ladies far exceeds that of the gentlemen."

"Still. You may have occasion to ride Tempest again sooner than you think."

If only. Unless her father changed his mind, she would have to deny herself the pleasure of riding Tempest again. She forced a smile at George's optimism, knowing she could not tell him of the consequences of her morning spill without embarrassing herself by crying during the reel. Then, everyone would want to know why she was upset, and she would spend the rest of the evening repeating the same wretched story.

She would not wallow in self-pity when Tempest was probably in a comfortable stall with fresh hay and kind stable boys to groom her. Mr. Bingley seemed kind. Unlike his sisters.

Elizabeth hated to think of Miss Bingley or her surly sister, Mrs. Hurst, using their whips on the spirited mare. They had looked down their noses at Elizabeth's friends and neighbors all evening, the few comments she had overheard as harsh as the crack of a whip. Miss Bingley had even brushed her sleeve off after a gentleman had passed too closely to her on his way to the refreshment table. As if she was above breathing the same air.

Elizabeth mostly forgot about Mr. Darcy for the rest of the dance, and so it was with great surprise she saw him rooted in the same spot where he had been standing before she flounced away.

George bent down and whispered to her, "Problems are best resolved quickly and directly. Allow him the opportunity to apologize. If he takes it, you might gain a friend … and a puzzle to entertain your intellect. If he does not, then you are better off without his acquaintance."

With a mischievous grin, he deposited Elizabeth beside Mr. Darcy and promptly excused himself on the pretext of seeking Charlotte for a dance. George took care of his family first and foremost. Elizabeth rather wished he would not treat her so much like he treated his own family when it left her standing beside the same gentleman who had insulted her so recently. It would have been much easier to think ill of Mr. Darcy and avoid his company, to call him proud and forget him.

But George was right. The easiest path rarely led to the best solution, and Elizabeth was not afraid of confrontation.

Mr. Darcy looked at her, then just as quickly looked away. Clearing his throat, he said, "You … dance very well."

His manners were so painfully awkward, Elizabeth thought that perhaps George was right. She would take George's advice and give Mr. Darcy the opportunity to recant his ill-chosen words and redeem himself, or to prove her right. Elizabeth would not mind being wrong about him. Still, she could not help but goad the poor man a bit. "It is a pity I cannot return the compliment. Do you not like to dance, Mr. Darcy?"

"I have little inclination for dancing with strangers."

There it was, that same unseemly pride she had sensed during the night. "Sir William introduced you to many of the families, Mr. Darcy. There is no lack of friendly people here who would be happy to welcome you to Hertfordshire."

Mr. Darcy fiddled with a fob that tucked into his

waistcoat pocket. It led to a compass with a monogram etched on the back of the casing. He must do a great deal of traveling to carry a compass on his person. If he proved at all agreeable, Elizabeth intended to set him on the subject of his travels.

He cleared his throat. "I do not have the talent which some people possess of conversing easily with those I have never met before."

Another point in George's favor. "What a conundrum you find yourself in, Mr. Darcy, for unless you make the effort to converse, strangers they will continue to be. I wonder how you befriended Mr. Bingley … or anyone else for that matter?"

Her question was impertinent, but she was genuinely intrigued.

Mr. Darcy had the grace to smile, and Elizabeth noted with some satisfaction that his shoulders relaxed. She also noticed a dimple in his cheek.

He said, "I prefer to keep my circle of friends small and made up only of those who have earned my esteem and trust."

Elizabeth saw the wisdom of his view, but it saddened her. She loved people, and she could not imagine walking through Meryton without greetings and friendly comments paving a welcoming path before her. "Sounds lonely," she said, then bit her tongue because she had voiced the wrong thought aloud. Covering her error, she added what she had intended to say, "I acknowledge the wisdom in your thinking. It is a great consolation to be assured of your truest friends — to know they would never betray your trust … or offend you." As he had offended her. Did that mean Mr. Darcy had no inclination of making friends in Hertfordshire?

His eyebrows drew together, and Elizabeth bit her tongue once again. She had not meant to refer, even indirectly, to his earlier offense toward her, but if he meant to apologize, she could not have made it any easier for him.

She held her breath and waited to see what sort of gentleman Mr. Darcy would prove to be.

Turning to face her, he met Elizabeth's eyes. They pierced hers with an intensity that made the noise surrounding them fade and the crowd disappear.

His voice was soft and smooth, as it had been earlier that day when he had pulled her out of the mud. Elizabeth's palms burned at the memory of his firm grip around her hands.

"Miss Elizabeth, I must apologize to you. I was frustrated and in ill-humor when I replied to Mr. Bingley as I did. It was not my intention to insult you so much as it was a poorly executed effort to—" He paused, searching for the words, and finally concluding, "—to continue as I was."

And what *had* he been doing? Elizabeth had noticed how he stood along the edge of the ballroom floor, but she did not presume he had occupied himself as she had. She had been listening unabashedly to her father's conversation with Sir William's eldest sons. She would rather divert her mind with a philosophical or political conversation than watch the dancers fortunate enough to secure partners. Anything to keep her mind off her own misery.

Had Mr. Darcy been listening too? Why?

Elizabeth did not know how long she was entertained in her own thoughts, but when she had come full circle, she found that Mr. Darcy was still watching her. His eyes searched her face, their concern far from the expression of a proud man. Proud men did not concern themselves with the feelings of others. Nor did they admit to their errors. It seemed to matter to him that she accept his apology. The idea was flattering, and it made it easier for Elizabeth to extend her forgiveness.

"Thank you, Mr. Darcy. I will accept your apology as well as your explanation for it. I will thank you in turn for not mentioning the incident of this morning to my mother and father when we were finally introduced."

"We are even, then?"

She had not considered him to be in her debt and found the notion pleasing. "If you were keeping score."

"Always," he said through a widening smile. Mr. Darcy had a nice smile — straight, white teeth and a twinkle that danced merrily in his blue eyes. And that unexpected dimple. "Might I inquire about this morning? Miss Lucas introduced herself after you ran off, and after observing her family this evening, I find myself perplexed. Perhaps you might offer your insight?" He stopped, waiting for Elizabeth to satisfy his curiosity regarding her neighbors rather than give an explanation for her behavior earlier.

She did not know whether she felt relieved at his quick acceptance or miffed at his disinterest after such a pretty apology. Given her forgiving nature that evening, she chose the former.

Perhaps Mr. Darcy's interest lay in Charlotte. Elizabeth determined to discern if that was the case. "You wish for me to explain the Lucases to you? I will warn you, I am hardly unbiased. Miss Lucas is my dearest friend, and you would be hard pressed to hear anything against her or her family cross my lips."

"I surmised as much, given that you were in each other's company at that early hour."

He did not press her concerning Charlotte, so

Elizabeth offered, "Miss Lucas is the most sensible lady of my acquaintance. Her logic defies emotion, making her a coveted confidante and brilliant strategist."

He raised his eyebrows. "You make her sound like a war general."

"And well she would do in such a role. I take your comment as a compliment to her steady character."

Again, his eyebrows met, and his gaze gripped hers. "Which is precisely how I meant it."

"Then we are in agreement," Elizabeth whispered, her neck growing warm.

"True friends are more valuable than gold. Miss Lucas is fortunate to have a friend who recognizes her value. How long have you known Sir William and his family?"

Mr. Darcy turned the conversation away from Charlotte too quickly for him to hold any particular regard for her. Interesting.

Elizabeth replied, "I have known them my entire life. My father's estate, Longbourn, is only a short walk from Lucas Lodge."

"They have always been situated at Lucas Lodge?"

"Sir William was formerly in trade at Meryton. He made a tolerable fortune, but his true pride was when he rose to the honor of knighthood by an address to the King during his mayoralty. It is a story you are certain to hear from Sir William himself eventually."

"I look forward to the occasion. It must have been difficult for him to remain in trade after the honor was bestowed upon him," he observed.

"He sold his business and residence in Meryton and removed with his family to his current estate outside the village. He has since occupied himself in being civil to all the world. He makes a splendid Master of Ceremonies, does he not?"

Across the room, Sir William roared with laughter — perhaps not genteel in its execution but genuine in its origin.

Mr. Darcy expressed no signs of disapproval. Elizabeth, who had been watching for them, would have noticed.

He said, "If only everyone elevated in society were so honest. From the little I have observed, Sir William's affability and interest in others has upset the overreaching ambition and excessive pride often felt by those who have likewise benefited from the King's favor. However, there is, I believe, in every disposition a tendency to some particular evil, a natural defect, which not even the best education or decorum can overcome."

Sir William, evil? Elizabeth could not take the suggestion seriously. Tilting her chin and peeking askance at Mr. Darcy, she replied with a question of her own. "Is it your defect, then, to distrust everybody?"

Mr. Darcy avoided her gaze, instead, peering at something invisible directly in front of the toes of his Hessians. "Is distrust a defect when the world is full of liars and traitors?"

"In Meryton?" she exclaimed in a mixture of laughter and wishful thinking. "Perhaps, where you are from, you are surrounded by criminals and spies, but Meryton is peaceful. Nothing ever happens here." And, oh, how she wished it would! Not involving liars and traitors, of course, but something exciting and out of the ordinary to break the tedium.

"You should consider yourself very fortunate, Miss Elizabeth." Now, he did look at her. The conviction in his firm tone and the sincerity in his expression convinced Elizabeth that Mr. Darcy knew danger.

Interesting. He did not trust easily. He was accustomed to danger. Who was Mr. Darcy? She searched his face for clues, not knowing what she looked for but enjoying the investigation.

He blinked, and his disposition lightened considerably. Looking about the room, he said, "I must thank Mr. Lucas for his attention to you after my blunder. He is the second son, is he not?"

Elizabeth arched her neck to observe Mr. Darcy better. He asked a great deal of questions about the Lucases. She had to wonder why he singled them out and how he had come to choose her for his source of information. The activities of the morning could not have left a favorable impression of her on him ... although his present manners indicated otherwise. Was that what this was? His effort to put her at ease by allowing her to speak of her friends?

She would not pretend to understand him, and so she said directly, "You take an acute interest in the Lucases. Why is that, Mr. Darcy?"

His pause suggested he had not expected her to take control of the conversation by asking a pointed question of her own. Elizabeth was too aware of her father's conversational manipulations to not catch on to Mr. Darcy's use of the tactic. He would extract information without revealing a single detail about himself, leaving a trail of unanswered questions and mystery behind him and robbing her of sleep when she would spend all night pondering them.

Distrust. Danger. Mystery....

He replied, "Mr. Bingley is a dear friend of mine, and the Lucases are his neighbors now, too. His nature is so affable and accepting, I have long since taken it as my responsibility to ensure he does not mislay his loyalties. They are too easily given."

In itself, the excuse was reasonable. Jane was very similar in disposition to Mr. Darcy's description of Mr. Bingley.

However, unlike his earlier conversation, there was no emotion in his words. It sounded odd in Elizabeth's ears when he obviously cared about Mr. Bingley's welfare enough to inquire about his neighbors. It was almost as if he had memorized his explanation.

Elizabeth pushed aside her reserve, for nothing she could say about the Lucases would lower them in the opinion of a just man.

Was Mr. Darcy just?

Intrigued to see how he would react, to see if the sketch she was making of his character was correct, she said, "Then I will reassure you on that front. Kinder neighbors cannot be found in all of Hertfordshire. Mr. George Lucas is the second son. He and his wife, along with their three beautiful children, live at the cottage near Lucas Lodge. He is responsible for raising the best horses in the county."

"Was that one of his horses you were riding this morning?" Mr. Darcy asked with a suppressed smile.

Elizabeth wrinkled her nose. He had to bring *that* up. "It was. He and Sir William have been generous in allowing me the use of their stable's occupants."

"Your father does not have horses?"

That was a question Elizabeth did not wish to answer. Searching for a way to redirect the conversation, she looked over the crowd until she found Mr. Bingley close to the refreshment table. He stood in the center of a cluster of laughing men and women. If Mr. Darcy had difficulty making new friends, then Mr. Bingley was his opposite. He had charmed everyone in the room. "Is there anything else you wish to know about your friend's neighbors? Or, perhaps, you would like to explain how Mr. Bingley came to let Netherfield Park? It has been vacant for a long time, and while we were thrilled to hear it was occupied, we were surprised to learn that a gentleman would choose to leave the entertainments of London in favor of a quiet country estate months before hunting season."

Mr. Darcy must have sensed her thoughts. He was looking at Mr. Bingley and his group when she turned her attention back to him. Again, he hesitated to reply, his manners guarded, though he attempted to disguise it with a smile. She had seen his real smile, and this one did not reach his eyes as that one had.

He stated an explanation for Mr. Bingley's uncharacteristic decision. Something about learning estate management. Something perfectly reasonable. Something rehearsed. What was he hiding?

Distrustful. Dangerous, or no stranger to danger — Elizabeth had yet to discern which. Mysterious. Secretive.

When Mr. Darcy smoothly extracted himself from her company, it was just the spark to light Elizabeth's imagination on fire. For the better part of the next quarter of an hour, she disregarded her thoughts as wishful fancy — a desire for some excitement in her dull life. A new way for her to distract her thoughts when she longed to run to the stables to ride with Charlotte.

However, the facts offered enough kindling to fan the flames of Elizabeth's growing suspicions. Her skin tingled and her pulse raced as she considered them one by one.

Mr. Darcy's determination to observe rather than dance or participate in conversation. His ability to extract information without revealing anything about himself. His careful thought before offering a reply. His prepared, practiced, and perfectly reasonable explanations. His sudden appearance at a place where he knew nobody at an unusual time of year. The hint of danger and mystery surrounding him....

Could it be that Mr. Darcy was a spy?

CHAPTER 7

"*A* spy, Lizzy? Really?" Charlotte whispered, for if Mr. Darcy truly were a spy, it would not do to blurt it aloud for all to hear. It was the reason why Elizabeth had sought out Charlotte before her family departed for Longbourn. Charlotte could be trusted for her discretion ... even if she was a touch more skeptical than Elizabeth had thought she would be after listening to her string of proofs.

Mr. Darcy had danced exactly twice and only with the members of his party (Miss Bingley and Mrs. Hurst) after parting from her company. That he had waited so long to dance at all — and only after she had questioned his motives in coming to the assembly — had offered further evidence to her growing list of reasons why she thought Mr. Darcy *could* be a spy.

Elizabeth knew her view might be wholly illogical, which was why she had sought out her more analytical friend.

Now, Elizabeth felt the ridiculousness of her suspicion, but pride prevented her from dropping the issue so quickly. "I am not saying he is. Merely, that he *could* be. That it is within the realm of possibility."

Charlotte heaved an exasperated sigh. "Very well, then. If Mr. Darcy is a spy, how can you be certain he is on the right side?"

Elizabeth nearly spouted an argument worthy of her father stating the relativity of justice and the subjectivity of right and wrong during times of war, but not even a war erased certain lines which ought to never be crossed. The line between enemy and ally, traitor and hero. How could she be sure Mr. Darcy was a British spy?

It was a fair question — one Elizabeth did not know how to answer. "I cannot find it in me to believe Mr. Darcy a traitor." She cringed at her weak reply. What did she really know of the gentleman? Hardly anything.

"And this is based on an impression formed from your inauspicious encounter this morning, one brief conversation at a crowded assembly, and your interrupted observations of the past few hours?" Charlotte twisted the corner of her lip and looked at Elizabeth with as much humor as she lacked judgment.

Elizabeth sighed, her dream blown to bits with rational thought. Hopeless and defeated, she said, "I sound as fanciful as Lydia."

"Not at all! Lydia would not have bothered to offer proof, while you have gone out of your way to substantiate your suspicion. Had you wished to continue in your fancy, you would not have told me and risked me challenging your view … which, I suspect, is precisely why you chose to discuss the matter with me."

"You know me too well."

"Which is why I insist you not allow yourself to feel foolish. Sometimes I envy your ability to infuse excitement into the dullest situations. Perhaps I would have enjoyed this evening's assembly more if I had your ability. Further, I will own that while your proofs were persuasive, my greatest reason for refuting your idea is the fact that a spy worth his salt would never risk his work, his very life, by arousing suspicions in clever maidens with active minds. He would have sensed your danger and done his best to stay away from you."

Elizabeth's pulse fluttered. That was precisely what Mr. Darcy had done! It offered a more flattering explanation for his insult, too. He had been avoiding her. But why?

She sighed, discouraged she should so easily fall prey to her own whimsy again. "Thank you, Charlotte. I am sure you are right about Mr. Darcy, and I thank you for disproving me so kindly."

Charlotte clasped Elizabeth's hands and leaned forward until their foreheads touched. "It is a romantic notion. Mr. Darcy is handsome enough to do the suspicion credit, I daresay."

They laughed together, and Elizabeth soon forgot her disappointment. Mr. Darcy may not be a spy, but there was no denying that his presence had sparked a change in humdrum Meryton.

DARCY WAS SHAKEN. He had asked too many questions. How easily Miss Elizabeth had seen through him! How quickly she had jumped to the right conclusion! It was all wrong. His mission was in jeopardy, and it was all his fault. Her charming, inviting manners had encouraged him to let down his guard. He had allowed her too great a glimpse into his character. He ought to have been more careful. Her humor was as disarming to him as her cleverness was dangerous.

It was a pity. He enjoyed her conversation. There was no guile or hypocrisy in Miss Elizabeth, but her curiosity and perceptiveness prohibited any further association. That, and her blinding friendship with the Lucases. While she had provided more information in a few minutes than he had gleaned since his arrival the afternoon before, Miss Elizabeth would be the first to warn them of his investigation out of a sense of misplaced loyalty. She would never believe Sir William capable of treachery, no matter how much proof was laid bare before her.

And there was proof.

Lucas Lodge was in debt. Heavily in debt. Sir William had cut off all his ties to trade too soon. He had not known how to manage an estate (and evidence suggested he had not gained much knowledge on that front since acquiring his property.) As a result, his farmland, and therefore, his income, suffered.

Without the money to be earned from proper administration of his estate, Sir William had mortgaged Lucas Lodge in order to continue living as the gentleman he strove to prove himself to be. Would that he had gathered more wealth before he retired from trade as Bingley's father had done! Sir William's children would be the ones to suffer his impatience for grandeur.

However, if Darcy was right about Sir William, he would come into a significant sum of money very soon. It only depended on Darcy to find out what service Sir William was willing to perform for The Four Horsemen before he went through with it.

By all appearances, Sir William was too involved with his acquired status and too determined to act the part to concern himself with something so vulgar as money. His attitude was perfectly reflected in his eldest son, whose preference for town living and higher society showed he was equally disinclined to take responsibility for his inheritance. The likeness lent credibility to Sir William's farce, making both the son and the father appear ignorant and harmless … when they could be anything but. The disguise was risky. And brilliant.

And there was more. Darcy must not forget George Lucas. The assembly afforded the perfect opportunity to observe the man. He was liked and respected by his peers. He was considerate, as Darcy's own experience with him had proved. No sooner had Darcy thanked George for his kindness toward Miss Elizabeth in the face of his own rudeness than George waved it off and praised him for being humble enough to admit his error. They had spoken of horses, then, and Darcy found George to be an excellent judge of quality horseflesh. It was, no doubt, the second son's attempt to save his family's estate which had led him to turn to horses. It was the only acceptable way for a gentleman to earn an income, the only one society and his own father allowed, and George did it all for a property he did not stand to inherit.

Therein lurked a powerful motive.

Like a loyal son, George kept within the strictures imposed upon him so that his father would not feel his failure, and society would not scorn their family. All of this done at the expense of George's own freedom. It was a lot to ask for so little return.

Darcy wondered how far George would go to secure his family's place and future, given what he had already sacrificed.

There could only be three explanations: One, George was unaware of his father's activities. Two, he was under his father's thumb and had little choice. Or three, he knew and was equally skillful at playing his part in throwing off suspicion through his role as the enterprising second son.

Was George so devious? Darcy wished to believe him honest, but he must set aside emotion and look to the facts.

He needed more facts. More clues to point him in the right direction.

Darcy's eyes roamed over the assembly, uncertain what he searched for until he saw Miss Elizabeth's eyes meet his.

Blast! Nodding his head as if their shared look had been a trifling coincidence, he forced his gaze to continue looking through the crowd. It was devilish difficult when he felt her observing him as intently as he avoided her.

He had to move. To do something.

He danced with Miss Bingley and Mrs. Hurst, but too often he felt himself drawn to Miss Elizabeth's smiling face. Darcy could not understand how, past midnight, she seemed to be enveloped in sunshine.

The harder Darcy exerted himself to stay away from Miss Elizabeth, the more difficult the task became when the hour progressed and the crowd thinned.

Bingley displayed a notable preference for Miss Bennet, and she, being a handsome lady with gentle manners, had also appealed to his sisters who believed themselves to possess the same qualities. Their acquaintance deepened quickly, as there was nobody else they could be presumed upon to befriend at the assembly. But it was ultimately Bingley's sisters who came to Darcy's aid and persuaded their brother to leave.

It was for the best. Darcy had a letter to write to Georgiana and another to Richard, one which he would have to phrase with care in case of interception. To an outsider's eye, it would appear as if Darcy merely wrote to his cousin about a ball and his new surroundings. To Richard, though, he would communicate his progress, relaying all the information he had acquired which might help complete their mission. Anything to capture The Four Horsemen so he would be free to return to Pemberley.

Yes, he must focus on his assignment. He must keep his eyes on the prize — and away from Miss Elizabeth Bennet.

ith renewed focus and vigor, Darcy aimed his full attention on his investigation.

He invited Sir William to fish on the largest of Netherfield Park's three ponds. Fishing lent itself to casual conversation, and Darcy had planned to make good use of it. He had hoped Sir William might relax his guard and loosen his tongue, but as it turned out, there had been no time at all for conversation. From the moment the first hook hit the water, Darcy and Sir William had been kept busy as fish after fish bit the bait. Evidently, the inhabitants of the pond had been at peace for far too long.

The successful fishing expedition was reciprocated with an invitation to a picnic at Lucas Lodge. Darcy had feared Miss Elizabeth would be there. He did not need her observing him as he tried to extract information from Sir William.

As it turned out, none of the Bennets had been invited. Darcy later learned from Miss Bingley, who scoffed and mocked the Misses Lucas, that Sir William and Lady Lucas had hoped that he or Bingley might form an attachment to one of their daughters. He ought to have known their reasons for extending hospitality to two newly arrived, unmarried gentlemen, but as always, Darcy took care not to give cause for encouragement. He had no business getting close to anyone. Not only would it complicate affairs, but it would endanger the life of the lady to whom his affections were attached. Now was not the time for love. Now was the time to capture The Four Horsemen and return to his normal life at Pemberley. Then, and only then, could he think of superfluous things such as love.

Not to suggest that Miss Lucas was not worthy of a good husband. Only that Darcy could never put himself in that role. Miss Lucas was as sensible as Miss Elizabeth had claimed her to be. If Richard were ever to settle down and marry, he would do well to seek such a wife.

Three days following the Meryton Assembly, Bingley's butler brought a letter to Darcy while he was dressing. It had been delivered by a messenger.

Wilson wiped the last of the lather from Darcy's chin. "Is it from the colonel?" he asked, cleaning the blade with a cloth.

"It is, though with its brevity, I wonder why it took him so long to send." Darcy read the page in a glance, then dropped the paper into the fire. Watching the flame consume the message until it was nothing more than a thimble-full of ash, he said in a low tone, "I must work fast, Wilson. The Four Horsemen were seen together at a club."

Wilson's busy hands paused. "They have never risked being seen together before."

"Exactly. I fear, as does Richard, that a grander scheme is afoot. We cannot allow them the upper hand much longer. We must discover what they plan and what Sir William has to do with it. I will own, Wilson, I have never met Sir William's equal. He does not crack or slip up. He seems to have no defects at all."

Packing the shaving utensils, Wilson stepped in front of Darcy to see to his cravat. "I have befriended the groom at Lucas Lodge as you suggested. Mercer is his name. A fine fellow so far as I can tell. He has nothing but kind things to say about Sir William and Master George, as he calls him."

"What of Mr. Lucas? John?"

"All I have learned of him so far is that Mr. Lucas

enjoys a lively fox hunt. He does not speak much of him. Either Mercer does not like the gentleman and, in good taste, denies himself the indulgence of speaking against Sir William's heir, or he simply does not have much to say about the man. It is my understanding that Mr. Lucas prefers the high society and comforts of London to the country and is not often in residence at Lucas Lodge." Wilson stepped back, surveying his handiwork.

Darcy rubbed his chin. "Very good. Keep up your acquaintance with Mercer. You might have greater success with a stable boy, but be cautious not to arouse suspicion."

"Of course," Wilson said with a bow.

Servants, unencumbered by the restrictions placed upon the gentle classes, were freer to discuss matters Darcy could never broach with a newly formed acquaintance. Many times, he envied them their candor. How much time it would save him! But he had to play by the rules others had made and passed down through generations. He could not rightfully scorn society's strictures — not when his previous successes could be credited, in great part, to his role in society. Few suspected a landed gentleman from a respected family who had everything to lose — a beloved estate which had been handed down through generations of Darcys, a sister under his protection, and no heirs to carry on the legacy of his family — of working as a secret government agent.

Time was of the essence, and if Darcy had learned nothing from Sir William in the past three days, he had to adjust his plan. He would spend more time around the gentleman's sons, and he had an idea of how best to do that.

Bingley was already in the breakfast parlor. To Darcy's good fortune, he was alone.

"Good morning, Bingley," he said, sitting at the table and pouring a cup of coffee.

Bingley looked positively miserable. "We are to have trout again today. Pray do not fish any more in my ponds, Darcy. You know I have an aversion to creatures with gills."

Darcy stifled a smile. Bingley had inadvertently given him just the entry he needed to affect his plan. "Then, we shall have to find another way to enter-tain ourselves. You ought to invite your closest neighbors to dine."

Bingley shot upright in his seat, his miserable mien transformed into his usual merriness. "What a splendid idea! I shall ask Caroline to invite the Bennets to dine with us this same evening."

Darcy's heart pounded against his ribs. Those

were not the neighbors Darcy had intended Bingley to invite.

Taking a deep breath, Darcy said, "Are not the Lucases closest?"

"Oh, yes. Of course." Bingley absentmindedly tugged his hair with a silly grin on his face. "Miss Bennet and Miss Elizabeth are good friends with Miss Lucas. They will enjoy her company as well as ours. I daresay the addition of Miss Lucas' brothers at the table will balance the numbers."

Darcy could not fathom how a table could be balanced with a family of five unmarried daughters occupying most of the seats, but if it got Sir William and his sons to Netherfield Park, Darcy was not about to argue the point.

Miss Bingley entered the breakfast parlor then, her stiff silk skirts abrasive to Darcy's ears.

"Caroline! Will you help me arrange for a dinner party this evening?" Bingley asked, eager to carry out his plan now that he had one.

She clapped her hands. "How lovely! Whom are we to invite? Has a new family of quality returned from town? I heard of a Miss King who seems promising." Picking up a plate on the sideboard, she turned to the platter of sausages.

"The Bennets and the Lucases."

With a resounding thud, Miss Bingley set her

plate down on the narrow table. She spun around to glare at her brother. "Have you gone mad, Charles? The Bennets are vulgar, and the Lucases are quite possibly the drollest family I have ever been forced to meet." She splayed her hand over her heart, her cheeks in high color. "Did you know that Sir William offered to show *me* around St. James? Me? As if he is of the first circles! As if he could possibly be of any assistance to me!"

Her brother's face darkened. "Have you forgotten our origins, Caroline? Sir William, at least, has a title."

"A bought one! It means nothing," she huffed.

"I find Sir William to be a pleasant fellow. Not one to give himself airs, though he very well might, given his knighthood," Bingley insisted. "Do not speak so unkindly of a gentleman I would befriend. As for the Bennets, what have you against them? You said you adored Miss Bennet. You and Louisa have been full of praise for her."

"She, I will agree to invite. She, at least … and Miss Elizabeth," she added begrudgingly, "did not make spectacles of themselves at the assembly. But even you must admit their younger sisters were as abominable as their mother. And did Mr. Bennet move one finger to subdue them? No. He was too busy in his own debates to care for the reputations of his daughters and anyone with whom they were in association."

Darcy had entertained similar thoughts about the Bennets, but it was unpleasant to hear Miss Bingley express them.

Bingley said, "Then, I insist you include Miss Elizabeth in your invitation, Caroline. You are too harsh."

"And should I lower my standards merely because we are not in town?"

Darcy exhaled. Had he not wished he could be free of the norms of high society only moments ago? While he would never act on certain desires, he realized the futility of casting judgment so quickly on a family who did — especially when they did not frequent town nor have the advantage of wider association. Really, what harm could Mrs. Bennet do outside of Meryton?

As for Mr. Bennet, Darcy did not know enough about him to form an opinion. His conversation had been diverting and well-informed, but his interest in academics and philosophy seemed to exceed his interest in his own family. That was a big point in his disfavor, but Darcy tried not to dwell on it out of a sense of rebellion. He would *not* imitate Miss Bingley's intolerant criticism.

Bingley drained his teacup. "Miss Bennet is a lady

through and through. I defy you to say otherwise. Miss Elizabeth is charming as well, although I will own that a lot of her conversation was over my head. You had best seat her next to Darcy at the table tonight … if she does not object. You seem to have made peace with each other even after your insult."

Darcy nearly choked on his coffee at Bingley's frank admission and the consequential horror twisting Miss Bingley's features. He might have laughed at the irony had the stakes not been so high. "I apologized, and Miss Elizabeth graciously accepted my apology," he replied.

It was settled. Miss Bingley would invite the two eldest Bennet daughters to dine at Netherfield that evening. Nothing, however, convinced her to include the Lucases, for boredom was a sin greater than a lack of connections when she had been put upon to suffer too much monotony in the country.

Not only were the Lucases not invited, meriting Darcy's scheme utterly useless, but now he would have to endure an evening in Miss Elizabeth's company.

An evening which had come about at his doing.

CHAPTER 9

*E*lizabeth tried not to watch the clock. She failed repeatedly as the hour for her and Jane to depart for Netherfield Park crept closer.

The moment eventually did arrive, finally, and they left Longbourn (an event which their lethargic horses extended to the best of their capabilities despite the alternating coaxing and threatening shouts of the coachman.)

Elizabeth peered up at the azure sky through the glass of the carriage window, her fingers rubbing over her colorful brooch. "Poor Mama was quite vexed at the lack of rain. There is nary a cloud in the sky."

It was a glorious day, and what was better, Jane beamed happiness. Elizabeth directed all of her own restlessness toward her anticipation of an evening away from Longbourn. Maybe, just maybe, she would catch a glimpse of Tempest. If not, she would content herself in her sister's contentment.

Jane leaned against the squabs, relaxing now that they were no longer under the scrutinizing stares of their mother (who held ambitious expectations for both of her daughters) and their jealous sisters. Kitty and Lydia because if they were denied diversion, they would deny everyone else of it, too. Mary because she resented not having been invited at all, though she would never admit it lest it sound sinfully covetous.

"I am so glad Papa allowed us to use the carriage, Lizzy. We would have arrived to dinner dusty and smelling of horses."

Her father had said nothing more about her riding, but his allowance of the carriage seemed to prove how seriously he took her prohibition. Elizabeth had not told Jane the whole of it, blaming her puffy eyes and red nose of three days before to the delay in her trip with Aunt and Uncle.

"We could have walked faster to Netherfield than the horses will convey us," she teased.

"And have us ruin our complexions?" Jane teased in turn.

Fanning her face with her hand, Elizabeth did her best imitation of Mama. "No gentleman of fortune would ever agree to marry a lady with sun-bronzed skin."

Contrary to her mother, Elizabeth held no lofty expectations for the evening. She did not anticipate a proposal of marriage, nor did she wish to impose that sort of pressure on what should be an enjoyable dinner — enjoyable for Jane, that is. It would be torture being so near Tempest, knowing she might see her but she could not ride her. What she would give for one more run across the fields.... She must not dwell on such things. Shaking off her melancholy, she concentrated on Miss Bingley's invitation.

Elizabeth did not know why she had been included. Mrs. Hurst and Miss Bingley had made their disapproval of her known at the assembly with their snide remarks and haughty airs. Mr. Hurst did not even merit consideration. There was Mr. Darcy, but the possibility of him wishing to include her at their dinner party was scanty. He had avoided her since their brief conversation at the assembly. That left only Mr. Bingley, and Elizabeth was pleased to credit him with her inclusion for all that it fortified her already favorable impression of the amiable gentleman.

Finally, the carriage came to a stop in front of

Netherfield Park. A footman handed her and Jane out. The polished front steps gleamed in the descending light of the setting sun. The entrance hall was bright and spacious, a few tiny rainbows reflecting off the prisms of the chandelier onto the walls. It was a lovely setting.

She and Jane smoothed their gowns in the reflections of the large gilded mirrors on either side of the wide doors where the housekeeper took their bonnets and spencers. Then, the butler led them into a parlor where Mr. Bingley paced in front of the window, flanked by his two sisters.

"Miss Bennet! Miss Elizabeth! How delightful you could join us!" Mr. Bingley welcomed, springing forward and bowing with a great deal of enthusiasm.

Mr. Darcy bowed elegantly. Of course.

Elizabeth tried not to notice that the dark blue color of his waistcoat matched the ribbon Emily had woven through her hair and tied around her waist.

Mr. Hurst inclined his head after his wife woke him with a nudge on the shoulder.

Pleasantries were exchanged, and after an extensive and highly proper discussion about the thunderstorms of the week before and the much-improved weather of the present, dinner was announced.

To Elizabeth's relief, she saw that while Jane was

not seated next to Mr. Bingley, the occupants of the table were so few as to merit their placement insignificant. Situated as Elizabeth was between Mr. and Mrs. Hurst, she was grateful for the intimacy of the setting. She did not know what she could speak of with the Hursts. They had already exhausted talk of the weather.

After the first course was served, Elizabeth reflected that she need not have worried about conversation at all. Mr. Hurst attended to his soup with a vigor which excluded speech. Mrs. Hurst only spoke when she could express support for her sister, which was often enough.

Miss Bingley expressed her numerous views with great intent, accenting each opinion with a glance at Mr. Darcy.

To the gentleman's credit, Miss Bingley's chagrin — and, therefore, to Elizabeth's gratification — Mr. Darcy did not flatter her empty expressions. To the contrary, he often asked for an explanation. Had her opinions been her own to defend, Miss Bingley's replies would have led to a lively discussion. But they were not, and after several repetitions of "I am sure I cannot say," Mr. Darcy stopped asking for explanations the lady was clearly unprepared to give, and Miss Bingley fell silent by the end of the third course.

Elizabeth suspected that Mr. Darcy had achieved precisely what he had set out to do, and she inwardly applauded his ability to silence pandering, gratuitous speech.

Mr. Bingley was not one to suffer silence. He took the lead at the head of the table, but unlike his sister, his views were his own and he discussed them openly, inviting discussion and even opposing views with good humor.

Jane hung on his every word, but spoke little, as was her custom when they were in company. Misunderstanding her timidity as disinterest in the topic, Mr. Bingley wove a varied tapestry of discussion, including everything from fashion to politics, house management to entertainments. He often dabbed his face with his napkin, so great was his exertion.

Elizabeth sought to give him a reprieve before he exhausted himself. "I understand Sir William helped you fill your stables, Mr. Bingley. Do you enjoy riding?"

It was a painful topic, but her desire to hear of Tempest was too great to ignore.

"Very much! In town, we are limited to Hyde Park, and it gets so crowded one must be careful. You cannot imagine how glorious it is to race over the hills," he replied.

Elizabeth smiled. It was no trouble at all for her to imagine such a thing.

Mr. Darcy, who had been mostly an observer rather than an active participant in Mr. Bingley's multifarious discussions, finally spoke. With one raised eyebrow, he remarked, "Miss Elizabeth is quite the horsewoman."

A scoff escaped Elizabeth before she could check it. "Quite the horsewoman" could mean anything from greatly proficient to the worst rider in Christendom. Covering her impulsive reaction with a cough, Elizabeth reached for her wine glass, sipping and peeking at Mr. Darcy over the rim. Was he mocking her? Mr. Darcy could hardly think her a skilled horsewoman with the image of her muddy face and riding habit staining his memory.

The corner of his lip curled upward.

She looked down at her lap, her wine glass clinking against the silver as she set it down blindly. He was teasing her, and while his attention was flattering, it also reminded Elizabeth of the embarrassing history she would rather he forgot. It was a vain hope, and one she must handle with care. If she looked at Mr. Darcy, she would laugh, then she would be forced to explain why she and Mr. Darcy shared a joke to which nobody else at the table was privy.

Miss Bingley said, "Every lady who would call herself accomplished must be able to ride well." She lifted her chin and smiled contentedly at Elizabeth. So self-satisfied was her expression, Elizabeth wondered what the lady knew to justify the airs she gave herself. Whatever it was, Miss Bingley seemed to think it significant.

Elizabeth could not think of anything the lady could use against her. She had not witnessed the accident, and though Elizabeth knew little about Mr. Darcy, she did not believe him to be the sort of man to revel in the misadventures of others.

Nor did she suspect Miss Bingley had overheard her father speak with Sir William at the assembly when the lady had done everything in her power to distance herself from the lowly locals.

Miss Bingley's lips curled back from her teeth. "We shall have to arrange an outing. Do you have a favorite horse at Longbourn, Miss Elizabeth?"

Elizabeth's stomach clenched.

Meeting the challenge in her hostess' eyes with one of her own, Elizabeth managed her reply as favorably as she could. "We do not keep riding horses at Longbourn. However, the Lucases have been kind enough to allow us to ride theirs on occasion. Sir William has the finest stables in Hertfordshire."

She felt Mr. Darcy's eyes on her, but she refused to look away from Miss Bingley.

The lady feigned shock. Grasping the gaudy necklace at her throat, Miss Bingley exclaimed, "How is that possible? How does your father expect you to be an accomplished lady if he does not supply horses for you to ride? How do you exercise?"

If her family's lack of horses shocked Miss Bingley, then what Elizabeth planned to say would certainly shock the lady further. With increased gaiety, Elizabeth said, "I assure you we do not suffer from want of exercise. My father makes up for our empty stables with a constant supply of books. Improving the mind through extensive reading is as important an exercise as that of a physical nature, although to allay your concern, please allow me to reassure you that I dearly love long walks and seek opportunities to indulge in them often." Alone — she added rebelliously in her mind. She had done enough damage without adding that little detail.

Miss Bingley looked horrified. Exercise of the mind? Books? What were those good for but to scatter across tables to give the appearance of intelligence? And walks? What accomplished lady would ruin her satin slippers to experience the beauty of nature when one appeared to greater advantage atop a horse?

Elizabeth bit her lips and looked away from Miss Bingley.

"You can hardly learn anything from a book," Miss Bingley opined.

Feeling impertinent and bold, Elizabeth said, "Then I must be very ignorant, indeed, for most of what I know has been learned from their pages." She smiled at Miss Bingley, who gasped between huffs.

"I applaud your father's foresight." Mr. Darcy's clear tone silenced Miss Bingley. It silenced everyone.

His eyes held hers. "Of all the accomplishments society requires of a lady, extensive reading is the most substantial and, therefore, the most beneficial."

His words warmed Elizabeth's heart. Mr. Darcy did not consider her an ignorant hoyden after all.

Miss Bingley exclaimed, "Of course, we all agree that there is no enjoyment like reading! How much sooner one tires of anything than of a book. When I have a house of my own, I shall be miserable if I have not an excellent library. However, you must admit that some things simply cannot be taught as efficiently from books, such as a lady's air or manner of walking."

It had never occurred to Elizabeth to wish to learn those things.

Mr. Bingley and Jane looked about them in acute

discomfort, no doubt equally distressed at the lack of absolute harmony in the dining room. Dear Jane never could endure a hint of disagreement, and apparently, she had met her equal in Mr. Bingley.

Snapping his fingers, he said, "I saw the most fascinating article about the traitor who was captured by the same British spy who took down a ring of smugglers only weeks before."

Did Mr. Darcy roll his eyes? Elizabeth would swear he had done it. However, the gesture was so unexpected from him, she doubted.

Miss Bingley snapped, "Ladies do not read the newspaper, Charles. It is too shocking for our delicacies."

Elizabeth raised her eyebrows and bit her tongue (her lips were getting sore.)

When Mr. Darcy cleared his throat, she held her breath, eager to hear what he would say.

"It is important for every citizen — ladies and gentlemen alike — to be informed of current affairs. Should the women be caught defenseless in ignorance and fully trusting the men in their families, who have been spoon-fed the rubbish in the papers, to make the best decisions for their wellbeing?"

A favorable view with which Elizabeth found no fault, but as was often the case with Mr. Darcy, his reply provoked more questions than he answered.

"You do not trust the accounts in the papers, Mr. Darcy?" Elizabeth inquired, wondering what information he might have which caused him to distrust the papers. Insider information, perhaps? While it was ridiculous to continue to think of Mr. Darcy as a spy, he might be acquainted with one.

Confidently, daringly, Mr. Darcy's gaze fixed on her. "The newspapers are more interested in increasing their circulation than they are in telling the truth. I suspect the British spy they like to write about is a fictional character, a trick to sell more papers. Nothing more."

He would deny the spy's existence altogether? If the newspapers sought to make money from spectacular spy stories, at least their ulterior motives were relatively transparent. What was Mr. Darcy's motive? What did he stand to gain by denying their veracity? Was he protecting someone?

Elizabeth shook her head. If she was not careful, she would fall victim to her imagination again.

"Be what they may, they make for entertaining reading," Mr. Bingley commented.

Jane said softly, "Our father likes to read them aloud to us when we are gathered around the table. It is so quiet in Hertfordshire, it seems strange that there are those who risk life and limb, facing danger every day."

Elizabeth's heart cheered at Jane's boldness.

Mr. Bingley brightened. "I am pleased you see the seriousness of the matter. We must not forget the sacrifice involved by this man ... if he exists," he added with a glance at Mr. Darcy.

"Well said, Bingley," Mr. Darcy acknowledged, raising his glass.

Miss Bingley raised her fingers and nodded at a servant nearest the door. Without a word, the servant slipped out of the room, and Miss Bingley smiled as warmly as her pinched face granted. "Just because we are denied the entertainments of town does not mean we must deny ourselves of all of its delights. I sent for some sweetmeats, the likes of which I am certain you have never tasted, along with a jar of preserves from Barton's."

Elizabeth did not know who or what "Barton's" was, but given the reverence with which Miss Bingley uttered the name, they must be something of consequence.

Mr. Hurst apparently knew Barton's, and the prospect of their preserves had him sitting up in his chair, provoking a belch which his wife ignored.

Mr. Bingley looked mortified.

For his sake, Elizabeth overlooked the voluminous exhale. It had not been aimed in her direction.

Mrs. Hurst, on the other hand, raised her napkin to her nose.

Not knowing to expect more food after their meal, Elizabeth was disinclined to consume a bite more. Jane, too, must have eaten her fill. She did not reach eagerly for the pastries or preserves as their hosts did.

"Will you not have one, Mr. Darcy? Georgiana told me these are your particular favorites," Miss Bingley said smoothly, batting her eyelashes and leaning forward against the table to display her … ahem, figure … to greater advantage.

Mr. Darcy's eyes did not drift downward. Elizabeth thought more highly of him for it.

"I have eaten my fill," he said.

Miss Bingley pouted, but Mr. Darcy would not be swayed.

With one more sweetmeat on the platter, Miss Bingley addressed Jane. "As our guest, I insist you try one, Dear Jane. You will thank me, I am sure." She slipped the pastry onto a plate, drowning the sweetmeat with several spoonfuls of apple preserves.

Too acquiescent to refuse as Mr. Darcy had, Jane accepted the plate. And, because it was expected and would please her hostess, once Jane swallowed her last bite, she professed the sweetmeat and preserves to be every bit as delicious as Miss Bingley had claimed them to be.

"My favorite is the strawberry jam, but this apple is superb," professed Mr. Bingley.

The Hursts' mouths were too full to offer their opinions, which was compliment enough for Miss Bingley.

The jar of preserves, which would have lasted a week at Longbourn (if kept away from Lydia), was empty.

Miss Bingley rose, signaling that it was time for the ladies to join her in the drawing room.

She and Mrs. Hurst doted on Jane, leaving Elizabeth to observe the room at her leisure. There was a card table set up on one end of the room, and a pianoforte occupied a prominent position in the center. There were no books to speak of, so Elizabeth inspected the landscapes on the walls and imagined herself wandering over the painted fields, picking wildflowers and dipping her toes into one of the ponds.

The men were not long in joining them, and it pleased Elizabeth to notice that neither Mr. Darcy nor Mr. Bingley reeked of cigars. Her father only smoked a pipe, and she had never grown accustomed to the pungent cigar smell as Charlotte had. Perhaps if her brother had lived....

Elizabeth squeezed her eyes shut, ridding herself of unpleasant thoughts. What place did cigar smoke and deceased heirs have in the charming room?

Miss Bingley played and sang while Mrs. Hurst turned the pages and watched for signs of Mr. Darcy's pleasure.

Said gentleman receiving so much attention, Elizabeth determined not to look at him at all. Instead, she pondered his character, frustrated she still did not know what to make of him despite hours of observation and more conversation.

As captivated as she was on puzzling Mr. Darcy's complexities, one look at Jane chased all thought of him from Elizabeth's mind.

An extreme change had come over her sister. Her cheeks were so pale, they looked green in the candlelight. A slick sheen of sweat glistened over her skin.

Elizabeth moved closer to the settee, her focus riveted on her sister. Clasping her hand, Elizabeth's concern grew. Jane's touch was cold and moist. Lifting her hand to her sister's forehead, she asked, "Jane, are you well? Shall we depart for Longbourn?"

The sheer misery reflected in Jane's face soon caught Mr. Bingley's full attention. "Miss Bennet, are you in need of rest? I daresay dinner was a touch too rich. I, too, am feeling its effects. Do you wish for a cup of tea?" he asked, already ringing for a maid.

Jane groaned in reply and leaned against Elizabeth.

"Jane!" Elizabeth wrapped her arm around her sister, holding her up before she collapsed completely.

Turning to Mr. Bingley, Elizabeth said, "Is there a room where she might lie down? Hopefully, her malaise will pass shortly." As quickly as Jane had taken ill, Elizabeth feared she was being overly optimistic about her recovery.

Immediately, he asked the maid to take them to the guest bedchambers. Following them out to the hall, Mr. Bingley said, "You must both stay the night. I will send a messenger to Longbourn so they know not to expect you."

"Thank you, Mr. Bingley," Elizabeth said over her shoulder, tightening her grip around Jane's arms as they navigated the stairs.

"Let me help you, Miss," the maid said, grabbing Jane's other side. Elizabeth was grateful. Her sister's weight grew heavier with each step toward the top of the landing, and her breathing became more labored.

Jane tripped over her feet as they dragged her

over the threshold into the bedchamber. Her eyes glistening, she covered her mouth and heaved.

Elizabeth dived for the wash basin at the same time the maid lifted the water pitcher out of it.

Poor Jane crumpled to the floor, but they reached her just in time.

Never before had Elizabeth seen anyone so violently ill.

CHAPTER 10

Which was worse — chill or fever? Elizabeth pushed Jane's hair away from her damp forehead and pressed her hands against Jane's cheeks to warm them, praying she was not doing anything to worsen her sister's condition. Oh, if only she had not been distracted by Homer and Shakespeare, then she might have dedicated more attention to the texts on medicinal herbs gracing Papa's bookshelves!

This incessant purging of bile was unlike anything Elizabeth had experienced or seen. If she did not know better, she would have thought Miss Bingley had poisoned Jane … but why would she do that? If anyone, the lofty lady would have directed her venom at Elizabeth. She might have won a defender in Mr. Darcy at dinner, but she had also won an enemy in Miss Bingley. It could not be helped, and Elizabeth did not have the energy to concern herself with Miss Bingley when her own sister was so ill.

Jane's condition was worsening. If Elizabeth delayed too long in seeking medical help, she might not improve at all.

The moment Jane collapsed against the pillows after another bout of choking dry heaves, Elizabeth ran out to the hall to send for the apothecary.

A tall figure in the dark hall moved toward her.

She came to an abrupt halt, her heart leaping into her throat.

"Miss Elizabeth," the figure said in a buttery baritone. He held the candle closer to his face.

It was Mr. Darcy.

Exhaling in relief, Elizabeth's heart suffered another round of palpitating spasms when she saw that Mr. Darcy was not wearing a waistcoat or cravat.

"The whole household has taken horribly ill," he said without preamble.

She tried to comprehend his words, but seeing Mr. Darcy in nothing more than shirt and breeches captivated her. She had always believed clothing's purpose was to feature one's best attributes and discreetly disguise everything else. Now, fully able to appreciate the strength of Mr. Darcy's shoulders, the flatness of his stomach, and the narrowness of his hips, she felt it a pity that he must always cover himself up with a waistcoat and cravat.

"I apologize for my state. I did not expect to see anyone," he explained, crossing his arms over his chest so that the linen stretched over his arms. Mr. Darcy had strong arms.

Elizabeth looked at the ceiling, then at the floor. She had been gaping, she was sure of it. What was wrong with her? As if she had never seen a gentleman in a shirt before! She had seen her father several times. Granted, he in no stretch of the imagination compared to Mr. Darcy, but that hardly excused her wayward thoughts.

What had he said? The entire household was ill? Yes, that was it. Remembering her purpose, and disturbed she had been so easily distracted, Elizabeth stepped toward the stairs. "I will send for the apothecary."

"I have sent for him already."

Elizabeth stopped, unsure what to do now that it had already been done. "Oh. Good. Thank you."

Handsome and thoughtful — a dangerous combination.

The furrow in Mr. Darcy's wide brow deepened. "How is Miss Bennet?"

Thoughtful and genuinely concerned. Oh dear.

"I have never seen her so wretched," Elizabeth replied, proud of the steadiness of her voice when she felt wobbly all over.

He bowed his head, his shoulders slumped. "I am sorry to hear it. Please, it would be a kindness for you to allow me to be of assistance. Is there anything you or Miss Bennet require?"

Thoughtful, genuinely concerned, and practical. He was willing to put himself at her and Jane's disposal when he had clearly been at ease in his bedchamber. Was it possible for any man to be more endearing than Mr. Darcy was at that moment?

Elizabeth pinched her eyes closed. She must focus on Jane, and not her growing admiration for Mr. Darcy. She and Mr. Darcy. Wait. They were not ill. Feeling as if she had stumbled over a clue to a mystery and unsure of its importance, Elizabeth asked, "Are you and I the only ones who are not ill?"

"Aside from the servants, yes."

Mr. Darcy had inquired after the servants? Did his thoughtfulness know no bounds?

He added, "One of Bingley's footmen helped me confirm that aside from Miss Bennet, the Hursts, and the Bingleys, nobody else has taken sick."

What was she supposed to make of that? There

must be a sensible explanation, but as upset as she was, it eluded her.

"Is there anything else you require? It would be my privilege to attend to it," Mr. Darcy repeated, shifting his weight and clasping his hands together as Elizabeth often did when she was anxious with pent-up energy. "A message to deliver perhaps?" he pressed.

His readiness to attend to her and Jane was kind, but Elizabeth could not accept. "The hour is too late. I would no more put you in harm's way—"

"The risk is nothing."

"I appreciate your willingness, Mr. Darcy, but I see no benefit causing my family unnecessary worry by asking you, a stranger to them, to gallop to Longbourn and wake them from a deep sleep with a letter from me conveying bad news. I will send them word first thing in the morning."

He pressed no further. Nor did he say anything else. He just stood there.

Elizabeth was tempted to send Mr. Darcy on a useless errand just to occupy him, but she had a sick sister on whom to attend — a sister she had been away from for too long. Jutting her thumb over her shoulder, she said, "I really must return to Jane."

With a curt bow, he said, "I will await the apothecary, then," and dashed out of view and into his room (where, Elizabeth bemused, he would no doubt don a waistcoat.)

ELIZABETH DID NOT KNOW if Jane's slight improvement the following morning could be credited to the apothecary's drought or to Jane's own purging of the evil sickness. But she finally rested.

Slipping away from her sister's bedside to the attached guest room Mr. Bingley had readied for her use, Elizabeth wrote to their mother, informing her of the current state of Jane's health (and happy she had waited to pen her letter so she had positive news to share.) She regretted having sent the coach back to Longbourn the evening prior to convey Mr. Bingley's message that they would be spending the night at Netherfield. Now, she had to request they send the carriage back to fetch them home.

Mama must have been thrilled to receive word of their stay. It probably had not occurred to her to wonder what had caused their delay when she could assume Mr. Bingley had been overcome by tender emotion and insisted they spend the night.

Poor Mr. Bingley. He must feel awful to have invited a young lady to whom he showed a notable preference only to have her fall ill at his table along with the rest of his household. Even in malaise, he was a perfect gentleman. He had insisted that the apothecary see to Jane before himself.

Elizabeth had not seen Mr. Darcy since their brief exchange in the hall. Netherfield Park was larger than Longbourn, but it was not so grand it prevented its guests from chancing upon each other. Was he purposely avoiding her? She could not conjure why. He had apologized for his state of undress (which she really must try to stop thinking about), but he had not seemed embarrassed.

Elizabeth did not want to flatter herself by supposing he thought of her at all, although she would not have minded if he did. No doubt, he had finally found an undertaking in which to occupy himself.

Pouring sand over the page and folding the paper, she carried her message to the footman sitting guard in the hall. He assured her a messenger would be sent post haste. Elizabeth wondered if this was the same footman who had helped Mr. Darcy inquire into the health of the servants.

Housemaids scurried up and down the stairs carrying chamber pots, pitchers of water, and clean linens. Each one paused to see if Elizabeth required anything for herself or Miss Bennet, adding that Mr. Bingley had impressed upon them the importance of seeing to their comfort. The servants' attentiveness was a testament to Mr. Bingley's kindness and his growing devotion to Jane.

Elizabeth asked one of the maids how the rest of the household fared, and the girl's hesitancy to reply offered little encouragement. Neither did the two recently cleaned chamber pots she carried.

Jane was too exhausted to speak when she woke, so Elizabeth told her stories and coaxed a couple of spoonfuls of broth past her lips. If their carriage delayed much longer, she would have to find the library.

Two hours later, just as Elizabeth was about to search for the book room, she received a reply from her mother.

CHAPTER 11

*A*t first, Elizabeth was pleased to see her family's carriage. But her contentment took a dramatic turn when she ran downstairs to see two trunks deposited in the entrance hall of Netherfield Park along with her and Jane's maid.

Two trunks! Was Mama trying to move them in?

Elizabeth would have run after the retreating carriage had Emily not stopped her. She held out a folded paper. "I have a letter for you from Mrs. Bennet." Emily's voice echoed in the marble hall.

Frustrated and confused at the sight of the distant carriage and crumpled paper, Elizabeth took the note begrudgingly and read her mother's scribble.

The contents of the note said what she had

expected, not that Elizabeth took any pleasure in being right. To the contrary, she was mortified.

Her mother demanded that she and Jane extend their stay at Netherfield Park as long as they can manage. A week's worth of clothing and whatnots had been packed in their trunks, and Mama trusted they would use the contents to their advantage. She hoped to hear of an engagement soon and would not think of receiving them home until at least one had been secured.

Elizabeth felt sick. Just when she was assured of Mr. Darcy's good opinion after their extraordinary first meeting, she was under orders to impose on Mr. Bingley's kind hospitality when he was as sick as Jane. How had this happened? Perhaps she had minimized Jane's illness too much for their mother to treat their impromptu stay like a house party.

The other side of the page contained instructions regarding Jane's care along with mention of a tin in Emily's possession containing a mixture of herbs Mama insisted Elizabeth make into a tea for Jane and any of the other residents still suffering from nausea. Elizabeth's faith in her mother's sense was restored to its usual place — that of a well-meaning but often presumptuous parent whose nerves would suffer endless attacks and spasms until all five of her daughters were settled.

Seeing the trunks upstairs along with Emily, who insisted Elizabeth leave Jane with her so that she might get some rest before she, too, fell ill, Elizabeth went to her bedchamber. The curtains were pulled and the bed looked soft and inviting. Elizabeth had not realized how tired she was until she saw the fluffed pillows and thick blankets. But though she laid down for several minutes, she could not sleep.

Concluding that her time would be put to better use finding the library than in tossing and turning, Elizabeth abandoned the comfort of her bed.

She riffled through her trunk, looking for a clean morning gown. Other than volume two of Mr. Pinkerton's *"…Best and Most Interesting Voyages and Travels in All Parts of the World"* there was nothing of interest to see. Mama had packed her bottle of Floris perfume and her nicest ball gown — because nursing was no excuse to neglect one's appearance evidently. Elizabeth imagined that the contents of Jane's trunk would be similar to her own. At least, Jane could be sick in style.

Emily must have packed the sensible gown layered at the bottom of the trunk. Elizabeth was grateful to see it. The soft fabric smelled refreshingly clean, like lye soap and lavender.

Donning her simple frock and dabbing the jasmine perfume onto her neck and the insides of her wrists, Elizabeth left her room and followed the sound of clanging keys until she found the housekeeper, Mrs. Nicholls. The gentle woman showed Elizabeth the way to the library, then left her to peruse the shelves.

Mr. Bingley's library was well-situated, with large windows overlooking the gardens and clusters of chairs and settees placed around them. The prospect afforded a lovely view and ample light by which to read. The bookshelves, however, were woefully understocked. It did not take ten minutes for Elizabeth to read the spine of every book in the room. Most of the tomes were on estate management, but she did find a couple of volumes of poetry she could read aloud to Jane.

Cradling the books in her arm, she was about to leave the neglected room when Mr. Darcy opened the door. She froze in place, unable to move.

He stopped abruptly, one foot poised in the air, when he saw her. He wore a waistcoat and cravat … more was the pity.

The hair at his brow and collar was still damp. Elizabeth appreciated how his dark locks curled every which way as hers did.

They stood in silence, contemplating each other. She knew her thoughts. They warmed her cheeks and held her slippers firmly against the carpet. What was Mr. Darcy thinking? He opened his mouth as if he intended to speak, but he said nothing. He just stood there uncomfortably, as if *he* had been the one to see her in a state of undress the night before. Or was he still embarrassed over the incident? Had he hoped to avoid her?

"I … had thought to find the library … empty," he stammered, already turning to depart.

He was definitely avoiding her. Far from being offended, Elizabeth was curious. She posed him no threat, and she thought no less of him for having seen him in his shirtsleeves. In fact, she was having difficulty not thinking of him a great deal more.

She took in a deep breath, eager to make her escape before her complexion betrayed her thoughts. "You soon would have found it so. I was on my way out." She drew closer to the door, her eyelids drooping when she was near enough to catch the scent of soap and shaving lather and something else she could not identify but which she would always associate with Mr. Darcy. It was agreeable whatever it was.

Shaking herself from her reverie, Elizabeth looked up at him expectantly.

Mr. Darcy did not remove himself from the doorway. "Is Miss Bennet improved?"

"She is a little, thank you." She cleared her throat,

her voice sounding too high in her ears. "What of Mr. Bingley and the rest of the household?"

"The worst is not yet over. The Hursts and Miss Bingley were affected most severely. Bingley has improved since last night, if only slightly. He has been able to drink some broth."

"The same with Jane."

He sighed, then removing himself from the doorway, he entered the room and sat in the chair farthest away from her. He crossed one foot over another, then tried to rest one booted ankle over his knee. When that proved unsatisfactory, he tried the other side.

So entertained was Elizabeth in watching him, she forgot she had meant to leave the room. It was obvious he was avoiding her, and now, it seemed that her presence made him nervous. Uncertain of how long her stay was to be, and not wishing to cause the gentleman more discomfort than necessary, Elizabeth thought it a kindness to address the problem directly.

"You seem unsettled, Mr. Darcy," she commented.

He shoved his hand through his hair, sighing audibly. "I am unaccustomed to inactivity," he said so grumpily, Elizabeth swallowed a chuckle. So, she was not the trouble after all.

Feeling much better, Elizabeth teased, "Then be grateful you are not a lady."

Mr. Darcy grunted. "I used to sit in on my sister's music lessons. Georgiana is very shy, and she would hardly speak to her tutor unless I was nearby. For her sake, I encouraged her through hours of endless scales and tunes I heard so many times I grew to despise them. I have never been so bored. I do not know how ladies endure spending all day indoors when there is so much to do."

Elizabeth tilted her chin. While the image of Mr. Darcy sitting beside his sister during her music lessons was precious, she was interested to know how he suggested a lady occupy her time. Crossing the room to the window, she asked, "What would you have us do?"

"Do ladies not enjoy such activities?"

"You did not. Why should I?" She sat opposite him.

He shifted his weight in his chair again. "It was my understanding that accomplished ladies have many activities from which to choose to keep them busy. Between developing their various arts, they have calls to make and their charitable causes to give them purpose."

Elizabeth snorted. "I have ripped my fair share of bandages, Mr. Darcy, but after a morning of nothing but stitching and polite conversation over sips of tea, I am so restless, I would rather poke my eyes out with a needle than re-thread it."

Most gentlemen were shocked to hear a lady complain so fiercely of lady-like pursuits. Mr. Darcy merely raised his eyebrows. "What of music, books, and painting? Do you not find them enjoyable?"

"Lovely pastimes, all of them. But would you be satisfied if you were stuck inside your house all day with nothing to do but receive callers who only talk of the weather and the styles of gown worn at the latest ball, practice the same music that is played at every social event, and paint the scenes you would rather see in person than painted on a table?"

Mr. Darcy frowned. "I have never considered that before. My sister enjoyed her music lessons so much, I never questioned that another lady might find them difficult to endure ... as I did."

Elizabeth held her peace. She had complained enough for one morning.

"Is that why you ride the Lucases' horses?" he asked, rubbing his side whiskers.

Elizabeth liked how his whiskers pointed at the end, angling to his lips and the small divot on his chin. She liked that they did not cover the dimple she had seen the day before. Hurrying to reply before she forgot he had asked her reason for riding the Lucases' horses, she said, "Excitement does not come to me, and so I must search for it however I can."

He frowned. "Excitement is overrated."

"How can you say that?" she asked.

"Too many young men throw away their lives in the pursuit of excitement."

Elizabeth understood the veracity of Mr. Darcy's statement, but she had had years to formulate a reply to that particular argument. "It is true, although it is their choice to do so. The fairer sex is not given that same consideration." Recalling Miss Bingley's comment from the night before, she added, "Our sensibilities are too delicate to even read the newspapers."

Mr. Darcy chuckled, granting Elizabeth a brief glimpse of his dimple. "Your sensibilities are not so delicate, I presume?"

She smiled in answer. She did not wish to be the topic of conversation when she had so much more to learn about him. "It is a good thing, I think, and I am tempted to return the compliment to you, sir, otherwise I suppose we both would have fallen ill along with the rest."

He nodded, his eyebrows furrowed.

Since she had raised the subject, she might as well ask his opinion. "What do you suppose happened to make everyone so ill?" As much as she had warmed to the idea, she did not think Miss Bingley was responsible. The lady was fickle-minded, but she was not stupid. Nor was Elizabeth so fanciful she would cry poison when there could be another more reasonable explanation.

"It was most likely the preserves. Consuming improperly prepared food is no better than imbibing poison."

"Really?" Poisoned preserves? Perhaps she should pay more attention to her initial impressions.

Mr. Darcy said impassively, "Most preserves purchased at the shops contain sulfate of copper. A gentleman interested in science has studied its effect on individuals after ingestion. He claims it is poisonous."

"I wonder at your knowledge of poisons, sir."

He shrugged his shoulders. "He wrote a pamphlet on the subject, and I like to read," he replied.

"As do I, but it has never occurred to me to read about poisons. Is that a common subject of study among gentlemen?"

He did not bat an eyelid. "An estate cannot run smoothly if the residents and animals are always sick."

"A poisonous herb in the grass, I accept, but that does not explain how you could link poison to a jar of preserves." Elizabeth realized how argumentative she sounded. Mr. Darcy could read whatever he chose. Who was she to question him?

He did not seem to take offense. Calmly, he explained, "Bingley and his household are not the first to suffer. I travel extensively and have met with several people who have been adversely affected by what appears to be a harmless delicacy. One elderly gentleman in particular, a Mr. Woodhouse from Highbury, refuses to serve them at his table. It was because of him I chose to read more on the subject to satisfy my curiosity."

For the second time since her arrival at Netherfield, Elizabeth wished she had availed herself of her father's medicinal books. She had not known what she was missing.

"What are you currently reading?" Mr. Darcy's question was so unexpected, Elizabeth felt as if she had been knocked off balance.

He nodded at her hands. She still held the two books she had selected for Jane.

"Oh, just some poetry for Jane. I am reading the latest published work of Mr. John Pinkerton." Taking a deep breath to recite the long title, she added, "*A General Collection of the Best and Most Interesting Voyages and Travels in All Parts of the World.*"

Mr. Darcy's lips twitched. "Impressive title. Are you enjoying it?"

"More than most, I suspect, not having been to any of the places he writes about. I find the author's description of Derbyshire and the Peak District thorough enough to form a picture of it in my mind." A picture she would have to wait a year to see in reality.

"You have not been to Derbyshire?"

She looked down at her hands. "I was supposed to travel there with my aunt and uncle this summer — my aunt grew up there — but the trip has been postponed."

Mr. Darcy leaned forward. "Where did she grow up?"

"A village called Lambton. Do you know it?"

He smiled. "My estate is near Lambton, along the edge of the Peak District."

Elizabeth's heart raced. Questions she had reserved for her aunt tumbled off her tongue. "Is it as lovely as my aunt has described? As I read about in Mr. Pinkerton's book? Is it true that England's largest natural cave is there? Does it make the strange sounds Mr. Pinkerton claims? Are there caverns with a unique blue and yellow mineral they call Blue John and make jewelry with? Did they really export it to France before the war? Are the gritstones as coarse as I have read about at the escarpment at Stanage? Oh, how I would like to see it for myself!"

Mr. Darcy pulled the compass out of his waist-coat pocket, moving it around in his hand and rubbing his thumb over the casing as he spoke. "It is a place you will forever carry in your most pleasant memories. Sweeping dales tucked under a blanket of velvety green grass. Craggy hills the more adventurous can climb." He nodded at her and continued, his voice softening as he spoke. "Peat-covered moorlands with henges cropping out of nowhere, as if they had been dropped from the sky. Limestone dales and wild woodlands, shimmering lakes and towering tors." Mr. Darcy's gaze fixed dreamily out of the window, his grip tightening around his compass. "And at its edge, proudly standing along the east bank of the River Derwent is Pemberley. Backed by dense woodland and rocky hills that rise to heather moorlands and surrounded by an immaculate parkland with terraces, ponds, and gardens, it is my vision of beauty and perfection. It is a place I am honored to call my home."

Elizabeth did not realize she had closed her eyes until Mr. Darcy's silence reminded her to open them. His vivid description had brought Mr. Pinkerton's book to life, and the longing to see such wonders for herself burned within her. She recognized the same yearning in Mr. Darcy. "You miss it. How long have you been away?"

"Too long." His reserve returned, his tone cold.

"Then, why are you here? Why do you not return to Pemberley?"

He winced. "I ought to see how Bingley is faring. Pray excuse me," he said as he stood, and with a curt bow, he withdrew from the library without a book.

DARCY COULD HAVE TALKED with Miss Elizabeth for hours, but he had already revealed too much of himself. She understood him well enough to question his motives, and the only explanation which would satisfy her — the truth — was forbidden.

He closed his eyes, the hint of her jasmine scent lingering in his senses.

There had been so much more he wanted to tell her. How the agent disguised as Bingley's footman had helped him determine the source of the household's malady. That Darcy had not endangered his friends to Sir William's retaliation as he had feared. That the reason he had been dressed down to his shirt the night before was because he had found a cat with its face stuffed inside the empty jar, licking the residue from the corners and covering its coat with the poisonous preserves. In typical cat fashion, the feline showed its appreciation for Darcy's extrication by vomiting all over his waistcoat and cravat. Not wishing to subject Wilson to the loathsome task, Darcy had chucked the offending items in the kitchen fire. His mistake had been to meet Miss Elizabeth in the hall when he ought to have stayed in his bedchamber. He had crossed his arms over his chest more out of a desire to hide the scent of cat vomit than a sense of modesty.

Darcy wanted to tell her not to call at the Lucases, but he had no right to make demands when he could give no explanation. And Miss Elizabeth would require one. Rightly so.

He wanted to keep his distance as he had done all morning. Miss Elizabeth's conversation, so honest and open and refreshing, had charmed him wholly. He had been wise to be cautious. Her rapid fire questions about Derbyshire, her slender fingers gripping the arms of her chair, her dark lashes splayed over her flushed cheeks, her lips parted in concentration on his every word, and the sparkle in her eager eyes as she listened to him describe the place he most loved — his home — were memories from which he had no inclination to part ... when that was precisely what he must do.

CHAPTER 12

*A*fter a difficult afternoon, Jane slept soundly through the night. Whatever evil had afflicted her had finally abated, leaving her weak and in need of rest.

Having stayed up with Jane so that Emily might sleep, Elizabeth, too, was tired. More than that, though, she was restless.

So, when the following morning dawned and Emily took over as nurse, Elizabeth donned her riding habit (for the warmth, nothing more) and slipped away from Netherfield Park for some much needed fresh air and a dose of Charlotte's good sense. She would look at the horses. That was all.

Unless her father had decided not to speak with Sir William after all…

Since the assembly, Elizabeth had been afraid to

ask Papa directly lest he forbid her from riding again. She had not had the opportunity to ask Sir William. She could have asked George or Charlotte, but Elizabeth had not wanted them to know anything was untoward. They would have felt guilty when she had been the one who had assumed nobody would be at the top of the knoll.

Elizabeth grasped at justifications as though they were straw, convincing herself that her father had not meant what he had said.

It took Elizabeth longer to reach Lucas Lodge from Netherfield Park than it did to walk from Longbourn, but she arrived at the usual time for her and Charlotte's ride. Only, this morning, there was no one to greet her when she arrived at the stables.

She had not come for five days. Had that been too long? Had Charlotte already left? Or was she riding later in the morning? Had she quit riding altogether? Had she quit out of undeserved guilt because Papa *had* spoken with Sir William? Each suggestion alarming her more, Elizabeth tapped her fingernail nervously against her brooch and waited outside of the building until Joe walked past.

"Good morning, Miss Bennet," the stable boy said, looking nervously over his shoulder.

"Good morning, Joe. Is Miss Lucas well?"

George stepped out from the shadows, and the

boy scurried off. "Miss Elizabeth, I am surprised to see you here. Did you not receive Charlotte's message?"

Elizabeth's heartbeat pulsed in her ears. "She is well, I pray?"

"She is. She only had some news to share with you."

News? Good or bad? Clutching her hands together, Elizabeth said, "Jane took ill at Netherfield, and I have been caring for her. She is improved this morning, and I have been trapped indoors for too long. I had hoped to join Charlotte for a few minutes before returning to the sickroom." If her father had spoken with Sir William, she would find out now. She held her breath, hoping.

George nudged a piece of straw with the toe of his boot. "I am sorry to hear of Miss Bennet's illness, but I am pleased to hear she is out of danger." He ran his hand through his hair and kicked a clod of dirt. "I hate to add to your troubles when you have been caring for your sister, but since you did not get Charlotte's message yesterday, I will have to tell you."

Dread twisted Elizabeth's stomach. Her father had meant his threat. "It is bad news."

"It is for you, though I hope you will be happy for Charlotte. Father engaged a dancing master, and

Charlotte has decided to give her full attention to her lessons rather than riding in the morning."

No sooner had hope sparked within Elizabeth than confusion damped it. She shook her head.

Charlotte loved to ride. She would not ignore her favored activity in lieu of dancing unless there was much more to the story than what George implied — something that had nothing to do with Elizabeth's father. "Charlotte decided this?" she asked.

"Yes. As you must know, she did not make the decision easily, and it was with great regret she penned the message for you yesterday."

Surely, it was only temporary. "How long?"

George kicked at the straw again. "Indefinitely, if our father has anything to do with it. Charlotte is to continue with music and language lessons after this."

Elizabeth could not think of a worse punishment. A horrible explanation arose in Elizabeth's mind. "She is not in trouble because of me, is she? My father said he intended to speak with Sir William about my accident, but Charlotte was not at fault. Not in the least—"

George held up his hand, shaking his head. "No. This has nothing to do with you, Miss Elizabeth. I would be the first to know if Mr. Bennet forbade your visits to our stables, and I would be quick to comply with his wishes."

Her father must have reconsidered!

Elizabeth's joy was short-lived. George continued, "Charlotte is not being punished. Our father merely wishes for her to add to her accomplishments so that she might… Well, you know."

"I see," Elizabeth mumbled. Now that her own concern had cleared her mind, she understood fully. Charlotte felt the pressure to marry well, and Sir William was doing what he could to raise her chance of making a better match.

Elizabeth's heart rebelled for her friend. Charlotte deserved so much better. Elizabeth herself could never be presumed upon to marry a gentleman who only saw her as a decoration who would reflect well on him through her superb display of talents. Why could a gentleman not simply admire a lady for herself — for her inner qualities? Must she also perform like a puppet, controlled by a society who cared nothing for her? Could she have nothing of her own to inspire passion and fuel her curiosities? Must she endure a lifetime of suppression and ennui?

Perhaps Charlotte could. Many ladies did. But Elizabeth could not stomach it. How grateful she was that her father, despite the limits he imposed, loved her enough to reconsider taking away the one freedom that fed her soul. She could still ride. Charlotte would want her to as would Mercer, who had difficulty ensuring that all of his charges received the exercise they required for their health.

"I do not suppose any of your horses require some exercise? I would be happy to help," she offered. It was too early to call on Charlotte, but she resolved to do so as soon as she could steal away from Jane's side during calling hours.

George's gaze had been fixed on the ground, but he finally looked up. Such sadness radiated from him, Elizabeth's eyes prickled and burned. She understood, then, that George had more bad news to deliver. Taking a deep breath, she wrapped her arms around her waist, lifting one hand to run her fingers over the familiar stones on her brooch and waiting for him to speak.

"I am sorry, Miss Elizabeth. Our father does not wish to receive visitors at the stables any more. Please understand it is nothing against you. He has hired a new trainer and does not wish for any disturbances among the horses."

Elizabeth had braced herself for disappointment, but her heart ached all the same.

"I see," she muttered, her tongue thick and her voice a weak whisper.

"I am sorry. Charlotte enjoyed your company, and Mercer will miss seeing you. We all will. I wish you could have read Charlotte's note instead of hearing about this from me. She would have known better how to tell you."

This truly was goodbye. No more horses. No more riding. No more freedom.

Elizabeth needed to leave, but her feet refused to budge.

"Mercer is still here?" she asked, blinking furiously so she would not make George feel worse than he already must by witnessing her cry.

"Yes. The new trainer is here to help him, not replace him. Mr. Robson trains racehorses."

"Mr. Robson?" Elizabeth felt foolish for repeating George, but once she left she would have no more reason for ever coming back to the stables unless Charlotte invited her … and it seemed that Sir William had his reasons for keeping her away.

"Mr. Robert Robson. You have probably read his name in the papers," George said with a confusing mixture of pride and concern.

What was going on at Lucas Lodge stables? Elizabeth felt like her world had been tossed on its head, and when she finally dismissed herself to walk away, she was not certain which direction she should go. The path blurred no matter how many times she rubbed her eyes.

As much as Darcy enjoyed Miss Elizabeth's company in his dreams, he was more determined than before to ensure that was where their acquaintance remained. In the confines of his dreams, in the safety of his thoughts.

Such was Darcy's plan until he heard steps in the hall. He did not need to peek outside his bedchamber to know it was her. She had a light, rhythmic step he would recognize anywhere.

He listened until her footsteps faded, trying to determine her direction, trying to convince himself it was nothing. But when he heard the front door creak to a close, and he confirmed with a glance out of the window that she was walking unattended, Darcy felt obliged to ensure her safety. Did she not know these were dangerous times? What if she called at the Lucases? What if she endangered her life when he could have prevented it?

Darcy's irritation at Miss Elizabeth's carelessness increased as he mounted his horse and rode in search of her. She could not have gone too far.

What was she thinking walking without company for protection? Was she so complacent, she believed herself immune to the evils of the world?

He found her near Lucas Lodge, but if she meant

to return to Netherfield Park or to Longbourn, she was walking in the wrong direction.

Gritting his teeth in agitation, Darcy closed the distance between them until a sound stopped him cold. Miss Elizabeth wept.

His gut knotted. Troublesome storm clouds did not belong near her when she was the sunshine.

Slipping down from his saddle, his anger forgotten, he reached her just as her foot caught against the ground and she lurched forward.

"Mr. Darcy!" she exclaimed, twisting in his arms to wipe her eyes and hide her face.

An overwhelming desire to pull Miss Elizabeth closer, to cradle her in his arms until her tears subsided, startled Darcy to his senses. Releasing his hold on her, he pushed his handkerchief into her hand, unsure what to say but wanting to make it better.

"...something in my eye..." she mumbled.

"I suspected as much," he agreed.

She made quick work of drying her face. When she finally turned to face him, she handed his handkerchief back with a weak smile.

Her self-possession filled Darcy with something he could not define nor adequately describe. It stirred him, and more than anything, he wished to restore her humor. There was little harm in that.

Right? His mind argued that he was playing with fire, but his heart insisted he was behaving as a gentleman ought. He prided himself in acting like a gentleman. His heart won.

Darcy returned her smile. "The fields are dusty. You may need it again."

She folded the handkerchief back into a square and held it out to him, avoiding his gaze. "Thank you, Mr. Darcy, but I am better now."

He tucked the silk square back into his pocket and turned to walk with Miss Elizabeth, directing her and his horse toward Netherfield Park. "Where were you going?" he asked.

She looked around as if she were seeing her surroundings for the first time. "I hardly know."

He waited for her to provide more details. When she did not, he asked, "Did you visit the Lucases' stables?"

"Yes." After a couple of steps, she added in a rush, "But Charlotte could not ride with me, and I was told I will not be able to continue my rides with her in the mornings." Another few steps, and her voice trembled as she added, "I shall miss them greatly. As you know, it was the one activity I truly enjoyed."

Darcy understood. For a lady who cherished her freedom as much as Miss Elizabeth did, taking away the one interest she loved would be a tremendous loss. No wonder she mourned.

With another smile brighter than the previous one, she added, "I am happy for them, of course. They have a new trainer — one I have heard about in the papers, though I cannot recall where — a Mr. Robert Robson. I am certain it means exciting things for the horses, and I hope it means good things for the Lucases."

Darcy's mind reeled. Robert Robson was not just any trainer. He was a racehorse trainer. He trained champions. His horses had won four Epsom Derbies, the last two being the most recent. He could not be bought easily, and with Lucas Lodge in debt, Darcy suspected he knew from whence the money originated. The Four Horsemen.

Darcy did not realize Miss Elizabeth had asked him a question until he felt her inquisitive gaze on him.

"You are out earlier than normal, Mr. Darcy," she observed, watching him keenly. Too keenly to hide the truth when it would not hurt her or expose himself to be completely honest.

"I saw you leaving Netherfield alone. I was concerned for your safety."

Her lips curled up, then she looked down. "Oh." A

becoming blush kissed her cheeks — a blush he had no right to put there.

Feeling uncomfortable, he said, "You ought not venture out alone. It is not safe."

There. Better to scold her than to continue in this precarious terrain.

"Am I not safe with you?" She arched her eyebrow impertinently.

Dear Lord. He cleared his throat. "Yes, though you would be wise not to take any man's word until his actions prove the integrity of his intentions."

She laughed. "Only a truly honorable gentleman would reply thus."

"You ought not trust so easily. How do you know I am not dangerous?" That had sounded better in his mind than it did aloud.

Again, that eyebrow. "Oh, I am convinced you are dangerous, Mr. Darcy. But you are not a danger to me."

Darcy gritted his teeth. He felt Miss Elizabeth's danger to him acutely. He found himself wanting to be too honest with her, and he liked her too much to endanger her in such a reckless fashion.

Changing the direction of their conversation, he asked, "Why do you like riding so much … other than the exercise and excitement?"

She sighed. "I love the wind against my face,

going so fast I feel tears pulling from my eyes. When I race over the fields, I feel free from inhibitions and expectations. I am allowed just … to be."

That was how he felt at Pemberley. It was the one place he could let his guard down and be himself.

She smiled. "Is that how you feel at Pemberley?"

Darcy startled. Of what use were private thoughts if she could read them? Or, had he spoken them aloud? He nodded, afraid to utter a word.

She said, "I heard it in the tenderness of your voice when you described your family's estate and in the rich details you gave which most people would not even notice. It sounded as beautiful as poetry to me."

If only she could see Pemberley. Miss Elizabeth was one to appreciate it.

She added, "You are fortunate to have a whole estate that lends itself to your happiness. The back of a horse is small in comparison."

Darcy bit his tongue. He wanted so badly to invite her to Pemberley, but he must maintain his control.

"Why does your father not keep horses?" he asked.

"Because of my older brother."

Darcy whipped his head around to face her. "You have a brother?"

"Had," she said softly, adding just above a whisper, "He was the heir to Longbourn and my only living brother. I know I ought to forgive him. It is not kind to hold a grudge against the dead, but my father sold all of our riding horses after his accident."

Darcy dared not ask what happened.

Elizabeth scoffed, the bitterness in her tone revealing a depth of feeling previously hidden to him. "You are far too mannerly to inquire, but I will tell you anyway, Mr. Darcy. You see, my brother — Thomas was his name — was indulged from infancy. Secure in his inheritance and with little regard for the future when he could find pleasure in the present, he was allowed to roam all over the country with his friends. It was on one such excursion he succumbed to pressure from his peers and accepted a foolish challenge."

Darcy recollected the senseless pranks and tricks in which his schoolmates had participated to prove their bravery. Some of them had been harmless; others had been deadly.

"The family where he stayed had recently acquired a difficult stallion. Despite the groom's warnings to stay away, Thomas' friends thought they would prove who was the bravest by entering the stall of the stallion while the family slept. Thomas went first." She looked down, her hands clenched together. "He never came back out. The other boys were too scared to help him. By the time the groom woke and got to them, Thomas was … gone."

"I am sorry." He could think of nothing better to say.

"Me too. Thomas dying away from home was awful enough. It left my father's entailed estate without an heir to inherit and secure the futures of my mother and sisters, but it also moved my father to prohibit travel and horses."

Travel and horses. Miss Elizabeth's two loves.

Darcy pressed his eyes closed briefly. How quickly he had judged Mr. and Mrs. Bennet when they had lost their only son and means of providing for their daughters after they were gone. He would always find Mrs. Bennet's manners brazen, but with knowledge came understanding … and acceptance. Even Mr. Bennet's seeming apathy toward his family was explained. Perhaps he distanced himself so that he would not have to face the pain of loss again. It did not justify his behavior, but at least it offered a strong motive for it.

Miss Elizabeth dabbed angrily at her cheek with her sleeve and forced a smile. "I have been fortunate to visit my aunt and uncle as far as London. Under the circumstances, I am grateful to be allowed to have gone that far. And until today, I was allowed to ride with Miss Lucas."

"How did you convince your father to allow that?"

"Quietly and without incident. My father has never said so aloud, but I suspect he has allowed it because he knows I am more cautious than Thomas ever was. That was why I ran off the morning we first met. I was afraid my father would take my spill too hard and forbid me from riding." She folded her arms over her chest. "It turns out, I need not have worried. I no longer have access to horses, and I am not so desperate as to attempt to ride our carriage horses."

Melancholy dulled her cheer, but only momentarily. She chewed her bottom lip and her eyebrows bunched together as though she was planning something.

Before her jaw could set in determination on an emotionally made solution which would surely bring on Mr. Bennet's displeasure, Darcy said, "The Lucases are not the only family with a stable full of horses requiring exercise. I am certain Bingley would wish for you, as his guest, to make use of his stables."

The brightness in Miss Elizabeth's face stirred Darcy's heart.

"Really? You do not think it in imposition? Could we go there now?"

There was too much hope in her question for him to deny her. What harm could possibly come from a brief jaunt over Netherfield's acreage?

CHAPTER 13

*E*lizabeth followed Mr. Darcy inside Mr. Bingley's stables, peeking inside each gated stall until she saw the familiar brown coat and black mane.

Tempest pushed her muzzle between the bars.

Reaching through them, Elizabeth touched Tempest's velvet nose. Contentment soothed her like sunshine soaking through her riding habit. "This one, please."

Mr. Bingley's groom cleared his throat and shuffled his feet. "Are you certain you want to ride this mare, Miss? She is a bit of a handful."

A stable boy stood behind him, holding a sidesaddle borrowed from one of Mr. Bingley's sisters. Elizabeth had seen the boy before, she was sure. Unlike the groom, the boy was not schooled in hiding his expression. He stared wide-eyed and open-mouthed between Elizabeth and the maligned mare.

"I am certain, thank you," Elizabeth replied.

The groom shook his head, but he led Tempest out of the stall to saddle her. "Easy, easy," he said calmly.

Elizabeth ran her hands over the mare's neck and down her flank, feeling her bridled energy and knowing Tempest was in as much need of a good run as she was. She needed to ensure the saddle was snug. "The girth will need tightened after she walks a few steps. Tempest has a bad habit of puffing out her stomach when she is being saddled."

The groom chuckled. "You are familiar with the troublesome minx, then? I am relieved, Miss."

Elizabeth smiled. "We are old friends."

The stable boy grinned. "The ladies of the house refuse to ride this mare after she unseated Miss Bingley then took a bite out of her bonnet … and all in front of Mr. Darcy."

With a groan and a sharp look which implied that the lad would get a good scolding regarding what should and should not be revealed about the master of the house's family, the groom led Tempest to the covered yard.

Elizabeth bit her lips together. She could not very

well laugh at Miss Bingley when it was that very lady's saddle she would be using. Thank goodness Emily had thought to include Elizabeth's riding habit in the trunk Mama had her pack. Elizabeth would use Miss Bingley's saddle and horse, but she drew the line at borrowing from her wardrobe.

After a few laps around the yard, the groom tightened the saddle's girth again, gaining two more notches in the strap.

"Blimey, just as the lady said! I bet she knows more about horses than Miss Bingley pretends to," the stable boy exclaimed to the groom.

The groom snapped, "I am tempted to send you back from whence you came until you learn to keep your mouth shut. No wonder they wanted rid of you at Lucas Lodge."

Of course! That was where she had seen the boy. If she recalled correctly, he was Joe's little brother.

Satisfied to have her memory restored, Elizabeth lifted a foot for the groom to help her onto the saddle just as Mr. Darcy and his groom, a man with light hair and a remarkably crooked nose, emerged from the stables.

Mr. Darcy's horse, a handsome gray thorough-bred, pranced impatiently, his brushed coat glistening in the morning sun. Such a striking creature would make most gentlemen appear shabby beside him, but not Mr. Darcy. Elizabeth had thought him handsome at first sight, but dressed as he was with a dark green coat, she could appreciate the width of his shoulders as she had the night she had seen him in his shirtsleeves. The fabric strained across his back when he pulled his gloves on. His buckskin breeches stretched over his thighs as he mounted the gelding with the agility of a cat leaping on top of a table. His was the physique of an athlete — strong and lithe.

The warmth crawling up her neck warned Elizabeth to look elsewhere before the blush reached her cheeks.

So Mr. Darcy was handsome. Many gentlemen were.

So he exuded an air of confidence and danger. That was merely the work of her unfulfilled longings and overactive imagination.

So he had proved himself reliable and principled. This thought gave Elizabeth pause. It was not easy to rebut admirable qualities, nor did she believe it just to attempt to do so. She would simply have to think kindly toward Mr. Darcy's character and superior figure and hope that he was in reality the man she was beginning to believe him to be.

He smiled widely at her. "I trust you know the best paths."

She arched her brow. Her earlier disappointment felt distant, and with Mr. Darcy as her willing accomplice, all Elizabeth wanted to do was chase her elusive dreams over the fields. One day, she would catch them. Maybe not today, but fulfillment seemed more possible right then than it ever had before.

Elizabeth nudged Tempest into a walk. "If it is the scenery you wish to see, I fear I will disappoint you. It is my intention to gallop Tempest so fast, the fields blur."

"Are you up to the task?" Concern contained his smile to his lips.

Elizabeth's pride puffed out like the feathers of a ruffled hen. Was *she* up to the task? She could very well ask the same of him!

But her offense was momentary when reason overtook her impulse. Mr. Darcy did not know whether she was a novice or an accomplished equestrian. His only observation regarding her skill had been the spill she had taken right in front of him. Of course, he would question her ability.

Well, she thought gleefully, she would simply have to correct his false impression. She would start out slowly, but Elizabeth resolved not to return to the stables until both she and Tempest were breathless and Mr. Darcy and his steed were several lengths behind them.

Tapping the mare's side, Elizabeth bobbed up and down to Tempest's trot. "I ought to ask you the same, Mr. Darcy. Do try to keep up."

He appeared at her side immediately, pushing his hat down firmly. The groom had already fallen behind.

It was a race, then. Elizabeth's body tingled in anticipation.

She nudged Tempest into a canter, and the longer legs of Mr. Darcy's thoroughbred easily matched them.

Tempest did not like that. She wanted to be out front. "All in good time, my friend," Elizabeth whispered. Truth be told, she was struggling to allow sufficient time for the horses' muscles to warm up. She wanted to run, but she did not want to provoke an injury.

When the flower-lined path opened up to fallow fields, Elizabeth leaned forward on her hip, tightened her grip on the reins, and clucked her tongue. It was time!

Tempest leaped forward, and Elizabeth lost sight of Mr. Darcy. Excitement surged through her veins. Crisp air doused her face and pushed against the pins holding her bonnet.

They flew over the field. The soft green grass blurred into a solid mass at Tempest's feet, the rapid staccato of her hooves beating in rhythm with Elizabeth's heart.

Out of the corner of her eye, Elizabeth saw a blob of gray and green. Mr. Darcy. She had not needed to slow down for him to catch up with her. Her limbs tingled; her concentration on the route to the path she sought intensified. *Let us see if Mr. Darcy can keep up now!*

One in thought with her mistress, Tempest stretched her legs, lengthened her neck, and kept their lead.

Elizabeth heard an inciting shout to the side, and Mr. Darcy's gray momentarily took the lead until Tempest gained on them once more. Elizabeth was not certain who was more competitive — herself and Tempest or Mr. Darcy and his thoroughbred.

Laughter echoed over clomping hooves and gasping breaths, and Elizabeth delighted when she realized it was her own. It felt divine to laugh.

Faster, faster she went, neck and neck with Mr. Darcy. He was a worthy opponent. He did not show her any advantage, and she reveled in the challenge. It would not last for long. She was determined to best him.

They were near the path now, and its rise and bend offered the perfect moment to make her move. If she could get in front of Mr. Darcy, there was no hope of him passing her until the path widened at the bottom. "Come on Tempest!" she shouted.

The spirited mare surged forward. She knew the path well, but evidently, so did Mr. Darcy. He made a move for the lead before the path narrowed.

Bunching her mouth, Elizabeth looked for another path with which he was not so familiar — one not so clearly tamped into the ground, one which provided an obstacle other than speed.

Rallying her counterattack, Elizabeth turned toward a copse of trees farther up the rise. She would see how well Mr. Darcy did with the fallen tree trunk crossing the grown-over path. His horse ran well, but could he jump?

Darting across the field toward the grove, Elizabeth directed Tempest toward the rotten timber. She cleared the obstruction with ease, sailing over it and lifting Elizabeth in her saddle.

At her side mid-air was Mr. Darcy and his gray. She could not shake him.

Elizabeth braced herself for the landing, preparing to call a truce before they exhausted their mounts.

Crack!

She winced, her ears ringing and her shoulders unable to cover them no matter how high she raised them and tucked her head.

Tempest's front hooves hit the ground, sending painful stabbing needles through Elizabeth's rigid limbs. She grabbed Tempest's mane, her grip around the reins so tight it hurt to loosen her fingers enough to gain hold on the coarse hair. She had kept her seat. Tempest had not panicked.

Elizabeth looked about. Burned gunpowder laced the air. The rifle crack echoed in her ears still.

She yelped when Mr. Darcy suddenly appeared at her other side, standing on the ground. He wrapped his hands around her waist and pulled her off her horse.

"Down! Get down!" he hissed, pushing her to huddle by the fallen tree on the ground and grabbing Tempest's reins. He held the uneasy horses as far away from them as his arm allowed while crouching in front of Elizabeth where the tree did not cover them.

Elizabeth's stomach lurched, her heart thrumming in her aching ears. Until that moment, until Mr. Darcy pulled her down and protected her with his own body, she had dismissed the shot as that of a hunter.

But it was not hunting season. And nobody in his right mind would shoot so near two riders in a field. This was horribly wrong.

She looked at Mr. Darcy for an explanation. His

jaw was set, but he mumbled through his teeth while his eyes searched. "Nobody there. No clear shot from there either," he said as calmly as if he were reading from a list. Mindlessly, he ran his hand through his hair, patting his head, as he muttered, "My hat," and began searching around them.

Elizabeth plucked it from a nearby hedge, prompting another "Get down!" but this time accented with a "Blast it all!"

Mr. Darcy snatched the hat away from her but not before she saw the hole. It was impossible to miss, being as wide as her finger.

Her breath caught as the pieces fell into place. "Your hat was shot! Someone shot at you! You could have been killed!" she gasped.

Mr. Darcy inspected his beaver hat, turning it around in his hands and tracing the holes with his fingers. "The lead came in this way and took its exit through here, which means…" He met her eyes. His skin was pale.

Elizabeth pressed her hand against her throat, trying to calm her racing pulse and roiling stomach. She thought she knew what Mr. Darcy had been about to say, and if he would not voice it, she would. "Which means I am fortunate it was only your hat that suffered a tragedy today, and not me."

His eyes darkened. "It could have been you," he whispered. "Blast it all, it could have been you."

Elizabeth shook her head. She was perfectly fine, only a bit shaken. What she did not comprehend was Mr. Darcy's reaction. He was the one who had been so nearly shot! Instead of yielding to panic, as most people in their situation would, he had immediately assessed the circumstances, taking shelter in the safest position available and shielding her with his own body when the shot had clearly been meant for him.

He was the one in danger, and instead of normal fear or shock, she sensed anger. It emanated from him, tempering her alarm and giving way to an intense desire to understand why someone would shoot at Mr. Darcy. Could it be that her fanciful instincts had been right, and the man crouching in front of her, protecting her, was, indeed, a spy? She could hardly believe it. Spies did not come to Meryton.

"Who *are* you?" she whispered.

He looked away, his eyes once again scanning their surroundings. "We cannot stay here." His face was devoid of expression, his voice distant.

Elizabeth tried to look about, but the width of his back blocked most of her view. "Is it safe to leave?"

"It is safer to move than to remain in one place.

We have the high ground, but there is little protection in these fields. Whoever fired that shot is either a poor marksman, or they only meant to give me a warning."

"A warning? For what? How do you know this?" she asked.

The muscles at his jaw clenched. "I would rather not wait around until the shooter becomes more serious. Let us go."

They raced back to Netherfield Park, but Elizabeth took little pleasure in it.

Who was Mr. Darcy, and what trouble was he in?

CHAPTER 14

*D*arcy dismounted as his gelding skidded to a halt. Several servants stood in front of the stables, gaping and staring. Given the frantic pace with which he and Miss Elizabeth had approached the house, Darcy hardly blamed them.

Tossing the reins to the stable boy, he instructed, "See that the horses are cooled down properly. Oakley will help you as soon as he returns." He had sent his groom to find where the shot had been fired. If there were any clues left behind, Oakley would see them.

Darcy stepped around Miss Elizabeth's horse. He could not look at her. Of all the people he could have endangered, it had been she. Most females would have fainted. Not Miss Elizabeth. Her insatiable curiosity demanded answers, and blast it all if he did not want to give them to her.

She deserved an explanation after what she had experienced. And yet, he must deny her. His was a secret too dangerous to tell, nor was it his alone to guard. He had sworn he would not reveal his role to anyone — not under capture, torture, or threat of death. Not even his sister knew. Had Darcy realized how long the war would last, he might not have agreed to join Richard so readily. He had no way of knowing how his secrecy would impact his life … and that of others.

Darcy shook his head. Wishing things were different helped nothing. He had chosen his path, and he must live with the consequences of his choice.

He held his hands up, a silent gesture of assistance.

Miss Elizabeth kicked her foot out of the stirrup and leaned forward to balance herself against his shoulders. Sweet jasmine enveloped him, making his head spin. The rich fragrance had always reminded Darcy of tropical climates, and with Miss Elizabeth's keen desire to see the world, he was not surprised she preferred the exotic scent of places she had never been nor was likely to ever visit.

He looked up at last, and though her eyes

reflected concern, she smiled at him. His heart clenched. So long as there was a war and she remained under her father's protection, she would never have her heart's desire. Darcy, on the other hand, only had to complete this last mission, and he could go where he pleased. He could return home.

It was not just.

Placing his hands around her waist, he carefully set her down. He noticed how large his hands were around her middle, how the soft velvet of her blue riding habit felt against his fingers. She was light, and soft, and delicate in his arms, and his heart yearned to protect her while his stomach felt sick all over again at the possibility that she might have come to harm because of him.

How could he keep her safe when it was his very presence which put her in danger?

"Mr. Darcy, you are in trouble. Please, let me help you," she said.

A cold sweat sent a tremble through him. His heart would convince him to protect her. Dread coursed through his veins. He had gone so far as to think, even briefly, that he could give her what she most wanted. Blast it, the journey to Pemberley would offer more opportunity to travel than she had experienced in her lifetime. But he was not free.

He could not trust himself. It was imperative he

depart immediately upon a thorough search of the grounds and surrounding area. He would go to London. He would follow the tidbit of information Miss Elizabeth had given him about the new trainer at Lucas Lodge stables. Mr. Robson. If there was a trail of money, it would most assuredly lead him to London.

"Mr. Darcy?" Miss Elizabeth repeated, her arms crossed over her chest.

He jerked away from her, jumping backward and removing his hands from her waist. He had held her too closely for too long. Her annoyance was justified. "Miss Elizabeth, I am sorry. I apologize—"

"I do not require an apology, Mr. Darcy, when it is answers I seek. You are in trouble, and I wish to help you, but I need to understand before I can be of any use."

He sighed in relief. He had not offended her, but he could not accept her offer. Not from her. Not ever. He cared for her too much. How had that happened?

She awaited a reply. Her eyes twinkled, bright with exercise. Her lips, which she chewed and worried, were as red as cherries. Her hair curled wildly around her shoulders. He would have to find her bonnet before he left. He did not want her roaming the fields alone. Not with a shooter on the loose.

Darcy groaned. Now was not the time to muse. Now was the time to act. Once he put himself to work, his thoughts would clear. He would go to London, and after a couple of days, Miss Elizabeth's hold on him would loosen. After a while, the inquisitive sparkle in her eyes and her nibble-reddened lips would dim from his mind until one day, he would not think of her at all — a prospect which left him empty and numb. It was necessary. As was her prompt departure from Netherfield. "You must leave this place as soon as you can."

Miss Elizabeth tightened her arms around her, her hands balled into fists. She did not like his reply, but it could not be helped.

When she started biting her lips again, Darcy was reminded of the urgency with which he must distance himself from the scheming lady. He would take Wilson and Oakley with him, leaving the footman and gardener to ensure that no threat remained after he departed for London. Looking behind Miss Elizabeth, Darcy addressed Bingley's groom. "Ready the chestnut stallion and two others."

"Your groom! The one who rode with us. Where is he?" Miss Elizabeth's eyes shone eagerly. Her wish to be of assistance, her resolve to involve herself despite his constant discouragement, confirmed to Darcy that leaving was the best course.

"He went to find the shooter. I expect him back shortly." Darcy offered nothing more. Taking Elizabeth by the elbow, he spirited her to the house, his eyes scouring their surroundings. Once they reached the landing, he grasped her hands — a precarious gesture given his current state but one he considered necessary in conveying the gravity of what he was about to suggest. "Is Miss Bennet well enough to return to Longbourn today? I wish to see you safely to your family."

"She was too weak to sit up this morning."

He gritted his teeth. "It cannot be helped. I will leave Wilson here to assist you safely to your family when she recovers." There was no one he trusted more. Wilson would protect Miss Elizabeth with his life, and he could be trusted to give a complete and accurate report to Darcy when he joined him in London. Very little escaped Wilson's notice. If there was any danger to the Bennets, he would sense it.

Miss Elizabeth's eyes widened. "You really do plan to leave, then. Where are you going?"

Would she miss him? Darcy shook his head and let go of her hands, shoving the thought away. So long as he was a danger to her, he had no right to encourage her affection.

"I must go to London. Promise you will speak of this to no one."

"I give you my word."

"And I trust you will keep it." He swallowed hard, then with a bow, he said, "Goodbye, Miss Elizabeth."

He turned to the stairs before she could ask any further questions. Before he could change his mind and stay. This was the right thing to do. He had to complete this mission. Her safety must come first. Miss Elizabeth would be safer at Longbourn.

Bursting through his door to see Wilson polishing his Hessians, Darcy said, "We need to ride." He tossed his hat to the valet by way of explanation.

Wilson blew a low whistle. "Warning or missed shot?"

"That is what I mean to find out. Oakley is already surveying the area, but we must make inquiries in Meryton. Perhaps a suspicious stranger has appeared in the village or someone saw a man riding through after the shot was fired. I need answers, and I need them now."

"You must be close to discovering the truth for someone to aim at you, sir. People get desperate and act rashly when their secrets are soon to be found out." Wilson rose, hobbling over to Darcy's wardrobe and pulling out a clean coat. "Let me help you change first, sir. We do not need to arouse suspicions amongst the villagers."

Darcy looked down. The knees of his breeches were damp and stained. His coat had a tear in the sleeve. Shrugging out of his coat while Wilson pulled the sleeves, he said, "We will ride over the property until we join Oakley. Depending on what he has found, we will continue to Meryton. Then," Darcy groaned. He had been about to say Wilson would remain behind to see the Bennet sisters home while he and Oakley continued to London. But he had overlooked one important detail. Miss Elizabeth had told him of Lucas Lodge's new trainer, and Darcy knew Richard would ask — and rightly so — what else he had found out from the stables. He could not continue to London until he had at least made a pretense of searching for other clues at the stables. And he could not very well do that in the light of day.

Frustrated he had been so intent on leaving Netherfield he had nearly neglected to inspect a key piece of evidence, Darcy continued grimly, "We will wait until nightfall to see what we can uncover at Lucas Lodge stables. They have a new trainer, none less than Robert Robson. I want to confirm his recent hire and see if there is anything else we might be able to learn."

Wilson held up another coat. "Do you have someone on the inside?"

Darcy remembered the talkative stable boy. "No, but did you know that one of Bingley's stable boys came from Lucas Lodge? I mean to have a word with Bingley to see about sending him back for a time."

Wilson brushed the lapels. "That may not be necessary. I learned from the groom — Mercer — that a mare is soon to drop a foal. If the lad was at all attached to the mare or if he is a curious sort, it would be easy to arrange. Mercer will be happy for the extra hands to fetch linens and clean water. He would not send the boy away."

"Excellent. I have no doubt the lad will be a valuable source of information."

"I will see to it immediately, sir."

"Good. Gain the boy's confidence, then you and I will go to Lucas Lodge stables tonight. He will not be so suspicious of your presence then, and you can ask what he knows while I see what else I can find inside. At daybreak on the morrow, Oakley and I will depart for London. I have a charge of the utmost importance to entrust in your care, Wilson."

Wilson stopped brushing to give Darcy his full attention.

Taking a deep breath, Darcy continued, "Miss Elizabeth was with me when I was shot at, and while

I have no other reason to believe her in imminent danger, I do not wish to take any chances. Will you keep a watch over her? And when Miss Bennet is well enough to return to Longbourn, will you see them safely returned to their family?"

Wilson stood taller. "I will not let you down, sir. I will keep watch until there is no more danger."

"Thank you, Wilson. Once she is returned to Longbourn, her father will keep her there. You can then join me in London ... unless you sense your continued presence is required here. I trust your discretion."

After Wilson made him presentable, Darcy departed. He looked in the direction of Miss Bennet's sickroom, but he saw no sign of Miss Elizabeth. His treacherous heart had hoped he might.

CHAPTER 15

*E*lizabeth did not set foot outside the rest of the day. She kept Jane company, conversing about the many kindnesses of Mr. Bingley and reading aloud.

However, had Jane asked Elizabeth what she was reading, she could not have told her. Words could not hold Elizabeth's interest when her thoughts were full of Mr. Darcy and the hole in his hat.

Why would he not let her help him? Why the secrecy?

Why did she care?

A knock at the door distracted Elizabeth from drawing any unsettling conclusions. It was not Emily. She would have entered after her usual five taps.

Could it be Mr. Darcy had come to explain the

strange events of the morning? Elizabeth rose to answer, holding her breath in expectation.

Dark curls and a brooding brow did not greet her. She tried not to show her disappointment at the sight of ginger hair and a bright waistcoat instead.

Mr. Bingley swayed weakly in front of the door, holding on to the casing to balance himself. He was as ghastly pale as Jane had been the day before. His grooved forehead and knitted brows gave him the doleful appearance of a sad puppy.

He must have used all of his energy dressing to check on Jane and had little left to hold himself upright. "Is Miss Bennet improved?" he asked between labored breaths.

Elizabeth burst with sympathy. Opening the door wider and stepping aside to allow him a glimpse inside, Elizabeth said, "She is, thank you, Mr. Bingley."

"Good. I am relieved to know it." His tender gaze fixed on Jane, and had he been any stronger, Elizabeth was certain he would have exchanged a few pleasantries with her sister. But Mr. Bingley had not recovered enough. He leaned against the doorway, his strength visibly spent.

Elizabeth reached forward at the same time Mr. Bingley's valet did. She had not noticed the man standing on Mr. Bingley's other side, and she appreciated his presence and attention to his master.

"Mr. Bingley, please rest. Here is a chair," she offered.

"No, no. I must use the little stamina I have left to return to my room. I just … I just needed to know she is better. To be near. That is all." Mr. Bingley supported himself against his valet, and slowly, they retreated down the hall.

What a lovely man.

While Elizabeth was overjoyed that such a fine gentleman expended himself on behalf of her sister, a gentle ping of jealousy made her wonder if she would ever inspire the same selfless interest in a man. A man such as Mr. Darcy.

She turned to Jane. Her cheeks were rosy pink; her eyes, a brilliant blue.

Elizabeth smiled. "He just *had* to see you."

Jane's blush deepened. She praised Mr. Bingley's fine qualities and amiable character until, once again, she succumbed to a tranquil slumber. Her dreams would be pleasant, and Elizabeth had no doubt she would wake greatly improved. One day more, or perhaps two, and Jane would be well enough to return to Longbourn where their mother would refuse to receive them from Netherfield Park before the completion of a week.

Elizabeth might have been tempted to extend their stay for the sake of Mr. Bingley and Jane's blooming romance, but it would be foolhardy to ignore Mr. Darcy's warning.

She chuckled. The gentleman would simply have to do without his valet until Tuesday. The idea of Mr. Darcy struggling with his cravat gave her pleasure. It satisfied her sense of justice knowing he would experience a level of harmless discomfort when he refused to confide in her even after the morning's ride had irrevocably involved her in whatever scheme had brought Mr. Darcy into her life.

How could she protect herself if she remained in ignorance? Elizabeth refused to allow a gentleman she had known for less than a full week, no matter how honorable she hoped he was, to be her sole source of protection when her dignity demanded self-sufficiency.

She was not weak, nor were her sensibilities too delicate. She proudly possessed a curious mind capable of more comprehension than society granted … or approved of. They patronized informed ladies, discounting their opinions and demeaning them for having an original thought.

While discouragement and condescension daunted some, it had never worked on Elizabeth.

Aided by her father's library and the skillful use of leading questions posed to the right people at the right time, she had become adept at finding answers and solutions on her own.

Why, then, should she not do the same with Mr. Darcy? Then, she would know once and for all if he was as trustworthy as her instincts were inclined to believe him. If Mr. Darcy's life was in danger, it was Elizabeth's moral responsibility to help him. If she was wrong, then she must strive to improve her character assessments lest she be misled again.

Whichever the answer, Elizabeth would find out that night. Mr. Darcy had spent the afternoon out — inquiring around Meryton as he had said, Elizabeth supposed. But he had returned later in the afternoon. He had returned her bonnet. Actually, Wilson had returned it, but she had sat reading to Jane by the window, and she had seen Mr. Darcy by the stables, holding her bonnet by its ribbons. She had hoped he would bring it to her.

Between Mr. Darcy's avoidance of her and his delay in departing for London, she suspected he had a matter to attend to before he could leave. Elizabeth determined to find out. She had little else to do.

Whatever the difficulty Mr. Darcy found himself in, it would not be a simple matter. If pride prevented him from allowing another to help him, well, then, he would simply have to overcome his fault.

With the assistance of Emily, the chambermaid, and Netherfield's many windows, Elizabeth kept watch, her dark riding coat and gloves draped over a chair beside the door. She was ready. If Mr. Darcy made a move, she would follow him.

She received her dinner in her room, not wishing to assault Jane's nostrils with smells that made her groan nor divert her own attention away from her vigil between the window and the door. "Is Mr. Darcy dining in his room as well?" Elizabeth asked the maid.

"He is, Miss. I will deliver his tray next." Bobbing a curtsy, the girl left to attend to her duties.

Elizabeth waited until the maid left, then peeked down the hall in the direction of Mr. Darcy's bedchamber. The maid knocked on his door, a footman holding a platter with a big silver lid behind her. Elizabeth strained her ears to hear Mr. Darcy's voice, but his room was too far down the hall.

Easing her door closed quietly (for Mr. Darcy would surely alter his plans if he knew she meant to follow him, and so it befell her to give him no indication of her intention), Elizabeth leaned against the barrier with her ear pressed against the smooth oak. Mr. Darcy had not escaped her, nor would she allow him to when every creak and thud set her nerves on edge.

She was too agitated to eat much, but she did her best. She would need the nourishment before the night was done. She hoped. Surely, Mr. Darcy meant to do something. She would if she were in his place.

Doubts began to chip away at Elizabeth's certainty, so much so, she thought she imagined the sound of a foot dragging over carpet. Tiptoeing to the door, Elizabeth tried to listen over the thrumming of her pulse. She dared not open the door until she could do so without being seen.

Step. Drag. Step. Drag. Mr. Darcy's valet, Wilson. Try as she might, she could not hear Mr. Darcy's steps, but then again, she had not really expected to hear them as it would defeat his purpose of sneaking out … and, once again, she was certain that was precisely what he meant to do.

Which gave her all the more reason to follow him.

Biding her time, Elizabeth counted. How many seconds would it take Mr. Darcy and Wilson to get down the stairs and out of the door? How long should she count? Mr. Darcy walked with a long, easy stride, but Wilson had a decided limp — not a usual choice for a gentleman's valet. She wondered how Mr. Darcy came to employ him.

Wilson's rigid posture suggested he had once been in the military. If that were the case, a man discharged from his duties due to an injury was fortunate to find steady employment in the respected position of a gentleman's valet. Had Mr. Darcy taken him on as a favor to another? Or was he really so kind?

How many seconds had gone by? Elizabeth gasped. Drat! She had lost count.

Frustrated, she reached for the door. It jumped back at her, smacking her against the forehead and sending Elizabeth reeling backward.

"Miss, he is gone! You had better hurry!" Emily whispered urgently, her eyes doubling in size when she saw Elizabeth rubbing her head. "Oh, Miss, that was you I ran the door against? I am so sorry." She rushed to Elizabeth's side, poking the tender bump.

Slapping her hand down, Elizabeth said, "Stop that! It hurts. Please hold me steady while I put on my coat. I am wobbly."

"Oh, Miss, I am sorry. Here, I am ready. I will go with you. I would never forgive myself if anything untoward happened to you after I had caused your injury. Is your vision blurred? Can you see well enough? I will be your eyes in the dark—"

"Hush, Emily. It is only a trifling bump. Let us go before they slip away from us. Only, promise you will be quiet." Elizabeth grabbed Emily's hand, tugging her as they sprinted down the stairs. Turning the corner and staying in the shadows, Elizabeth pulled Emily toward the kitchen at the back of the house. There was less of a chance of being seen escaping through the kitchen door leading outside than through the front door where any number of servants might observe them.

The kitchen also had the advantage of being closer to the stables. Not that Elizabeth could sneak Tempest out now that she had Emily with her. They would simply have to do their best to keep up on foot. If Mr. Darcy went too far, they would have no choice but to return to Netherfield. However, if he only went so far as Meryton, then they could follow him without being seen. The shops would be closed, and most families would be gathered around the fire in their parlors.

The cold night air stirred the loose ringlets around Elizabeth's face and sent a shiver through her to her fingertips. She would be plenty warm soon enough, she thought with growing delight as she wondered what Miss Bingley would think of this sort of exercise. No doubt, she would not approve … which made Elizabeth all the more excited to begin the chase.

"Come!" she whispered, catching a glimpse of

Mr. Darcy and Wilson's retreating backs in the darkness. With an unknown shooter on the loose, they would stay as close as they could to the gentlemen. "Keep your head low," she whispered to Emily, just in case. Standing out in the open as they now were, Elizabeth suffered another onslaught of doubts. How wise was it to tramp about in the dark when she had so nearly been shot earlier? Her hands trembled, and her breath quickened at the memory.

She looked at Mr. Darcy. He was not afraid, and atop a horse, he offered a much easier target. Surely, he would not take such a risk if he believed his life still endangered. Perhaps he had already found the shooter and chased him off?

Strange, the men did not ride to the main road but chose to cut over the field that led to Lucas Lodge. If that was their destination, Elizabeth and Emily would have no trouble following them. But why would Mr. Darcy go there?

Elizabeth recalled his questions about the Lucases at the assembly. And while her fancy had temporarily led her to believe him a spy, now that she had her senses about her, she could not fathom how that would lead him to Sir William. Sir William did not have the duplicitous temperament necessary to involve himself in a plot which would draw the notice of a British agent. Nor, Elizabeth had to admit, did he possess the intelligence to design a plan worth the government's attention.

Neither could she imagine how anyone else in the family could have involved themselves in a dishonest or traitorous design. John Lucas lacked the initiative to do anything at all, much less engage himself in a scheme in which a great deal would be demanded of him. George Lucas was too busy with his family and his horses. Also, he lacked malice. While he complained about taxes (as many did), he would never risk losing the very estate he sought to help his father protect.

No, Mr. Darcy's business at Lucas Lodge had to stem from another source. The horses? The new trainer?

The new trainer! That must be it. Had she not noticed George's mixture of pride and concern that morning when he had told her of the racehorse trainer? Perhaps Mr. Darcy had lost a great deal of money at a race. Perhaps he was friends with Mr. Robson. Or enemies. The hole in Mr. Darcy's hat suggested an enemy, but Elizabeth did not know enough about Mr. Robson to decide if he had put it there.

"They are slowing down, Miss," gasped Emily between breaths.

Mr. Darcy and Wilson were barely visible ahead of them.

"Please, may we slow down, too?" she added.

"Let us get a bit closer. Stay down," Elizabeth replied, slowing her pace when it became apparent Emily would complain more unless she did. They were too close to risk exposing themselves with the moonlight or her maid's grievances.

The men had dismounted their horses, leaving them tied up at a thicket a short distance from the stables.

Mr. Darcy said something to Wilson, but Elizabeth was not close enough to hear. She watched the valet limp away from Mr. Darcy, passing the outdoor paddock and skirting around the stables in the shadows.

Whatever their business was, they did not wish to be seen. Truth be told, neither did she.

As for Mr. Darcy, he peeked into the open door of the building, then prowled past the lit aperture to look through a window. Had she not been watching him from the start, she would not have noticed him dressed as he was in black from top to bottom. Had she not known better, she would have thought him a spy. But that was preposterous. There had to be a reasonable explanation.

"Stay with the horses," she instructed Emily.

Creeping forward with her eyes fixed on Mr. Darcy, she heard someone approaching before she saw who it was. She spun around, looking for a hiding place and seeing only fence posts.

It was George. The lantern he carried illuminated the scowl he wore as he juggled a stack of linens in his arms.

Mr. Darcy leaped forward, reaching for the pile before they fell to the ground. "Good evening, Mr. Lucas," he said.

Elizabeth released her breath, relieved Mr. Darcy had not kept himself concealed from George. She would have doubted his intentions had he tried. (And this from a lady ducking behind the paddock's fence post.)

"Mr. Darcy, what brings you here at this time of night? I hope all is well at Netherfield Park?" George looked around.

Before Mr. Darcy could reply, a large figure loomed in the entrance of the stables — a man Elizabeth had never seen before. It had to be Robert Robson. He held Mr. Bingley's stable boy by the scruff of the neck. "This boy does not belong here. What are you about, Sir? I will not allow for any of your neighbor's spies to creep around while I am here." He shoved the boy forward so that he landed in a heap at Mr. Darcy's feet.

Elizabeth's dislike of the trainer was immediate.

Mr. Darcy helped the stable boy to his feet, dusting him gently and placing one hand protectively on the boy's shoulder.

George said, "He is harmless, Robson. He is Joe's little brother, Jim. He only came to help with the foaling."

The boy straightened his coat and rubbed his ear gingerly, wisely keeping behind Mr. Darcy. "Blimey, you has a rough grip, sir."

"See I am never put upon to use it against you again, lad."

"I only wanted to see the new foal. That's all. I didn't mean no harm."

Mr. Robson stepped toward the boy, which promptly sent Jim scurrying away into the darkness.

"Curiosity is not a crime," Mr. Darcy commented, stepping in the trainer's path and making it clear that Mr. Robson would have to get past him first if he wished to pursue the boy.

Elizabeth huffed her agreement, then promptly covered her mouth with her hand lest she reveal her presence and add to the famous trainer's consternation.

Mr. Robson turned his ire on Mr. Darcy. "And who is this, then, Mr. Lucas? I told you before I signed on to work with your father, that I will not have strangers — especially gentlemen — snooping about while I am trying to work. They steal my methods for their own gain and cause more trouble than they are worth. We had an agreement."

What a horrible, disagreeable man. First, he threatened and scared Jim. And now, he cast doubt over George's word and Mr. Darcy's honor. As gruff and unpleasant as Mr. Robson was, Elizabeth could easily imagine him firing at Mr. Darcy. That explained Mr. Darcy's sneaking of earlier. He had wished to speak to George without the wary trainer present. It made perfect sense. It also meant Mr. Robson was a threat.

How could Mr. Darcy extricate himself without raising further suspicion from the trainer, endangering both himself and George?

Elizabeth had an idea. With one flick of the loose clasp, she flung her brooch toward the stable door where she had spoken with George that same morning.

Bolstering her courage, she straightened her shoulders and charged out from behind the post. "Mr. Darcy, I told you it was by the main entrance, not along the side of the building." She propped her fists on her hips and huffed for good measure.

All three men gawked open-mouthed at her.

Taking advantage of their shock, she continued,

"Must I again explain how precious my brooch is to me?" Rolling her eyes, she turned to George, explaining as quickly as she could form the words, "It went missing today, and I have searched all over Netherfield. The only other place I might have lost it was here, and seeing how I would have no peace until it was restored to me, Mr. Darcy was kind enough to offer to fetch it."

"At this hour?" George asked, looking between her and Mr. Darcy.

Elizabeth crossed her arms over her chest. "Would you have me wait and risk never finding it again? I could not sleep knowing my beloved token from my dearest uncle might be trampled by a horse."

"But it is dark. How did you plan to find it?"

She shrugged. "Your lantern will do nicely."

Mr. Darcy crossed his arms and glared at her.

As if he had been doing any better! At least, she had given Mr. Robson a valid reason for them being there — far more than Mr. Darcy had done.

Arching her neck away from him to address George, she said, "You told me you had a mare about to foal. I knew you or Mercer would be awake tending to her. Mr. Darcy was merely looking for you so that he might request the use of a lantern if the moonlight did not suffice. I do not see why you are in such an upheaval. You know how dear my brooch is to me."

"I know how impatient you are when an idea takes root in your head," George countered.

She was in no position to defend herself on that point, so she merely said, "Then, you had better let us look for my brooch so we can be on our way. My maid is waiting by the horses. I do not want to make her wait long."

Lantern light cast altering shadows over Mr. Darcy's face. Was he gnashing his teeth or trying not to grin?

"I will look where you indicated," he said, turning and inspecting the ground by the door with George following him with the lantern.

Mr. Robson grabbed the linens and grumbled all the way inside the stables. Good riddance. Elizabeth was content he seemed to accept her excuse for their presence.

It was not difficult to find the brooch. The light glistened on the aventurine.

Picking it up, Mr. Darcy said, "Here it is. Let us not disturb Mr. Lucas and Mr. Robson any more."

Elizabeth cheered. "Oh, wonderful! It was here all along! I knew it! You cannot imagine how relieved I am."

She did not pause long enough to take the brooch

Mr. Darcy held out to her. Her aim was to leave before the murderous Mr. Robson made another appearance. With a quick curtsy and "Good evening," to George, she spun on her foot and took off across the yard to Emily and the horses.

The hairs on the back of her neck prickled at Mr. Darcy's nearness, but she kept walking.

"That was a very foolish thing you did," he scolded.

Her irritation flamed. "No less foolish than you prowling around the stables at night." She kept going. Emily was in view, as was Wilson.

Mr. Darcy took her hand, spinning her around to face him. For a moment, he looked as if he would grab her by the shoulders and shake her, but instead, he released her hand and crossed his arms over his chest. "It could have been dangerous."

"More so than our ride this morning? Mr. Darcy, I just extracted you from a compromising situation. I think the trainer was the man who tried to shoot you. The least you can do is say thank you."

"Thank you," he seethed through his clenched jaw. His arms tightened around him.

Gratitude was gratitude, even if it sounded painful to give. Elizabeth ran with it. "I am happy to help, and as you have witnessed for yourself, I can be of greater assistance if you would only let me. I know the people around here much better than you do, and I have their confidence. A couple of questions to the right person, at the proper time, and whatever you are involved in can be cleared. Besides, if Mr. Robson is a criminal, I do not want him near my friends."

"I do not wish for your help."

Stupid pride. Elizabeth had little patience for it. "Why? Because I am a young lady? Do you believe me incapable?" She mirrored his rigid posture.

"That is not it at all."

"What is it, then? Pride?"

"No!"

Elizabeth stepped closer to him, dropping her voice. "Then pray enlighten me, Mr. Darcy, for I refuse to remain under your protection when I am capable of defending myself. I am not the sort to back down when I see someone in danger."

She saw his nostrils flare and felt the hard stare in his eyes. Undaunted, Elizabeth returned Mr. Darcy's glare.

He held his ground. Leaning forward, he enunciated, "You refuse? Are you so obstinate and headstrong you would endanger your life—"

"So, I am in danger, then? Thank you for clarifying the matter, Mr. Darcy. Now, you see, you owe me an explanation. You cannot deny me."

Closing the distance so that he loomed in her view, Mr. Darcy seethed, "Then, you will have to accustom yourself to feeling disappointment, Miss Elizabeth, for there is no circumstance which could convince me to confide in you."

He was so near, Elizabeth felt his warmth. It became increasingly difficult for her to focus on her anger when he smelled so good.

"None at all?" she whispered, trying to catch her breath.

His eyes held her mesmerized. So dark and deep and tender. So close.

She lifted her chin, her eyelids drooping of their own accord as his breath brushed like a feather over her lips.

CHAPTER 16

Moonlight gleamed against Miss Elizabeth's creamy skin, adding a lustrous sheen to her chestnut locks and a dangerous glint to her cocoa brown eyes before her thick lashes fell like tasseled curtains over them.

Her lips parted — plump and red.

Darcy stared at them, caught between his honor and an overwhelming desire to gather her in his arms and press his lips against hers.

He had sworn an oath to protect, an avowal which prohibited him from allowing anyone to get so close as Elizabeth was to him at that moment.

How had he allowed it? How had she won his respect, laying inroads into his heart where they could not lead anywhere but to their mutual suffering? How could he keep his word and keep her safe? It was impossible.

He pulled away, forcing himself step-by-step to continue onward to the horses. Wilson nodded at him. Darcy rubbed his chest. He had done the right thing, small consolation though it was. Botheration, that sounded bitter.

Elizabeth deserved better — a secure place in the heart of a man who could make her happiness his purpose; honest conversation without the taint of lies and secrets; the happy prospect of a long life free from strife and villainous traitors. Darcy could give her none of that.

He shoved his hand through his hair and repositioned his hat. What was wrong with him? He was not one to pine when he must keep his senses sharp. The shooter could make another attempt, and he now had two extra females to return safely to Netherfield. He had seen firsthand where that led when too many of his acquaintances at the agency allowed a woman to cloud their vision and jeopardize their missions. Too many times, the lady ended up being used as a lure. The fortunate ones survived. Most did not.

Elizabeth was too full of vivacity to suffer such an early end. Darcy could not do that to her.

If he was really a gentleman, he would end this

now. He would keep her safe. He hated lying. He especially hated lying to Elizabeth. But he had no other choice. The mission must always come first. He would complete his assignment, then he would return to Pemberley. All would be better at Pemberley. He would know what to do once he was home.

The maid and Wilson fell in behind Darcy, his valet leading the horses and his free hand hovering near the pistol he kept at his side. He would protect the maid. Which left Darcy with Elizabeth.

Darcy's skin tingled, and he knew she had caught up with him before he saw her beside him. He squinted his eyes in the dark, searching for movement or out-of-place shadows. "I must leave for London at first light." Taking a deep breath, he added in a rush, "I doubt I shall return. My business will take some time."

"Oh," she said softly. Was that regret he sensed? Lord help him, he wanted it to be.

Darcy continued before his resolve weakened. "We tracked the shooter back to Meryton." His first untruth of the night. They had not found the shooter. "He was seen leaving on horseback." He stopped there. Not too many details. Just enough information to be convincing.

"Toward London?" she asked.

He nodded.

"Then, why did you not follow him immediately? Why go to Sir William's stables?"

She was quick, but Darcy had an explanation ready. "We learned that his business in Hertfordshire involved Sir William's new trainer."

"I knew it!" Elizabeth exclaimed, the glint in her eyes restoring her usual vigor. She was charming. Enchanting.

Darcy had to look away. He would not see the shooter if he was gawking at Elizabeth.

She continued excitedly, "Mr. Robson's arrival at Lucas Lodge was so unexpected, I suspected there was more to his sudden presence than Sir William's horses. When Mr. Lucas told me of it this morning, he bore a troubled expression which has bothered me since. This explains it! Mr. Robson is not to be trusted—" She came to a sudden stop. "Oh, but you said he had business with the shooter. You did not say he was the shooter himself."

It would be a greater challenge to get Elizabeth to believe his lie than Darcy had imagined. He would have to be more convincing.

Redirecting her line of reasoning away from the identity of the shooter to the harmless trainer, he said, "There is nothing untoward with Mr. Robson. He may not react well to strangers in his stables, but he is not a danger to your friends." The last thing

Darcy wanted was for Elizabeth to continue probing into the matter after he had left. He did not think the trainer himself had anything to do with The Four Horsemen's scheme with Sir William, but he would not risk Elizabeth trying to find that out on her own.

She was silent for a few paces. He prayed they would reach Netherfield and part ways before she had too much time to find the flaws in his makeshift excuse. Such as his connection to the trainer…

"So, the man who tried to kill you was *not* the trainer, but he had business with him," Elizabeth puzzled aloud.

Darcy held his breath, knowing the folly of hoping she would not ask the question he most wished her not to ask when she was intent on getting answers.

"The trainer has nothing to do with you, then?" she asked.

Drat.

"The shooter's business with the trainer was an unfortunate coincidence." Darcy clamped his mouth shut. He did not believe in coincidences. How could he expect Elizabeth to believe him when he didn't believe himself?

Wilson cleared his throat. "Pray excuse me for overhearing your conversation and intervening where I ought not, Mr. Darcy. But Miss Elizabeth is too astute. You must tell her the rest."

Darcy scowled at his valet. Wilson clearly had more confidence in his arts of deception than Darcy did. He abhorred disguise of all sorts.

Elizabeth looked at him expectantly.

Only one explanation presented itself, and Darcy's pride rebelled. He would rather die than cast that shade over his character.

But as the seconds passed, and no other reply came to him under Wilson's encouraging nods and Elizabeth's watchful (and growingly impatient) eye, Darcy had to swallow his deuced pride. Anything to protect her.

The conviction that this unflattering fabrication was for her benefit helped Darcy choke out the words. "You will understand why I do not wish to reveal the whole of it when you see how poorly the truth reflects on me." He took another deep breath, trusting the momentum of his exhale to force the repugnant lie past his lips. "I am deeply in debt to a gentleman I suspect of sabotaging the horse I had bet on. He is an unscrupulous man I knew better than to cross, but my horse was certain to win, and I took the risk. I bet heavily. Too heavily."

He looked askance at Elizabeth. What did she think of him now?

"You did not pay your debt?" she asked.

"I asked for time, allowing the gentleman to believe I needed it to gather the money I owed when in reality, I have been investigating."

"Then, why did you come to Hertfordshire?"

Darcy's muscles were so tense, he thought he might snap. Forcing his voice to relax when his body could not, he said, "I heard from a reliable source that Mr. Robson was to accept Sir William's offer of employment at his stables. You can imagine my disappointment when I arrived before he did."

She arched her neck and peeked up at him. "Is that why you were asking all those questions about the Lucases on the eve of the assembly? Did you think they were involved somehow with this unscrupulous gentleman?"

He nodded, determined to hold his silence as much as he could to allow Elizabeth the opportunity to fill the story in on her own. She was doing a much better job of it than he was.

She chewed on her bottom lip, her eyebrows bunched together. "I gather that Mr. Robson was at the same race, and you intended to ask for his help?" she asked.

"Yes." He wiped his brow. Would she never stop asking questions?

"Then, why did you not ask him if he saw

anything untoward at the race while you had the chance, Mr. Darcy?" She gestured behind her. "He was right there."

Dash it all, was she incapable of accepting anything without proof?

He almost scoffed. Of course, she could not. Nor would he wish her to. Her intelligence had been nurtured and developed by her inquisitive nature, and he would not change her ... no matter how inconvenient it was to him right then.

It was time to change tactics. He had to take control. To attack.

Assuming a stoic expression, he turned to her. "I would have done so had a certain young lady not interrupted and caused an unnecessary scene."

She gasped, but her bravado fizzled as he saw doubt enter her mind.

He struck again while she was unsteady in her understanding. "You saw how cross Mr. Robson was. He would have refused to answer, and I would have guaranteed his unwillingness to cooperate at all had I pressed and worsened his opinion of me."

Elizabeth's downcast posture suggested she believed him, but Darcy felt no victory of triumph. He felt wretched.

They continued across the field. Netherfield was in view. Five more minutes, and he would have to put Elizabeth out of his mind indefinitely. His feet dragged. Only Wilson's constant pace behind him kept Darcy from prolonging the inevitable. The necessary.

Grass turned to gravel as they neared the stables. Wilson turned the horses over to Oakley, and Elizabeth's maid waited by the door to the kitchen.

Darcy waited for the ladies to precede him into the house, but when he saw how woeful Elizabeth looked, he regretted the gentlemanly gesture. He ought to have stormed inside the house like a brute without seeing to their welfare. Then, he would not have seen Elizabeth's insecurity. It was too late. Her dismay was branded on his mind's eye where it would haunt him because he had been the one to put it there.

"Would it not be better to approach Mr. Robson again on the morrow? I promise not to interfere. Surely, he will be more agreeable, and you could find out what you need from him without leaving for London," she said, her eyes searching him.

She wanted him to stay. The realization was a dagger to Darcy's gut.

"Under the circumstances, it is more urgent for me to pursue the henchman. I am still within the time agreed upon to pay my debt, so I am determined to learn why he was sent. Perhaps he will provide what I need to expose the gentleman and put an end to this wretched business."

Elizabeth stepped closer to him, twisting her fingers in front of her, the night breeze rustling her hair and granting Darcy another hint of jasmine. "This is where we part ways, then." She extended her hand.

Darcy lifted her hand in his, her touch gripping him so hard, it knocked the air out of his lungs. With a bow, he brushed his lips over her glove. "Goodbye, Miss Elizabeth," he whispered.

Dropping her hand, he stormed inside the house.

CHAPTER 17

*E*mily made no observations, though she frequently sighed and looked dreamily off into the distance with her hands clutched at her heart.

Elizabeth's life had become one big adventure since she had landed at Mr. Darcy's feet, and she did not know if this was a cruel blow from fate or a gift from the gods. She did not want to believe he had irresponsibly gambled away a fortune. That he would allow the "gentleman" (whoever he was) to believe he lacked the ability to pay his debt went contrary to the pride she had discerned Mr. Darcy to possess. Then again, pride had prevented him from telling her about the loss … which added credulity to his account along with Wilson's knowledge of his debt.

And then, there was the kiss. The almost kiss. Elizabeth was not artful in feminine manipulations, and yet, her body had reacted of its own accord — rising to her toes, tilting her chin, and closing her eyes.

After Mr. Darcy had walked away from her, she had felt foolish. But when he had caressed her hand so gently, melting her limbs and sending delightful shivers through her, she knew she had not imagined how closely he had come to kissing her. She did not believe in coincidences.

If he held her in any regard at all, why had his goodbye sounded so final? Why had he offered no reassurance of returning to Netherfield after sorting his affairs in London? Why did he not stay and ask for Mr. Robson's help?

Elizabeth almost wished he had admitted to being a spy. It might have made more sense — outside of Sir William's involvement. In that, she could more readily accept Mr. Darcy's explanation of his debt and Sir William's trainer's connection to the ill-reputed "gentleman."

She sighed. Mr. Darcy was a study of contrasts. Elizabeth was fascinated. And now, he was going away.

Soft gray light peeked through the edge of the curtain. Throwing off her blanket and wrapping it around her shoulders, Elizabeth ran out to the hall.

Mr. Darcy's bedchamber door was open. The room was empty except for a packed trunk Wilson would no doubt take with him when he joined his master in town.

Mr. Darcy was gone. She was too late.

What a silly goose she was for hoping he would stay, or at least bid her farewell before he departed.

She shook her head. *Foolish, foolish girl.*

Only the day before, Mr. Darcy had narrowly escaped a bullet to the head, and she wanted him to stay at Netherfield Park? Of course, he had to leave! He had a henchman to catch and a reputation to repair. He had no time for a moonstruck maiden when his life was in danger. No wonder he had left so quickly! She would have done the same in his position. She would stop at nothing until she got to the bottom of the affair.

Hope fluttered in Elizabeth's breast. That was it! Mr. Darcy had gone to London in pursuit of the henchman, but she was not useless. She had better ways of gaining information about Mr. Robson. She had Charlotte.

Feeling lighter now that she had a purpose, Elizabeth cheerfully tended to Jane. She was much improved, and it was not difficult for Elizabeth to suggest they depart for Longbourn on the morrow. Mr. Bingley was sad to hear it, but he was overjoyed that Jane was well enough to travel, going so far as to offer the use of his carriage, which Elizabeth accepted readily (knowing how unlikely it was that her mother would send theirs.)

Mr. Bingley, too, had improved. He offered to sit in the garden with Jane, claiming that the fresh morning air was just the thing to restore their strength. Elizabeth did not disagree with him. In her mind, sitting in the warmth of the sun in a blooming garden was just the thing to encourage their blossoming affection.

While Miss Bingley and the Hursts showed signs of improvement, none of them felt strong enough to venture out of doors. *Pity that*, thought Elizabeth sarcastically.

Given her activities, the morning mercifully passed, and Elizabeth left Jane to rest while she walked to Lucas Lodge.

Charlotte was embroidering in the drawing room, the picture of an accomplished lady. Sir William would be proud.

"Good afternoon, Lizzy. I am glad to see you. Is Jane any better?" Charlotte set aside her white work.

"She is. We plan to return to Longbourn on the morrow."

"Before a full week has passed? What will your mother say?" Charlotte asked with an impish grin.

"She would have refused us the carriage had I asked her to send it. Mr. Bingley offered his, and I gladly accepted."

"Very sensible of you." The arch in Charlotte's eyebrow asked what she did not voice.

Elizabeth would not do as her mother often did and pronounce victory in an assumed engagement before an offer was made. She said, "He and Jane conversed for quite a while in the garden, and I suspect both of them are well enough to find their way to the drawing room during the course of the afternoon."

Charlotte smiled. "I am relieved to hear she is offering him some encouragement. If things progress as we hope, they will be happy."

"What of you? It has been ages since we have talked. What with—" Elizabeth bit her tongue. She was about to mention Sir William's prohibition of his stables to her.

"My father means well, Lizzy, though I have to remind myself of his motives often as I face hours of instruction in all manner of accomplishments I have little interest in mastering. Of what use is it to me to speak French in running a household smoothly? And while I am capable enough on the pianoforte, I do not share his ambition in learning to also play the harp." She reached across the settee and squeezed Elizabeth's hand. "I am sorry for your sake, Lizzy. I know how important our morning rides were to you. I miss them, too. Now that I am trapped indoors, I can better understand your restlessness, although I am much better suited to it than you will ever be."

Elizabeth squeezed her hand in turn. "Thank you, Charlotte. I hold no grudge against your father. He is only trying his best to see you well settled, as any good father does."

"Remember what you just said when it is your time." With another squeeze, Charlotte released her hold. Sitting back with a sigh, she added, "Things are changing at Lucas Lodge."

Elizabeth practically felt her ears perk up. If the conversation turned to Mr. Robson, now was the perfect time. Trying not to sound more excited than she ought to be, Elizabeth casually asked, "How so?"

"Father and George have acquired a new horse. I expected it, as they could not hire a famous horse trainer without a thoroughbred worthy of his attention, but it still came as a shock. They leave for London on the morrow. I am glad they are taking

John with them. He has been particularly restless, not being accustomed to our quiet country life."

A new horse! Now, she was getting somewhere. Where had they acquired enough money to buy a thoroughbred? What did they intend to do with it? She assumed, with the presence of the trainer, that George had something other than merely breeding in mind. Did he intend to start racing?

"Really?" Elizabeth interjected, holding her tongue to avoid overwhelming Charlotte with all the questions she wanted to ask.

"He has been quieter than usual, surlier. He wavers between snapping at us for no cause at all to apologizing profusely. It is disconcerting."

Elizabeth contemplated how to steer the conversation away from Charlotte's eldest brother to the topic in which she was most interested — horses. "How strange," she acknowledged.

"I have given the matter much consideration, and the only satisfactory explanation is that John resents George for always coming to the rescue when he is the one to inherit."

"He has never troubled himself over it before," Elizabeth said absently. She did not wish to seem inconsiderate by changing the subject when Charlotte clearly wished to speak of her brother.

"True, but we have never been so close to losing

Lucas Lodge before either. And now, it seems that whole affair has been resolved. While my father carries on as if all is well no matter what befalls us, George is too responsible to invest in a thorough-bred and trainer unless he had sufficient funds to cover the cost. My hope is that this turn of fortune has been extreme enough to awaken John's conscience. He has to face his own deficiencies, but he will be a better man for it."

Elizabeth could not count how many times she had wished the same for her older brother. But he had not learned from his scrapes, and he had paid for his foolishness with his life.

"For all of your sakes, I pray you are correct, Charlotte. Are they collecting the horse in London to bring here?" Elizabeth hoped her redirection was not too abrupt.

"Father mentioned something about the races. He wanted Mama, Maria, and I to join them. It is said the Prince Regent will be there, and you know how my father never misses an opportunity to attend to royalty. But John argued that my presence at the races would ruin my prospects. George was hesitant for us to join them, too."

Elizabeth gasped. "But ladies attend the races all the time! Why should they not wish for you to go?"

"John considers it the height of vulgarity to discuss

financial affairs with anyone, much less with the women in his father's household. Since this is a venture for gain, he does not wish to draw attention to it by having us underfoot. George agreed with him."

Elizabeth rolled her eyes. Why should a lady not be concerned with her family's fortune if it affected her future? "I am happy to hear Lucas Lodge is no longer in danger, but I do not understand how the reverse in circumstances could happen so quickly."

"Nor I, to be honest. It is hardly fair. The gentlemen of the house hide the affairs which most affect the women who occupy a goodly portion of our time in their houses. They seem to believe we are immune to concern regarding our security and the stability of our residence." Charlotte smoothed her skirts. "Perhaps John learned his lesson on seeing how close he was to losing Lucas Lodge for us all. Perhaps his luck has changed."

Her choice of words captured Elizabeth's attention. "You do not believe in luck. It is too romantic a notion."

"All the same, I am grateful for our turn of fortune — whatever it was." With a knowing smile, Charlotte asked, "And what of your romantic notions of spies? Does Mr. Darcy meet your expectations?"

Chuckling at her own whimsy, Elizabeth said, "I was often in Mr. Darcy's company at Netherfield Park, and while I admit he would make a dashing spy, I cannot fathom how such an activity would lead him here." She said no more, not wishing to mention his debt.

Charlotte leaned forward, her eyes sparkling. "You make a handsome pair. I thought it at the assembly when I saw you conversing with each other."

Elizabeth's face caught fire (or, at least, it felt like it!) "He is easy to converse with, and I will admit I enjoy his company." She liked Mr. Darcy. She liked him very much, and unless she could find a reason to entice him back to Netherfield, she had little hope of ever seeing him again.

The realization smarted too much for her to share with Charlotte, and Elizabeth soon bid her farewells to her friend before she revealed her melancholy.

Mind muddled and heart-sore, Elizabeth departed from Lucas Lodge. She had sought clarity and clues, and now, she realized her folly. Mr. Darcy would not come back to Hertfordshire no matter what she found out.

"Miss Elizabeth!" called Mr. Lucas as she crossed

the drive. He dismounted his horse, an elegant stallion Elizabeth did not recognize.

She bobbed a curtsy, hoping she would not be kept long. Elizabeth was in no mood for conversation, and she had so little in common with John Lucas, she could not fathom why he had stopped her.

He bowed, swooping his hat off his head and shuffling it between his hands until Elizabeth longed to snatch the item away from him. His eyes widened, and it was then Elizabeth noted how feverish his complexion appeared. Charlotte had said he had been acting strangely.

Thinking it best to dismiss herself, Elizabeth curtsied again. "Good day to you, Mr. Lucas. I am expected back at Netherfield Park."

He reached out as if he would stop her, but quickly retracted his hand. "Be careful whom you trust, Miss Elizabeth. There are those who carelessly put a price on life, and they do not realize what they will lose until they are called upon to settle their debts," he said in a rush of agitated breath.

She stood frozen in place. He was warning her? He had hardly uttered more than a few sentences to Elizabeth directly in her entire lifetime, and his agitated manners combined with his choice of words sent chills through her. Price on life? Settling debts?

He could only be referring to Mr. Darcy. What did John know? Seeking more information, Elizabeth said, "I do not understand."

Mr. Lucas shuffled his hat again. "These are dangerous times, and the people you are inclined to trust might very well betray you."

Elizabeth balked at the insinuation. Mr. Darcy was not the sort to betray a trust. By his own reluctant admission, Mr. Darcy had told her of his senseless, outlandish bet. It had pained him to reveal the truth to her. Was that not proof of his honesty?

Was it fair of her to alter her regard based on one poorly made decision when she was far from perfect? Or were her emotions too involved for her to see Mr. Darcy for anything other than what she wanted him to be?

Oh, confound this wretched doubt!

The breeze ruffled Mr. Lucas' disheveled hair. Charlotte was right. He was not quite himself. Given his vague warnings, agitated state, and feverish complexion, Elizabeth thought it prudent to continue on to Netherfield rather than press for more details. "Charlotte told me you will accompany your father and brother to London on the morrow. I wish you a safe journey."

The pained look he gave her moved her to continue. "I pray all will turn out well."

He frowned. "It will be well. In the end. Very well indeed. I thank you, Miss Elizabeth. Good day to you." Spinning on his boot, he walked away, smacking his hat against Lady Lucas' rosebush and sending several leaves fluttering to the ground.

CHAPTER 18

*E*lizabeth crawled on her hands and knees on the floor, looking under the bed, the armoire, and checking under the rugs. "I am losing my mind, Emily."

The maid closed the trunk and latched the lid. "You will not find it on the floor, Miss."

Standing and brushing off her hands with a chuckle, Elizabeth said, "To be sure, I do not remember Mr. Darcy returning my brooch, but I cannot imagine him keeping it either, so I must assume he left it behind." The mention of Mr. Darcy brought on an onslaught of mixed emotions Elizabeth would rather not think of right then. She was about to return home with Jane before their mother's appointed time. Elizabeth would need all of her fortitude.

"He did not leave it with me, and Mrs. Nicholls assured me he did not leave anything with her either," Emily reassured her again.

"He must have left it with Wilson, then." It was the only explanation that made sense. The others, Elizabeth had to admit, were not nearly so plausible. She could not imagine Mr. Darcy purposely keeping her brooch as a token to remember her by. While the idea appealed to her vanity, she could not rationalize turning Mr. Darcy into a thief of feminine fripperies. Especially when he knew how much she valued the item. Its worth was not so much intrinsic as it was symbolic of her desire to see the world.

Mr. Darcy had already seen much of the world and could have no use for it. He clearly had no use for her. Now, that was a dismal thought if ever she had one.

He had probably forgotten it in the deep pockets of the greatcoat he had worn the night he had—

Elizabeth stopped the thought before she could finish, though that did nothing to stop warmth from enveloping her whole body. If she closed her eyes, she could still feel his breath tickling her lips. She fanned her face with her hand until Emily gave her a funny look.

"Miss, are you certain you wish to leave today?" she asked.

"Jane and I are decided."

Emily clutched her hands together. "It is only that … perhaps Mrs. Bennet is correct in assuming a connection."

Elizabeth shook her head vehemently. "Jane does not wish to be a burden to Mr. Bingley when he and his family are still recovering. Longbourn is not far, and he has already said he will call as soon as he has strength enough to ride a horse."

"I was not speaking of her." Emily looked up, and Elizabeth felt the color drain from her cheeks.

She could easily dismiss Mr. Darcy's attention by pretending her imagination had exaggerated it. But Emily had been there. She had seen. Elizabeth could not pretend she had not come a whisper of a breath away from her first kiss.

Mr. Darcy had done well to step away. Had he kissed her in front of his valet and her maid, he would have had to honor his attentions with a proposal. And while there were worse things in life than marrying Mr. Darcy, Elizabeth had not yet had enough adventure to be willing to settle into the life the wife of a gentleman of the first circles would be expected to live — no matter how willing she had been at the moment to receive his attentions. Besides, she needed to be certain her attraction to him stemmed from a deeper source.

Now that Mr. Darcy was miles away, he might regret his actions. Were Elizabeth as accomplished in the manipulative arts as her mother wished her to be, a word would secure her engagement. But she could not do that to Mr. Darcy any more than she could to herself. She did not want her marriage to come about by accident or force. She wanted love — true, constant, ardent love. The kind that grew stronger through tribulation and deeper over the passing years.

She wanted to marry a man who would ask her to be his wife so that he would not have to suffer a day apart from her side; who would keep her awake late just so he could converse more with her; who valued her opinions as much as his own; who would steal glances at her in a crowded room and seek out her company because he truly enjoyed being in her presence. All things her mother would deprive Elizabeth of if she knew how easily she could secure Mr. Darcy for her son-in-law.

"Please, Emily, do not tell Mama. Please promise me you will not." Elizabeth wrung her gloves in her hands.

"I will not breathe a word to her, I promise, Miss," Emily said, one hand over her heart. "Oh, but the way Mr. Darcy looked at you, Miss, it was like to make me melt."

"Let us speak no more of it," Elizabeth mumbled. Mr. Darcy was gone, and there was little chance she would see him again unless he returned to Netherfield Park.

The footmen came to take her trunk down to Mr. Bingley's carriage.

Mr. Bingley and Jane were out in the hall. They both stepped away from each other and jerked their hands back with telling blushes.

Wilson, who emerged from his room just then, reached out to steady Mr. Bingley, who was still weak.

"Thank you, Wilson," Mr. Bingley said, "Are you certain you, too, must leave today? I had hoped Darcy would return."

"I am certain he would have liked that, Mr. Bingley," Wilson said, his eyes flickering to meet Elizabeth's before returning to his host, "but I am afraid it is impossible."

Impossible was such a definite word.

After a brief visit to Mrs. Hurst and Miss Bingley's rooms to express their gratitude for extending their hospitality in Jane's distress, and, in turn, wishing the ladies prompt recoveries, Elizabeth and Jane joined Wilson at the bottom of the stairs.

Mr. Bingley, kept at the top of the stairs by his vigilant valet lest he should attempt to navigate them in his weak state, waved from the top of the landing.

"Pray return any time," he invited, his enthusiastic voice echoing in the entrance hall.

Pink-cheeked, Jane curtsied. "We would be delighted to. You are always welcome at Longbourn, as well."

Her boldness made Elizabeth wonder how many times Jane and Mr. Bingley had "chanced" upon each other once they were recovered enough to leave their sickrooms. Evidently, they had made good use of their time for Jane to feel comfortable enough to speak so invitingly.

Wilson handed them into the carriage.

Taking advantage of her opportunity, Elizabeth asked, "By any chance, did Mr. Darcy leave my brooch with you to return to me?"

"I am afraid he did not, Miss Elizabeth. I will inquire of the other servants before I depart for London." He turned to the front of the coach, extending his hand for the coachman to pull him up and revealing a pistol hidden under his coat.

Right. How could she have forgotten? Wilson had stayed behind to ensure her and Jane's safe delivery to Longbourn. Elizabeth did not feel herself in danger (the danger, apparently, being meant for Mr. Darcy and not for her), but she did feel better knowing she and her sister had Wilson's protection.

Was Mr. Darcy safe from harm? Had he found the henchman and acquired the proof he needed against the unsavory gentleman? Elizabeth's stomach tied into knots. So many things could go wrong chasing after a lawless thug with no respect for life. A ruffian such as that would think nothing of shooting Mr. Darcy, picking his pockets, and leaving him in the street for dead. Things of that sort happened all the time in London. She read about them in the papers.

Before she had a chance to prepare herself to face her mother, they were at Longbourn.

Wilson handed them out. Elizabeth wanted to ask him about Mr. Darcy, but what could he know?

The valet smiled. "I will inquire about your brooch, Miss Elizabeth."

"Thank you, Wilson. I hope you have a safe journey to London."

He nodded, then ensured the trunks were gently handed down to carry inside Longbourn.

Mama burst out of the house, handkerchief in hand. Aside from fans, handkerchiefs were her favored accessories. One could dab delicately at the eyes to suggest tears, or drop it as a means to command attention, or wave it about like a victory flag. So versatile was the handkerchief. Mama waved hers about when she saw Mr. Bingley's carriage sitting in her drive.

Then, when she correctly discerned that it was only the gentleman's carriage and not the gentleman himself come to convey Jane home so that he might request an audience with Mr. Bennet in which he would ask for his blessing on their forthcoming union, she began dabbing at her eyes.

Jane and Elizabeth looped their arms through their mother's, encouraging her with gentle pulls to enter the house.

"Where is Mr. Bingley? Mr. Bennet is at his leisure and quite able to see the gentleman." Mama looked between Jane and Elizabeth, adding as an afterthought, "Or Mr. Darcy, perhaps? He is not so agreeable, but he has more carriages than Mr. Bingley."

There being no reason to delay the inevitable, Elizabeth said, "Neither of us is engaged, Mama, but Jane is fully recovered. Are you not happy to see her well after her horrible illness?"

Their mother's face scrunched. She whined, "I would much rather have seen her engaged. Did you not read my instructions? You were not to return before the end of a full week. I sent enough gowns. I can understand this willful rebellion from you,

Lizzy, but I cannot believe it of my sweet, beautiful Jane." She hid behind her handkerchief and sobbed.

Jane embraced her, giving Elizabeth an apologetic look over their mother's bowed, weeping form as she led her into the drawing room.

Papa joined them, but he was little consolation to his grieving wife. "There, there, my love. No harm is done."

"No harm, you say, Mr. Bennet? Oh, my poor, poor nerves! My heart! Such spasms! Lydia, bring Mr. Jones' draught! Hurry before I am overcome! Oh, I fear it is my time! Dear Lord in the Heavens, help my daughters settle where I have failed them!" she cried out in another fit of sobs and wails which lasted until the calming draught the apothecary had given her for such occasions worked its effect. Snivels turned to snores and tears to spittle soaking her pillow.

Father lit his pipe and called for tea. "I am happy to have my two sensible daughters restored to Longbourn. Your mother has talked of nothing but lace, wedding gowns, and cake since you left. I daresay all of Meryton expects to hear an engagement announced or a reading of the banns on Sunday." He chuckled. "I am sorry for you, Jane, but your mother is resilient. She will find a way to come out triumphant or, more likely, she will forget the shame of her presumption altogether when she finds another unmarried gentleman upon whom to cast her ambitions."

He asked about Netherfield Park, and Jane spoke kindly of everyone in the household, making sure to mention the great care they took to see to her health even while they were ill.

Elizabeth's gaze wandered to the window. It had started to rain. Was it raining in London as well? She imagined Mr. Darcy roaming through narrow streets and alleys in a relentless search for the henchman. It still bothered her that he had gambled an exorbitant sum. And yet, it must be true if Mr. Lucas knew of it. Perhaps there was more to the matter than Mr. Darcy had hurriedly explained—

"Lizzy?" her father's voice interrupted.

She blinked, clearing her vision and momentarily disoriented until she saw Papa looking at her with his bushy white eyebrows raised in question marks. "Yes?" she said.

"You did not hear my question?"

She had not heard anything at all. "I am afraid not."

"Jane told me you were an exemplary nurse. I suppose Netherfield offered enough to explore within its walls to keep you occupied?" he asked.

What could she answer? She could not tell the

truth — that her time at Netherfield had been full of adventure and mystery … and Mr. Darcy. "The library was woefully neglected, an oversight Mr. Bingley assured me he means to put to right."

Father bunched his cheeks and chewed on his pipe. "Yes, Mr. Bingley seems to be of the sort who is easily distracted from books. However, I suspect he is a quick student of experience and chooses to learn by observing others. I imagine he is unafraid of a bit of trial-and-error, but does so only when the stakes are small, otherwise he would have purchased an estate rather than lease one. It is a recommendation to his caution."

Stakes. Caution. Elizabeth knew it was accepted — expected even — for gentlemen to gamble. But she never would have put Mr. Darcy in the same lot as Beau Brummel and Scrope Davies.

Could she trust a man who admitted to losing such a large sum? Who gambled away a fortune?

"Lizzy? Are you well?" her father asked.

Elizabeth blinked. She had been staring out of the window again.

"You keep sighing," he said.

"I am sorry. I am only tired, and the rain makes me restless." Tired was not the right word. Perplexed was more suitable. Consumed, better still.

"Understandable, I daresay, my dear girl. You

have been too long away from Longbourn, but now that you are home, all will be well."

That time, Elizabeth noticed the sigh escape her. Tempest was lost to her. The stables at Lucas Lodge were forbidden her. Mr. Darcy was gone. And, once again, she was stuck at Longbourn.

CHAPTER 19

*D*arcy paced in the front parlor, avoiding the mirror every time he passed it. He was not so adept at tying his cravat as Wilson was, and every look at the uneven folds and creases reminded him why his valet was not with him at Darcy House.

Elizabeth.

His cravat reminded him of Elizabeth. As did the preserves on the breakfast table that morning. As did every bookshop he passed. And the copies of Mr. Pinkerton's books he had purchased the day before. And every blue riding habit.

Darcy saw Elizabeth everywhere, and his heart grew heavier every time it was not her. Georgiana had noticed when he had called at Matlock House. She noticed everything.

It was Tuesday, now, and unless Wilson had suffered an accident, he ought to be arriving soon. Better a miserable man with a neat cravat than a miserable man with a crooked one.

Darcy shoved his hands through his hair. His plan was not working — not in the way he had needed. He was closer to finding the source of the Lucases' new fortune, and he was more convinced than ever it would lead him to The Four Horsemen … but how could he keep his mind on his mission when his thoughts constantly turned to Elizabeth?

What he would give to hear her laugh right now or see her bright smile.

He shook his head and resumed pacing. He would not hear her laughter anytime soon. She was safe at Longbourn, where Mr. Bennet would ensure she would stay — like a princess held captive in a tower waiting for her knight in shining armor to carry her away on a grand adventure.

Darcy chuckled brittlely at his error. The Elizabeth he knew would wait for nobody. She would find a way to scale the walls. She would find a horse and ride to her freedom without help from anyone. He hoped she would … someday … so long as it did not happen right now … so long as she did not come to London or anywhere near him.

No, Mr. Bennet would keep her at Longbourn. Elizabeth was safe.

He would catch The Four Horsemen red-handed, and he would return to Netherfield Park to restore Elizabeth's brooch to her. Darcy had forgotten it was in his greatcoat pocket until he had ridden several miles past Meryton. If she did not despise him for his abrupt departure and his many secrets, perhaps she would forgive him when he returned her treasured brooch….

He stopped. A commotion outside his bedchamber door and the familiar step-drag sound of Wilson's walk alerted him that his carriage and valet had finally arrived.

Darcy opened his door before Wilson knocked.

The good man winced at the sight of Darcy's cravat, and he immediately went about the business of untying and refolding it as he gave his report. "There were no sightings of anyone out of place at Netherfield Park, though the footman and gardener you installed at the house know to remain alert. Mr. Bingley insisted the ladies use his coach instead of yours, but since it was arranged yesterday, I was able to hide the usual munitions in his carriage without being noticed."

"Very good. Did Bingley's coachman give you any trouble?"

"I had a word with him before we departed. Like most of the servants out in the carriage house and stables, he knew about the shot at your hat, so he was obliging when I asked to ride with him up top for the safety of the Bennet ladies."

"He did not ask further questions?"

"Not after Mr. Bingley made such a fuss about seeing to Miss Bennet and Miss Elizabeth's comfort."

God bless Bingley. Darcy had hated to leave his friend, but he had little option when Elizabeth was endangered because of him. "Bingley is recovered? The rest of his household as well?"

Wilson stepped back to allow Darcy to admire his handiwork in the mirror. He was now a miserable man with a neat cravat.

The footmen came in carrying Darcy's trunk, and Wilson saw to its placement. Once the servants had left, Wilson said, "They are recovering nicely. Mr. Bingley will call at Longbourn as soon as he is strong enough to make it down the stairs and atop a horse. No later than Saturday, I suspect. Not a day more."

Would that he was free to call on whomever he wished. Jealousy gave Darcy's thoughts a bitter turn. He had better focus on what he must do rather than on what he could not. "You saw nothing suspicious around Longbourn?" he asked.

"No, Sir. Nothing."

"And … and Miss … Elizabeth?" he asked, stuttering over her name. "Was she…?" Darcy could not find a way to appropriately finish his question when Wilson could not possibly know what he burned to hear confirmed. Did Elizabeth think of him at all, as he thought of her?

Wilson squeezed Darcy's shoulder. "I left her well and safe with her father. She was, however, saddened at the loss of her brooch."

Darcy grimaced. "It was in my greatcoat pocket."

"Too bad it is too valuable to entrust with the post, or you could send it to her directly," Wilson said with a glint in his eye.

"I could send one of my messengers…" Darcy mused, finding the solution both practical and entirely disagreeable.

"You could. But you will not." Wilson shook out a dress shirt.

Darcy sank onto the nearest chair, pressing his fingers against his temples.

"Do you mind if I ask you a question of a personal nature, Mr. Darcy?"

"What could it hurt? You see a great deal too much as it is."

Wilson draped a waistcoat over the lid of the trunk. "It is why you employed me, and it is because of my gratitude, I wish to see you happy when all this is done."

"I am happy enough," Darcy quipped half-heartedly. Happiness had never left him so dissatisfied and hopeless.

Wilson raised his eyebrows but did not contradict him. Instead, he continued unpacking the trunk. "You have sacrificed your happiness for years. For so long, in fact, you have convinced yourself that you can only be happy at Pemberley."

"Because it is true. It is where I was last happiest." Darcy pulled out his compass, turning it in his hand. But instead of the calm it usually restored, Darcy became more acutely aware of an incompleteness. He turned it again in his hand to the same effect.

Wilson hung the greatcoat up, brushing the capes until he found what Darcy had left in the pocket. He smiled at the colorful item and nodded as if it represented the solution to Darcy's dilemma. In a way, it was as much of the solution as it was the problem. Holding the brooch out to Darcy, Wilson said softly, "All the same, it seems you might have found happiness elsewhere. In someone."

Darcy rubbed his chest. Happiness was a dangerous subject for men like him. He grabbed the brooch, the bright mosaic pieces uneven under his thumb, unlike his smooth compass. He and Elizabeth were too different. She craved the life from which he longed to retire. She wanted an escape from her home, and all he ever wanted was to return to Pemberley. How could he ever make her happy?

The ache deepened. Hope was a double-edged sword. One side made a man soar. The other sent him plunging into the depths of despair. The Four Horsemen had escaped his capture before. What if they escaped yet again? Darcy could not think of a future with Elizabeth while those wicked men were still a threat. And he would rather die than endanger her any more than he already had.

"You know the rules, Wilson. I cannot risk the lives of the people I … greatly esteem … to suit my own wishes. It would be selfish."

"When this is over? What then?"

Placing Elizabeth's brooch in the secret drawer of his writing desk, Darcy stared at the monogram on his compass. *Home is where the heart is.* Therein lay his predicament. His heart was no longer at Pemberley.

THE FOLLOWING MORNING, Richard walked into

Darcy's study without so much as a warning from the butler.

Dropping unceremoniously onto a chair and stretching his legs out before him, Richard grimaced. "Why are you here when your assignment is in Hertfordshire?"

Darcy turned the ledger he had been pouring over for the past few hours and pushed it toward Richard. "An informant in Meryton disclosed to me that Sir William recently came into a large sum of money. I am here to trace its origins."

Richard sat forward, all attention. "This is from the bank? How did you get this?"

"You know I cannot reveal my sources."

"Right, right. I am merely astonished. This is a quick bit of work, Darcy," Richard said, running his finger down the ledger.

Darcy pointed at the pages. "As you see, several deposits were made into an account with the name Smith. Not the most clever alias, but unless someone were searching for something unusual, it would easily go unnoticed. One of my contacts is inquiring into the true identity of the account holder. I am convinced it is Sir William's and that the funds are coming from The Four Horsemen."

"Four deposits of equal amounts to a John Smith? I should say you are onto something, Darcy. You said you learned this from your informant in Hertfordshire?"

Darcy nodded. If Richard knew his greatest source of information was a curious female, he would pull Darcy off the case quicker than he could draw his pistol. Richard had too recently lost an agent whose head had been turned by a clever lady working for The Four Horsemen. Apparently, the lady had not been completely devious. Her body had been dredged out of the Thames two days after the agent was found stabbed to death and left in a pile of refuse outside a pub by the river.

Richard rubbed his chin. "I am impressed you were able to gain the confidence of an informant so quickly when Sir William has the advantage of being a local with an established reputation. How did you manage it?"

"I prefer not to reveal my methods." Again, Darcy had to give credit to Elizabeth. However, falling in love with the best friend of the villain's daughter was not something he cared to admit to his prying cousin.

Darcy's breath caught in his throat. He loved her. He loved Elizabeth.

"If this person is a reliable source of information, do you think you might recruit him? We will need—"

"Absolutely not!" Darcy exclaimed too passionately. Taking a deep breath to calm himself, he added, "That is, I have come to know this person well enough to recognize that … his … value would be wasted in the field."

Rubbing his chin still, Richard said, "You will be a difficult one to replace."

"There are other gentlemen more than willing to take my place."

"Too many of them want notoriety. After all, what is the use of being a hero if nobody knows about it? Your type is rare, Darcy."

"What of you?" As much as Darcy wanted out from under the thumb of the war office, he dearly wished it for Richard, too.

"Ah, as for that, my mother has made it clear to me that she will see me settle before I am thirty years of age … or else."

"That is this year."

"And well I know it," Richard grumbled.

"Do not fret. When the right lady enters your life, you will know it." Darcy had never put much credence in such romantic notions before, but he was a believer now. His attraction to Elizabeth had deepened with all the strength and subtlety of a rafter beam to the head.

Richard looked up at him.

"Or so I have been told," Darcy added quickly, pulling the ledger back to him. "Until this business is done, let us not speak of mundane affairs. We have work to do."

Richard sighed. "Yes. There is always work to do." He looked so tired. So weary.

Darcy knew the feeling. He had been jaded before he had met Elizabeth. She had reminded him of how joyous life could be. He missed her vivacity, her spark.

Pushing himself up, Richard said, "I will leave you to it, then. Keep me informed of your findings so I can be ready should you require me and more men." Walking to the door, he turned, adding, "And Darcy, like you, I am ready for this sordid business to be done. We cannot let these devilish rascals roam at large. This time, we must capture them, or we will never gain another advantage. The war with France is nothing compared to the enemy we face within our own borders. Stay close to this informant of yours. We cannot afford to let a good asset go to waste. Not when we are so close. Do what you must, but do not let them slip between your fingers." He gripped the door, sighing and shrugging his shoulders. "All is fair in love and war."

A fortnight ago, Darcy might have agreed with the axiom. Now, he would much rather face The

Four Horsemen than he would Elizabeth. He stood a chance against the criminal minds, whereas he had already lost his heart to a fine-eyed maiden he could never make happy, a lady to whom he had lied. Far from considering his actions fair, Darcy despised himself for them.

CHAPTER 20

*M*ama waved her handkerchief from the doorway on the chance Mr. Bingley might look back from his withdrawing carriage, elbowing Jane to do the same, and saying, "Mr. Bingley is so charming! And his sisters! Absolutely lovely. They will introduce you into their society in London once you are married, Jane. Oh, the pin money you shall have! I do hope you do your duty by your sisters and invite them to stay at his townhouse. Oh! To think my daughter will marry a gentleman with a townhouse and a country estate! I would just like to see Lady Lucas do better, although Charlotte is well on her way to being shelved if she is not careful. It is a pity she is so plain."

Elizabeth rolled her eyes, stepping back inside

and leaving her mother and sister to watch Mr. Bingley's carriage. She was happy for Jane.

Mr. Bingley had clearly dragged his sisters along with him. It had been diverting to see how expertly he soothed over his sisters' jabs at her mother and younger sisters' silly comments while securing her family's good opinion. Even Papa, who was disinclined to favor anyone with such a pitiable library as Mr. Bingley's, found himself quite taken with the gentleman.

Elizabeth was thrilled for Jane. Really. Simply ecstatic.

She settled on the settee, folding her feet up under her and reaching for the book at the top of the pile on the table.

Father sat by the fire with his newspaper folded out so that only a puff of smoke from his pipe was seen drifting into a cloud above the page.

Kitty and Lydia were upstairs, and judging by the ruckus they created, they were ransacking everyone's rooms for ribbons and hat trimmings. They had convinced Mr. Bingley to throw a ball to which Jane need only name the date, and as they would naturally see that the ball would happen sooner rather than later, they had begun their preparations for the blessed event.

Mary read aloud from one of her books,

attempting to instill in her impetuous sisters the benefits of study and reflection.

Wiggling her toes, and still feeling happy for Jane, Elizabeth flipped blindly through her book. Would Mr. Darcy return for Mr. Bingley's ball? If he had forgotten to leave her brooch at Netherfield — which she must assume since Wilson had left for London three days ago, and it had yet to appear — would Mr. Darcy deliver it back to her possession himself? Had he forgotten her brooch in his pockets? Had he forgotten her?

She set aside the book, reaching for an embroidery hoop of white work instead. The linen was soft, but not so soft as Mr. Darcy's silk handkerchief. She ought to have kept it. She could have held it hostage until he saw fit to return her brooch.

Mama barged into the drawing room. "Oh, my dearest Jane! I just knew you could not be so beautiful for nothing!" Sitting triumphantly in the chair opposite Papa, she pronounced, "I would not be surprised if Mr. Bingley proposes within the week. What do you think of that, Mr. Bennet?"

Papa lowered his newspaper. "Mr. Bingley is a fine young man. If he wishes to marry Jane, it would please me to give my consent."

Mama clapped her hands. "What do you say,

Lizzy? You had more occasion to observe the two at Netherfield than anyone."

Unprepared as Elizabeth was for the conversation to turn to her, she said the one thought she had been forcefully repeating through her mind since Mr. Bingley's arrival with his sisters. "I am very happy for Jane."

Her mother was too pleased with her success, and her sister was too enchanted by Mr. Bingley's attentions to notice the hollowness in Elizabeth's tone.

For a moment, Elizabeth feared her father had noticed, but she must have imagined his frown and drooping pipe. He left for his book room. And just in time, for Mama was like a dog with a bone, and Elizabeth was incapable of hiding her reactions fully from her father. He knew her too well.

"It is too bad you could not entice Mr. Darcy to stay longer at Netherfield. You must not have been tempting enough to encourage him to stay," Mama said, clucking her tongue.

Elizabeth clamped her jaw tight, her fingers pressing against the cold metal of the needle until it left marks on her skin.

Jane rose to Elizabeth's defense. "Lizzy was so busy nursing me, and Mr. Darcy was equally occupied. You heard Mr. Bingley recount how indebted he is to Mr. Darcy for coming to his aid when he fell ill."

"All the more reason to stay," Mama grumbled.

Jane persisted. "Mr. Darcy is a busy gentleman with an estate of his own to manage. No doubt, business took him away. He will return for Mr. Bingley's ball."

Elizabeth smiled her thanks to Jane, though she was not as optimistic as her sister was that he would attend the ball.

"Mr. Bingley must have been very ill, indeed, to have waited three whole days to call," Mama complained, fanning her face. "I was beginning to worry he would never call."

How quickly their mother waved between ecstasy and anguish.

Elizabeth said, "Mama, Mr. Bingley nearly fainted the last time he dragged himself to the door of Jane's bedchamber to inquire about her health. When we left, he had to lean against the banister."

"I do not understand how his recovery delayed longer than Jane's. It is a bad omen. Oh, Jane, you had better secure the ball in haste, or the event will lose its importance and he will never propose! And Mr. Bennet will die, and we will be tossed out of Longbourn to live in the hedgerows," Mama wept, fanning her face and dabbing her cheeks with her handkerchief.

Jane reassured her. "Pray do not trouble yourself so, Mama. Mr. Bingley ate more of the preserves than I did and was much more ill than I was."

Their mother pshawed. "Mr. Darcy did not fall ill. What is his excuse for preferring London over our company?"

Elizabeth could not recall telling her mother of his whereabouts. "How did you know Mr. Darcy was in London?"

Mama sniffed. "Mr. Philips saw him riding through Meryton. He was on horseback, accompanied by his groom with the funny nose. Where else would he go without his luggage and valet but London where one assumes that a gentleman as wealthy as Mr. Darcy must have another house?"

Most assuredly, the henchman Mr. Darcy pursued was not a single gentleman of fortune. Otherwise, her mother would have tracked him down as easily as she had Mr. Darcy.

Elizabeth sighed, plunging her needle into the linen. She wished she knew more. All she saw were loose threads which led nowhere, and Mr. Lucas' warning only added to her confusion. She could not believe Mr. Darcy capable of perfidy. Nor did she think him a liar. Neither explanation settled well with her, which, after several days of pondering the conundrum had led her to the conclusion that Mr. Darcy was protecting someone. That was what she hoped. It added integrity and virtue to his actions.

Had he not seen to the needs of everyone sick at Netherfield? Had he not shielded her when their lives had been endangered, putting her life ahead of his own? While a pinch of jealousy prayed the individual under his protection was not another lady, Elizabeth took comfort in her reasoning. It was the only thing that made any sense at all.

Mama's grievances trespassed on her thoughts. "If only you had stayed longer! You did such a good job securing an invitation to stay at Netherfield by falling ill, Jane. Why could you not have stayed a few more days? Then, I am certain Mr. Bingley would have felt well enough to propose. You could already have been engaged. Oh, I am so disappointed! My poor nerves! How will you ever marry, Lizzy, when you insist on scaring gentlemen away? And how nearly you ruined Jane's chances with Mr. Bingley by leaving before a week had passed."

Elizabeth clutched her embroidery, stabbing the needle back and forth. Nothing she or Jane could say — had said over the past three days — would convince their mother that they had acted sensibly.

Still, Mr. Darcy's absence and her mother's

constant lamenting gave rise to Elizabeth's growing discontent. Jane's happiness only emphasized her distress ... no matter how glad Elizabeth tried to be for her.

What did she really know of Mr. Darcy? Less than she liked. She had been convinced of his character until he had told her of his debt. That piece did not fit in her puzzle.

Jane gently tugged the embroidery from Elizabeth's hands. "Perhaps you should set the needle down, Lizzy. Your finger is bleeding."

Elizabeth looked down. Gracious! Blood rimmed her fingernail.

Not knowing what to do with herself, Elizabeth went to the one serene place in the house, and the only room where her mother would not follow her.

The door to Papa's book room was closed. Elizabeth tapped on it.

Emily opened the door. "Miss Elizabeth," she said, bobbing a curtsy and brushing past her with her eyes firmly on the ground.

Elizabeth watched her scuttle off, then turned to her father. "Is Emily in trouble?" she asked.

Father rubbed his side whiskers. "No. Nothing of the sort. I merely wished to consult with her ... about Mr. Bingley. To know what sort of man he is when he thinks nobody is looking."

Elizabeth exhaled, sitting in the chair across from him and resting her elbows against his desk. "I cannot imagine she had anything disagreeable to say."

"True—" Papa stopped short, looking as though he wished to say something more. Instead, he took off his glasses and polished them, his lips pinched closed. When his glasses reflected the sun coming in through the window to crystalline perfection, he filled his pipe and settled against the back of his chair. "Your mother planned Jane's wedding trousseau while you were away. It was insufferable. Nothing but lace and bonnets and speculations on the number of carriages and the amount of pin money she would have."

That sounded about right. Elizabeth smiled, but ended up sighing yet again.

Looking at her askance, Papa said, "It has been difficult for you, too. You are very distracted of late."

She did not wish to discuss the greatest source of her restlessness until she understood herself better. So, she told him what she could with confidence. "I know you would rather me never ride a horse again, to keep me at Longbourn and away from danger. I do not begrudge you your reasons, knowing them to be borne from love and concern. But I miss riding. And I dearly wish to see something of the world."

Papa's eyes misted. "You are too good to me, my dear girl. I know it is unjust of me to make you pay for Thomas' foolish choices. I am not completely blind. I know you have suffered the most for it, and for what? I am the father to three of the silliest daughters in Hertfordshire despite the limits I have placed on your freedoms." He looked out of the window and tugged his side whiskers.

Elizabeth's eyes burned and blurred. Father had never recognized how his way of mourning his only son's death had affected her before.

When he turned his gaze away from the window to her, she blinked furiously and rubbed her sleeve over her cheeks.

"I call you my favorite, and yet, I have allowed your mother to torment you over the past three days. I have watched your lively nature turn listless, and I cannot continue to ignore it. How can I make reparation, Lizzy?" he asked.

Blindsided by his question, Elizabeth sat with her mouth open. There was so much she could say, and none of it seemed appropriate.

Waving his pipe in the air, he said, "I know what! Why did I not think of it before? Please forgive me for being such a foolish father, Lizzy, but I promise I will do my best to make amends. I will try."

Elizabeth rushed to his side of the desk and

kissed his cheek. "That you wish to try is enough for me," she said, her heart so full, emotions pooled in her eyes and spilled down her face.

Papa chuckled, dabbing at his eyes and handing her another handkerchief. "I will do better than that, dear Lizzy. Tell Emily to pack a trunk for you and Jane. On the morrow, we will leave for London."

CHAPTER 21

*M*r. Carton did not often work on Saturdays, so when Darcy received a note requesting his immediate presence, Darcy knew his man of business had discovered the provenance of Sir William's new fortune.

Not only had Carton acquired a reliable informant inside London's largest bank office, he had also procured copies of four separate transactions for the precise amounts deposited in Sir William's account in the names of Sir Leonard, Sir Benedict, Sir Harcourt, and Sir Erasmus. The Four Horsemen. Darcy had the documents in his satchel. He had already sent a message to Richard.

If brought to court, The Four Horsemen would argue that the amount was nothing more than a coincidence. They would contend that however the evidence was obtained was unlawful and therefore inadmissible. But to Darcy, the information was priceless. He was on the right track. And as soon as his carriage conveyed him to his residence, he would focus his energies on finding Sir William.

Wilson had told him that Sir William and his two eldest sons had departed from Lucas Lodge, but finding them had proved to be a daunting task. Now, it was a priority.

Before the carriage came to a complete stop, Darcy hopped out of the conveyance, taking the stairs two at a time. He would be anxious until he handed the satchel over to Richard, who would hand it over to the higher powers at Leo.

Crossing the entrance hall, Darcy instructed the butler, "Colonel Fitzwilliam will arrive shortly. Please send him to my study directly," and he proceeded up the stairs.

Floor-to-ceiling bookshelves lined the walls surrounding the mahogany desk commanding the center of his study. Taking several books off a shelf, Darcy entered a combination in the safe hidden in the wall and gently placed the satchel inside.

He had just slid the last book into its position on the shelf when there was a knock at the door. The butler peeked inside.

Anticipating him, Darcy said, "If it is Richard, see

him in immediately. And send up a bottle of my best brandy."

"It is not Colonel Fitzwilliam, Sir. A Mr. Bennet from Longbourn in Hertfordshire is here to see you."

Darcy leaned against his desk.

"Shall I tell him you are out?" the butler asked.

Nausea churned Darcy's stomach. Mr. Bennet should not be in London. Why was he here? Was something wrong? Was Elizabeth safe? Good God, what if she was in London, too? Wiping his palms against his breeches, he said, "No. No, I will see him. Please bring him here."

Darcy sat behind his desk. When that felt too formal, he stood in front of his desk. Too stiff. He leaned against the front of his desk. Too informal. Trying to calm his rising panic, Darcy looked about the room, seeing it through the eyes of a newcomer.

The trio of chairs arranged around the fireplace offered a welcome compromise. He would greet Mr. Bennet standing beside his desk and invite him to have a seat in one of the cushioned chairs.

That only left the salutation. How did you greet the father of the woman you loved when you both feared and craved her presence more than anything? *Good day. Good morning. Welcome. Greetings.* He had not yet exhausted the list when Mr. Bennet walked in.

Darcy bowed, his tongue tied.

"Good afternoon, Mr. Darcy," Mr. Bennet said with a bow. "I thank you for receiving me."

His manners were too light to stem from concern. Perhaps all was well in Hertfordshire. "It is my pleasure," Darcy said, gesturing toward the seating area (rather smoothly, he thought.)

Mr. Bennet rubbed his hands against his breeches several times and looked about the room. The tell-tale nervous gesture increased Darcy's own anxiety. He reached for his compass, turning it over in his hand and waiting on pins and needles.

"You have a great many books here. I am always inclined to think kindly of well-read gentlemen," Mr. Bennet commented amiably.

Darcy smiled, somewhat relieved. "If you like this room, you would love the library, although it pales in comparison to my library at Pemberley."

Mr. Bennet's eyes lit up with an energy Darcy was shocked to see the gentleman possessed. Darcy saw where Elizabeth got the twinkle in her eye, and it made him miss her all the more.

As his own had done, Mr. Bennet's smile faded. He patted his pocket until he found his pipe. Had the gentleman asked for permission to light it, Darcy would gladly have given it, but Mr. Bennet seemed content to fiddle with the object — much in the same manner Darcy fiddled with his compass.

Realizing how anxious he must look, Darcy tucked the keepsake into his pocket and clasped his hands together.

"I suppose you are wondering why I am here," Mr. Bennet finally said.

Yes!

Darcy nodded, using every trick in his possession to keep his voice steady and his heart from leaping out of his chest. "You are not in difficulties, I hope?"

Mr. Bennet tucked his pipe back into his pocket and tugged on his side whiskers. "No. Nothing like that, I assure you. I only wished to have an excuse to bring Lizzy with me to London."

Darcy's stomach dropped, and his heart raced. Elizabeth was in London.

"She has seen so little of England," Mr. Bennet continued, "and she has been more restless than usual lately."

Really? Did she miss him? Vain hope rose within Darcy even while rational thought told him this was a disaster. She was supposed to forget him. He was supposed to forget her.

Mr. Bennet smiled, completely unaware of the turmoil he had stirred. "As her father, I am doing my best to see to her happiness."

Now? He chose to see to her happiness now? Darcy breathed deeply. He must relax. "Your attention on her behalf is certain to give her cheer," he said, only a little stiffly.

"Thank you, Mr. Darcy. I hope so. She is dearer to me than anyone." Mr. Bennet looked at him intently, as if inquiring where Elizabeth stood in his affections.

Darcy clamped his teeth shut. That she was also dearer to him than anyone on the earth, he had no right to say. Not yet. Perhaps not ever. It was the saddest reality Darcy had contemplated since his father's death had left him without his most-trusted adviser. What would his father have counseled him to do now?

He exhaled slowly. Darcy knew the answer. His father had ensured his son never forgot the solution to all his troubles. Placing the compass in Darcy's palm and wrapping his hands around them, he had said, "This will guide your path to home. Keep it close and you will never be lost or alone."

That was the answer. Darcy needed to go home. Pemberley had always been his fortress, his safe place. It was where his favorite memories were, where his aspirations had been inspired.

But Elizabeth was not there.

So entangled was Elizabeth in his visions of the

future, Darcy could not think of Pemberley without imagining her there with him.

Would the excitement of Pemberley wear off, leaving her as dissatisfied there as she was at Longbourn? Would she resent what he cherished?

Mr. Bennet did not continue. He watched Darcy over the rims of his spectacles. Darcy needed to say something, but he could not without exposing his heart to the father of the young lady he was certain to disappoint. Tongue thick and throat dry, he finally said, "That is how it ought to be, Mr. Bennet."

"I am glad you agree, Mr. Darcy. Lizzy has not had the advantages most ladies of her station have had, but she is an intelligent student and learns more quickly than most. She is a credit to me through no effort of mine. She will be a credit to the young man who wins her heart."

Darcy thought his heart would crack his ribs, it hammered so violently. "I am certain you are right," he muttered.

Mr. Bennet seemed pleased with his reply. He visibly relaxed. "We are staying at The Stratford Hotel. Do you know it?"

"Of course." Darcy had walked by there from his residence at Mayfair many times.

"We would have stayed at Gracechurch Street with Mrs. Bennet's brother and family, but they are away at the present, and I thought Lizzy might fancy staying in a more fashionable part of London. I find the location convenient. My favorite bookshop is only a bit over a mile away, and Hyde Park is a comfortable walking distance. Perhaps you would agree to dine with us tomorrow evening?"

Darcy wanted to accept so badly. Clearly his heart was treacherous where Elizabeth was involved. If he could just see her…

He had to change the topic without giving offense. He could not accept Mr. Bennet's invitation, but he could not bring himself to refuse it either. "You did not bring the rest of your family? It is just you and … Miss Elizabeth?" Even saying her name was difficult.

"Mrs. Bennet would not leave Longbourn when Mr. Bingley is so recently courting Jane. He had already called twice before we departed for town. Otherwise, I had hoped Jane would accompany us."

Darcy tried to be content for Bingley. "I wish them both well and happy." He tried to cover the bitterness in his tone with a smile he hoped did not look as forced as it felt.

"Mrs. Bennet is very happy, although my younger daughters were cross with her for insisting they stay behind while Lizzy and I came to enjoy the enter-tainments of London with our acquaintances. To be honest, I am relieved they did not come. I am not brave enough to venture out with my youngest daughters quite yet."

Before Mr. Bennet could repeat his invitation, Darcy asked, "What do you plan to do while in town?"

"Sir William invited us to see his new racehorse."

Darcy sat forward in his chair. If he could find out where they were from Mr. Bennet, he would have more time to figure out how to lay a trap for The Four Horsemen. "He is in town?" he asked casually.

"They have been for nearly a week. I am not one to appreciate horseflesh, but I know Lizzy will like to see the animal." Mr. Bennet shivered.

Darcy appreciated the sacrifice the father was willing to make for his daughter's pleasure, but he must find out where the Lucases were staying.

"Sir William is more than happy to show off the creature — presumptuously named Trophonius, I might add. I am certain he would welcome your inspection, Mr. Darcy. Perhaps you would like to accompany us. I have arranged to meet them at their inn on Monday."

"Where are they staying?" Darcy held his breath, trying to relax his fingers when he felt them grip the arms of his chair.

Mr. Bennet bunched his cheeks. "I cannot recall. It was not a name I recognized, though I recall his assurance that it is not a difficult place to find, being on the road to Epsom."

Drat!

"I will consult my schedule," Darcy said noncommittally, disappointed Mr. Bennet had not remembered the details he needed but grateful for his forthrightness. Men who had nothing to hide often revealed what Darcy needed to know without any prompting from him, but he wondered how Sir William would react if he found out how readily his neighbor revealed his whereabouts.

All Darcy had to do was inquire at the inns along the road to Epsom, and he would find Sir William. It should not be difficult, as proud as he was of touting his title and his prized horse.

"Good. Then I expect to hear from you soon. The invitation to dine stands, Mr. Darcy. I ought to have known that a gentleman as busy as yourself would have other obligations, but I do hope you will choose to join me and Lizzy before too long." He rose.

"Thank you, Mr. Bennet." Darcy stood to see the gentleman out before he had to evade another invitation. His resolve was wearing thin.

CHAPTER 22

*D*arcy had only just caught his breath and calmed his mind when Richard burst into his study. Hoisting the bottle of brandy Darcy had asked the butler to bring up, he said, "I take it we are celebrating?"

That had been the idea, but that was before Mr. Bennet had called.

Richard jutted his thumb over his shoulder. "Was that your informant? The older gentleman? He was leaving as I came in. He is the perfect type to avoid suspicion — scholarly and countrified. Nobody would suspect him of anything. He is perfect, and you, cousin, are brilliant."

Darcy shook his head. He did not wish to involve Mr. Bennet in his activities, nor did he wish to mislead his cousin. "To the contrary."

"You deny brilliance? What is wrong with you, Darcy? I have never known you to refuse a compliment when it has been earned."

"That is not it at all—"

Richard interrupted. "Then let us not mince words about it. It is due in large part to your diligence that we have a chance at capturing our foe. Now, tell me what you and your secret informant have discovered. I know you are onto something, or else you would not have sent for me to come here."

Typical Richard. The man insisted Darcy speak but never shut up long enough to let him.

"Are you done?" Darcy asked drolly as he sauntered over to his safe.

Richard grinned. "I am all ears."

Darcy handed the satchel to him. "Take this with you. It is proof The Four Horsemen have dealings with Sir William. Given the exorbitant amount their deposits add to, I believe you were right to suspect that Sir William is at the center of their big plan."

"And I suppose you know where he is?"

"At an inn on the road to Epsom."

"There are a great number of inns there. Do you know which one?"

Darcy did not, and he hated how his mind immediately turned to the quickest way to find out. Mr. Bennet. Elizabeth.

Richard raised his eyebrows. "No matter. I know you will find out. Was that another morsel from your informant?"

Darcy glared at Richard.

He raised his hands. "Forget I said anything, and I will try to forget whom I saw leaving here and his connection to you. Tell me nothing more about your sources. You can trust that my lips are sealed."

"Impossible. But there is more I must tell you. It is the reason Sir William hired Mr. Robson."

Richard leaned forward in his chair.

Darcy continued, "Sir William has acquired a racehorse."

"Now, that is interesting. Why would he invest in a racehorse when he has a promising breeding farm going?"

"He bought Trophonius."

Richard's jaw dropped. "Black Trophonius? Winner of the 2000 Guineas and the Newmarket Stakes?"

"The very one."

Rubbing his chin with a long whistle, Richard said, "A three-year-old in his first racing season in the midst of a winning streak. Sir William must have paid a fortune. The timing is highly suspect. Trophonius is the favorite to win the Derby this coming Thursday. His odds are three to one."

"Aside from the investment, there are other obstacles which add to the mystery. The Derby is five days away. The Lucases know nothing about racing horses, and they are new to The Jockey Club's rules and regulations."

"Do you think they will be allowed to race? It seems impossible."

"And yet, they are staying at an inn on the way to the racetrack. I suspect their reasons for purchasing a horse practically guaranteed to win the Derby are strong enough, they would not hesitate to pay the club whatever price the officials named to allow them to participate."

Richard's eyes widened, and the color drained from his face. "You do not think—?"

Darcy nodded somberly. It had been his first suspicion as soon as Mr. Bennet had told him the name of Sir William's horse. As audacious as his suspicion seemed in his mind, he could not fully voice it aloud. "We cannot afford to overlook the possibility, however outlandish it seems."

Richard remarked, "When have The Four Horsemen ever been discreet?"

Rising from his chair, his posture rigid and alert, Richard added, "If you are right about this, Darcy — and I fear you are — I must insist you get to the bottom of this by any means necessary. We cannot afford a treason of this magnitude—" he stopped, finishing his sentence with a groan. "This is worse than I thought it would be. This is … this is anarchy."

Watching Richard draw the same conclusions he had minutes before impressed upon Darcy the gravity of the situation. This was not the stuff of a melodramatic novel. This was real. And it was up to him to prevent it.

Richard walked over to the door. He took a deep, shaky breath. "We have five days. We cannot fail. Use your informant to get close to Sir William. Find out where he is staying. Do not let him out of your sight until we can formulate a plan."

He left, the bottle of brandy unopened and forgotten.

ELIZABETH WAITED for her father in the parlor facing the street's corner, the book in her hand failing to hold her attention at the sound of every approaching carriage or footstep on the other side of the glass.

Where had Papa gone? He had left suddenly, only saying he had a call to make before he disappeared and offering no explanation or hints.

She tried to shrug off his whereabouts, but too

much time spent in solitude with an overly active imagination conjured up a bevy of possibilities. He had gone to purchase tickets to the theater. He had finally accepted an invitation from one of his university friends to call. He had a business matter to attend to and was taking advantage of their time in town to see to it. Or, more likely, he had heard of a new bookseller and wished to explore the shop at his leisure.

By the time a hackney carriage stopped in front of the hotel, Elizabeth expected to see her father carrying a stack of books in his arms. But he did not. He was smiling, however, so whatever he had done must have brought him some satisfaction.

Closing her book, Elizabeth met him in the entrance hall.

"There you are," he said, as if *she* had been the one wandering about London.

Elizabeth smiled. "Did you not expect me to be here?"

Papa chuckled. "It could not have been easy for you to stay behind while I went out, and now that my business has been seen to, I will not exclude you from any other outings."

"What business was that?" Elizabeth asked demurely.

He waved his hand flippantly. "Nothing to concern yourself with, my dear girl. Only a small matter between gentlemen."

"Between gentlemen?" She was more intrigued than ever. She knew he could not mean Mr. Darcy, but he was the first gentleman she called to mind. And, she had to admit, her father was not the only one she had been looking for through the parlor window.

What was it she felt for the gentleman? She hesitated to name it mere attraction. It felt more intense than anything she had felt before, and it grew in intensity with each passing day. Each passing hour. Even in his absence. Was that love? Could she love a man she had known for such a short time? What did she really know about Mr. Darcy?

There had been his description of Pemberley. His love for Pemberley was genuine, of that she was certain. Could he love her enough to think of her at his most treasured home?

Therein lay another problem. Elizabeth had wanted adventure so badly — as badly as Mr. Darcy wanted to return to Pemberley — she did not realize until her mother attempted to make her feel guilty for not securing a proposal from Mr. Darcy that she would not have minded receiving a proposal from him. She had not realized how deeply she had come to … esteem … respect … care for … love … the man who had brought adventure into her life. But which did she love more: the promise of excitement or the man? How could she be sure? And what if she did love Mr. Darcy only to find out he did not love her in return? After all, as her mother so plainly and repeatedly pointed out, he had gone.

Papa removed his pipe from his pocket, polishing the ivory bowl and tapping it against his palm. "Now, I am free to spend the day as you please. What would you most like to do? I am a servant to your whim," he said with a gallant bow of his head.

So lost in her own thoughts had Elizabeth been, she only then realized he had avoided answering her question. Why did he wish to hide the identity of the gentleman he called on from her? Was it worth pursuing the topic when she kept her thoughts of Mr. Darcy to herself? Hardly. Elizabeth let go of her curiosity with a chuckle, determined to give her dear papa her full attention. "You are in high spirits, and if you do not wish to tell me why, then I am content to enjoy your happy mood and attentiveness."

Papa bowed his head repentantly. "I know I have not been so attentive as a good father ought to be. I am poor company compared to Jane or the

Gardiners. I have not given you a proper season as you deserve—"

Elizabeth stopped him. "That was not what I meant to imply at all, Papa. I do not want to dwell on the past. It will only ruin today and any chance of a glorious tomorrow."

Folding her hands inside his, he said, "Allow me to do this one thing for you and ease the guilt on my old heart." His eyes misted, and his voice trembled. Clearing his throat and patting her hands, he said, "So, what is it to be? Do you wish to go to the theater tonight? Perhaps we might take a leisurely stroll down Bond Street? I hear the fashionable set like to eat ices at a place called Gunther's. We could try that."

Her father's willingness to please her brought tears to Elizabeth's eyes.

"I would love to do all of that, but do you know what would please me the most?"

He did not guess, so she continued, "I should very much like to walk with you to Hatchards. I asked the proprietor of this hotel, and he informed me that the bookshop is a comfortable distance to walk. Then, if we require nourishment for the return here, I should very much like to visit one of the chocolate shops nearby." She would have crammed her days with one activity after another, but she did not wish to overwhelm her father. Small steps.

"That sounds delightful. I will wait here while you fetch your pelisse."

Elizabeth wasted no time. Hastening upstairs, she tied the ribbon of her bonnet as she returned to her father.

He frowned when she drew near. "Where is your brooch? I had noticed you did not wear it yesterday, but I thought you did not want to risk losing it during our travels. It is odd to see you without it."

Elizabeth's pulse raced. She did not wish to explain how her brooch came to be lost, for then she would have to speak of Mr. Darcy, and she did not trust herself not to betray her sentiments regarding the gentleman to her father.

"I must have left it behind in all the excitement. We did leave in a hurry," she said vaguely. It had certainly been exciting when she had left her brooch behind. Every night when she closed her eyes, she relived the moment. She felt Mr. Darcy's closeness, the crispness of the breeze wisping between them, the magic of the moonlight bathing them in its glow… It was no wonder she had forgotten all about her brooch until the next day.

Her father's forehead wrinkled as he considered her explanation, but then, he shrugged and held his arm out for her. "Maybe we will make our way to Piccadilly. We can find you another one."

Elizabeth would not dream of replacing her treasure, but she smiled and took his proffered arm, content to spend the afternoon perusing bookshelves and glancing out of the window glass on the chance Mr. Darcy might walk past.

CHAPTER 23

$\mathcal{D}$arcy did his best to stay away from the Stratford Hotel. He and Oakley crossed the river, riding South along the road to Epsom, asking for Sir William, John Lucas, George Lucas, and even Trophonius at every stable and inn along the way … with no success.

Undaunted, he tried again the next day, but as the afternoon sped by with no sign of Sir William, Darcy had to admit defeat. The gentleman and his race-horse had vanished.

There was no way around it. Darcy would have to ask Mr. Bennet.

Even if he had found Sir William on his own, Darcy would have been hard-pressed to explain his appearance without mentioning the Bennets. He could not afford to arouse alarm this close to the

Derby, which was now only four days away, lest The Four Horsemen change their plans and escape capture yet again.

He had no other choice.

Knowing the desire of his heart was to see Elizabeth, Darcy took pains to ensure his motive for accepting Mr. Bennet's invitation to dine with them was not entirely selfish.

And so it was with eager footsteps and cautious, watchful eyes that he made his way to Oxford Street at the appointed hour.

The Stratford Hotel was a fine establishment in a respectable neighborhood not far from his own residence. The public dining room, furnished with several tables in which guests could converse and enjoy a meal, hummed with polite chatter when he entered the hall and the houseman took his coat, hat, and gloves.

He followed the man to a separate parlor where a table encumbered with flickering candles, crystalline wine glasses, gold-rimmed porcelain plates, and polished silver sat in the soft glow of the fireplace.

Mr. Bennet stood to meet him, and Darcy did his best to give the gentleman the attention his due. But it was difficult to look at anyone other than Elizabeth when she was in the room. She looked so lovely with her mouth open and her eyes wide, as if his presence was a most welcome surprise. Her smile reached her eyes, and Darcy's heart fluttered in his chest.

"How good of you to join us, Mr. Darcy. This is a pleasant surprise," Mr. Bennet said, leading him to the table where only two chairs were nestled cozily around the table. Mr. Bennet called for another to be brought.

"How did you know we were here?" Elizabeth asked. Clearly, she did not know her father had called at Darcy House the day before.

Mr. Bennet blushed, preoccupying himself with the even placement of the three chairs around the table.

Under the circumstances, Darcy felt it best for the gentleman to respond.

With a sheepish grin, Mr. Bennet said, "A happy coincidence helped us cross paths, and I saw fit to invite Mr. Darcy to dine with us — an invitation I am pleased he has graciously accepted."

Darcy was unsure what to make of the gentleman's secrecy, but he had enough secrets of his own to keep without bearing the burden of Mr. Bennet's. He would stay out of it as much as he could.

"Is the rest of your family in good health?" Darcy asked, aware of the need to include Mr. Bennet in his conversation.

"They are, I thank you for asking. You will be pleased to know that Mr. Bingley and his household are fully recovered from their illness. They had called a couple of times before we departed for town, and I daresay he, at least, has called once more since. Mrs. Bennet could not be happier."

Darcy could easily imagine so, especially when Mr. Bennet had already assured him of Mrs. Bennet's felicity during his call at Darcy House. However, Darcy had hoped Miss Bennet would be more pleased to receive Bingley's attentions than her mother. A week ago, Darcy would not have concerned himself in his friend's affairs, but that was before he understood the power of a young lady over a man's heart. He would find out for Bingley's sake. "And Miss Bennet? Is she as happy to receive his calls?"

It was a forward question he knew, but while Bingley's eye had led him to believe himself in love many times before, he had never truly fallen in love. His was a tender heart, easily hurt if the one lady to win his love did not wholly return his fondness.

Elizabeth replied, "You wish to discern my sister's sincerity in receiving Mr. Bingley's attentions?"

"I will own that is my intention. I saw firsthand how important your sister's welfare is to you. That which affects her happiness, affects you. I would do no less for Bingley. He is one of my dearest friends."

"Fair enough," said Mr. Bennet, looking to his daughter with a nod for her to expound on the subject.

"I cannot find fault with you protecting Mr. Bingley as I do Jane. She is often misunderstood because she is so shy. The more she feels, the less she says."

Hearing an explanation Darcy had uttered many times about his own sister eased his concerns. Miss Bennet was not indifferent. She was shy.

Elizabeth continued, "Jane hated falling ill at Netherfield. She worried about what you and Mr. Bingley's sisters would think of her. She could not bear to suffer criticism or be accused of using artful designs against him when she is too sincere and kind to act deceitfully. It was why she insisted on departing when we did." She clasped her hands and looked down at them. "And I will admit, Mr. Darcy, that while I find Mr. Bingley's character to be every-thing agreeable, I held some doubts about his constancy. I feared his fancy fickle. Suffice it to say, I was pleased to have him prove me wrong when he braved his sisters' disapproval and called shortly after we had quit Netherfield."

"His sisters do not have the advantage of tact or

delicacy. I hope they did not alter your sister's view of Bingley."

"No more than my mother and sister altered Mr. Bingley's view of Jane."

Mr. Bennet chuckled. "It would appear that both young people have been blessed with blinkers where their relations are concerned. They are fortunate, indeed, for every family has at least one ridiculous member."

Darcy thought of his aunt Lady Catherine de Bourgh. If she and Mrs. Bennet stood side-by-side, Darcy would find it difficult to select which one's company he would suffer from more. It was a humbling realization.

Unwilling to think of those who made him cringe, he changed to a more agreeable subject. "I have a sister who is as shy as you describe yours. She is but fifteen."

Mr. Bennet clucked his tongue. "A troublesome age. If she is as sensible as my Jane, then she will not give you too much trouble."

Darcy sympathized with him. If Georgiana acted like the two youngest Bennet daughters, he would be tempted to lock her in her room until she developed a modicum of sense.

"Is Miss Darcy at Pemberley?" Elizabeth asked.

Darcy's chest tightened. He cleared his throat.

"Not presently. She is with my aunt, who has two daughters about her age." He cleared his throat again. "I hope she will want to return to Pemberley with me once my business in town is done."

A shadow of sadness passed over Elizabeth's countenance, but she overcame it with a smile. "I am sure she will like that very much. Have you had success in arranging the affair which brought you to Hertfordshire?"

Mr. Bennet's eyebrows shot up.

For his benefit, Darcy explained, "I told Miss Elizabeth my reason for coming to Hertfordshire was to investigate a failed bet which I suspect was sabotaged. I will pay my debt and be done with the business, but I do not wish for another unsuspecting gentleman to fall into the same trap I did if I can expose the scoundrel." Lies tasted sour on Darcy's tongue. He took a sip of wine to wash it down, but the aftertaste lingered.

"I would not have taken you for a betting man," Mr. Bennet said.

"I am not usually." At least that was true. Darcy was not one to frequent the gambling houses. He could not help but think how hard his tenants worked for the same wage many gentlemen thoughtlessly squandered on one bet.

Mr. Bennet shrugged. "Ah, well, it is a gentlemanly pastime. I once indulged in a game of dice to see what it was all about. I won twenty guineas, then lost the entirety of my winnings within the next quarter of an hour. The whole experience was too volatile for my taste, and I have never cared to repeat it. When I think of the books I could have bought with that sum, it makes me ill."

Darcy laughed. He liked Mr. Bennet.

Mr. Bennet looked about. "They must be very busy in the dining parlor. I fear they have forgotten us. Pray give me one moment to remind them of our presence. I am getting an appetite." With a large grin at his daughter and Darcy, he left the room.

Darcy was alone with Elizabeth.

Fumbling in his pocket, he pulled out her brooch. "I am sorry I kept this for so long."

She covered his hand, pushing the brooch away.

His eyes fixed on their hands. Her fingers were long and thin, her palm narrower than his. Her skin was soft, and though her touch was gentle, the effect it had on him was not.

"Please, Mr. Darcy, will you keep it a while longer? If you return it to me now, I will have to explain to my father how it was lost ... and I think that is a conversation best kept between ourselves for now." She pulled her hand away.

Not knowing what else to do with himself, Darcy

did as she asked and put the brooch back into his pocket. "As you please," he mumbled.

"Thank you." Her lips captivated Darcy. He had not appreciated how perfectly formed her Cupid's bow was or how the corners curled upward at the edges. And her chin. Elizabeth had a strong chin (which often revealed her agreement or disagreement with its angle), but the point at the tip gave her a constantly impish, mischievous look. The urge to trace her chin with his finger grew, and Darcy clasped his hands together lest he give in to it.

She glanced toward the door her father had disappeared through. "My father does not know how to hurry," she said apologetically.

Darcy was not sorry.

She looked down at her lap, her eyelashes splaying over her cheeks. "I hope you do not think his invitation here an imposition."

Was she nervous? Did she doubt him?

"I would not have accepted had I thought so."

"You are kind."

"Not that kind. It is not my custom to act contrary to my instincts or imply agreeableness unless it is genuinely felt."

She looked up, her pupils rimmed in chocolate brown. "I am relieved to hear it," she whispered, nibbling on her bottom lip.

Mr. Bennet returned just then. "Our meal will arrive shortly. Apparently, some Lord something or other is dining in the main room, and he has kept the servants occupied with his many demands."

He resumed his seat, and pulled out his pipe to fiddle with, looking at it in his hands and guffawing. "I have this bad habit when I am nervous, Mr. Darcy. I believe I rub the ivory with my thumbs more often than I actually smoke from the thing. But I noticed I am in good company. I saw you do the same earlier with a timepiece ... or is it a compass?"

"It is a compass," Darcy said, pulling it out of his pocket and rubbing his thumb over the mono-grammed case. "It was a gift from my father. He gave it to me the day I left Pemberley for Eton — my first extended stay away from my family. I was anxious, and though I confided my fears in no one, my father knew." Darcy smiled at the memory. "He was a great man. And insightful. He took me aside the morning I was to depart, and he gave me a box wrapped with a green bow and lined with satin. Inside was this compass." He handed it to Mr. Bennet.

"Home is where the heart is," he read. "Pliny the Elder. A wise quote from a wise man."

Darcy smiled. "Pemberley was always a happy place. When my father gave me the compass, he told me it would always guide me home, to Pemberley. So long as I carried it in my pocket, I never felt lost."

Mr. Bennet handed the compass back. "How extraordinary you should carry a symbol of home with you always. My dear Lizzy has a brooch she usually wears, but I have long suspected that hers is a symbol of her desire to venture *away* from her home. I suppose Mr. Darcy had the right of it, my dear. Home is where the heart is."

Elizabeth jutted out her chin. "And who defines what home is? If home is where my heart is, then I can feel at home so long as I am with the people I love."

Her words knocked the breath out of Darcy's lungs. Had that been what his father had meant when he gave the compass to Darcy?

The food arrived, and as hearts and stomachs filled with good food and excellent company, Darcy found himself laughing and talking more than he had since he had sat around the table with his mother and father.

He felt as though he was at Pemberley.

CHAPTER 24

*D*arcy's heart was so light, he finally understood the expression "walking on the clouds." Or was it "head in the clouds?" Either one would do. The slightest gust of wind would send him floating into the heavens.

He waited in the entrance hall for the maid to bring his hat and coat. Soft laughter echoed in the hall. Candlelight flickered from the crystal chandelier above him and reflected on the mirrors flanking the room.

It was a perfect night. He had found out why Sir William had been so difficult to find. Fearing trouble for his newly acquired racehorse, he had checked in under an assumed name. John Smith (the same name from the incriminating ledgers) and his horse

Blacky. He and his two eldest sons were staying at The Golden Crown.

The Four Horsemen were within his grasp.

Brimming with hope, Darcy dreamed of his life after years trapped in a cloak-and-sword existence. He imagined riding over the fields at Pemberley with Elizabeth. He wanted to show her every inch of his family's legacy, knowing that not even Pemberley would feel like his home without her there with him. He understood that now.

He would show her his favorite places in England, and they could discover new places together. Then, when the war was over, he would show her the world. He would travel to places he had never seen before, not so much for a desire to see them, but so that he would have the joy of experiencing Elizabeth's wonder and delight.

He would give her what she wanted so long as she was with him. Their needs were not so different after all. She needed adventure. He needed her. It was so simple now, Darcy wondered how he had ever thought it complicated.

Bursting with optimism, Darcy peeked over to the busy dining room, wishing he could profess his happiness to the world, for such happiness must be shared.

Several met his gaze with smiles of their own, as one person's cheer often inspires cheer in another.

However, his gaze froze at a table in the back corner of the room where a gentleman sat alone. A gentleman Darcy would know anywhere. A gentleman who did not belong in the crowded hotel.

Sir Erasmus nodded at Darcy, his face devoid of expression, his eyes as dark as coals.

Darcy tensed, resenting how quickly the Horseman robbed him of his euphoria. There could be no light, no smiles or dreams while that man was free to use others' suffering for his own gain. He was a viper.

"Allow me to assist you with your coat, sir," the attendant said behind him.

Only then did Darcy break eye contact with Sir Erasmus. With a quick look toward the stairs to reassure himself that Elizabeth and her father, who had retired for the night, remained upstairs, he donned his coat and hat.

How had Sir Erasmus come to dine at the hotel the same night he had dined with the Bennets? Were The Four Horsemen and their lackeys onto him? He had been pursuing them for months, and they were not so foolish as to ignore threats to their evil empire. Had they followed him? Had he inadvertently led them to the Bennets?

Darcy's stomach lurched. If his real identity was laid bare, he was being watched, and, now, the Bennets were in danger. He would take no risks. He had to send help — another agent The Four Horsemen would not know — to watch over the Bennets at the hotel.

Careful to appear unaffected under the watchful stare of Sir Erasmus, Darcy kept himself from running up the stairs lest Sir Erasmus see confirmation of Elizabeth's importance to him. He would have to treat her like a stranger. He would have to distance himself.

Waiting until his carriage pulled up in front of the door, Darcy had a quick word with one of his footmen. The young man would remain behind to watch over the Bennets until Darcy arranged for more protection.

Darcy hopped inside the carriage and waited. If he was being followed, he wished to cause as much confusion and distraction as he could create.

When the carriage slowed at a crossing, Darcy saw his opportunity. Quietly, he slipped from the carriage. His coachman would continue as if nothing were untoward. He was accustomed to Darcy's ways and would alert Oakley, who would ensure that Wilson knew they were no longer unknown to their enemies. It was best to assume the worst and act accordingly. It meant Darcy could not accompany the Bennets to admire Sir William's horse, but that could not be helped. He had the information he required, and he only needed until Thursday to capture his prey.

Sticking to the shadows, Darcy walked, pulling his hat down and tugging his collar up. He would run, but that would only draw more attention to himself. His residence was not far.

He came to a street crossing. Looking about, he wished he could make better use of his senses over the sounds of carriages, clattering of horses, and boisterous dandies celebrating the late hour with their packs.

Two more streets, and Darcy House would come into view. He looked around again, hastening his step now that there were fewer passersby to take notice of him.

To the right was clear. The left, too.

Darcy turned to face forward, the hair on his arms prickling as the hairs rose. His pulse beat wildly. He looked left.

A sharp blade pressed against his exposed throat. "I would not turn if I were you, Mr. Darcy. One flick of my wrist, and you are a dead man." The voice was rough like gravel.

Darcy twisted, but the man held him fast.

"What do you want?" Darcy asked slowly. Was the man alone? Did he have another weapon? Could he overtake the man? He must be tall. That limited Darcy's options. If the man was taller than he was, butting his head back would be ineffective.

The blade dug into Darcy's flesh. A trickle of hot blood trailed down his neck. Wilson would be cross with him for staining his shirt again. Dirt was one thing, but blood was another matter.

The man pulled Darcy's left arm back, freeing his other side but giving Darcy no time to make use of it when he thrust Darcy's arm upward until his shoulder pierced in pain. "My boss wants you to quit interfering in his business. He saw you with that young lady and her father. It would be a pity if something were to happen to them."

Bone-deep terror gripped Darcy. "Your quarrel is with me. They are of no use to you."

"Ah, but methinks they are very useful. Back off, or I will hurt the girl."

"Not if I get to your boss first." Darcy could not allow the ruffian to think his threats had hit their mark. Slowly, he moved his free hand toward his pocket. If he could reach inside without being detected…

"You make one move against my boss, and she will pay for your mistake. When you think she is safe, we will strike. We will make you regret you ever tried to stop The Four Horsemen."

Darcy grabbed onto the chain of his fob. Dropping his compass so that it dangled from the end, he swung it around and let the compass fly at the face of his assailant.

He heard the thud and felt the sharpness of the blade dig into his neck. But the man's hold loosened around Darcy's arm. Wrenching himself free, Darcy pivoted around with his fist raised to strike a blow.

The man was taller than Darcy. His knuckles smashed and tore against the assailant's chin. However, Darcy could run with a throbbing hand much easier than the ruffian could with a swollen eye and a dislocated jaw.

He ran until Oakley met him on the sidewalk, pistol in hand.

"They are onto us," Darcy gasped, pressing his hand against his neck and praying he would not lose consciousness before he could send an agent to watch over Elizabeth and her father.

"I already told Wilson something was off. The coachman told us you left the footman behind and slipped out of the carriage on the way. What do you want us to do?"

Darcy kept moving, not stopping even when they

entered Darcy House, and Oakley noticed his injury. "Good Lord, Mr. Darcy. You need a surgeon."

Gritting his teeth and continuing up the stairs to his study, Darcy said, "I need you to deliver a message. Not to Richard. I do not know if he has been discovered yet, and I do not want to lead The Four Horsemen to him. Take it to Mr. Carton. He will know what to do."

Carton was the first step in Darcy's emergency protocol. He would be at home, but his clerk kept a room at his office for precisely this purpose. The clerk would hear the knock and see the note slipped under the door, and he would take it to his employer. He would keep Richard informed through Darcy's messages.

"Stay with me while I write the message, Oakley. We can lose no time," Darcy said, clenching his jaw when his heart cried out. "And bring Wilson to me. He will be my surgeon. I must consult with him on a matter of utmost importance." If his cover was unreliable, Darcy could not trust that The Four Horsemen would not know the identities of Leo's other agents. He needed a soldier. A trustworthy, trained soldier capable of watching over what Darcy could not protect.

He had endangered Elizabeth. She could die because of him — another tragic fatality through no fault of her own. It was his fault. He had thought he could be happy with her after this mess was resolved. He had deceived himself into thinking it could ever be resolved. He had hoped, and because he had let his guard down enough for Elizabeth to become a part of his life, he would have to be the one to disappoint her ... if she loved him. There were times he thought she did, but until he heard her say the words, he dared not believe. He would never hear them now. He had no right to.

God, what had he done?

Darcy steadied his hand and wrote a concise account of what had transpired, sealing the page and handing the note to Oakley to deliver to Carton. "Be cautious. You will likely be followed."

With a nod, Oakley departed. He would be swift.

That left only one more letter to write, and a guard capable of defending Elizabeth to find. Someone unassociated with Leo, someone unknown.

Wilson's uneven steps carried from the hall. Darcy wiped his knuckles with a clean handkerchief. The blood at his neck had dried enough to glue his collar to his neck. He could not move for fear of ripping the wound open again.

After his customary double knock, Wilson entered the room with a medicinal case and several towels in hand. A maid scurried in behind him, leaving a water pitcher and bowl on the edge of the desk.

On catching sight of Darcy, Wilson heaved a sigh. "You know how I hate cleaning blood, but I would rather scrub a shirt than bury you, Mr. Darcy. Oakley spoke to me, and I see for myself that the tide has shifted against us. Tell me what I can do while I clean you up, and I will see it done."

"Thank you, Wilson. I do have something I cannot trust with anyone else." He paused, the ache in his heart consuming him. "And something I am not brave enough to do even if I were able to."

"I doubt that, but it will be an honor for me to be of service," Wilson said, calmly pouring water over a linen cloth and holding it against Darcy's collar.

Wilson's faith in Darcy deepened his wound. His worst fear had been realized. He had made Elizabeth a target. Honor, justice, and decency demanded that Darcy sever all connections to her. But writing that letter would kill a part of him he had only recently found. With her, he felt complete. Without her, he would be lost.

His future was determined. He would not return to Pemberley. He could not burden Georgiana with his grief. She would be better off remaining with their aunt than with her shell of a brother. He would continue working for Leo until he drew his last breath.

If Darcy could never be free, he would fight for Elizabeth's freedom. He would make sure England was a safe place for her to travel. He would smooth the way for her to travel the world.

Darcy would see her happy from afar. It would have to be enough.

He pulled another sheet of paper toward him and began writing.

CHAPTER 25

*E*lizabeth slept a little later than normal the next morning. With such delicious dreams, she was not in a hurry to wake.

Fitzwilliam Darcy. Fitzwilliam. Last night, even before her dreams, he had been charming and interesting and … exciting. She could have talked with him for hours. Her father had been enchanted with his company as well, conversing at length about his favorite topics, to which Fitzwilliam replied with greater insight and more passion and conviction than even Elizabeth could have envisioned. It was a side of him she looked forward to drawing out.

Washing her face and dressing, Elizabeth took her second volume of Pinkerton's travels down to the front parlor where she could reread the sections on Derbyshire with a cup of tea. She did not expect Fitzwilliam to call so early in the morning, but she would not mind it if he did. Hope reigned eternal, and she chose to sit at the small table placed in front of a window overlooking the street.

Captivated by Mr. Pinkerton's description of Derbyshire, which came alive to her now that she heard Fitzwilliam's baritone reading it, Elizabeth was startled when a maid approached.

"There is a man to see you, Miss," she said.

Elizabeth's heart leapt into her throat. How had she missed him? Some sentinel she was!

She followed the maid's gaze to the entrance hall where a man stood. It was not Fitzwilliam. It was Wilson. He held his hat in his hands and stared down at the carpet.

Her heartbeat slowed. Was something wrong? Where was Fitzwilliam?

Leaving her book on the table, Elizabeth rose. "Thank you. I will see him," she muttered to the maid.

Wilson bowed his head, his stance repentant. "Good morning, Miss Bennet," he said, his eyes flickering upward to meet hers before returning to their downcast position.

Elizabeth's fingers reached for her brooch, settling for fiddling with her fichu when the familiar stones were not there to soothe her. "Good morning, Wilson. Is all well?"

He lifted a folded, sealed paper. "I was asked to deliver this. It is not my place to interfere, but—" He shook his head, his cheeks bunching up. "But I wish for you to know how difficult this was for Mr. Darcy to pen."

Elizabeth stared at the letter, alarm stirring her stomach. She did not want to take the letter, but neither could she expect Wilson to stand in the entrance hall all day.

She took the missive, not knowing what to say.

Wilson looked at her, his soft gray eyes imploring. "Would that life were just, Miss Bennet. Would that the people who most deserve happiness could attain it." With a quick bow, he whispered, "Good day to you. God bless you," and limped away.

Tongue-tied and feet-frozen, Elizabeth stood in the middle of the floor until people started trickling into the parlor from their chambers. Her cheeks burned and her eyes clouded, but she smiled and nodded to them until she closed the door of her room behind her.

Hands trembling, she opened the letter.

Miss Bennet, it began. She had hoped to see an endearment. "Dear Miss Bennet" would have been satisfactory. "Dearest Miss Elizabeth," even better.

"My Dearest Elizabeth" better still. "Miss Bennet" was too impersonal. Too distant.

She crumpled onto the edge of her bed and continued reading.

MISS BENNET,

I REGRET *to inform you that I must depart from London immediately. I will not bore you with details. It is enough to tell you that decisions I have made in the past do not allow me the freedom to live as I would wish. The blame is mine, and I accept it fully. I have been selfish, and for that I must beg your forgiveness knowing how undeserving I am.*

Goodbye, Miss Bennet.
Pray forgive me. Pray forget me.
Forever Yours, Faithfully,
Fitzwilliam Darcy

HER HAND DROPPED to her lap, limp. *Forever yours, Faithfully.* How could he write that after telling her to forget him? Did the ease with which he begged her to dismiss him from her heart suggest she was so easily forgotten?

Elizabeth looked about the room, but if the answers were there, she did not see them. She hardly saw anything at all. She did not feel anything. A void swallowed her whole, leaving her empty and more alone than she had ever been.

The man who had given her a taste of the life she had always wished had snatched her heart away, and now he wanted to return it?

Hot tears spilled down her cheeks as her anger rose.

He said he had been selfish. Elizabeth looked down at the page, taking note of how many times "I" was written. "I" cursed every sentence. If Fitzwilliam was so concerned about her, he had an odd way of showing it by writing a note focusing solely on himself.

Granted, his focus was on his faults (which no genuinely selfish man would do), but all Elizabeth could see was that cursed letter "I."

He did not bother to offer an explanation. The nerve! He claimed it would bore her as if he understood her better than herself. As if she were like Miss Bingley. What a pompous, arrogant brute!

She crumpled the paper in her hands, the creased wads and folds piercing her palm. The dreadful note would not disappear no matter how tightly she squeezed it.

Oh, she could strangle Fitzwilliam Darcy! How dare he presume to order her about as if he were the master of her emotions!

Unless…

Was it possible there was a perfectly reasonable explanation? The prior evening had been marvelous. Elizabeth had imagined how it would feel to spend every night in thoughtful conversation and meaningful gazes with Fitzwilliam. She was convinced it had been real for him, too. He had shared stories of his youth, of growing up at Pemberley with a loving mother and father. He had spoken of his little sister, whom it was clear he missed dearly. That had been real. More real than the letter balled up in her fist.

She uncurled her hand, folding out the letter and smoothing the paper. Had she missed something?

No, there was nothing more to see. If only she had read it in front of Wilson, she would have insisted he tell her what had happened between dinner last night and this morning. Something had happened. Fitzwilliam had to have a reason — and it had better be a very good one — for writing such a horrible letter. For saying goodbye and trying to convince her to forget his existence.

Well, the damage was done. She could no sooner forget Fitzwilliam and erase his impact on her life than she could forget Charlotte or Jane or her own father. He was a part of her whether he wished to be or not, and she would not be dismissed with a letter. A gentleman would have told her directly, not sent his valet to deliver a message … no matter how difficult said message had been for him to write. Had he told Wilson to put in a good word for him?

She dismissed the thought. Fitzwilliam may not have acted as she would have preferred, but he was not devious. She would not berate his character until she understood his reason for distancing himself. She had to know. Otherwise, (she swallowed hard) she would never be able to accept that he truly wished her to forget him. It would haunt her. This need went beyond her normal curiosity. It was necessary.

But what could she do? She could not call at Darcy House. Nor could she invite him to dine with her and her father again so soon, and certainly not without arousing Papa's suspicions. He had already exerted himself so much to give her an adventure away from Longbourn, she could not repay his kindness by turning her attention to another.

Steady enough to stand, Elizabeth walked over to the wash basin. Dipping her handkerchief in the cool water, she pressed the soft linen against her face. Once the redness in her eyes disappeared (mostly), leaving a brightness she doubted her father would notice, she placed the hateful letter inside her book, which she placed inside her trunk. She had no desire to read either of them again, but something prevented her from tossing the cursed page into the fire.

She opened her door just as her father was about to knock on it.

"Perfect timing," he said with a happy grin, lowering his fist and extending his arm gingerly. He patted her hand when she wrapped her arm through his. He was in an exceptionally good mood.

"I am famished. Let us see if the breakfast is as delicious as dinner was," he said, leading her into the main dining room. "Let us join the other guests. We can watch them and poke fun at their odd habits and extravagant fashions." His eyebrows wiggled, and Elizabeth caught herself smiling when she followed his line of vision to a woman wearing a stuffed bird on her shoulder.

Papa whispered into Elizabeth's ear, "I am sorely tempted to say 'Ar, me matey,' as we pass. Or perhaps, I would do better to offer her bird a cracker? What do you say, Lizzy?"

Elizabeth began to see the difficulty before her. She felt miserable — somewhere between wretched and vengeful — and yet, she must pretend to be happy for her father's sake. Without humor, she lacked her customary wit, and she was certain he would notice that before he noticed the red rimming her eyes.

"I must be as hungry as you, Papa, for I cannot settle on a retort worthy of such a sight." Of all the excuses she could have given! Now, she would have to eat when she had absolutely no appetite.

He smiled and patted her hand again. "I will see if they have any chocolate, then. That will do the trick. I find chocolate appeases the soul as well as it satisfies the stomach."

"That sounds delicious," Elizabeth said, meaning it.

Settling at a table for two, Papa requested a banquet.

"Papa, I do not know how we shall fit all of that food on the table, let alone eat it," Elizabeth said, her smile feeling less forced as she focused on her father to the exclusion of everything else. If she could only go the entire day without thinking of Fitzwilliam, she would manage.

"Your mother is so worried about my health, she insists I avoid certain foods that I, as a result of her prohibition, particularly crave. It is my intention while I am away to partake of as many sausages, pastries, and so-called unwholesome foods as I can."

Elizabeth raised her cup of chocolate, the rich

aroma teasing her nostrils. "I will drink to that. Why do we always want that which we cannot — or should not — have?"

Father sighed. "Human nature. Dissatisfaction has been passed down from one generation to the next, intensifying with each passing, I think. Which is why we must find happiness where we can. We must latch on to it, for it is precious."

The conversation was taking a serious turn.

He laughed. "Your mother is a testament to tenacity regarding her happiness. She determined that I was the one to make her happy, and Lord love her, she did not give me a moment's peace until I relented and proposed."

"And have you been happy?" Elizabeth asked, setting down her cup.

He considered for some time, then said, "I believe from the depths of my heart that I am as happy with her as I could have ever been with anyone else. She gave me a son and five healthy daughters. She manages our household as well as she can, and she allows me more freedom to pursue my own interests than I deserve. Your mother is very good to me." He paused, his eyebrows drawing together until he nodded. "I can do better by her. She loves shiny baubles and fluffy fripperies. Would you help me select a gift to bring back to Longbourn for her?"

Elizabeth smiled. "She would love that."

Leaning back in his chair, he said, "This has proved to be an eventful trip so far. I can hardly wait to see what else transpires. Take Mr. Darcy, for example. He was exceptional company, do you not agree?" He sipped his tea, squinting his eyes at her through his fogged spectacles.

"I enjoyed his conversation very much." Her tightening throat did not permit a longer reply, nor did she wish to encourage her father in this topic. It made her chocolate taste bitter.

"So well-informed, and his ability to defend his views was admirable. And yet, I would not describe him as close-minded. I felt his rapt attention where our views differed, and I will admit that while we were not like-minded in some areas, I still felt that his heart was every bit as sincere and as passionate as mine in defending my opinions. It was refreshing."

Elizabeth reached for her chocolate with every intention of hiding behind her cup.

Papa added, "I am of a mind to call again at Darcy House."

Her fingers fumbled around her cup, spilling some of the chocolate onto the tablecloth. "Call *again*?" she squeaked.

Papa looked as though she had caught him

sneaking into Longbourn's pantry to eat something Mama would certainly disapprove of. "About that. I told you I had chanced upon Mr. Darcy, and while that is true, it is not the complete truth." In a quieter voice, he said, "A gentleman is far more likely to 'chance' upon another if he calls on him at his residence."

She stared at her father, stunned.

He continued, "I noticed how out of sorts you were when you quit Netherfield Park. So, I asked Emily—"

Elizabeth dropped her head into her hands and groaned. "What did she say?"

"Only that she was convinced that you and Mr. Darcy seemed well-suited to each other."

She prayed that was all Emily had said.

"Do you love him, Lizzy?"

She lowered her hands from her face. Papa's eyes looked like shattered glass, shimmering and fragile. How could she tell him that she loved a man who wanted her to forget him? But she did love Fitzwilliam. And she would not lie to her father about it.

Nodding, she simply breathed, "Yes."

His chin quivered, but his voice was bolder, braver. "And so it begins. I had never thought I would lose you, dear girl, but I could not give you up to a better man. It is clear to me, especially after last night, that he adores you. As he ought to. I could not approve otherwise."

Hearing her father praise Fitzwilliam when she wanted nothing more than to think of anything but him was the worst torture. Pretending to be happy when she was miserable and confused would be a formidable challenge, but she was determined for her father's sake — and her own — to hold herself together.

Their breakfast arrived, and fortunately for Elizabeth, Papa was distracted from further conversation by the delights crowding the small table. She pushed food around her plate and tried not to think of Fitzwilliam.

Finally, when he had eaten his fill, he rubbed his hands together. "I apologize for the lack of conversation, Lizzy. I have been deep in thought, and I believe I have come up with a promising theory. It is no secret that I do not often agree with Mrs. Bennet's methods, and so, I am tempted to treat Mr. Darcy very differently from how she is enticing Mr. Bingley to Jane. While she stays at home and waits for him to call, making Jane an easy catch, I believe an opposite approach is more suitable for Mr. Darcy. He seems to be more of a sporting man, a gentleman who enjoys the chase more than he triumphs in achieving his prize."

Elizabeth chafed. "I am not a fox to be caught, Papa."

"Of course not. Please forgive my overenthusiastic use of the hunting metaphor, but the idea is similar enough to prompt its use. You are my favorite daughter, and if I can in any way ensure that your happiness lasts, then I would like to see if my theory works in your favor."

"Thank you, Papa," Elizabeth started, shaking her head, "but—"

"But nothing." He rubbed his hands together, the twinkle returned to his eyes. "Of what use is it for me to hypothesize if I never test my theories? I have dozens, if not hundreds, of them I have never tried to prove, and if I am to begin now, it might as well be with a theory which will benefit you."

She knew she would regret it, but Elizabeth said, "What is it you plan?" Only in a bookshop had Elizabeth seen her father so excited.

He rubbed his hands again. "I am glad you asked. We shall make ourselves scarce. If Mr. Darcy is sincere in his affections, he will pursue you. The effort he must exert on your behalf will strengthen his love. Years from now, when you have a squabble over some trifling matter, he will remember how hard he worked to win your heart. He will remember how precious you are, and his upset will subside. You, in turn, will remember his exertions, and you will not be able to remain cross with him for very long. You will appreciate each other all the more for having endured a ... strenuous ... courtship."

"You make it sound like we will spend all our time fighting."

He grinned. "You will, but if you are wise, you will learn to make the most of it." Clearing his throat, his cheeks pink, he added, "We will join Sir William later today. Then, I think, we shall quit London for a spell. We will give Mr. Darcy a bit of a chase." Papa stabbed a piece of potato with his fork and popped it into his mouth, chewing gleefully.

A chase. Elizabeth tingled with anticipation despite her misgivings.

CHAPTER 26

A sign rimmed with gold-colored paint distinguished The Golden Crown from the other hip-roofed shops and residences along the road leaving London for Epsom. Two dormers peeked through the rusty bricks on their upper floors like a pair of gossips spying through their windows at the lane.

Sir William clapped Papa on the back. "It is good to see friends." Dropping his voice, he added, "I fear I will have no peace until Blacky—" He winked markedly. "—is secured at Lucas Lodge. Allow me to remind you to address me as Mr. Smith. We do not want to risk drawing attention to ourselves."

Elizabeth felt as if she was watching Sir William enact a scene from a melodramatic novel with his grave, cloak-and-sword manners. Sir William — mysterious spy. Now, that was a diverting image! She imagined him with a large mustache and an eye patch. He would befriend both friends and foes, but his cover would be blown the second someone mentioned St. James, whereupon he would forget his disguise to relive his glory days.

She bit her lips together. Sir William could never act in deceit purposely, nor was he capable of injuring anyone … not even a villain. She stifled a chuckle as she imagined Sir William stopping in the midst of a duel to ask permission to strike the evil fiend down.

Papa played along nicely. Squeezing Sir William's shoulder, he said, "You may trust us to keep your identity secret, Mr. Smith." He tapped his nose, to which Sir William nodded somberly and tapped his nose in turn.

Elizabeth tapped her nose for good measure, receiving a nod of approval from Sir William and an exaggerated roll of the eyes from George, who said, "Would you like to see…" He scowled, adding reluctantly, "…Blacky?"

Sir William took a deep breath, his voice piercing. "He is hardly worth crossing to the stables to see. Such a temperamental brute." After a look around the room to ensure his resounding proclamation was overheard, Sir William gave them the clear to leave.

If anyone had not thought to doubt his true identity, or that of his horse, they certainly did now.

George fell in beside Elizabeth. "My father has been insufferable since we fetched the stallion. He is so afraid someone will attempt to steal his prized racehorse he has had us all use assumed names, and he disparages his champion at every opportunity."

"I am surprised nobody at the inn has offered to take him off your father's hands."

"One gentleman did offer, but Father pretended not to hear him."

Elizabeth laughed. "And how are you faring, Mr. Smith? What do Mrs. Smith and the little Smithlings think of your new acquisition?"

George grumbled, "Smith, of all names. I do not believe my father gave the matter much thought before he selected the surname."

She heard the embarrassment in his tone and could no longer tease him. "To his credit, it is a common name."

"Commonly used by criminals and those who wish to hide who they are."

"Anyone who spent more than five minutes with Sir William could never believe him of that sort."

"True, though he unwittingly does his best to arouse suspicions. I think Mr. Robson has worn off on him."

Elizabeth did not look forward to seeing the trainer again. "I had forgotten he would be here, but of course he would wish to protect his new pupil. Is he as disagreeable as he was the other night?"

George looked at her askance. "You have to admit the circumstances were suspect, Miss Elizabeth. The hour was late, and your excuse sounded rather far-fetched to believe … even for me."

Elizabeth shrugged. She was not about to explain that night to him when she did not completely understand it herself — when it brought up thoughts of Fitzwilliam.

Would he follow her as Papa thought he would? Did she want him to after he had said goodbye in a letter? A letter! Who did that? He ought to have told her in person … unless he had not been able to meet her and a letter was his only option. Perhaps he had come to harm. Maybe he was not able to settle his affairs to satisfaction with the dishonest gentleman and his henchman.

In the blink of an eye, her anger turned to concern as the justifications excusing Fitzwilliam's behavior piled up, constructing a tower of wishful thinking that had no other option but to topple over for lack of a solid structure. She could make a million excuses for Fitzwilliam, but all she needed was the one answer he had denied her.

Did he not trust her? Did he not care?

Elizabeth's eyes burned, and she told herself it was pure anger causing her upset. Anger was easier than hurt.

"Are you well, Miss Elizabeth?" George asked, his eyes full of concern.

She was not well at all, and she was wounded enough at that moment to wish Fitzwilliam was as miserable as he had made her, too. Not that she would explain that to George.

Would that Fitzwilliam had spoken with her directly. In sending a letter, she had been deprived of the opportunity to demand an explanation. Or, had that been his purpose, cowardly though it sounded? She could not believe him a coward. He had not recoiled when a bullet ran through his hat. His first thought had been for her safety. He had shielded her with his own body. He had gone without his valet for her and Jane's benefit. Hardly the acts of a careless coward.

Elizabeth was too conflicted to be well. "I wish Charlotte was here," she replied.

"She will be shortly. John does not know, but Father is traveling to Lucas Lodge on the morrow to fetch the rest of our family and return in time for the race."

Elizabeth's spirits rose. Epsom was not far from London, but — she recalled, her spirits falling — Meryton was another half a day's ride beyond London. It would be an arduous journey for Sir William. "He must really want all of his family there."

"He insists on making it himself. I offered to go in his stead, but he says I am needed here to keep John from discerning his plan, knowing he would not approve, and to keep an eye on … Blacky."

Elizabeth smiled in earnest. Her father had already suggested they quit town. Perhaps they would go to Epsom. Charlotte would help her see things more clearly. "His secret is safe with me. The distance is nothing when one has a motive."

Papa came to an abrupt stop at the entrance of the stables, his shoulders hunched up to his ears.

Had she not been wallowing in her own troubles, she would have had more compassion for her father before. She would have been at his side already, knowing how difficult it would be for him to set foot inside a stable when he had avoided horses for so long. She went to him, wrapping her hands around his arm and leaning against him, wishing she could absorb some of his fear.

"I had thought I could manage it, but I … I

cannot. This is as far as I can go." His voice shook, and he tried to cover it over with a smile and a pained chuckle. "Given the animal's name, I suspect his coat is black. What else do I need to see when I am sure he is a fine specimen?"

Elizabeth's curiosity to see the stallion dissipated under her need to comfort her father. "I will stay with you."

Sir William huffed and puffed. "I dare not have … Blacky brought out for everyone to see. Rest assured, he is safe in his stall."

It was not the horse's safety her father feared. Who knew what horrible recollections had been dredged up to torment him already?

Papa squeezed Elizabeth's hand against his side, holding her to him. "You should go, Lizzy. We have come all this way. I do not mind, only take caution. Pray be careful."

She looked down at his grip on her hand. His knuckles were as white as his face. She could not leave him.

George moved to his other side, shielding his view of the offensive building. "If I ensure all the other horses are tied up or inside their stalls, would you agree to come in, Mr. Bennet?"

Elizabeth watched her father struggle between

the present and his memories. He had changed so much over the past few days, making choices where he had sought solace in avoidance before. If he could just walk inside a stable, then perhaps, some of his fears would loosen their hold on him.

"If you do not feel safe, then I will return with you," Elizabeth said, holding her breath and trying not to place too much importance on this moment.

Her father nodded reluctantly, and George lost no time running inside to secure the lodgers. Sir William paced and smiled encouragingly at Papa.

Elizabeth cradled her father's hand between her own. He was cold, but there was a determined set to his jaw she had not often seen from him in her lifetime.

After some time, George returned. "The groom made sure all the horses are tied, and they will remain so until we depart. Blacky is in his stall with Mr. Robson and Joe holding him with a halter." He extended his hand. "Are you ready, Mr. Bennet?"

Papa took his arm, keeping his eyes fixed on the ground in front of him as he placed one foot in front of the other. He was going to try.

Elizabeth thought she would burst with pride.

Sir William pranced ahead of them, spinning in place and bobbing up and down on his toes with his thumbs tucked into the pockets of his waistcoat until he paused in front of a closed stall. "This is Blacky." Looking about and lowering his voice, he added, "He is a beauty, is he not?"

Elizabeth could not spare a glance until her father looked up. Uncertain how he would react at seeing the trainer and stable boy in the stall with the stallion, she breathed an immense sigh of relief when he seemed to relax at her side.

"As gentle as a pussy cat," Joe said, rubbing one hand down the horse's neck.

Trophonius was the handsomest horse Elizabeth had ever seen. His ebony coat shone in the light peeking through the narrow window above. His mane was brushed and his hooves polished. From his muscled shoulders, down his long back to his sinewy thighs, he was built for speed. "He is perfect," she whispered in awe.

Mr. Robson, who had worn a scowl, almost appeared to smile at her favorable assessment. Joe grinned happily at Trophonius' other side, proud to stand beside the famous racehorse.

Elizabeth resisted the urge to lift her hand to the bars. Her father was inside the stables, and she would not do anything to cause him to regret it.

Sir William rambled about "Blacky's" finer

points, until Mr. Robson cleared his throat. "Miss Elizabeth, if I may have a word. I wish to apologize for my behavior the last time we met."

Elizabeth was stunned. "Think nothing of it, Mr. Robson. My timing was abominable."

"Ay, that it was. However, Mercer explained to me how often you used to frequent the stables, how he taught you to ride along with Sir William's children. He praised not only your skill, calling you an accomplished equestrienne but, what is even more remarkable to one such as I — whose life revolves around these marvelous creatures — he praised your understanding of the horses you ride. You challenge them without abusing. You notice when they are not up to their normal standard and tell the groom, thus allowing him to see to the health of his charge." He bowed his head. "Mercer is a trustworthy man. He would not say these things about you unless they were true, and so I apologize for accusing you of spying on me with that other gentleman."

"Other gentleman?" Papa asked.

Elizabeth cringed. She had not told him about the brooch, and now it looked as though she would have to explain everything to him anyway … after blatantly avoiding the topic earlier. "Mr. Darcy. He accompanied me to fetch my brooch."

Her father raised an eyebrow. "The one you said you left at Longbourn?"

She gave him a nervous smile.

He patted her hand. "You can explain the whole of it to me later. Now," he turned to Sir William, "I am curious how you came to possess this fine animal."

Elizabeth's pride tempered her remorse. Now that her father had ventured where he had not dared go in a decade, he seemed determined to extend his visit beyond a mere passing through. It was far more than she could have dreamed was possible.

Sir William was happy to explain, and he did so with great alacrity and attention to detail, mentioning as many important names as he could in his narrative. The only one Elizabeth recognized was a Sir Erasmus, but she could not remember where she had heard the strange name before. Probably from Sir William himself.

She was more interested in Trophonius. She enjoyed seeing how Mr. Robson took Joe under his wing, treating him more like an apprentice than an errand boy.

Her father asked, "And where is John? I had thought to see him here."

Instinctively, Elizabeth looked about the stables.

Sir William blustered, so George answered for

him. "He is probably with his set, which is for the best. He has been in a surly mood of late."

Papa raised his eyebrows in question. "I imagine it would weigh heavily on a gentleman to possess such a magnificent racehorse."

George said in a low tone, "I fear he has already bet a substantial amount on him to win the Derby."

Sir William chuckled. "An investment, my dear boy. Why should John not wager on our stallion when he is certain to win? The odds are markedly in his favor."

George clamped his mouth shut and stared straight ahead.

Elizabeth sympathized with him. Gambling was never a wise investment, nor was any horse a sure win when so many things could go wrong between now and the race. As had happened to Fitzwilliam. The thought rankled her mind. He and Mr. Lucas were nothing alike, and while she believed Mr. Lucas capable of gambling away a fortune without regard for the consequences, she could not accept it to be true of Fitzwilliam.

"When is the race?" Papa asked.

"Three days hence, on Thursday," Sir William replied proudly, his face lighting up as he added, "You should come! We would be delighted for you to witness our first race along with us, would we not, George?"

Papa, no doubt having had enough of the stables, set foot in the direction of the doors. "Lizzy and I would enjoy that very much. She has never been to a race before, and Epsom Downs is a lovely bit of country." Looking down at Elizabeth with a gleam in his eyes, he said, "I think Epsom will suit our purpose perfectly."

It would take a miracle for Fitzwilliam to find out they had gone to Epsom, much less chase her there. She dearly wished to speak with him — to know once and for all if there was some explanation for his behavior. Something she could believe. She wanted to trust him. Her inclination told her she could. But that sliver of uncertainty chafed against her perception.

A movement in the last stall caught her attention. Once their party had passed, a man spun deftly out of the stall to walk in the opposite direction. She recognized his face.

Turning around, she was prevented from calling after him when Sir William exclaimed, "I have had the most splendid idea! Please say you will join us to dine at the inn tonight. John will be here, and I am certain your company will improve his spirits."

Her father accepted, and the gentlemen made

plans while Elizabeth looked back toward the stables.

The man was gone, but Elizabeth was certain she recognized Oakley accurately. Two men could not possess the same crooked nose. It had to be him.

What was Fitzwilliam's groom doing at the stables?

CHAPTER 27

*E*lizabeth's father listened with rapt attention to her explanation for the events she ought to have confided in him earlier. Leaving the emotion out of her telling to describe the facts as they had happened, her apprehension grew. What if she had read too much into Fitzwilliam's conversation and actions? His had been the reaction of a gentleman. Would he have done the same for any lady? Was she no more special to him than any other? Was that why he had sent the letter?

She traced her fingertips over her lips, trying to remember if she had really felt his breath feather against her skin or if she had imagined it. Did absence make the heart grow fonder ... or forgetful? If only she could converse with Charlotte. Her friend's vision was never clouded by emotion, unlike Elizabeth, who felt herself in a fog.

Papa, believing that all young ladies should find themselves crossed in love, was of no help at all. Elizabeth supposed she ought to take comfort in his decision to persist in his theory, but he also brushed off Fitzwilliam's excessive gambling when she could not so easily dismiss it. The shot in the field was not so easy for him to dismiss, though Elizabeth took care to provide only the scantiest detail and most minimal risk to herself. She elaborated on the lengths Fitzwilliam went to in securing her and Jane's safe return to Longbourn, but she took little satisfaction in it. Any gentleman would have done the same.

Her father went silent for some time, but upon deciding it was best not to dwell on what could have happened, he chose to dwell on what brought him pleasure. Elizabeth had not been harmed, and he was enjoying his time in London all the more now that he had a theory to prove.

Elizabeth exerted herself to be good company for her father as they left the hotel to stroll through Hyde Park, observing the passersby as much as they did the scenery — Papa for entertainment; Elizabeth in an attempt to not think of Fitzwilliam. At least she had a clearer conscience now. She kept no secrets from her father (aside from the near kiss she now questioned, that is.)

They ate ices at Gunter's, sitting by a window. Elizabeth's neck prickled and her cheeks warmed like they did when someone tried to catch her attention from the other side of an assembly room. She glanced around, but nobody met her eye.

When offered the chance to return to Hatchards to peruse his favorite section of books on philosophy and horticulture, Papa decided that if he were to purchase a gift for Mama, they had better head to Covent Garden before the good intention faded into inaction.

The piazza and surrounding streets bustled with basket-women hawking their wares, costermongers selling fruit, vegetables, and fried eels, market boys pushing wheelbarrows, and pedestrians trying to cross through without trampling on anyone's toes or losing the coins in their pockets.

Several times more, the prickling at her neck had Elizabeth turning to look over her shoulder, but with so many people milling about, it was no wonder. Her imagination was once again at work, creating excitement where there was none.

She shook her head. No excitement? At Covent Garden? What was wrong with her? Was she so restless not even London could satisfy her craving for adventure? Was somebody watching her or not? Was her imagination trustworthy or misguided? This uncertainty was driving her mad.

She grasped for a rational explanation and nearly laughed in relief when she settled on Oakley.

Of course! The sight of Oakley at the stables earlier that morning had set her dreaming. Where Oakley was, Fitzwilliam was certain to be nearby.

Elizabeth groaned inwardly. That was her answer. She had not been hoping to see some stranger following her. That would have been unnerving, and she did not feel scared. No, she had been looking for Fitzwilliam. It was not excitement she craved. It was him. She missed him.

Melancholy slowed her steps and calmed her smile. When Papa proudly purchased a fan with a handle embellished with mother of pearl for Mama, Elizabeth thought she would cry.

Fortunately, Papa was too distracted getting them away from a persistent flower-girl pushing a bunch of violets into his back, until he finally gave in and bought the blooms, to notice Elizabeth's deteriorating merriment. If only she could stop looking over her shoulder. After so many unsuccessful turns and side glances, she began to fret that she would never see Fitzwilliam again. That perhaps he *had* meant every word of his letter. That he had departed from London. That it had *not* been Oakley at the stables, but merely a flaxen-haired man with a remarkably crooked nose just like his.

She had no appetite by the time they reached the inn. The warmth, laughter, and smells of beef stew and freshly baked bread wafting from the kitchen did not soothe her. Not when she could not help search the room for Fitzwilliam and face another disappointment when he was not there.

When her father suggested they pack their things to leave the hotel for The Golden Crown, she did not object.

Travel offered a brief respite, and Elizabeth endeavored to appease her bruised heart and uneasy mind with her father's eagerness to please her and with Sir William's jovial reception later that evening.

"I am sorry John and George could not join us this evening. John had some pressing matters in town, and George is with the horse." Dropping to a whisper, he added, "We cannot be too cautious, you know?"

"Your company is pleasant enough to make up for their absence, Sir— ahem, I mean to say, Mr. Smith." Papa looked about the room. "It is quite crowded here tonight."

Sir William blustered, his face beaming bright red. "Yes, I had not accounted for how many would be staying here on their way to the Epsom Derby. You were wise to request rooms when you did."

Elizabeth had seen the sea of strange faces, but so intent was she on who was *not* there, she had not thought to question the presence of so many people.

Casting a weary glance about, Sir William leaned closer. "Poor timing, indeed. Had I been able to use my status freely, I should have been able to secure a private room in which to dine with facility. However, as I am only Mr. Smith, I am afraid a small table against the far wall was the best I could do."

Papa squeezed his neighbor's shoulder. "I often find it more enjoyable to dine surrounded by strangers moving to and fro and conversing. It feels as if one is being entertained at the theater but with the advantage of a meal at his table."

Pleased with Papa's reaction, Sir William looked at Elizabeth.

"Satisfying on multiple grounds, as my father says," she reassured him. "Besides, if anything were to befall Blacky, I daresay you take comfort in being more easily reached here. We can see everyone entering by the door."

Sir William brightened considerably. "I had not considered that, but it is true."

They walked to the far wall, passing tables with

travelers crammed beside each other on benches and barmaids weaving through them with heavy trays.

Between bites of stew and sips of wine, Sir William told them his plans. "My sons will travel on the morrow to give Blacky a day to rest before the big event while I return to Lucas Lodge. John does not approve, but I wish to share this joyous occasion with all of my family. I do hope you accept my invitation to join us. Miss Elizabeth can share a room with my girls, and you would be quite comfortable sharing with my boys, Mr. Bennet," he said to Papa, adding, "You will be quite safe in the stands. Close enough to see well, but far enough away from the horses to appease you. Really, you cannot beat the view. Not to mention how you avoid being jostled by the crowds. I was assured that only the upper circles are able to procure a stand, but with my position and our champion racehorse, John had no trouble securing one."

Papa smiled. "Your offer is kind, Sir— Mr. Smith, and we will accept it gladly." He glanced at Elizabeth, wiggling his eyebrows.

Elizabeth smiled. Truth be told, she would rather be away from London where she both hoped and dreaded she might see Fitzwilliam. Hoped he would smile at her. Dreaded he would turn away. At least, at Epsom, she could only hope he might follow her. And she would have Charlotte.

A nearby table of officers cleared, and a gentleman reading a newspaper moved closer to them, angling his paper for better lighting. With his worn brown velvet coat, disheveled hair, and over-grown sideburns, he reminded her of what her own father might have looked like some twenty years ago. He caught Elizabeth's eye and nodded politely before returning his attention to the paper, ignoring the new set of travelers moving in on his recently vacated table. Sir William had done well to secure a private, albeit small, table for them.

"George holds high hopes for the race," Sir William confided, the hint of worry in his tone restoring Elizabeth's attention back to her party. "He is concerned we will not win, but with odds of three to one, I say we cannot fail. John agrees with me." The way he looked at Papa for confirmation troubled Elizabeth. She wondered how far into debt Sir William had gone for his prized horse. What if he did not win the race? Would it mean ruin for her friends?

Papa rubbed his chin. "The Jockey Club is known to be strict. How did you manage to convince them to let you race so soon after changing ownership on the horse?"

Sir William puffed out his chest. "I did not present myself as Mr. Smith to them, you may be certain. During my interview with them, I ascertained that the gentlemen and I shared several acquaintances in the first circles. They know better than to question quality. John assisted me with the arrangements, of course, and everything turned out swimmingly. George does not give his brother enough credit, but John will do well by his family."

The more Sir William talked, the more profound Elizabeth's concern became. Poor Charlotte. She must feel the burden of her father's vainglorious choices. If his venture failed, his whole family would suffer. And for what? To prove himself to a class who would never invite him into their circles nor spare him a parting glance?

After Sir William had retired to his room to rest for his journey on the morrow, Papa rubbed his hand over his face, his brow furrowed. "I pray they will not lose their estate over this. Your mother will miss presuming over Lady Lucas, you will lose your close friend, and without Sir William, I fear I shall be presumed upon to step in as Master of the Ceremonies at the monthly assemblies." He shivered.

Elizabeth tried to smile at the irony of her father, who missed as many assemblies as he could, becoming the host of the affair. But the stakes were too high for humor. Papa must have felt it, too, for though he spoke in jest, the furrow in his brow remained.

The Epsom Derby was no longer just a race. It was going to alter lives.

CHAPTER 28

*A*ll the pieces had fallen together. Thanks to Oakley's reconnaissance, Darcy knew what The Four Horsemen were planning. How they planned to do it would be revealed through Sir William. Darcy had to stay close. He had to get Elizabeth far away from Sir William.

Already, Richard had a small army of men in place at Epsom, with more to come. The end of The Four Horsemen's reign was in sight, close enough to touch. Close enough for Darcy to dream of his own future — a future he had not allowed himself to ponder for years. A future he wanted to share with Elizabeth.

He could not lose her.

But he must wait. Darcy had too many enemies who would think nothing of using Elizabeth to manipulate him and kill her when they were through.

He must be patient. He would protect her until this sordid affair was done and The Four Horsemen's cutthroats were convinced they could gain nothing by harming her. However long it took, Darcy would watch over her. It would be agony, but he would do it for her.

Then, he would explain why he had written that wretched letter. He would tell her why he could not give her the answers she deserved. He would beg for forgiveness. He would befriend Mrs. Bennet, and he would help Mr. Bennet improve his younger daughters' prospects. All this and more, Darcy would do gladly.

What he could not do was return to Pemberley without Elizabeth.

Wait and watch. Out of sight, but always close.

Oakley had nearly been caught that morning. It had been too close a call. Thank goodness Elizabeth had not suspected that another man followed her.

It had been difficult to find a capable guard with no connections to Leo to watch over Elizabeth and her father at the last minute — as difficult as it had been for Darcy to secure a room near The Golden Crown.

Wilson had called in a favor from an old friend,

and despite the short notice, Lieutenant Croft had been happy to oblige.

At the sound of a knock on his door, Darcy glanced at Wilson, who stood in front of the barrier with his hand at the latch until Darcy sealed the message he had been writing to Richard.

It was Lieutenant Croft. With his overgrown hair, worn velvet coat, and the newspaper tucked under his arm, he gave the appearance of a country gentleman (much like Mr. Bennet might have appeared some years before.)

Wilson greeted his friend and took the envelope from Darcy. "I will dispatch this immediately and send for some tea. Or would you prefer coffee?"

"Coffee, please, and three cups." Darcy looked at Croft, who nodded his approval.

"A gentleman who shares a cup of coffee with his valet? It is an uncommon, but not unwelcome sight, sir," Croft said once Wilson had closed the door behind him.

Darcy motioned to the chairs arranged before the fire. "Please have a seat."

The soldier set the newspaper on the table and sat with his boots firmly planted on the wood plank floor.

Darcy sat opposite him. "I trust you left Miss

Bennet and her father well? They have not noticed you?"

"Miss Bennet is as perceptive as you said. She did not notice my presence in London, but she did see me sitting at the table beside them tonight."

Darcy froze, his body tensing.

Croft crossed one booted foot over his knee, a relaxed pose in stark contrast to his vigilant gaze surveying the room. "I nodded and resumed reading my paper, taking care not to make eye contact again. I am certain she suspected nothing, and I only left to report here after she, her father, and the other gentleman with whom they dined retired to their rooms."

Darcy finally let out his breath. "Well done. I cannot thank you enough for agreeing to help me."

Croft considered Darcy, his calloused fingers scratching against his scruffy side whiskers. "Mr. Darcy, I am not new to surveillance work. It is my habit to take in all of my surroundings — a habit I have formed since the day Wilson was shot."

"I did not know you were there."

"He took three bullets before we even realized we had walked into a trap. I dragged him back to the camp, but the damage was done. He considers himself in my debt, but I cannot agree. He was left crippled while I escaped unscathed. There is nothing fair about war."

"No, there is not." Darcy understood the guilt. He had escaped more than his fair share of scrapes without a mark on his skin. He understood that the invisible burdens were often the heaviest to bear. Croft could no sooner recover than Wilson could from such an injury. "Wilson is a good man. There are few I trust more."

"He speaks highly of you. It is for that reason I will share what I observed and overheard."

Darcy kept his posture relaxed, though his nerves snapped to attention.

"You were clear regarding my duty to watch over Miss Bennet and her father, to prevent anyone from approaching them to do harm, and to fetch you should I suspect anything untoward. As I mentioned, I have made a habit of observing certain things — scars on knuckles indicating a fighter, a building's handiest exits, the nearest horse, where a weapon is most likely to be hidden…" He waved his hand in circles. Darcy could have added more items to Croft's list. Those were things he noticed, too.

Croft leveled his eyes at him. "There were two men sitting on either side of the Bennets' table. They stayed as long as I did."

Darcy shrugged. He could not tell the man that

Richard had a handful of men watching Sir William and a whole contingent waiting at Epsom Downs. "It is not unusual for some to prefer the warmth and noise of the tavern in favor of their rooms upstairs."

Croft uncrossed his foot, leaning forward. "Neither of them drank more than one tankard of ale in over three hours."

If Darcy blew the mission when he was this close, he was not clever enough to capture The Four Horsemen. The success of his trap depended on secrecy. He had to stick to the story he and Wilson had told Croft.

His gaze never wavering from Darcy's, Croft said, "It was a prop. The men were watching the same party you hired me to protect."

Wilson had said Croft was one of the best. He was too good. However, he was wrong. The other agents' interest lies in Sir William, not in the Bennets. And Darcy meant to keep it that way. The less he could involve the Bennets with Leo, the better. It was why he had asked Wilson for help hiring a reliable guard.

Carefully weighing his words, Darcy said, "Anything is possible in these times, Croft. I can neither confirm nor deny what you saw, not having been present myself. My only interest is to keep the ruffian who threatened me away from Miss Bennet."

"Yes, Wilson told me how you were accosted. Your neck appears to be healing nicely."

Darcy touched the tender skin. His collar chafed against it. "You do not think the two men meant any ill-will, do you?" He knew they did not, but it seemed like the most natural question to ask.

"I do not, otherwise I would have stayed until they departed. Their purpose might have more to do with the other gentleman at the table than with the Bennets. He was a suspicious sort, going by the name Smith."

Resisting the urge to grit his teeth, Darcy said, "Really?" Sir William had been too clever to travel by his real name. It was the reason why he had been so difficult to find after he had left Lucas Lodge for London. Another clue handed to him by the Bennets.

"Mr. Bennet had trouble remembering not to call him 'Sir' on several occasions. The sarcasm in his tone was unmistakable at every utterance of the assumed name."

"That sounds accurate. What else did you observe?" Darcy's patience wore thin. He did not wish to dance around the topic of Sir William or Mr. Smith or whatever he chose to call himself. He wanted to know when the Bennets planned to return to London or, even better, return to Longbourn. Oakley had overheard Sir William invite the Bennets to join him at the Epsom Derby. A brazen offer. Only a madman would want a larger audience for the traitorous act he planned to attempt.

Darcy needed Elizabeth far away from Epsom. Far away from Sir William.

"The Bennets accepted Mr. Smith's invitation to join him at Epsom for the race. They will depart on the morrow, staying in the same inn as the gentleman."

Blast! Darcy clenched his fists and held his breath until his lungs screamed for air. Blast it all! "Tell me everything," he forced past the knot in his throat.

He listened while Croft spoke, taking in every detail and doing his best to pretend it did not matter until Wilson returned, they drank their bitter coffee, and Croft resumed his post at The Golden Crown.

Darcy had felt misery before — when he had lost his mother and again when his beloved father died. Their loss had created a void he had been unable to fill … until Elizabeth tumbled from a horse at his feet and conquered his heart. With her he had hope, happiness, and the home he had never thought he would find again. He relived his time with her in Hertfordshire in vivid detail, his longing to see her aching in his bones.

He had thought himself wretched the night he

had penned the letter for Elizabeth, but even after that odious message had been delivered, embers of hope burned within him. If he did his job, their separation was temporary.

If he could not do his job… He would lose Elizabeth.

He did not hear the knock at the door until Richard came into his room and sat down in the chair Croft had occupied hours before.

"I am tired of being at your beck and call at all hours of the day and night. Do you know I have not slept soundly since I recruited you? Had I known I would have to take on the role of the mooching cousin, I might not have recommended you at all. Do you have any brandy? I am parched. Some of the good stuff, maybe?"

Darcy raised his eyebrows. "You only have to assume the role of the leeching—"

"Mooching," Richard corrected. "Leeches are repulsive."

"Whatever you wish to call it, you do not need to pretend when there is nobody to see your performance. My brandy will be available to drink another day."

Richard raised a finger. "Ah, but I prefer to immerse myself in my role fully. Otherwise I risk giving a less than genuine reaction when it matters, or worse, being observed by a foe when I thought the coast was clear."

Darcy sighed. "My brandy will never be safe from you."

"I doubt it. Now, on to business. I know I grumble and complain, but that is only to ensure you do not get too full of yourself. The truth is, you brought us to Sir William after we had lost him. This operation would not stand a chance without you."

"I want to be done with The Four Horsemen as much as you do, but I cannot take credit for any of the information I've relayed to you." Darcy had to tell Richard. He needed someone else on his side, someone who would help him see clearly when emotions clouded his judgment.

"Ah, the informant." Richard raised his hand. "Do not tell me who it is until this is done. You know the rule: The less we know, the better—"

"But Rich—"

"I will not hear it. It is as much for your protection as mine."

"I must tell you—"

Once again Richard interrupted him, prattling on and on about the importance of their mission. Darcy was sick of the mission. Sick of The Four Horsemen. Sick of all of it.

"Blast it all, Richard! Will you shut up and listen?

Will you forget the mission for a moment and just be … my friend?"

Richard pinched his lips closed and watched Darcy expectantly.

Having expected a retort, Darcy felt his silence acutely.

"I am quiet. It is your turn to speak, Darcy," Richard finally said drolly.

Darcy ignored his impertinent cousin's remark. His revelation would be shocking enough. "My informant is a young lady from Hertfordshire."

"A lady?" Richard gasped.

"The daughter of a landed gentleman and a close friend to Sir William's eldest daughter. Elizabeth Bennet is inquisitive and lively and," he sighed, his voice going soft as the image of her grew stronger in his mind. "And mischievous. She is witty and too clever by half. She finds joy in the smallest things. She laughs when she is covered in mud or when a frustrated fool insults her vanity. Her whole face smiles, and her laughter would provoke the grumpiest growler to smile with her." He paused for a breath, his vision clearing to see Richard staring at him, gaping with his mouth wide open.

"You love her," Richard said through a wide grin. "You love a country maiden with fine eyes and a trilling laugh. I am delighted to hear it! I had been worried about you. When I saw you lonely and floundering at Pemberley after your father died, I had thought I was doing you a favor by recruiting you. I had thought you only needed to be kept busy, to have a purpose, but as the years went by, I thought I might never see you content again. But, look at you now! You are a simpering man mooning for his lady love! This is excellent! We will finish this assignment, and you will retire to marry your Miss Elizabeth."

He would have continued, but Darcy stopped him. "The Four Horsemen know she's important to me. One of their men threatened to hurt her unless I back off." He pulled his collar away from his neck.

Richard's smile faded until a thought brightened his aspect. "Yes, that. You are fortunate to have thick skin, Darcy. However, did that not happen in London? And you said she is from Hertfordshire? She is safe there, far away from Sir William and this whole affair. Did you not leave a footman and a gardener behind for Bingley's protection? You can send word to them immediately, and I will arrange this same night for a couple more men to travel to Meryton where they will remain watching over your young lady until The Four Horsemen are locked up. They will have no influence when the court convicts them of treason and their ill-gained fortunes are seized. So you see, it is no trouble at all." He rose. "I will see to it right now." He looked so pleased with himself.

"She is here. With Sir William."

Darcy heard the breath hiss out of Richard and watched him sink back onto his chair. It was the longest stretch of silence Darcy could recall between him and his boisterous cousin, but Darcy said nothing to disturb him. Richard had a mind for strategy. He might see something Darcy had missed. His situation might not be as bleak as he feared.

Richard slowly began. "Sir William is asleep right now. I only just sent my men to rest so that they are ready in the morning when he travels to Epsom. That gives us one full day before the race. There is plenty of time. You only need to convince your young lady to stay here, return to London, or go back to Hertfordshire."

Darcy shoved his hand through his hair and groaned. "I wrote her a letter severing all connection."

Richard threw his hands heavenward. "Only you could be so daft! What were you thinking?"

"I had just been attacked!"

"And?" Richard exclaimed sarcastically. "What? You could not think of something more dramatic to do?"

"If you could have heard that man breathing threats against the woman you loved with a knife cutting into your throat, you would have reacted the same. All I wanted to do was keep her safe. Everything I do is done to protect her, Richard. That is why I confided in you. I feel like I am drowning, and I refuse to drag her down with me. If this operation fails, I die alone. She needs to be able to move on. To be happy without the burden of guilt or wondering if things might have been different had she tried to stop me." Darcy's chest tightened, his throat squeezing around the words until he could say no more.

Leaning against the back of his chair, Richard massaged his temples. "I am sorry. You need help, not insults. I daresay that when it is my turn to fall in love, I will not fare any better." He took a deep breath and let it out. "You sent her a letter. If she is half as spirited as you described her to be — by the way, I expect an explanation of the mud and the fool who insulted her vanity at some point."

Darcy nodded. Richard would laugh at him, but he did not care.

Richard continued, "Good. As I was saying, if she is as you described, she will be angry with you. You will have to go to her and beg for forgiveness. Once you are restored to her good grace, you can convince her to leave without arousing her curiosity."

"Easier said than done."

"Which will be easier? The apology or the convincing?" Richard teased, a smug look on his face, so certain he was of the reply. *Prepare yourself to be shocked, know-it-all.* "The apology." The stunned expression Richard held encouraged Darcy to continue. "I am prepared to beg, to grovel if I must, for her forgiveness. Anything to get her away from Sir William."

Raising his sagging jaw, Richard shook his head. "I never would have believed it had I not heard it with my own ears. Darcy apologize? Beg and grovel? If this young lady is responsible for this change in you, you simply must marry her." He grinned. "She does not by any chance have any unmarried sisters, does she?"

"Four of them."

Richard's countenance brightened considerably. "Of the same caliber as your Elizabeth?"

"Her eldest sister does her credit, but Bingley is quite taken with her. And before you inquire after the younger sisters, I think you would find them … too young."

Richard grunted. "That will not do. I desire a lady with a bit more sense and maturity. Someone who would think this plain face handsome, and who would not mind my lack of fortune. A lady who would be content with a comfortable cottage and my constant heart."

Darcy smiled at him. "Someone who will not mind your incessant prattle."

"That too." Richard chuckled.

The air was lighter. Darcy could breathe now. His problems were still present, but he had a plan. "The hour is late. I will have to wait until the morning to speak with Elizabeth."

Richard rubbed his hands against his breeches and stood. "Try to sleep."

"Not likely."

Boom, boom, boom, vibrated the door. The hair on Darcy's arm stood on end as he jumped to his feet. Richard turned to him with wide eyes. He opened the door.

An agent burst into the room, panting heavily. "Sir William is gone!"

Darcy clutched his stomach, dragging himself behind Richard, who ran outside, yelling for their horses while Darcy raced to The Golden Crown.

CHAPTER 29

*E*lizabeth watched the sunrise from her window, relieved to climb out of her sleepless bed, anxious for no reason she could explain.

When her father tapped on her door, she was eager to join him downstairs to watch the goings on while they broke their fast.

The same gentleman with the worn velvet jacket she had seen the night before sat in a corner, his newspaper folded on the table beside his steaming cup and chunk of bread. He nodded at Elizabeth, and she nodded back as her father guided her to a table near the windows facing the street at the opposite side of the room.

A barmaid asked if they wished to eat.

Papa rubbed his hands together, ordering another feast he would surely regret when it came time to travel in a bouncy coach down a rutted road. Before she left, he added, "Do you have a current newspaper I might read?"

"It is too early yet for today's morning paper, but *The Times* came in last night's evening post. I will see if it is still behind the counter." She spun around to leave when the gentleman in the corner spoke.

"If it is the newest paper you wish for, I have it here." He walked over to them, extending the folded pages to Papa.

"I do not mean to rush you, good sir. I will only accept it if you are finished reading."

The man moved the paper closer. "I am done. Most of it is about the Epsom Derby, if that is of any interest to a gentleman traveling with his daughter."

Her father smiled. "I doubt it is of more interest to us than it is to a gentleman traveling alone. Please allow me to present my daughter Miss Elizabeth Bennet. And I am Thomas Bennet. We hail from Hertfordshire, and while it seems an unlikely place for us to go, we are, in fact, on our way to Epsom."

The gentleman bowed. "I am honored to make your acquaintance, sir. Miss. I am Lieutenant Abraham Croft of His Majesty's Army most of the time. Today, I am employed as I have been for the past three days by Mr. Fitzwilliam Darcy."

"Mr. Darcy!" Elizabeth exclaimed, her cheeks

burning when Lieutenant Croft and her father turned to look at her.

Papa wiggled his eyebrows. "Mr. Darcy, eh? I do believe my theory will prove itself, Lizzy." Motioning for the lieutenant to sit with them, he asked, "Is Mr. Darcy here, then?"

That was exactly what Elizabeth wanted to know. Her vision wandered about the room, through the window to the inn-lined lane, and back to Lieutenant Croft again.

"Thank you, Mr. Bennet," said the lieutenant, fetching the rest of his breakfast and settling at the table beside them. "Mr. Darcy was here, but he is not presently. He was called away, and given the rapidity with which events occurred, I can attest to the urgency surrounding his departure."

Elizabeth frowned, her forehead tensing. Was he in danger still? Had another attempt been made against his life?

Lieutenant Croft paused, securing her and Papa's rapt attention before he continued. "He gave me a message for you. He said: *I beg you not to travel with Sir William. You must not go to Epsom.*" He clasped his hands together. "Those were his exact words. He wished to explain more, but another man called him, and he had to rush away. I saw him gallop with another man in the direction of London and another two men gallop in the opposite direction toward Epsom. I do not know any more than that."

At least he was not alone, Elizabeth thought. But what was he doing? And why the need to warn her? "Why did Mr. Darcy hire you to work for him?" she asked.

"To protect you."

"Protect us? From what? Or whom?" Elizabeth clasped her hands in her lap to keep from wringing them. Her heart was flattered that Fitzwilliam had not forgotten her, that he took an interest in her welfare, but that he saw the need to hire a military man for their protection was alarming. Had the lieutenant been the reason why she had felt someone was watching her in London? He said he had been working for Fitzwilliam for three days.

"I did not ask particulars, Miss. In my profession, you learn when to question and when to follow orders. A man I trust with my life, a dear friend of mine who fought at my side until an injury forced him to retire, sought me out. He told me his employer had been attacked near his residence, that his assailant not only threatened Mr. Darcy's life, but he also threatened the young lady he had recently dined with along with her father."

Elizabeth went cold. "He was attacked? Was he harmed?"

Lieutenant Croft's smile reassured her. "Only a nick of the knife, an insignificant scratch. He is much more concerned with your safety."

Right. The threat. The letter. The dear injured friend. Elizabeth was on the brink of understanding. "Your injured friend. Was he the one who approached you on Mr. Darcy's behalf? What did you say his name was?" The connection between a man Fitzwilliam trusted would go a long way in ensuring Lieutenant Croft was trustworthy as well.

"I did not say, but I will tell you his name is Wilson."

Good. This fellow was honest. "You said Mr. Darcy was accosted in the street? Who was responsible? What provoked the attack?" Elizabeth's heart drummed against her ribs.

He shook his head. "I am not privy to the details, Miss. What I do know is that Mr. Darcy bears the mark at his throat and that his first concern was for your safety. I beg you treat his message with the seriousness with which it was given."

Elizabeth reached up, touching the tender skin where she imagined an evil ruffian pressed a knife against Fitzwilliam's neck. That was why he had written that letter. That was why he had not dared deliver the message himself.

Once again, he had been protecting her.

She ought to have known.

They fell silent while the barmaid emptied the dishes burdening her tray onto their table. Grabbing a loaf, Papa broke it in half and spread a generous portion of butter over the warm bread. "Mr. Darcy told you to tell us not to travel to Epsom with Sir William," he said, taking a large bite and chewing heartily.

"Not exactly. His exact words were: *I beg you not to travel with Sir William. You must not go to Epsom.*"

Her father gulped down his bread. "I have a theory about his reasons for prohibiting the trip, but that is neither here nor there. What he does not know is that we do *not* intend to travel with Sir William to Epsom, as the gentleman is not here. So, you see, there is no problem. We are quite safe." He stabbed a piece of sausage and popped it into his mouth.

Elizabeth had no appetite. "Papa, Mr. Darcy was attacked, and I have been threatened. Surely, if he has gone to the trouble of engaging Lieutenant Croft to protect us, then it would be wise to heed his plea."

The lieutenant nodded in agreement. "Mr. Darcy is an honorable gentleman, and whatever he is involved in must be a grave matter indeed for him to take responsibility for your welfare. Pray do not take his warning lightly. It was given for your benefit."

Father drank deeply from his tankard, lifting one finger into the air after setting the pewter down. "I have a theory about that. Rest assured I will not do anything foolhardy. It is in my nature to be cautious."

Theories, theories, and more theories. Elizabeth was concerned his recent success proving one of his precious theories had gone to his head.

Lieutenant Croft did not look convinced. Looking at the rest of his roll and coffee as if he did not have much of an appetite any more, he picked up his cup and plate. "Then, I will not take up any more of your time but will leave you to break your fast. Thank you for your attention, Mr. Bennet. Miss Bennet." Bowing, he retreated to the corner from whence he had joined them, his back against the wall to face them.

"Papa," Elizabeth hissed. "You cannot be serious. Do you not see the danger?"

"With our own guard to protect us, it is not likely anyone will attempt to harm us. Besides, the haste with which Mr. Darcy departed, leaving you under the watchful eye of a trained veteran soldier, implies he is very near to resolving his debt with that unsavory gentleman."

Elizabeth could not keep the sarcasm from her

tone. "And Epsom? Do you have a theory about why he does not wish for us to travel there?"

Her father's eyebrows shot up. "I am surprised you have not drawn the same conclusion I have, my dear. Why go to Epsom if not to attend the Derby? As a gentleman who recently succumbed to a moment of weakness, gambling too much and losing to a dangerous man, it stands to reason that he would not wish for us to go there. He would hesitate to follow."

Elizabeth stared at her father.

He chuckled. "It is not often I have followed through in proving a theory. They normally take a great deal too much time and effort. But my courtship theory is coming along nicely, and I daresay that if Mr. Darcy overcomes his vice to follow you to Epsom, then I proclaim him a gentleman deeply in love, and I will gladly give my consent when he asks me for your hand."

Taking another bite of sausage, he snapped the pages of the paper open. "Look at this, Lizzy. I do not know how today can get any better. First, proof of my theory and Mr. Darcy's genuine interest, and now this." He folded the page and pointed to the article he wanted her to see before snatching it away to read himself. She was still too stunned to complain, so she listened as her father read another account of the brave spy's heroics.

"They are calling him The Red Campion. Not quite as catchy as The Scarlet Pimpernel, but a dignified name all the same if one is to be called after a flower."

Elizabeth tried to eat. It was going to be a very long day.

The chair groaned when her father leaned against the back sipping his coffee. "Red campions are native to Derbyshire, as is the scarlet pimpernel. I have neglected my studies of horticulture, but if my memory serves, it is also home to the more unfortunately named pignut, petty spurge, twayblade, and navelwort. Whoever this spy is will be pleased one of those was not chosen as his *nom de guerre*."

She was supposed to laugh, but Elizabeth could not even manage a smile. Another thought, a theory as outrageous as her father's, had taken hold of her mind, and the more she pondered the possibility, the more convinced she became of its truth. The more convinced she became that the danger to them was, indeed, great. But if she was in peril, at least she knew of it. The risk to Sir William was far greater, and he had no idea of it, Elizabeth was certain. Otherwise, he never would have fetched his family to join him at Epsom.

Her misgivings against her father's choice to continue to Epsom waned, pushed out of her concern at the suspicion that her friends were soon to walk into a trap they had no idea existed.

Elizabeth needed to talk to Charlotte. She needed to warn her.

But, of what?

THEY ARRIVED at the inn in Epsom without any tragedy befalling them. Elizabeth had held her breath, her heart leaping to her throat at every bend in the road while she kept watch out of the window opposite Lieutenant Croft whose hand, she noticed, hovered near the bulge in his coat. It was not fanciful to assume he carried a loaded pistol.

She could not wait to talk to Charlotte. What would she say when she heard this crazy story?

On arrival, Elizabeth saw no need to put her or her father's safety to the test. She stayed indoors, and her father was happy to follow suit so long as he had people to watch, worthy conversations to engage in, and the newspapers to read.

Elizabeth occupied herself as well as she could, but the hours stretched endlessly until late the following afternoon when the Lucas coach finally arrived, and Charlotte stepped inside the inn. She took one look at Elizabeth, and asked, "My dearest Lizzy, whatever is wrong?"

"You arrived without incident?" Elizabeth asked, her relief so great, she felt warmth flood her face.

"Of course. My poor father is exhausted, but Mother is so pleased he decided to come for us. But what of you, Lizzy? You appear anxious."

"I have been, Charlotte. Let us go upstairs, and I will tell you all about it." She tugged Charlotte up the stairs to the rooms Sir William had arranged for them to share.

Calmly, Charlotte sat, perching her hands in her lap, her eyes focused on Elizabeth. "I am ready," she said, pursing her lips together.

Elizabeth loved how seriously her friend took her concerns. What she was about to reveal was shocking, and she needed Charlotte's level-headed sense.

She had rehearsed how best to present her thoughts to Charlotte, so Elizabeth lost no time beginning. "I will state the facts, as free of emotion and my own opinions as I can state them, and then I wish to ask your view to see if it matches the same conclusion I have drawn."

Charlotte nodded.

Elizabeth took a deep breath. "Suppose there is

a gentleman who attends a ball. He is new to the area and knows nobody. After he has been introduced to most present, he engages another attendee in conversation. The conversation is light, as is appropriate for two people who have only recently met. However, this gentleman cleverly extracts information about one family in particular."

"A family present at the ball? And, Lizzy, if you are not to infuse your own opinion, you ought to avoid describing him as clever. Already, I know this gentleman is someone you admire."

Elizabeth twisted her lips. If she was not more careful, Charlotte would see right through her. "I will try to leave my own impressions out of this supposition. To answer your question, the family he inquired about *was* present at the ball. That is the first event involving this gentleman, and on its own, not significant to merit further analysis."

"You will let me be the judge of what is significant or not. What is the next event?"

"During a leisurely ride over the countryside, the gentleman's hat was shot off his head."

Charlotte inhaled sharply, but she said nothing.

Elizabeth continued, "His first reaction was to pull the lady he was riding with off her horse and shield her between his body and a rotten tree stump while he calculated the approximate location of his shooter."

"Oh Lizzy." Charlotte pressed a hand over her heart. She knew.

Elizabeth pressed on. "They raced back, the gentleman riding between where he thought the shooter had been and the lady. He provided a guard to keep an eye on the lady, and later, to secure her safely to her family."

The more she talked, the more convinced Elizabeth was of her conclusion.

"That is not all, is it? There is more." Charlotte still clutched her heart, her eyes brimming with sympathy. So much for keeping things hypothetical.

"This same gentleman dressed in black, blending into the darkness and slipping around the property of the same family he had inquired about at the ball."

Charlotte frowned, her eyebrows forming a deep V.

"He offered a logical explanation, but given the impression of his character from previous actions, it was difficult for the lady to believe he had fallen into a gambling debt he had yet to pay."

Now, Charlotte chewed on her lips. Elizabeth could tell she did not believe the excuse either.

"Then, this gentleman joined the lady and her father for a mediocre meal made spectacular with the quality and abundance of the conversation. The gentleman was charming and attentive and … perfect … in the opinion of the lady. And then, when her hopes were soaring, she received a letter the following day in which the gentleman broke all connection with the lady without any reason offered. He merely sent his servant to say goodbye." Even knowing his reason, it still pierced Elizabeth's heart to relate the event.

Charlotte squeezed her eyes shut, as if she, too, felt the pain.

"And finally," Elizabeth added, "she later found out that the gentleman had been attacked after leaving the dinner. The lady he had dined with was also threatened by his assailant. She learned this from the guard he hired to protect her and her father while he galloped off into the night from whence she has not seen him. Now, Charlotte, I beg your sensibleness and ask you to what conclusion you are led?"

"I would assume you are describing a novel about a spy and his true love."

Elizabeth sank into the nearest chair. "You must know I was describing Mr. Darcy."

"I supposed as much, and it appears I must apologize to you for accusing you of falling prey to your fancy at the assembly. It seems outrageous, but for a man as serious as Mr. Darcy to act as you have described him, he must be using his position in society to hide his true identity. As thoroughly as he has protected you, I cannot believe him a villain, though I cannot imagine why he was snooping around someone's property."

"That is why I had to speak with you Charlotte. It was your family he asked about and your stables he was snooping around. If Mr. Darcy truly is a spy, then he is investigating your father."

Charlotte shook her head. "I cannot fathom why. You know I love my father dearly, Lizzy, but he simply does not possess the qualities required of a hardened criminal, nor the intellect to effect any evil plan."

"That is what concerns me, too, Charlotte. If Mr. Darcy is investigating your father, it means that the real threat is going unchecked. He is in peril, and so is your father."

"We all are," Charlotte said with admirable coolness. Her eyes narrowed, and her lips pursed together for several minutes. Then, she said, "We must develop a plan to help Mr. Darcy and acquit my father from suspicion. We must find what is going on and catch the real culprit."

"That was what I was hoping you would say."

CHAPTER 30

*D*arcy worked out a knot in his shoulder, feeling every hour he had spent in the saddle since Sir William had disappeared from The Golden Crown and sent him on a wild goose chase lasting two days.

Richard was in no better shape. He leaned against the brick wall of the cart shed, but his eyes never stopped scanning the rectangular building. It was the perfect location, wedged as it was between a stone wall marking the edge of the property and the back of the racehorses' stalls. A long, skinny corridor with an entrance at both ends, it was the only building available for their use during the frantic minutes counting down to the time when the race would begin.

"Why did Sir William bring his family here?"

Richard asked the question which had kept Darcy awake all night. "He is either the boldest, most shameless man in Christendom, or..." He stopped, the alternative being too horrible to speak aloud.

If Sir William was only a ploy to distract them, if he was unbelievably oblivious to the role he played in the final act of the dramatic play they were engaged in, then Darcy did not know who their target was. And, now, he only had one hour to find him. "I have thought of little else since I caught up with Sir William. Until he reached Meryton, I had not once doubted his involvement with The Four Horsemen. The money leads to him, as does his presence here with a new horse when he has no history of racing. We must acknowledge the possibility that he is a red herring. While I have believed him to be a highly skilled and accomplished villain, I cannot believe him so callous as to involve his wife and children."

Richard rubbed his chin. "It is a vicious circle, is it not?"

Not knowing what he meant, Darcy watched Richard until he spoke again.

"The one person who could help us is the one person we do not dare approach today. I bet you a year's salary that one candid conversation with Miss Elizabeth would lead us right to our man."

"Out of the question," Darcy snapped. "She is in enough danger as it is, thanks to me." He had known she might not heed his warning, but nothing had prepared Darcy for the anxiety he had felt when he had seen Croft standing outside the inn one of his men had tracked "Mr. Smith" to. And he knew. Elizabeth was at Epsom. The thought made his stomach sink again.

Holding his hands up, Richard said, "I would never suggest you tell her the whole truth unless it was the absolute last recourse. However, you have to admit, she has been essential to the success of this mission thus far. You will have a clever wife."

Darcy sighed, beating his fist against the brick wall. "If we seize The Four Horsemen. If she will have me. How can I expect her to love me as much as I adore her when I have done everything possible to earn her distrust?" He winced. That harked of despair, and if he was desperate about anything, he was desperate to win Elizabeth's heart. "If it takes years, I will do what I must to be what she deserves."

Richard squeezed his shoulder. "I wish you success and happiness, Darcy. As much as I hate to admit it, I will miss you … and your fine brandy."

Darcy squeezed Richard's shoulder, and they stood together in silence in a sort of embrace which communicated everything their tight throats kept them from uttering.

Finally, Richard smacked Darcy's arm and cleared his throat. "Your retirement will be a loss to our organization."

Gone was the brotherly camaraderie. They were colleagues again, working together to achieve a common goal.

Darcy followed suit, crossing his arms over his chest and stepping back. "You might consider recruiting Croft. He has the advantage of military training, and he is discreet. Throughout this ordeal, he has followed orders without asking questions I suspect he is wise enough not to ask even though he must suspect there is much more at stake than his task to watch over the Bennets."

Richard rubbed his chin again. "Yes, I had noticed. I took the liberty of asking Wilson about his family." He paused so long, Darcy rubbed his chest and braced himself for tragic news.

"His wife and child died of smallpox while he was on duty."

Darcy sucked in breath, his gut twisting. He could not imagine the pain Croft must have endured. It was enough to break a man.

"That is not the worst of it," Richard continued. "The letter from his father-in-law informing him of their passing was lost. He returned home expecting to find his family and, instead, found strangers living in his residence."

"Dear Lord."

"Since then, Croft only takes leave when he is forced to, and then, he is known to take on other employment. Anything to occupy himself and busy his mind; anything to keep from wondering what might have been had he been with his family instead of away at war."

Those unanswerable questions drove men to madness. What if? What if Darcy could not save the Prince Regent? What if he could not capture The Four Horsemen? What if he could not protect Elizabeth? What if his archenemy hurt her to get to him? What if after all his effort, the Prince refused to listen to reason and let his traitorous friends free? What if Darcy had to live the rest of his life waiting for them to retaliate? Acid churned in his stomach, burning his heart and stealing his breath. He could not fail. Not today. Not when it meant losing Elizabeth forever.

He had to focus. He had to control his fear, or risk losing his reason for living.

Standing to his full height, Darcy forced his shoulders to relax and his mind to concentrate on one objective. "One more hour. Then, we will be done with The Four Horsemen."

A movement caught the corner of his eye, charging Darcy's blood and steeling his nerves.

It was Oakley. He looked over his shoulder, then advanced toward them. "I will not stay long in case I was followed. As many men as we have stationed around the grounds, you can wager The Four Horsemen have at least as many."

A charged calm fell over Darcy. He stood with his weight evenly distributed between his feet, his hands loose and ready at his side. His senses heightened like a soldier ready for battle. "You were able to replace Sir William's jockey?"

"It is done."

"He is fully aware of what is expected of him? We do not know how many riders The Four Horsemen have placed in the Derby, and we cannot risk permitting anyone but our man near the Prince. He *must* win."

"He knows."

Richard stepped forward, his arms crossed over his chest, his eyes narrowed. "You ensured that the real jockey will not be found until after the race?"

Oakley smiled. "I left him bound and gagged in a privy."

Richard clapped him on the shoulder, his grin wide. "Good man."

Darcy had no space for humor. He pulled out his timepiece. "Three quarters of an hour left. Where is your jockey? He should be here."

Oakley looked about, his eyebrows furrowing. "I expected to find him here. He already weighed in, although there is not much there to weigh. I left him not five minutes ago, and he was on his way here for final instructions. I had thought perhaps he had already left, there not being much more to say."

A sense of foreboding gripped Darcy. Their replacement jockey had been difficult to find. Not only did they need someone of the same stature and slight build as Sir William's rider, but they also had to find a skilled horseman who resembled the jockey enough to be mistaken for him. If he met with any trouble, their entire mission would be compromised.

Darcy looked at his timepiece again. Forty-three minutes and one missing jockey. "We cannot take any chances. I will go see what has happened."

Oakley stepped in front of Darcy. "Let me go. You need to stay out of sight. They know you." His gaze flickered down to Darcy's bandaged neck which served as a reminder of how easily the tide could turn.

Richard nodded. "I had best take my position. All

my men are in place, awaiting your signal, Darcy." He charged past Darcy and down the corridor.

Darcy hated staying behind when there was so much to do, but Oakley was right. His greatest advantage was in remaining unseen. He was about to tell his groom as much when he heard a scuffle from the other side of the cart building, the side where Richard had gone through.

Oakley's eyes widened. "They followed me."

Darcy spun around just as Richard stumbled in, one cheek swollen, the blade of the knife he held bright red.

Four men blocked the exit. One of them held his arm to his side, his fingers drenched in blood. But it was the tall one with the blackened eye who demanded Darcy's attention. He pointed his finger at Darcy. "I will make you pay for this," he seethed, plucking a dagger from his boot and running past Richard straight toward Darcy.

CHAPTER 31

"*H*ave you ever seen so many people in one place?" Charlotte asked, tightening her grip around Elizabeth's arm as they strolled over the grounds.

With Papa on her left, Charlotte on her right, and Lieutenant Croft always nearby, Elizabeth felt safe. What danger could befall them in the midst such a large crowd?

"I will appreciate the relative quiet of Longbourn all the more for it," Papa commented.

Elizabeth laughed. "So long as Lydia is not bemoaning the loss of her spent pin money, Kitty is not agitating Mama's nerves with her incessant coughing, and Mary is not practicing to exhibit her skills on the pianoforte."

Her father smiled. "Books provide an admirable

sort of barrier to excessive sounds. It is why my library is my favorite room in the house." He looked about, jolting forward when a gentleman clipped his shoulder in passing.

Elizabeth wrapped her free hand around his arm. "It is excessively crowded." It was no wonder she had not seen Fitzwilliam despite her and Charlotte's best efforts to find him. Elizabeth had even asked Lieutenant Croft, but he had been no help at all. If he knew where Fitzwilliam was, he was not telling — assuming Fitzwilliam had returned from wherever he had run off to. He may not be at Epsom at all, but that did not discourage Elizabeth from constantly looking over the crowd.

Her father patted her hand. "You will strain your neck if you continue in this fashion, Lizzy. If I am right about Mr. Darcy, I do not suspect he will make an appearance until after the race is done, at which point he can see you without the temptation to gamble. Besides, Mr. Darcy is tall. Even in this crush, you would not fail to see him." Despite his warnings and arguments, he stretched his back and lengthened his neck to look about them.

Elizabeth lowered herself from the balls of her feet. Her father was right. If Fitzwilliam was at the racecourse, she would have noticed him. Had she not felt his eyes on her from across the ballroom at the Meryton Assembly? Even if she did not see him, she would sense him. Her skin tingled, and once again, she rose to her toes to look around.

Papa came to an abrupt stop. "Has my mind created an apparition to further prove my courting theory, or is that Mr. Bingley in the flesh?"

"Mr. Bingley?" exclaimed Elizabeth as she followed her father's line of vision.

Charlotte saw him, too. "What is he doing here?"

"My theory is more effective than I gave it credit for," Papa said with a chuckle.

At first, Mr. Bingley seemed relieved to see them approaching, but his satisfaction quickly turned to nerves. Brushing his hat off his head, he twisted and bent the brim.

Peeking around from behind Mr. Bingley was Jim. On seeing them, he stepped around his master, grinning from ear to ear. His presence puzzled Elizabeth, but she returned his smile. She enjoyed the stable boy's chatter.

Her father greeted Mr. Bingley warmly, inquiring politely after the health of his family before adding, "You are not here to bet on the horses, too, are you?"

Mr. Bingley blushed. "Me? No. And you, Mr. Bennet? I would not have taken you for a gambling gentleman."

"Indeed, I am not. I only refer to your friend, Mr. Darcy."

"Darcy?" Mr. Bingley's eyebrows shot upward. "He rarely gambles. This would be the last place I would expect to see him."

Elizabeth exchanged a look with Charlotte. Her father's theory might have its flaws, but hers was gaining strength. Fitzwilliam did not gamble. He could not be deeply in debt. Then, why had he lied to her? The only explanation that satisfied, that added the weight of honorable intent, was that he was a spy. Once again, he had been trying to protect her.

Papa, having had so much success in proving his theory up to that moment, did not take well to Mr. Bingley's proof against it. He forgot to carry on conversation when he had a new twist to ponder.

Addressing Mr. Bingley, Elizabeth said, "We are pleased to see you. If you are not here for the horses, then how did you come to the Derby?"

Mr. Bingley's blush spread from his cheeks to cover his face.

Jim blurted, "Blimey, Miss, we've been chasing you all over the country! First that fancy hotel in London, and then The Golden Crown, and finally here. If me throbbin' feet is any indication, we've been walking for hours, and I still haven't seen me brother. That's why we were walking toward the stables. Have you seen him? Have you seen Joe? Is he with the racehorse and the famous trainer? Golly, I hope Sir William's horse wins today."

Hat mangled between his hands, Mr. Bingley jumped into the conversation before Jim could take another breath and continue. "Thank you, Jim, but you really must not interrupt."

Jim's eyes widened. "Did I bungle things up again?" His face twisted. "I am sorry. I'll try harder, I swear it."

Elizabeth wondered how many times Mr. Bingley and Jim had had this same conversation. The kindly rebuke of the master and the repentant remorse of the boy tugged at her heart and pulled her lips into a smile. That, and her complete joy for Jane. Why else would Mr. Bingley chase them all over the country if not for her?

Papa bobbed up and down on his toes, once again pleased with himself. "That is quite a trip."

Mr. Bingley dropped his hands to his side, a nice reprieve for his hat, Elizabeth thought. "There is a matter of vital importance I wish to discuss with you," he said.

"Vital?" Papa repeated.

"To me, yes," Mr. Bingley said with so much misery, Elizabeth took pity on him. She understood the feeling.

"Well, then," Papa replied, "I invite you to call on me at the inn once this race is over. I will admit that despite my nature and better judgment, I am much too excited at present to give you the attention you deserve. But the race will be done in an hour, and we can discuss your vital matter then."

"Thank you." Mr. Bingley bowed, trying to look grateful when he was clearly disappointed.

Charlotte must have noticed, too. She changed the subject, asking, "How is it that you came to bring Jim?"

Jim opened his mouth to speak but thought better of it when Mr. Bingley shot him a look. The boy really was trying.

"His brother is here with your father's trainer, Miss Lucas. Jim has talked of nothing else since Sir William left, and when it was suggested to me that I bring him along and allow the rest of the household to recover, I relented … er, accepted."

Elizabeth bit her tongue to keep from laughing. She imagined the chattering lad following Mr. Bingley around the Netherfield Park grounds whenever he required a mount, irritating everyone in his path with his exuberance. "I imagine so," she said vaguely, smiling again at Jim.

It was too much for the lad. He looked as though he would burst with unspoken words.

"Golly, it's a pity the ladies can't race. You'd give all these gents a run for their money on Tempest, Miss Elizabeth."

Mr. Bingley blushed scarlet. "I am so sorry, Miss Elizabeth. I am certain Jim meant it as a compliment."

Elizabeth chuckled. "And so I will take it, Mr. Bingley. Please do not trouble yourself." To Jim, she added, "I will stick to the fields, all the same. Any lady who attempted to ride in the Derby would be ruined if she were found out."

He frowned. "'Tis not fair."

Charlotte intervened. "We are close to the stables. Would you like to see Trophonius?" she asked Mr. Bingley as much as she asked Jim.

"We would be delighted to," Mr. Bingley replied. Jim's grin was answer enough.

Papa leaned toward her. "I might have been mistaken about Mr. Darcy, but my theory stands. Poor Mrs. Bennet's nerves must be fraught! She will scold me sharply when we return, but I will have the satisfaction of informing her of my part in securing a young man's proposal for my daughter. Perhaps two by the time the day is over." He wiggled his eyebrows at Elizabeth, and they fell in behind Mr. Bingley, Charlotte, and Jim.

So distracted were they, Papa almost trampled

over Mr. Bingley, who had stopped and was pointing at a small building behind the stables.

"That is Colonel Fitzwilliam, Darcy's cousin. I would not have thought to see him here."

Charlotte glanced over her shoulder at Elizabeth. Perhaps the colonel would help them find Fitzwilliam.

They turned toward the building to see four rough-looking men round the brick building from the other side, surrounding Colonel Fitzwilliam. One of them held a knife.

Elizabeth's breath caught in her throat. She no longer felt safe any more.

"Blimey," exclaimed Jim, charging forward.

Mr. Bingley grabbed him by the back of his jacket. "You stay here with Mr. Bennet and the ladies."

In the split-second Mr. Bingley's back was turned, the colonel lunged forward, and one of the men screeched in pain as he grabbed his arm. The colonel took a hit to his face, but he retreated inside the long, narrow building before they saw more.

"We ought to call for help," Papa said.

Elizabeth was already walking toward the building with Jim. Fitzwilliam was inside. She knew it.

"The altercation will be over by then," Charlotte

said behind her.

Papa continued protesting. "I do not know what help you think we will be."

But Elizabeth was already at the side of the building, peeking in and squinting until her eyes adjusted to the darker interior.

"Blimey," Jim said in breathless awe.

Elizabeth could not have expressed herself better. And when her father and Charlotte saw what they did, they gaped and stared, too. The shape of Oakley's nose made perfect sense now.

Mr. Bingley did his best to be of assistance, but the ease and agility with which Oakley, Fitzwilliam, and his military cousin received their assailants was thrilling to behold. It was like one of the stories she loved to read of The Red Campion.

Swing, kick. Down dropped one.

Jab, punch. Down went another.

As the third dropped to the floor, her father turned to her. "Who *is* Mr. Darcy?"

Lunge, thrust. The last henchman fell.

Jim ran past the open boxes into the shed. "That was amazing!" He flung his fists in the air in imitation of his new heroes.

Fitzwilliam looked panicked, and when he noticed them standing at the side entrance, he looked crestfallen. "You cannot be here."

The colonel pressed his hand against his swollen cheek. "It is too late, Darcy."

"Excuse me, please," said a deep voice behind her.

Elizabeth stepped aside to allow Mr. Croft to pass. His swollen lip signaled that he had also met with trouble.

Jutting a thumb over his shoulder, he said, "I caught two trying to sneak up on Miss Elizabeth from behind."

Elizabeth gasped. "I saw no one."

Fitzwilliam's nostrils flared. "It is as I feared. They will try to capture her. Anything to keep me from—" He stopped, shoving his hands into his hair and pacing.

Charlotte grabbed a couple of lead ropes hanging in the box stall and breezed past Elizabeth. "Unless you want these men to cause more trouble, you had better tie them."

The colonel jumped to action, taking the rope. "Of course! Thank you, Miss—"

Fitzwilliam offered hasty introductions.

"Lucas, you said?" The colonel raised an eyebrow and shot a glare at Fitzwilliam before swooping an elegant bow. "I am honored to meet you, Miss Lucas. And the Bennets. I am pleased to finally make your acquaintance."

Elizabeth stepped farther down the corridor,

stopping when she did not feel her father by her.

He shook his head. "I think I will stay here at this opening. If any other rough types come near, I will shout a warning." He looked around the inside wall, his face brightening when he saw a shovel. Grabbing the tool, he held it like a club, his knuckles white. "If anyone tries to kidnap my Lizzy, they will have to get past me first."

She could not help but smile … and pray he would not have to use his rustic weapon.

The colonel cut the leads in half, tossing the lengths to Fitzwilliam, Oakley, Mr. Bingley, and Mr. Croft. "Tie them tightly. We have no idea how many more are out there, but at least we may be confident knowing there are fewer now than there were before."

Once the ruffians had been dragged to lean against the darkest far wall with their hands tied, the gentlemen found another rope with which to secure their feet. Fitzwilliam moved with the same agility Elizabeth had seen outside the Lucases' stables. Not one movement was wasted.

"I was right. I thought you were, but I talked myself out of it, believing that I suffered from fancy." Elizabeth stood still in the middle of the shed, numb with emotion.

Charlotte wrapped her arm around her. "That

was partly my doing." Turning to the colonel, she asked, "Why were you investigating my father?"

"Come no closer!" Papa shouted. "Halt, I say!"

Clang!

Elizabeth whirled around to see a jockey with a switch in his hand drop to his knees.

"No!" shouted the colonel and Fitzwilliam in unison, running past Elizabeth to where her father stood. The colonel caught the jockey before he fell forward on his face.

Her father mumbled, "He was trying to sneak up on you like those others. He raised his switch."

Fitzwilliam rubbed his hands over his face. "He was our jockey." He helped his cousin drag the man over to the wall and gently lower him down.

The colonel waved his hand in front of the jockey, but the man was out cold.

Papa tugged his side whiskers, utterly confused.

Standing up, Fitzwilliam pressed his palms together in a plea. "Please, I beg of you to leave."

Elizabeth crossed her arms over her chest. "I am sorry if our presence is an inconvenience, but it is clear to me that you need our help. Let us help you."

Fitzwilliam pleaded. "You do not understand. It is too dangerous. You could get hurt." The pain in his eyes convinced her of the gravity of their situation, strengthening her resolve to stay.

"You are right. I do not understand. But I see that you are in trouble, and I care enough to want to help. You never were in debt, were you? You are a terrible liar, but I know you well enough to trust your reason was honorable."

Fitzwilliam gritted his teeth, his hand pressing against his chest.

Elizabeth felt her father's sleeve brush against her arm as he stood beside her. He still held the shovel, which he handed (quite sheepishly) to Oakley when he motioned for it. Papa said, "If someone has attempted to take my daughter away from me, I do not trust them not to attempt it again. I would rather she stay close to a gentleman more capable of protecting her."

The colonel spoke. "They are right, Darcy. There is no hiding it any more. Tell them. Tell them you are The Red Campion."

Elizabeth felt her jaw drop.

Fitzwilliam groaned.

Jim grinned. "Blimey!"

Her father's breath whooshed in an exhale. "Native to Derbyshire. I said that only recently but did not connect him to you, Mr. Darcy."

"That was you? All of it?" Elizabeth winced. She may have found her tongue, but eloquence still evaded her.

"All that, and more," the colonel said, shrugging when Fitzwilliam glared at him again. "What? What harm can it do to tell them the whole of it now? Your cover is blown. If they can tell us anything to ensure the success of this mission, it will not be for nothing."

"All I have tried to do is keep those I most care about safe, and here they are. The only one missing is Georgiana, and the damage would be complete."

A man ringing a bell clamored, "Thirty minutes! Jockeys, mount your horses! The race begins in thirty minutes!"

Oakley knelt in front of the jockey, smacking his cheeks to no avail. "We need a replacement," he said.

Fitzwilliam resumed his pacing, mumbling, "Thirty minutes," while his cousin rubbed his temples. The bell faded into the distance.

"I suggest you talk fast if you wish for us to be of any use," Charlotte encouraged. "Tell us what is going on so we might help."

The colonel nodded in approval, his eyes smiling at her.

Stopping with his feet firmly planted and his arms crossed over his chest defensively, Fitzwilliam said, "I was sent to Netherfield Park to investigate Sir William. He has ties to four notorious gentleman who together have formed a traitorous agency called The Four Horsemen."

Papa shook his head in disbelief. "Sir William — a spy? I would no sooner suspect the Archbishop of being an atheist."

Elizabeth agreed.

"Names please," Charlotte demanded.

"Sir Leonard Sharp, Sir Benedict Voss, Sir Harcourt Grant, and Sir Erasmus Clark."

Charlotte nodded. "All names I have heard from my father, although I doubt his association is as intimate as you claim. He drops names in conversation to impress others. It does not always mean he enjoys a close friendship with the individuals of whom he speaks."

Fitzwilliam's posture was so stiff, Elizabeth worried he would snap in two. He continued, "Your father came into a large sum of money I traced back to The Four Horsemen. He purchased a racehorse to secure a spot in today's Derby, thus allowing him access to the Prince Regent when he congratulates the winner out on the field."

Charlotte stilled, her voice cool. "You believe my father means to assassinate the Prince Regent?"

"I did. Until he brought his family. The worst criminals are as deceptive as they are cruel, but most of them are fiercely protective of their families. Your presence here casts doubt over his direct involvement."

"But you think he is indirectly involved?" Charlotte arched an eyebrow.

"He has to be, as difficult as it must be for you to accept. There are too many coincidences otherwise," the colonel said.

Stiffening her back and jutting out her chin, Charlotte said, "Then we must get to the bottom of this. I have a father's name to clear and a dear friend to protect from those who would snatch her away."

Elizabeth heard the bell. It grew louder as the caller drew nearer. "Twenty-five minutes! Jockeys, take your positions at the starting line!"

Oakley knelt before the jockey again. The man had regained consciousness, but he could not correctly name how many fingers Oakley held up in front of his eyes. "He cannot ride in this condition. It would be suicide."

Fitzwilliam resumed pacing. "Where are we going to find an experienced jockey his size to take his place? We had a hard enough time finding him!"

They fell silent, the only sound being Fitzwilliam's boots scuffing against the straw on the tiled floor.

A wild idea occurred to Elizabeth. The jockey was about her height, and he could weigh little more than she did. If she tucked her hair firmly under the cap and tied down her breasts, she could wear the silks. If she was caught, she would be ruined. Dressing like a man was bad enough, but riding astride in public with the Prince Regent and the cream of high society to witness her shame would ensure it. Fitzwilliam would not be able to marry her. Society would ostracize not only him but his family. Her own family would never recover. Her ruin would doom her sisters to the shelf. Her mother would never forgive her. Longbourn would be lost to them.

It was audacious, but it would afford them more time. Locking eyes with Fitzwilliam, she asked, "If you prevent these evil men from murdering the Prince, can you ensure Sir William's name is not dragged through the mire if he is innocent?"

"I would have to catch the man they have bribed to assault the Prince. If Sir William has nothing to do with their plan, then there is no need to sully his name."

"Fair enough. What of you? What do you gain if you imprison these men?"

He rubbed his face. "Freedom."

Elizabeth took a deep breath. Once the words were said, there was no taking them back. "I will do it."

CHAPTER 32

"Out of the question," Darcy boomed. He could not agree. This was his mission, and he refused to expose Elizabeth when the risk to her was far greater than it was to him.

Miss Lucas cleared her throat, clasping her hands in front of herself primly. Surely, she would help her friend see the harsh reality. "We must not allow emotion to cloud good reason when we must think sensibly. As Mr. Croft pointed out, Lizzy is already in danger. She could be kidnapped and used by these heartless criminals against you, Mr. Darcy. Would she not be safer disguised? And if she is to be disguised, why not as a jockey? She is as accomplished on a horse as any of those other equestrians riding in the race today."

Darcy was stunned. Now *he* was the one thinking irrationally?

Richard was no help. He grinned open-mouthed at Miss Lucas.

How could Darcy make them see? He did not doubt Elizabeth's ability to ride against the best jockeys in the nation in the Derby, but the risk was too great. If anything went wrong — if her cap slipped, or the silk shirt clung to her form, or the breeches ... Dear Lord, the breeches. Darcy swallowed hard. Elizabeth was slight, but she was unquestionably a woman. Her ruin would be public, and nothing he could do would shield her from the harshness of Society's rebuke. Her sisters' prospects would be ruined, and her mother would never let her forget it. While Bingley's attachment to Miss Bennet seemed genuine, Darcy did not know if Bingley could withstand the pressure his sisters would place upon him. Elizabeth would shoulder all the blame, and Darcy would always wonder if he could have come up with a better solution. Why could he not fix this?

"There is no time. We must act now," Richard stopped ogling at Miss Lucas long enough to say.

Fitzwilliam stepped closer to Elizabeth. She nodded, her chin firm and determined. For him. For his freedom. Well, he cared for her freedom, too. His gain should not be her loss.

He grabbed her by the shoulders, her closeness grounding him while his head spun. "Do you not understand that it would kill me if you were hurt … or killed? I will not lose you. I love you, Elizabeth. I love you so much it hurts."

Her eyes met his, their clarity blurred with tears. She smiled, and he felt her hands at his cravat, her fingers trailing up his lapel to his collar. Darcy sucked in his breath, his body trembling with the restraint it took not to pull her into his arms.

A finger brushed against the bandage at his neck, her eyes widening and a tear spilling down her cheek. He pulled her hands away, enveloping them in his own, his heart wrenching in agony as the clock ticked away the minutes and he had no better solution to offer.

Mr. Bennet appeared at their side, placing one hand on Darcy's shoulder and the other on Elizabeth's. "My Lizzy can do it." He wiped his cheeks, his voice strong. "I have tried to shield my girl from harm, and yet, without knowing it, I am the one responsible for dragging her into the middle of this dangerous web. We cannot always protect the ones we love, but if we let our fears guide us, then we miss out on living. On loving. Do not make the same mistake I have made, Mr. Darcy. Let her help you. Let her ride in the race."

"Oh, Papa," Elizabeth cried, burying her face in her father's chest and wrapping her arms around his middle.

Bingley sniffed at his side, dabbing at his eyes. "It is a beautiful moment."

Richard cleared his throat excessively. "Beautiful."

Miss Lucas kept looking up and down the corridor. "I hate to interrupt a tender scene, but if I am to help Lizzy get ready for the race, you gentlemen must leave."

Croft helped the jockey into the box stall, draping the silks over the wall as he removed them.

Oakley ran inside, holding up another change of silks in the same color and handing them to Croft. "I apologize for the odor, but we cannot leave our man naked. I stripped these from the other jockey in the privy. He has no use for them right now."

ELIZABETH'S HEART jumped wildly in her chest.

The men got ready to leave, but Fitzwilliam held back. Turning to her, leaning close and speaking in a low voice, he said, "The Prince Regent presents the award to the winning rider and his owner. You cannot merely run the race. You must win. Whatever you do, stay away from the podium. You must stay out of the line of fire, if it comes to that."

Elizabeth took her role seriously, but she was so full of joy, she had little room for failure in her mind. "You really *are* a spy. I knew you were not trying to get out of a debt." She stopped, the words striking her like a bolt of lightning.

There never had been a debt. What were the words? She squeezed her eyes shut, trying to remember. Something about putting a price on life … settling debts … people being betrayed by those they trusted.

Oh no.

She reached out blindly, latching on to Fitzwilliam's coat lapels. "Wait. Wait, I have it. The only reason I even considered your story might be true was because of what John said to me outside Lucas Lodge. I thought he spoke of you, but he could not have been." Her vision cleared, and she sought out Charlotte. "His strange behavior. His warning not to trust anyone. The horse and this race. It is not your father at all. It is your brother. It is John."

Charlotte pressed her eyes closed. "He sold his soul to pay our debts. I cannot deny the possibility.

He was furious when we arrived here with Father. He did not want us here."

Fitzwilliam asked, "The shot fired at my hat? Could that have been a warning from him?"

Charlotte blinked hard again. "John is an excellent shot. Mr. Darcy, if my brother is involved in this scheme, I beg of you to stop him before he does something for which we could never forgive him."

In four long strides, Fitzwilliam had run the length of the corridor. "We will find him." Bending over to Jim's level, he said, "I am trusting you to keep Miss Elizabeth from being discovered. You will go with them to the stables and distract anyone from getting too close to her. She must make it to the starting gate."

Jim nodded solemnly, placing one hand over his heart. "I swear on me life."

Oakley and Jim stood guard at the open ends of the shed while Papa chased behind the pack of gentleman.

With Charlotte's help, Elizabeth dressed in the breeches and silks in short time. The piece of wardrobe that proved most difficult was fitting the cap over Elizabeth's hair. Charlotte removed several of her own pins to secure the cap to her head.

When that was done, Elizabeth walked between

Charlotte and Jim on one side and Oakley on the other.

"Mr. Robson and Joe are the ones most likely to recognize you, Lizzy. Jim and I will keep them busy and away from you," Charlotte said.

Oakley said, "Try not to sway when you walk, and keep your head down, Miss."

Elizabeth's heart leapt into her throat. "You had better not call me that."

"Right, you are. I will not make the same mistake again. We all know what is at stake."

"Disqualification and absolute ruin," Elizabeth mumbled.

They walked in silence the rest of the way to the stables. To save the Prince Regent and put the bad men in prison, so Fitzwilliam was free to live without fear of their retaliation — Elizabeth's reputation was the least of her worries.

True to his word, Jim chattered nonstop from the moment they entered the stables, and Joe was surprised to see his little brother there. He asked questions, always pointing away from Elizabeth. He was such a darling sport, Elizabeth was sorely tempted to kiss him on his freckled cheek.

She flung her leg over Trophonius, letting Jim help her feet into the stirrups. Trophonius sensed her nerves, growing as uneasy as she felt perched precariously atop the ebony giant.

Oakley disappeared, but with the ease with which Elizabeth made it to the starting line, she knew he had smoothed the way. It felt surreal, like a dream.

The track circled around a verdant field where a grand procession led by matching white horses pulled the Prince Regent's carriage to a platform covered in red velvet and cluttered with enormous arrangements of flowers.

The other horses pressed around her, and she kept her head down to keep from being noticed.

Elizabeth wiped her palms against her breeches and tried to calm the fluttering in her stomach before she got sick. Taking a deep breath, she recalled the memory she most cherished. In a flash, she was racing Fitzwilliam over the fields. She laced her fingers through Trophonius' black mane, pretending it was Tempest's, the treasured memories turning her fear to unbridled joy, her nerves to excitement. She was ready.

The pistol cracked through the air. The race was on.

Trophonius leapt forward, and Elizabeth clung to his back with all her might. He was much bigger than Tempest. The jolt of his stride might have unseated her in a sidesaddle. But she straddled the stallion, holding herself up as the other riders did, clods of dirt and grass flinging into her face.

They flew down the field. Tears pulled from her eyes, blurring her competition. Her vision unreliable, she tried to listen, but between the roar of the crowd, the thunder of dozens of hooves, and her own galloping heart, Elizabeth heard nothing.

She was surrounded, deaf, and mostly blind. She needed to break away from the pack and get into the front. Blinking furiously, she tried again to look ahead.

A rail to her left, a horse to her right, and two horses blocking her from the front as best as she could tell. All she saw were the bright colors of the silks bobbing around her.

Her face stung from flying debris. Her legs quivered and burned. What if she did not win? What if they were too late? What if John could not be stopped? What if The Four Horsemen escaped capture again? What if Fitzwilliam was never free of them?

Elizabeth gritted her teeth together. She would not succumb to fear or doubt. Not when she had so much worth fighting for. Fitzwilliam loved her.

And she loved him.

The two horses blocking her vied for the lead,

pushing against each other and creating a gap at the rail. If she squeezed between the rail and her competitor, he could easily dismount her. Riding astride required muscles she had never developed. It was a tremendous risk.

The gap widened.

She went for it.

CHAPTER 33

*D*arcy ran, shouting and pushing his way through the milling crowd, clearing a way for Mr. Bennet, Bingley, Croft, and Richard toward the row of stands spotted along the edge of the field.

"There they are," panted Mr. Bennet, pointing two more stands down the length of the track.

Sir William saw them before they climbed up the steps to the stand. "Mr. Darcy! This is a surprise! You are just in time. The race is about to begin. Would you like to join me and my family, sir? Along with the rest of you? I daresay I had expected Mr. Bennet to be here already, but I do not see Miss Elizabeth or Charlotte." He craned his neck on the chance the ladies were hiding behind the gentlemen.

Darcy held up a hand. "Where is Mr. Lucas?"

"John?" Sir William asked in surprise.

"Yes. Where is he?" Darcy pressed.

Richard mumbled something to Mr. Bennet in a low voice, causing the older gentleman to slip past Darcy. Bowing to Lady Lucas, he said, "Lady Lucas, I beg of you to return to the inn with your children."

"And miss the race? It is about to start!" exclaimed Sir William, his face turning a purplish-red.

The shot of a pistol cracked, and Darcy's cry was drowned out by the excited crowd. Calming his panic, for it was only the starting pistol, he shouted into Sir William's ear, "Where is your son? It is urgent I find him!"

Not taking his eyes off his horse in the field, Sir William shouted back, "How am I to know? I supposed he was with another acquaintance or with George at the stables. Look how grand Trophonius looks on the field. He is a champion!"

Mr. Bennet stood at the other end of the platform, his hands gripping the railing, his focus intent on Elizabeth. Darcy could not ask him to leave his post to search for John Lucas when he feared for his daughter.

Darcy turned to Croft and Bingley. "Stay here with the Lucases and Mr. Bennet. Keep an eye out. We do not know if their lives are in danger."

Croft nodded. Bingley looked as pale as a table-cloth, but he swallowed hard and went to stand on the other side of the platform by Mr. Bennet.

Darcy glanced out to the field. Staying to watch was a luxury he could not permit himself.

The crowd shouted and cheered, their fists pumping the air as they called the names of their favorite horses.

Richard was already at the bottom of the steps when Darcy joined him. Jutting his thumb over his shoulder, he said, "I will go this way. If we do not find him before the race ends, we must force our way to the center of the field."

Darcy was already searching, pausing to look at each face in the sea of people clamoring and pushing their way for a closer look. It would not be easy to claw his way through them if it came to that.

Face after face, he examined until they all started to resemble each other, and he had to remind himself of Mr. Lucas' light brown hair, straight nose, and pinched features.

The noise of the crowd rose to a deafening roar, a mix of dismay and pleasure.

The race was over.

John was nowhere in sight.

Darcy was too late.

ELIZABETH DROPPED down to the saddle, her legs screaming and her limbs shaking. She had done it. She had won.

Hands trembling, she checked her cap. It felt loose, but her hair had not escaped.

Oakley appeared at her side. "If you will give me the reins, I will lead you to the winner's circle."

Of all the questions she wished to ask him, she would not waste the little time she had by asking, "How did you get here?" Instead, she asked, "Did they catch him?"

The grim look on Oakley's face made her stomach plummet to the ground. She looked around from the vantage point of her tall perch atop Trophonius and was instantly disheartened. How could she possibly pick out one man from a vast multitude?

"Keep your head down," Oakley said, walking as slowly as they dared toward the podium where the Prince waited.

Elizabeth peeked through her lashes at the opulent carriage. Only royalty could afford such luxury. Gleaming gold, sparkling stones, and creamy white with a red velvet carpet running from the top of the platform to the height of the conveyance's first step. Vibrant flower arrangements perfumed the air and cluttered the stand. It all looked so serene.

Several guards dressed in livery surrounded the winner's circle. Elizabeth prayed they would prove themselves fit for their duty.

"Whatever you do, do not step in front of the Prince. Stay out of the line of fire," Oakley instructed, stepping to the side to allow her to dismount.

If The Four Horsemen had not yet been captured, Elizabeth did not know what other option she had. She could not allow the Prince to be murdered in front of her, nor could she allow the villains responsible to go free when she might stop them.

Slipping her foot out of the stirrups, she slid down Trophonius' side and would have tumbled straight to the ground had Oakley not steadied her.

"Are you steady enough?" he asked.

She nodded, feeling like a toddler taking her first steps as Oakley let go of her elbow and led Trophonius off to the side where the Prince could admire him without getting trampled.

Slowly, precariously, Elizabeth advanced to the podium, her steps slowing the more she concentrated on the faces and shouts around her. Where was Fitzwilliam? Or Mr. Lucas?

"Stop!" she heard a deep voice exclaim behind her. Her heart skipping a beat, she turned.

Fitzwilliam jumped over the fence, crossing the beaten track and racing toward her, arms waving and shouting. Several guards ran toward him.

"The Prince is waiting for you," another guard boomed in front of her. She nearly gave her sex away when she nearly took his extended arm. Men did not take each other's arms to help each other navigate stairs. They did not have gowns to trip over or wobbly legs to contend with.

She nodded, intent on keeping silent, and continued to the top of the platform where the Prince waited to make a show of presenting her with an award.

At his signal, a hush fell over the crowd.

Elizabeth prayed Fitzwilliam had made it past the guards.

"Over there! The shooter!" rumbled a voice from the murmuring crowd.

Elizabeth looked behind her to the stand. Mr. Croft pointed. "Over there!"

Mr. Bingley and Father dropped to the floor of the stand.

"Get down!" Mr. Croft shouted again, pushing Sir William and Lady Lucas down just as the wood railing in front of them burst into splinters. A puff of smoke lingered near them.

Screams and cries filled the air, the crowd seething.

Crack!

Crack!

The shooting had started. They were too late.

Elizabeth saw Fitzwilliam out of the corner of her eye and the Prince in the other. She had one chance, and she had to take it.

Stepping in front of the Prince Regent, she shoved him with all her strength, sending him tumbling backwards into his carriage.

CHAPTER 34

*E*lizabeth saw the shock on the Prince's face. She would hang for what she had done, but he was out of immediate danger.

Just one more look at the crowd, then she would get off the platform. If the guards did not seize her first.

"No!"

Elizabeth turned in time to see Fitzwilliam jump in front of her.

Crack!

He stiffened in the air, and Elizabeth watched in horror as Fitzwilliam dropped with a deep thud to the platform. She screamed, but the Prince's guards held her fast. She struggled and writhed, screaming for Fitzwilliam.

He lay there, just out of her reach. Limp. Lifeless.

Colonel Fitzwilliam appeared, and the next thing Elizabeth knew, the guards had released their hold on her, and she stumbled forward. To Fitzwilliam. Collapsing at his side, she ran her hands over the tear at his chest. There was no blood. Where was the blood? Why was there no blood?

A warm hand touched her fingers, and she cried when she heard Fitzwilliam groan.

"You are alive!" She showered his face with kisses, wiping her tears off his cheeks.

"I say!" a nasal voice protested from behind them, but she did not care. Fitzwilliam was alive, his hands were in her hair, and his lips were pressed against hers. Heaven surged through her, and she forgot their audience as his strong arms pulled her closer, his ragged breath teasing her skin and lighting her on fire.

A perfect first kiss. Achingly sweet, and much too short.

Fitzwilliam sat up, cradling her face in his hand, chunks of dried earth falling off her face as he rubbed his thumb over her cheek. "Just like the day I met you," he said. "Covered head to toe in mud. Part of me fell for you right then."

Elizabeth emerged from her glorious haze with a delighted sigh. "And now?"

"Now, I love you with all my heart."

"I love you, too," she said through her beaming smile.

No sooner had she said the words than the same nasal voice which had impertinently tried to interrupt her kiss said, "This is an unexpected sight, but a welcome one given the circumstances." His shadow covered them. He was none other than the Prince Regent.

"Rise," he ordered.

Fitzwilliam pulled Elizabeth to her feet. Her hair curled wildly around her, and for a brief second, she did not know if she ought to bow or curtsy. Her cover was blown, but Fitzwilliam still held her hand. "Your Royal Highness," they said.

The Prince looked down his nose at their stooped figures, his gaze narrowing at Elizabeth. "You pushed me."

Elizabeth bit her tongue.

Jim's childish voice rose in protest. "She saved your life, by golly!" Guards seized him, but he shouted louder, "And then, Mr. Darcy jumped in front of Miss Elizabeth and saved her! They're heroes!"

Who knew what Jim's fate might have been had several cries and a grievous wail not drowned out their interview?

"Darcy! Darcy, quick!" Colonel Fitzwilliam shouted from across the track.

DARCY HELD his breath until Prinny signaled he could go. Elizabeth's hand firmly in his, he pulled her along as they crossed the racetrack to where Richard knelt on the ground over a recumbent figure. The crowd thinned, allowing them to pass.

Croft shouted, "Bring a surgeon!"

Lady Lucas knelt at her son's side, crying, "My dear boy, my sweet John!" She stroked his face, kissing his forehead. "Hold on, my child. Stay strong a bit more until the surgeon comes." As if his injury was no worse than a scraped knee, nothing a kiss could not cure.

Sir William stood behind her, stunned, held upright by George on one side and Miss Lucas on the other.

Darcy asked Richard, "What of The Four Horsemen?"

"My men have them surrounded, but unless we can tie them to this act of treason, we do not have enough proof to hold them."

John's breath rattled. "My hat?" he whispered.

"I have it." Charlotte held it out for him to see.

A peaceful expression crossed her brother's face. "Keep it." His gaze wandered wildly until he settled on his father. "They said they would kill you. I am so sorry." His breath wheezed, then stopped abruptly as he relaxed against the ground.

"John!" wept Lady Lucas. Sir William bowed his head, his shoulders slumped and shaking.

Miss Lucas embraced her mother. George wrapped his arm around his father, supporting him while looking at the lifeless form of his brother with a blank expression.

"Bring The Four Horsemen here. Let them see what they have done," Richard ordered.

Darcy heard Elizabeth gasp as the four men were brought forward. She whispered, "Evil men wear black and trim their side whiskers at sharp angles. These men look like grandfathers."

"They seem harmless until you look them in the eyes." He felt their flint-like glares on him.

"I see what you mean," Elizabeth whispered, clasping his hand more firmly.

The Prince, surrounded by dozens of guards, approached. "What is the meaning of this?" he demanded. "These men are my friends. I demand you release them at once." Pointing at John, he said, "You have your assassin. I will order an investigation to be conducted on his family, and they will be charged with sedition for their role in my attempted assassination."

Sir Erasmus bowed. "You are wise, Your Royal Highness. The evidence against them is great. A last-minute entry in the Derby. The horse alone must have cost the family a fortune, not to mention the trainers and fees the Jockey Club would impose upon them."

Sir Harcourt added, "I would not be surprised if you found a large deposit in his bank accounts made just before the race."

Against the canvas of his blanched complexion, Sir William's cheeks appeared strikingly red. "Preposterous! There must be a mistake."

Elizabeth rose onto her toes, whispering in Darcy's ear, "Why did John want Charlotte to keep his hat? Might he have hidden something in it?"

Elizabeth's instincts had proved to be correct too many times to be ignored.

"Miss Lucas, would you be so kind as to search your brother's hat?" he asked.

The crowd went silent around them, collectively leaning forward as Miss Lucas released her hold on her mother and turned her brother's beaver hat around in her hands. With anxiety inducing slowness, her fingers prodded over the hat and around the band, tugging at the lining and tearing it from the crown.

Finally, when Darcy's lungs screamed for breath, she pulled out a folded paper and held it up. "A letter!"

"Allow me," the Prince said, holding out his hand.

Reluctantly, Charlotte gave him the letter.

Squinting at the page, the Prince's eyes roved over the page rapidly until they widened at a certain passage. He paused, peering over the page at the four gentlemen he called "friends," and then resumed reading more deliberately.

When he was finished, he folded the letter and tucked it up his sleeve. Raising his bejeweled hand, he pointed at Sir William.

Elizabeth clutched Fitzwilliam's hand.

"Sir William, you and your family are free to go. Your son has paid for his sins." The prince swiveled until he aimed at The Four Horsemen. "Seize them!"

In a frenzy of activity that was over in a blink, the Prince's guards closed around the four men, clapping irons on their hands and feet, and leading The Four Horsemen to a barred carriage with a locked shacklebolt door.

Darcy watched in a dreamlike silence as the carriage jolted into motion, rolling away, rolling out of his life.

"It is done. You are done." Richard said.

Darcy could hardly believe it.

With a departing jab on his shoulder, Richard turned to Croft. "Have you ever considered a different kind of assignment?"

Still, Darcy stood there, watching the carriage get smaller until it disappeared down the lane.

It was not until Mr. Bennet stepped in front of him that his wits returned to him fully.

Looking pointedly between Darcy and Elizabeth, he said, "I suspect there is something you wish to discuss with me?"

Darcy bowed his head, lifting Elizabeth's hand and cradling it to his chest. "Mr. Bennet, I love your daughter. I wish to spend the rest of my life with her if you will allow it."

Mr. Bennet smiled, his eyes glistening. "I could not consent to a lesser man. It would be my honor to include you in our family, Mr. Darcy. Now, if you will excuse me, I do believe there is another young gentleman eager to make a similar request."

Sure enough, Bingley was on his way over.

Leaving Bingley to Mr. Bennet, Darcy returned his full attention to Elizabeth. He reached into the pocket under the tear in his jacket. Emerald malachite, bright turquoise, and yellow and orange aventurine glimmered in the springtime sun. He rubbed his finger over the lead bullet lodged in the middle of the tranquil scene.

"My brooch!" Elizabeth reached out for it.

That was what he thought she reached for until her arms wrapped around his neck and her fingers wound through his hair.

THEY ALL GATHERED AROUND TROPHONIUS' stall, a motley assortment of friends and family with much to attend to and no desire to part from one another's company. Elizabeth had pinned her hair up and changed back into her gown, tucking the jockey silks into her trunk as keepsakes … and on the slight chance she might need them again. One never knew…

Sir William had arranged for a cart to convey his eldest son to Lucas Lodge. He would be buried on their land. They would depart for Hertfordshire on the morrow.

Trophonius, ridden by Miss Elizabeth Bennet, was disqualified. The winner of the Epsom Derby was Phantom, ridden by a male jockey whose name Elizabeth did not care to remember. She knew the truth, and no official could take her win away from her.

Sir William was disappointed. "All the investment for naught," he said, sadly shaking his head.

George draped his arm over his father's shoulders. "Not all is lost, Father. The events of the day were so spectacular, our horse is certain to make the papers as the first to cross the finish line. We may not get to keep the winning title, but he will earn us a fortune in our breeding stables."

Sir William cheered remarkably. "True! They are as much yours as they are mine, now." His melancholy returned, and a silence fell over the group.

Many times, Charlotte had expressed her wish that George would be the one to inherit rather than John. Their estate was more secure, but they would all suffer the loss of the price.

Papa leaned closer to Elizabeth. "I believe it best for us to take our leave, Lizzy. We must let the family mourn."

Fitzwilliam bowed. "Pray excuse me as well. I must meet up with my cousin. We still have a great deal of work to do."

The three of them turned to leave but were prevented from going very far when the Prince's carriage drove up the narrow path in front of the stables, blocking their way.

They stepped close to the building to allow him to pass, but the Prince seemed to have a different idea. The carriage came to a stop, and the door opened.

"Rise, please," he insisted when they dropped into bows and curtsies. "I must depart for London, but I had hoped to address you before taking my leave. It would have been a horrible blow to England to have their monarch taken from them only months after the beginning of my regency. Mr. Darcy, Miss Bennet, I owe you my life. I have learned the details surrounding your roles in my rescue and am well aware of the sacrifice you were willing to give on my behalf. People accuse me of being extravagant in taste, but I will never allow them to accuse me of being stingy in praise and gratitude to those deserving of it."

At this, he looked directly at Elizabeth. "If anyone questions your reputation, they may answer to me. You are to be proclaimed a hero in the newspapers along with The Red Campion, to whom I am deeply indebted."

Fitzwilliam shook his head, but the Prince anticipated his refusal to accept more than the monarch's gratitude.

"I wish to bestow upon you a knighthood, Mr. Darcy. Parliament will be certain to approve my petition once they are told the particulars."

Sir Fitzwilliam. That had a nice sound to it. Sir

Fitzwilliam and Lady Darcy sounded even better, Elizabeth mused.

Looking past them to Sir William, the Prince said, "I wish you to know that I harbor no grudge against you. Thanks in great part to your eldest son's letter, I now know who the traitors were who have been selling secrets and jeopardizing my men for their own gain. They were false friends, and it was your son who helped expose them. I will remember where your loyalties proved to be when you handed his letter over to me."

Elizabeth thought kindly of the Prince for granting Sir William a brief exchange, a full pardon, and another story he would entertain his guests with for years to come.

The door closed, and the Prince Regent departed.

Only Jim had words. "Blimey!"

"*A* wedding and a knighthood ceremony in the same week! I never thought I would say this, but I very much look forward to some calm and quiet." Elizabeth smiled at Fitzwilliam from across the carriage and wondered how long it would take until he joined her on her side.

It did not take long.

Slipping beside her, he raised his elbow so that she could wrap her arm through his and lean against his shoulder.

He kissed her forehead. "Your wish is my command, Lady Darcy. Although I believe our families have other plans."

Elizabeth groaned. "My mother wishes to parade through town so she can presume just as she did three weeks ago at Mr. Bingley's ball."

"She had much to celebrate," Fitzwilliam teased.

"At least she has finally forgiven me for returning to Longbourn before either Jane or I were engaged."

Fitzwilliam chuckled. "I will never forget how she stood up to my aunt Catherine at our wedding, threatening to send for Prinny when my aunt tried to stop the ceremony."

That had been a sight. Her mother had come dangerously close to tackling the imperious woman to the floor. Lady Catherine would never stoop so low when she could order a servant to do it for her. "They are not so different, are they?"

"Mercenary regarding their daughters' prospects?"

Elizabeth chuckled. "Precisely. I was happy to meet Anne and see for myself that she was as determined to avoid the assumed engagement as you were. Had my mother been in Lady Catherine's position, I have no doubt she would have presumed an attachment despite your repeated proclamations that you did not intend to ever marry." She peeked up at him and continued, "I am so glad you changed your mind."

"You convinced me." He tilted her chin up.

The Four Horsemen had been tried and convicted as traitors. They were drawn and quartered publicly, a warning to those inclined to follow in their footsteps or avenge their gruesome deaths on those responsible for their capture. She and Fitzwilliam had read about it in the newspapers. One journalist pointed out that loyalties to The Four Horsemen would dry up once their fortunes were seized. And so it proved to be. They truly were free.

The carriage came to a halt outside Darcy House.

Fitzwilliam's smile faded. "What is he doing here?" he growled.

Elizabeth peeked out the window to see Richard wiping his boots. She was perplexed, but the colonel was always good company. That, and he had taken a noticeable interest in Charlotte, who seemed equally content to receive his attentions. Elizabeth could not imagine a more suitable match.

The colonel chattered until Fitzwilliam led them upstairs to his study. Elizabeth would leave if she was asked, but she had no desire to part from Fitzwilliam.

Closing the door and helping himself to the brandy on the sideboard, the colonel said, "Leo would like to make a proposition."

"Leo?" Elizabeth asked.

"The name of our organization. It is short for Leonidas."

"The warrior king who held off a Persian army

with only three hundred men?" Elizabeth had always loved that story and admired the men in it.

Richard grinned. "A small but powerful and effective force. Just like us."

Fitzwilliam glared daggers at his cousin, who chose to ignore him and continued, "Leo wishes to arrange your wedding tour on the continent. As a newlywed couple, you would prove invaluable in infiltrating another organization they have their eye on. It would mean a great deal of travel, but you would have many adventures to relate to your grandchildren one day."

Elizabeth watched for Fitzwilliam's immediate dismissal, but it did not come. He hesitated.

Taking her hand, he kissed her palm. "I make no decisions without first consulting my wife. If a life of travel and adventure would make her happiest, then I am willing to accept."

He was doing this for her! Elizabeth's heart brimmed with joy. What a wonderful, magnificent man! Her choice was an easy one. With immense pride and complete sincerity, she replied, "I have always craved adventure. Fitzwilliam knows that, and I love him for putting my desires before his own. But we cannot accept. I long for a different sort of adventure, of a long life together with my husband and the family we will have. That is my greatest wish."

Fitzwilliam pressed her hand against his cheek. "Do you mean it?"

"With all my heart."

"Then you will be content with a wedding tour around England? I thought we could start at Ramsgate. Georgiana has taken an acute interest in the place. I had thought we might help her set up a residence there before continuing on our tour."

That reminded Elizabeth. She had met most of Fitzwilliam's family and a great many of his friends at the knighting ceremony, one of them a man she did not think it wise to trust. "About that. Did you notice the way Georgiana blushed whenever Mr. Wickham addressed her?"

Richard exclaimed. "Wickham? He and Georgiana are childhood friends. She would never—"

Fitzwilliam shushed his cousin. "I want to hear. Do you not think it wiser to listen to my wife's intuition when it comes to the happiness of Georgiana? After all, she suspected I was a spy from the start."

They faced Elizabeth, lips shut, eyes intent, and hearts on their sleeves.

She tried to be tactful and kind. "I only wish to warn you not to trust Mr. Wickham so much around Georgiana. She is young and impressionable, and he is charming, handsome, and attentive. Even with me, a recently married lady, his manners were flirtatious. I do not trust him."

The colonel rubbed his chin. Fitzwilliam massaged his temples. Their concern for their charge was adorable, their ignorance regarding the workings of young ladies, endearing.

Finally, Fitzwilliam said, "I suppose Georgiana can stay with your mother until Elizabeth and I return from our tour."

Richard nodded. "She would love that. Georgiana has become a daughter to her over the years."

Elizabeth admired her husband all the more for always thinking of her and his sister foremost, but she would be his champion as much as he was hers. "What about Pemberley?" she asked.

He squeezed her hand. "Pemberley will still be there when we return."

Elizabeth's heart was so full, she thought she would cry. "Why wait when we can go now? I would love to see my new home, to have you show me all the places you have described to me and others I have read about. And, please, let us bring Georgiana if she wishes to come. Do you not think she would love to hear why you have been away so long? You could reassure her that you intend to be more constant in her life."

Fitzwilliam leaned forward, his forehead touching hers. "Every day I wake, I cannot imagine happiness greater than I feel at that moment. And yet, you always surprise me by proving it possible."

"I am only returning the favor," she teased.

Richard stood and bowed. "I believe I have my reply. Shall I tell my mother to prepare Georgiana for travel?"

"Please do. We will leave within the hour," Fitzwilliam proclaimed.

WHILE ELIZABETH WOULD HAVE PREFERRED NOT to share her husband with her new sister, if she could do it over again, she would have made the same suggestion. On the first day, Fitzwilliam and Georgiana's conversation had been a trifle forced and awkward. So accustomed were they to communicating by letter or with the company of their aunt Matlock, they struggled on their own. But by the final day, their conversation flowed without any help from Elizabeth. They teased and laughed and cried, and by the time they reached Derbyshire, they were as close as any brother and sister who had never spent a day apart could be.

Today was their last day of travel, and their

shortest. Fitzwilliam had insisted they stay at an inn a short distance from Pemberley the night before.

Georgiana gazed out of the window on her side of the carriage. "Switch sides with me," she said to Elizabeth. "I do not want you to miss the prospect from the top of the hill."

"Are we nearly there?" Elizabeth asked, clambering over Georgiana. Three days inside the enclosed conveyance, listening to stories that took place at Pemberley, had heightened her anticipation.

Georgiana smiled impishly but said no more.

Fitzwilliam merely smiled, but with the way his gaze fixed on the view through the window, Elizabeth suspected they were very near indeed.

The forest of trees cleared, and as beautiful and parklike as Pemberley was to see nestled in a valley surrounded by forests, gardens, and lakes, the happiness on her husband's face was perfection.

The servants lined up to welcome their master and meet his bride. It would take Elizabeth a while to remember their names.

"I have your rooms ready and water heating for baths," Mrs. Reynolds, the housekeeper, said.

A bath sounded divine!

Elizabeth went to follow her up the stairs, lured by the promise of a luxurious bath and the tour she planned Fitzwilliam would give her.

He caught her hand, and she looked back at him.

"We will join you in a minute," he said.

With a sly smile at her brother, Georgiana headed up the stairs with Mrs. Reynolds.

"I have something to show you — something for you to remember Hertfordshire by." Fitzwilliam tugged on her hand.

"We already plan to receive my family shortly. What more could I want that is not already here?" Elizabeth asked, her pulse racing in excitement.

Pemberley's stables were nearly as large as Longbourn and every bit as stately. Had the aroma of hay and manure not identified the building, Elizabeth might have thought it the dowager house.

"Lady Darcy!" exclaimed a young voice from the side of the building.

Dropping his wheelbarrow to wave enthusiastically, Jim ran over to them. "Can you believe that Sir Fitzwilliam hired me on? Mr. Bingley took on another one of me brothers, and Joe is busier than ever at Lucas Lodge. Your mare didn't like the bumpy roads one bit, but she settled in nicely when she saw her open stall. It's much larger than the one at Netherfield Park."

Elizabeth's breath caught in her throat. Her mare. She looked at Fitzwilliam.

He held out his hand. "Come. I want to show you your wedding present."

She had so much, she was speechless at the thought of more.

Jim pranced like a playful foal in front of them, stopping at the largest stall at the back of the stable. Plucking an apple from his pocket, he handed it to Elizabeth.

Tempest raised her head, objecting when Elizabeth wrapped her arms around Fitzwilliam rather than feeding her the sweet treat in her hand.

"She is perfect! Thank you! Oh, thank you!"

"I could saddle her for you in a jiffy, Lady Darcy," Jim offered.

Elizabeth pulled away to look at Fitzwilliam. Arching an eyebrow, she asked, "What do you say, my love?"

The corner of his lip curled up and mischief glinted in his eyes. "I have envisioned many happy days chasing you all over the grounds of Pemberley."

"A race? I accept," she exclaimed, adding with an arched brow, "Do try to keep up."

Fitzwilliam's laugh echoed through the stables. "Pray tell me what my reward is to be if I catch you?"

"A well-deserved kiss, I should think," Elizabeth said, rising to the tips of her toes to give him a taste of his prize.

Her husband's hands circled around her waist, his sweet breath brushing over her skin, his soft lips teasing hers until her legs felt as wobbly as they had at the Derby.

The beloved mare, impatiently seeking her treat, nudged Elizabeth. Jim had already saddled her.

"I checked the girth just like you said to back at Netherfield Park, Lady Darcy," he said with a toothy grin.

Holding the apple out on her palm, Elizabeth moved Tempest's forelock over to rub the star underneath. "Thank you, Jim."

Oakley joined them, leading the gorgeous gray thoroughbred.

Already, Elizabeth had a treasure trove of memories with Fitzwilliam — enough to cherish for a lifetime. But today … she would remember today forever. Marriage had not bridled or bound her at all. Fitzwilliam had caught her heart, but his love was so complete — so generous, honest, and accepting — he had given her a gift greater than her wildest imagining. He had given her freedom.

For that, she would give him a good chase. And then, at least for today, she would allow herself to be caught.

Can't get enough of Darcy and Elizabeth? Read on to find your next book!

Can curiosity and crimes lead a young lady to the altar? Join Elizabeth Bennet as she finds out!
Read all the standalone books in the Mysteries & Matrimony series here!

Follow Fitzwilliam Darcy as he overcomes various challenging roles on his path to love.
Read all the standalone books in the Dimensions of Darcy series here!

Darcy and Elizabeth form a formidable investigative team as they work together to bring enemies to justice and forge unbreakable bonds with their newfound family.
One-click the complete Meryton Mystery series here!

A hidden letter that rocks the Darcy cousins' world. Will it ultimately lead them to their own happily-ever-afters?
One-click the complete Darcy Cousins series here!

THANK YOU!

Thank you for reading *Chasing Elizabeth*!

Did you enjoy the story? Then, please leave a review.

Reviews spread the word and help like-hearted readers find their next read. They're also a great way to say "thank you" to an author.

Want to know when my next book is available? You can:

* Sign-up for my newsletter
* Follow me on Twitter
* Like my Facebook page
* Follow my Author page on Amazon

ABOUT THE AUTHOR

When Jennifer isn't busy dreaming up new adventures for her favorite characters, she is learning Sign language, reading, baking (Cake is her one weakness!), or chasing her twins around the park (because … cake).

She believes in happy endings, sweet romance, and plenty of mystery. She also believes there's enough angst on the news, so she keeps her stories light-hearted and full of hope.

While she claims Oregon as her home, she currently lives high in the Andes Mountains of Ecuador with her husband and two kids.

Made in the USA
Monee, IL
17 March 2021